DAYS OF LONG SHADOWS

DAYS OF LONG SHADOWS

TIM FRANKS

Crescent Swan
Publishing

Copyright © Tim Franks, 2024

The right of Tim Franks to be identified as the
author of this work has been asserted by him in accordance
with the Copyright, Designs and Patents Act 1988.

Cover copyright © Stuart Bache, 2024

All rights reserved. This book or any portion thereof
may not be reproduced or used in any manner whatsoever
without the express written permission of the publisher
except for the use of brief quotations in a book review.

First published in Great Britain in 2024
by Crescent Swan Publishing.

ISBN 978-1-8383084-3-8
Crescent Swan Publishing
www.crescentswan.com

*To Teresa, Laura and Kate:
for the disappeared hours at a keyboard.*

A year before the torso.

Some days morality is a bastard. Under his desk, Jamie Seagrief unfolded a single sheet of paper – a printed, grainy image of a girl: pretty, smiling and, seemingly, a bleached blonde babe, like so many other Baltic exiles. Then he began reading her file. She was educated, an engineering degree, some specialism in plastics. She'd written *none* in answer to the question of any previous police incidents, but that wasn't what the background check said. Her offences were just kid's stuff; a warning for shoplifting when she was thirteen and a something-and-nothing drunken affray at university – but it was enough. She would show up.

Seagrief texted back the innocuous message that meant *take her off the transport*, then looked up. Across the office he stared at a huddle of Peepos; shaven-headed immigration officers. The Peoples' Police.

'First line of defence for the United Twatdom of our glorious Great Britain,' he hawked up a gob of phlegm and swallowed it.

Seagrief tried not to think about the girl in the file; tried to forget her face, because somewhere, on a long, flat East European road, Liliana Normova would be screaming, swearing, pleading for her dreams, as the lorry drove away.

'All over for Normova.' He tried to detach.

He knew there were so many more. He couldn't risk the dodgy cases, couldn't get involved with those who might flash up on a fingerprint or DNA database. He had to make sacrifices, so he could save others. He knew he had to protect himself. Arrested heroes save no one. And it was a calculation he knew he'd get wrong. There would always be some he threw back that he could have got away with – but he could only weigh the odds and go with his head.

Always keep your own oxygen mask on, so you can save others. He'd seen that on an aeroplane safety leaflet once, but it brought him no comfort. The Peepos' noise, laughing and pushing each other with mock-macho good humour, made him flinch. Seagrief looked at the brutish faces, heard the loud vulgarities and knew, unfortunately, they weren't stupid; knew they were experienced, cunning and never to be underestimated – not if he wanted to keep his oxygen mask on.

1

'So it's not just the head that's missing?' Jamie's phone was by his ear as he walked along the corridor. 'Nothing to give us any clues?' He opened the door of the large, square briefing room and headed towards a row of desks, parting the dark herd of uniformed Peepos grazing in the central space. 'A woman and she's white. Is that it?' Jamie was still walking.

'A woman and she's white. My dream date,' a squat Peepo smirked and deliberately remained in the path between Jamie and his desk.

'Clues to age?' Jamie kept on his line, leaning into the man just enough to imply no weakness, but not so aggressive as to spark confrontation.

'Fat Manc twat.' The Peeopo glanced to the herd. 'That's all we need, a fat Manc twat with his flat Manc vowels polluting our ears.'

Jamie lifted a middle finger, without bothering to look back. The squat Peepo blustered out some more attempted gibes, but Jamie's body language shut out the room. Leaning on his desk, he picked up a pen, monosyllabic as he rechecked details. Finally, he tapped *End Call*, stood and was moving again.

'What is it?' the squat Peepo probed again. 'Lollipop lady

phoned in sick?'

'Something like that,' Jamie's hand was deep in his pocket, searching for car keys, as he reached the door.

He knew where he was going. It was one of his places, though not one he'd chronicled. He'd walked it, scouted it out. His places; edgelands – every city has them – the secret green spaces that hide beyond the lines of buildings; the fields that are just there, behind a fringe of trees that separate scrubby, briar-clumped patches from the garden-ends where the civilised people live.

Jamie drove east, tracking the Don Valley. Turning off before the Rotherham frontier, he parked, then walked past a line of tall, terraced houses, their once pale limestone blackened by decades of Steel City soot. The last had been converted into a funeral director's showroom, with a few sample memorials on display behind an expanse of plate glass. *That's handy* ran through his mind. A narrow drive led him down to a hidden enclave of three houses, neat and ornamentally gardened as if trying to claim some honorary rural status. The building-line ended at a disused railway bridge. Then the land opened up.

Jamie moved quickly, taking in the selection of mixed flora; brown barbed brambles, leafless and spiralling across grass, pale and ochre-streaked in the winter's sun-starved days. Last vestiges of a December afternoon; a time for long shadows. Jamie was used to those.

Beyond, where the canal escaped from the urban sprawl, willows rose tall along the bank, thriving with their roots drawing on the constant water. Reaching lock gates, he crossed via a narrow ledge, using the iron sluice-rods as a handrail. Below, a cascade of water spurted into the chasm. Next to the open bottom gate was a white tent and a jumble of ripped plastic sheeting. Behind him, substantial concrete pillars framed a dark arch where the canal tunnel surfaced from beneath a huge brick wall. Jamie walked down to the tent. The paper-suited Scene of Crime Officer pointed at a plastic box.

'What you got?' Jamie picked up latex gloves and began pulling elasticated bags over his shoes.

'Piles and a sore throat. Too many fags and sitting on cold, concrete walls.' The SOCO had wispy hair and his eyes and nose reminded Jamie of a Christmas turkey.

'Yeah, well, bound to have consequences; that and spending years talking out your arse.'

Both men grinned.

'We've got a body,' the SOCO was accidentally accurate, because it was just that: body. No head or limbs, just a torso. 'Scared the shit out of the two old dears when they saw a pair of tits and a bloated belly bouncing off the pointy end of their barge.'

'Remind me again why you chose a career in the police instead of the navy.'

A single middle finger rose to the vertical from the end of a paper-suited arm.

Jamie looked back towards the tunnel and its hidden span. 'Clever,' he said, almost to himself.

'What?'

'The tunnel,' Jamie continued. 'No line of sight for prying eyes from up there.'

The SOCO's gaze followed Jamie's towards the dark arch.

'Easy to drop her off, or even kill in there. Clever.' Jamie finished his train of thought.

'Not that clever,' the SOCO replied. 'She's popped up again.'

'Clever, if that's what you wanted. Tie weights on her, but not too tight, then drop her somewhere she'd get pulled downstream, a lock-full of water at a time.'

Jamie knew whoever did it was professional; someone who knew the body would stay in the water long enough to contaminate anything incriminating, but would float up eventually as a grisly warning to anyone who thought of copying whatever offence this remnant of a girl had committed.

'Been a bit quicker in the summer.' The SOCO looked into the lock. 'Not many barges passing through this time of year. Still, the cold water's kept her fresh. Every cloud…'

The torso lay on blue brick paving, white-grey with blackened circles where the limbs and head had been detached. Strips of green algae and dark dots where collisions and scavengers had pierced her skin had left trails across her flesh, like bizarre staves of music.

'Any clues?' Jamie asked.

'Well, I wouldn't want to over-commit,' the SOCO leered. 'But I'm ruling out suicide.' Then, sliding a forensic sheet alongside and holding the remains between his latex-gloved hands, he turned the torso onto its front.

Jamie looked at the stub of neck. 'Some kind of metal cable.' He pointed at a thin indentation that ran close to a severed vertebra, then disappeared into the circle of blackened flesh. 'So, cause of death, garrotte?'

The SOCO bent down to look then shrugged.

'Could be kill. Could be control. Or torture,' Jamie said, tracing a finger over a small tattoo on the shoulder.

Two words and a stylised stickman, sword in hand, mounted on a horse.

A few minutes of professional observation followed. Voices became quiet, factual. Smart-arse remarks were parked for a while.

'Not much else obvious,' Jamie bent down by a pack of forensic sheets. 'Tell the photo boys I want every angle and copies emailed to me, soon as.' He threw the man an end of a sheet. 'Come on. Get her covered before those other bastards turn up and start gawping.'

'For fuck's sake,' the SOCO chuntered, his neck nodding rhythmically, adding to Jamie's sense of a Christmas turkey.

As he stepped out of the lift from the police station's basement car park, the duty sergeant on the front desk called over.

'Cleggy's messaged down. Wants an update before you sign off.'

'Thanks, will do,' Jamie mumbled to himself. 'Like I was going home without telling the boss about the headless corpse that's been found on our patch.'

Clegg's office was one in a line constructed of glass and cheap veneered plywood that formed the far wall of the briefing room. Jamie knocked.

'Yes,' the voice was loud through the glazed door. 'And hold your nose. I'm not putting my shoes back on. My feet are killing me, and I won't be opening the window before Easter.'

Jamie entered. His nose twitched. 'Nice, boss. Mind if I keep things brief.'

'Alright for you. I bloody hate wearing heels all day. Sodding pointless, glad-handing the mayor and his police committee. Sit down and don't look up my skirt. You'll only be disappointed.'

Inspector Clegg was in a smart, winter-weight two-piece, but had her legs stretched with her feet angled up onto her desk. Jamie could see little worms of black and sweat where her toes met the seam at the foot end of her tights.

'So, what've we got? I'm not going to have to close the beaches am I?'

Jamie's face didn't register.

'Like in *Jaws*. When they find that girl's bits washed up on the sand.'

'Don't get much of a tide on the canal, boss,' Jamie smiled. 'Initial impressions look—'

'Professional. Sends a message. But not to us. Hence the lack of head and fingerprints.'

'That's the way I see it too, boss.'

'So, details so far?'

Jamie outlined the events of his afternoon.

'OK. I'll draft a press statement; get it out ASAP. Better if we're in the driving seat, rather than having to fend off rumours and shit.' Inspector Clegg eased her feet from the desk and wiggled her toes. 'Right. And bollocks to these.'

She held up her shoes and dropped them into a supermarket carrier, then opened the bottom drawer of her filing cabinet and took out a pair of white trainers.

'There. Adidas and Harris Tweed. Classic combination for the more mature, but still sexily athletic woman.' Easing the trainers onto her feet, she stood and flexed her toes. 'Anything else?'

'Possibly, but not for the press, boss. Can I check it out before I run it past you?'

'So long as I don't have to run after it. Not if I'm wearing those bloody heels.' She leaned on the desk and stretched. 'Okay. But let me know straight off if it turns out to be something.'

2

The central heating had reached lethargy point. Jamie's eyelids were already sliding into several second blinks and he knew a television-induced semi-coma was imminent if he surrendered. But he would never surrender. He hated this sluggishness and his answer was simple. He got off his arse.

Jamie gathered his clothes and equipment, like a priest with vestments and chalice. First, his coat. Berghaus; expensive, but it held him in a bubble of body heat even in the depths of winter. His rucksack contained a notebook, assorted pencils, micro-towels, maps, and two torches: head and hand. His phone's GPS provided the grid references for notes and sketches.

Once home, his edgeland chronicling would be written up in hard-covered journals on high quality paper. Text and illustrations were always pristine; two pens, black ink, one fountain, the other an artist's needlepoint.

'Like a *Wainwright's Guide* to dogging sites,' his sister had said when she'd seen it open on the kitchen table one morning.

Outside, he banged together ski-gloves, stamped mud-crusted boots and began to stride, inhaling life from the winter night.

He'd always done it. Gone out. The millions who spent their nights sofa-stretched and plasma-bathed were a mystery to him.

For Jamie, television was an irritant, soon turned off in favour of books. He savoured maps and illustrations of flora and fauna, as if they were menus of landscapes he might be tempted to try.

Tonight, his walk took him deep into the pockets of hidden green; the spaces forgotten by all but day-time dog walkers and night-time drug-takers and drinkers of plastic-bottled cider. He needed to be tired. He knew that broken, drifting sleep held the danger of infection from the events of the day, so he relied on the dopamine of movement to wash the canal-side torso from his inner eye. He needed distraction; the collision of nature with urban, the green with the galvanised and grime-caked, where plants and animals refused to be disheartened by pyramids of fly-tipped rubbish, or bound by the antiseptic boundaries of parks and gardens.

Winter. Jamie didn't mind. He enjoyed the rotation of light and dark, of creation and decline. He'd hated that about Africa and the Tropics. The sameness of it all; hot and wet, or hot and dry; the almost equal day-nights, the air devoid of vigour. And the relentless colour. But at night, he missed African skies; big, dark and star-clouded. This sky was narrow; cut short by tight-terraced roofs and diminished by streetlights bleeding into the night.

Jamie turned into the blackness of a passage between two gable ends, but his LED torch spread across a path and he strode out. Two garden walls enclosed a corridor of total shadow. Briefly, in the darkness, the torso flickered in his mind, but then, behind one of the walls, he heard a chain running, then clanking into stillness, then dragging across the ground again. With the chain came a snuffling and padding of paws. He waited for the inevitable bark.

'Quieten down Kaiser, it's only me,' Jamie hissed and the paws slowed. Jamie knew Kaiser well. In the daytime hours he was a gentle, lolloping presence in the shop that sat within one of the gable ends, but at night, when Mr Abdullah put him in the yard and gave the order "Kaiser, guard," Jamie was glad to have the wall between himself and the padding Rottweiler.

Soon the walls turned at right angles, stretching into a stark frontier between the street and the unruly thistle and scrub land beyond. A few metres on, close-packed silhouettes of hawthorn rose and enclosed a long-dismantled railway line. Beyond their skeletal arches was an open space, punctuated with clumping grass and low bushes. Shuffling into the shadow of shrubs, Jamie pulled a small square of carry-mat from his rucksack and knelt down, hoping the life of the night would wash his mind clear of the death of the day.

He focused on a series of mounds. Rabbit country; worn grass patched with sandy soil where warrens could run, dry and cosy. Sand beef, that's what his grandad used to call rabbits. It was only later, when Jamie read about their habitat, that he understood why.

After a few minutes, he saw the tails, white, bobbing exclamation marks in the dark, casually upright as heads went down to graze. Jamie smiled to himself. He was downwind and still. No cause for concern. Almost by touch, in the darkness, he began to write scruffy notes. Look and write, look and write, that was his routine. Then the day invaded the night and the bobbing white shapes resembled an earlier shape; a shape that Jamie had imagined bobbing in dark water. Any amusing cuteness was lost as Jamie looked into his mind's eye. Movement pulled him back into real-world focus as the white tails disappeared, directed down as all heads went up, sniffing the predatory air. Jamie's eyes were well-adjusted to the dark now. Two, three seconds and fast-bobbing white scattered in diverse curves, all arcing towards the sandy rise. One by one each tail blinked out as various entrances of the warren were reached. For a few moments, all was still. Jamie scanned the sky for the hovering ghost of a barn owl, but then movement in his peripheral vision made him turn and he saw the fox; its light-trotting, white-socked feet moving towards the rabbits' colony. Against the pale jaw fur, he could see the fox's tongue casually bouncing and, even in the dark, its eyes glinted with a hunger-born alertness. Reaching the first hole, the fox began to dig, sand flying backwards between his hind legs. Jamie watched. It was natural – the food chain in action. *It'll only come back tomorrow, dig out the young while the adults are away*, went through his mind. Not my place to intervene.

Then he was up, running, clapping his hands and the fox was wheeling away, scampering back into the night. Jamie reckoned it would take at least an hour of total stillness before the life of the edgeland would return.

He rolled up his carry-mat, re-packed his rucksack and began walking. Tapping the index finger of his right hand on the back of his left, he tried to occupy his mind, but when he reached the track and its arch of trees, the world went darker. The torso could not be resisted now. In his mind a young woman re-humanised, slim and bleach-blonde, moving through her last moments on Earth. Not just images, her thoughts were with him too. Jamie walked on, torch-led and steady, but in his mind he was racing, pursued by footsteps and muffled voices, bellowing above the sound of his own heart-pumped blood drumming in his ears. His feet moved automatically across the ground. Now Jamie was conscious only of his inner world and it was filled with the sound of predators; pursuing shouts, taunts, threats, breathing and feet closing the distance between hope and terror.

At the edge of the bramble scrub, the garden walls formed a corridor where shadow and fear became solid. Jamie stopped. But closing on his back, he felt them. He stood. He paced. He looked into the blackness. Breathing deep; deep and again, he focused on the distant gap between the gable ends and its promise of light. Holding his breath at the base of his lungs, he stepped into the darkness. Thought-borne pursuers closed in, their breath tangible, heavy with a butcher's casual disdain for the dismemberment of flesh.

Then a chain rattled and pulled him into the outer, conscious world.

'Quiet Kaiser, quiet,' Jamie whispered, but the dog's bark intensified as it sensed his panic. The chain rattled louder and faster and, as Jamie moved forward, the thud of paws moved along the wall, as if the enraged dog was following the track of his fear.

Jamie held himself to his steady walk. Then, a few paces from the wall end, in sight of the light beyond the gable ends, a thunderous impact sounded. Disorientated, almost vomiting, an age of seconds was broken by a second impact. It shook him back into coherence. With full force, the Rottweiler was hurling himself against a wooden gate. Now, finally running, Jamie sprinted the ten or twelve strides that pulled him into the safety of the streetlights where, hands on knees, he gasped.

Suddenly self-conscious, he looked around. No one near. Trying to walk naturally, he sucked in air. He could feel the throb of his carotid arteries and the tightness eased at the back of his tongue as the impulse to be sick abated. Stride by steady stride, oxygen began to win its battle. By the end of the street his breathing was normal and stability returned to his legs.

'Free and clear,' he whispered to himself on his front step, but then his fingers panicked, fumbling keys as the compulsion to look behind pulled at his shoulders.

Inside, leaning against the front door, he closed his eyes and became aware of his own back. Within his expensive, climate-controlled coat, he could feel sweat.

Folding, filing, tidying, he replaced all his ritual equipment, then made a cup of tea. He would clean his teeth and shower in the morning. Still in shirt and jeans, he lay on the bed and turned on the news. He wasn't interested in the world, but he needed speech-based radio, other people's words to fill his mind. He didn't want thoughts. No thoughts. He wanted sleep. He wanted his eyes to close without seeing the bloated torso, without imagining what went before. The radio droned on and he droned too; droned out his mantra.

'Tomorrow I'll phone Baggage. Tomorrow I'll phone Baggage,' tapping the index finger of his right hand on the back of left, syllable by syllable until the several second blinks came and lengthened.

3

Jamie's head was muzzy. Sleep had been short and surface only. He had a sense of dreams, but no memory of them and had woken before his alarm, anxious not to sleep beyond the time when he could speak to Baggage. He wanted to catch her before she went to school. Sierra Leone and UK time was synchronised in winter, though in Sheffield no one was awake early to avoid the heat of the day.

He waited anxiously as the tablet beeped.

'Jamie. How are you?' An African woman in her sixties appeared.

'Fine, Claudette, fine. And you're looking well.'

'Are you sure your screen is in focus?'

'You've never been lovelier. Don't look a bit pixelated.'

'Pixelated. I wish it was just pixelation I had to worry about. Still, I know you aren't interested in the aches and pains of an old lady. Let me call her. Give you a pretty face to look at… Emmanuella, Emmy. Daddy's on the iPad.'

Suddenly Jamie's screen filled with a new face; eight years old, with hazel eyes and skin much lighter than the old woman's. The ribbons in her plaits matched the maroon and white gingham of her dress and, for all the miles in between, she could be on her way to any English primary school, dressed in her summer uniform.

'Hello Baggage,' Jamie's smile was wide and natural, and so was the one that grinned back from the screen.

'Daddy.'

'You've lost another tooth,'

The girl's smile widened even more. 'Nanny says the tooth fairy keeps moaning because she has to give me too much money.'

'The tooth fairy?'

'That's what Nanny says, but I know it's just her really. I pretend I believe, in case she stops putting the money under my pillow.'

'Clever girl. Like your mam.'

'*Mum*, not mam. We're going to mass for her tonight. Are you?'

'If I can get away from work, but I'll say some prayers. Definitely.'

'I do keyboard after school. Been learning for a month.'

'You didn't say.'

'Nanny,' the girl called. 'Hold up the iPad, so Daddy can hear me play.'

The old lady came into view as Baggage turned her keyboard on.

'How much? I'll do a wire transfer.'

'Don't worry,' Claudette said. 'I got it second hand.'

'Still, let me know – and the lessons. There's all her clubs. I'll send—'

'Listen. Stop now Daddy, and listen.' The voice was beyond the screen. 'Bring it over Nanny, so he can see me.'

Jamie watched and listened as Baggage played her obvious learner's repertoire: *Twinkle, twinkle*, *Skip to my Lou* and *Chop Sticks*. More general chatter followed, school and friends and parties, then Claudette came back into view.

'Time to say Goodbye now. Time we were on our way to school.'

And the little girl waved and smiled.

'Upstairs now. Get your books.'

And the girl was gone.

The old lady looked into the screen. 'Good to see you Jamie.'

'Wish I was really there with you both. Maybe try to find a way.'

'Not in Sierra Leone. Too many people still know your face here… One dead parent is enough for that child. Especially today.'

Jamie's eyes closed as Claudette spoke again.

'We'll all think of each other today. Try and get to mass. Even if you don't believe in God, Jamie, he believes in you.'

4

Leaving his flat, Jamie's mind had been lightened by his call to Baggage, but, nearing the city centre, where parked cars formed unbroken lines in front of shabby terraces, he became oppressed by the day.

Walking towards the lift in the police station's underground car park, his feet slowed and his shoulders hunched. Knowing the macho fest that would greet him, Jamie inhaled as he approached the briefing room door. He was well-practised at oxygenating his bravado to fend off the Peepos' sniping words. The briefing room was mainly open space where people could stand to receive instructions and intel, but folding tables and chairs were stacked at the side, ready for occasional use.

Jamie's was the single police desk squeezed against the back wall and he reached it unnoticed by moving along the room's edge, while the Peepos were focused on ripping the piss out of the shortest one of their group.

As he checked his emails, the shaven-headed herd continued to mill, mocking and point-scoring, oblivious to the silhouette on the translucent door.

'Twat.' Jamie recognised the shape of the man who was leaning on the outside of the frosted glass talking to another foggier, smaller shape that was distorted by distance.

The door opened and, for a second or two, the noise level held constant. Then, one by one, mouths closed and body language shifted. Eventually, one voice remained, self-absorbed by the opportunity to be the centre of attention.

'And did you see when—'

'Yes, Hobbes, I'm sure he did.' The officer was behind him now.

The solitary speaker turned and shrank, becoming even more squat.

'Now gentleman, if we're ready?' The officer wore a similar uniform to the herd, but with embroidered gold insignia on his collar points and epaulettes, while – unlike the herd – from one shoulder a leather strap crossed his chest diagonally and clipped onto his belt. Stepping onto a lectern on a small platform, he faced the room, while his lanky second-in-command linked a laptop to a wall-mounted plasma screen.

'Target for tomorrow.' The officer stood to the side and a map appeared, then photographs. 'So, these are workers' transport and this is their destination.' A slide of transit vans was followed by a series of farm sheds. 'Information received identifies this as one of biggest operations in the area using illegal, foreign labour. Every day they're processing over a thousand chickens for distribution to small retailers.'

'Chickens,' Jamie sniggered to himself.

'Yes, sergeant?'

'Nothing, sir. Just my cold, bit of a cough,' Jamie faced the officer. 'Thank you for your concern, Group Leader Moonlight.'

'Personal health not one of your strong points, is it?' Moonlight's eyes became slits.

'Comes with the job, sir. Too many meals on the move and doing surveillance in bad weather.'

'Such dedication. Puts us all to shame.'

'Not just me sir. We all do vital work. All maintaining the rule of law. My murder case and your chicken operation.' Jamie leaned low over the papers on his desk, ending the encounter.

Moonlight straightened and a new slide appeared. 'If we can refocus gentlemen. Need to be on the ball. Efficient. Show them what justice means in this country. Hit them hard. Nasty, brutish and short. Job done, eh Hobbes?'

Jamie registered the remark, but his eyes didn't lift from the desk until Moonlight had finished and left the room.

'Bit of action,' one man rubbed his hands.

'Yeah, real military operation,' Jamie was on his feet, moving through the clump of dark shirts and shaved heads. 'Up against a crack squad of chickens. Let's hope they're not being led by Colonel Sanders.'

The Peepos stared, hoping one of them could say something smart. Eventually, the short one spoke into the silence. 'Why does Moonlight call me Hobbes? It's not my name. Why—' but the others just started talking and, as he faded into the acoustic background, Jamie was beyond the door.

When Jamie returned with a coffee, doughnut and a packet of throat lozenges, the Peepos were gone. Then his phone beeped.

'Yeah, it was on the briefing, few days back,' Dave Collins looked up as Jamie opened his door. 'So, I thought I'd honour the plain clothes glory boys with a call.'

'Great. What you got?'

'One of the mini-markets,' Dave was scrolling across a screen. 'They were fencing a load of knock-off burners and SIM cards. Uniform picked a couple up on a stop-and-search. Anyway, I've sent you this audio file.' There was a voice: female, East European echoing from his laptop.

She second to go. They say watch news. Help you work harder.

'It's all muffled now, listen. My guess? She's had to hide it, fast. Dropped it in a bag or pocket.'

'All talking English,' Jamie leaned forward to listen.

'Probably don't speak each other's languages.'

'But tracking it? How'd you...?'

'Burner. Cheap crap. Traced the batch number for the SIM cards,' Dave shrugged. 'What can I say? I'm a geek and it was a slow day.'

Jamie waited.

'Old Androids,' Dave continued. 'If the phone's on you can send a tracker app remotely and—'

'And she hadn't hit end call properly.'

'I was just playing about with it. Like I say, slow day. Seems the precinct was a go-to destination. Anyway, my guess is she must've seen someone.'

'And some shops could have CCTV,' Jamie joined the dots. 'Brilliant, Dave, brilliant. I owe you a pint.'

'Great. I'll hold you to that. But not with your mate – that barmy bird-watching pathologist. Evening with a pissed twitcher? Not my idea of life in the fast lane.'

Back at his desk, Jamie had the audio file on his phone. He listened a few more times then pulled his coat on.

As he crossed the car park he saw a black Merc, top of the range. 'Bastard Moonlight.' He reached for his key fob. Then he noticed the number plate. The car was identical, but this one had the latest registration. 'Fuck sake,' he stopped and looked. 'Same as last year. Third Merc in a row. All the same... except for a couple of digits.'

Jamie's car beeped and he got in. He knew the way to the precinct. Every copper in the city did. It was shithole central.

5

Jamie hated this estate. Late twentieth century pebble-dashed crap, tiny slit windows street-side and floor to ceiling glass at the back, with a sweeping view of five yards of concrete and a low wooden fence that everyone looks over and watches you eating your tea in front of the telly.

'You know when you live on a shit estate,' one of his mates had once told him. 'When your local pub has a flat roof.'

Jamie looked around as he was driving. This was shit in spades. The scruffy, Victorian terraces towards the city centre were luxury compared to these tight-packed, thin-walled boxes. Jamie remembered life in a noise sandwich, blaring music, screaming arguments, the occasional shagging if you woke in the early hours – and the casual morning conversations with the prat next door, as if you'd never heard him screaming death threats at his wife and children the night before. He'd seen a documentary on BBC4 once: scientists investigating how close rats could be crammed together before they began killing each other.

'Could've just driven to Manchester,' he'd told one of his mates on the refugee boats. 'Caught a bus to my old street in Collyhurst and looked around... Irk,' he said. 'A river ran through it – The

River Irk. Look it up… Geography and onomatopoeia.'

Pulling up on a patch of crumbling tarmac, he walked into the precinct. Low, flat grey shops around a litter-strewn square of paving slabs. People milled about in various versions of tracksuits and leggings.

'Like an Olympic Village for fat bastards,' Jamie muttered to himself. 'Feels like home.' A woman in jogging bottoms and stilettoes looked at him.

Scanning the garish shop signs he spotted the one he wanted: a mini-market with every window covered by security grills. Beyond the papers and magazines by the door, rows of general groceries and Asian ingredients stretched away deeper into the building like some retail version of Dr Who's Tardis.

A woman, somewhere between twenty-five and forty stood by the till. She too wore the obligatory elasticated sportswear, with her hair scraped back in a tight, greasy ponytail.

Jamie took out his police ID. 'I'm looking for a woman.'

'Nice of you to ask love, but I'm stuck here till six.'

Jamie couldn't help smiling. 'No, I'm trying to trace someone.'

'Yeah, I did guess.'

'East European,' he continued. 'Probably in her twenties. Bought a pay-as-you-go SIM card.'

'Well, you've come to the right place. They're always in here. Loads of them.'

'Where would I find them?'

'You don't work this patch then?'

Jamie waited.

'Somewhere on the industrial estate.' The woman looked towards the door.

'That's where they work?' Jamie asked

'You could call it that.'

'Have you got CCTV?'

'Yeah,' the woman pointed just above her head.

'And I could look at your recordings?'

'You could if I were the boss love, but he doesn't let me near it. Everything's in the back with the safe he's got concreted into the floor.'

'And if I wanted recordings from a month back?'

'You'd be out of luck. It's cheap knock-off, like half the stuff in here. Only has it for the insurance premium.'

'Thought you weren't allowed near it?'

'He talks. Thinks I'm deaf and daft.'

'Isn't he worried about theft?'

'Never keeps anything in the till more than a couple of hours. We do a lot of cash business, if you know what I mean. Him or his wife keep emptying the till and putting everything in the safe at the back.'

Jamie looked around. Cash business. The bottles of spirits had familiar brand names, but there was something about the letters and colours on the labels. The woman saw him looking and rolled up the shutter on a cupboard, then stepped to the side so he could see the packets of cigarettes and tobacco. He didn't need to look for the missing health warnings, or the Greek and Arabic lettering. He knew what she was saying.

'Caring employer is he?' Jamie asked.

'Shit, and I'm moving on. Bettering myself. Going for the big money. Starting at Lidl soon. Proper pay... Tax and National Insurance. It'll be a bit of a bastard, long term investment-wise. And not much chance of getting it back in pension payments, what with the life-expectancy round here. Still, sets an example to the kids... and it's a chance to diversify my portfolio.' The woman grinned. 'There's lots of them come in here, love, but I can't help you with names. It's all Nadia this, Irena that. Like I say... industrial estate.'

'So you don't think the East Europeans are taking your jobs then?'

'Not taking a job I want, love… Not taking a job any girl should have to do.'

As Jamie sat in his car he made a note about the shop. He'd pass the details on to the tax office and trading standards in a few weeks. Give the woman time to be clear, so no one would tie her in with the shop or his visit. He'd start helping to catch poor sods who earned a bit of cash to bulk up their benefits when the government started nicking their tax-dodging mates with off-shore accounts.

Back outside Jamie sat on a concrete bench in the concrete expanse of the precinct and opened Google Maps on his phone. When he looked up he saw a uniform on foot patrol. He walked over and showed his ID.

'Oh yeah,' the uniform said when Jamie mentioned sex workers. 'Down the far end. It's a knocking shop. Shag City as the locals call it. Been reported,' the uniform carried on. 'Ages ago. But…?'

Jamie waited.

'Yeah. I play badminton with one of the civilian admins. He collates stuff for vice. Said it's rated low priority. Unofficial line is, turn a blind eye if it isn't causing problems. Better than creating a vacuum for some real bastard to fill.'

'And it isn't causing any hassle?'

'Bit more than it was. Bigger volume of punters by all accounts, but nothing major.'

'Any reason for the change?'

'Under new management, as the saying goes.'

'So, there's a new owner?'

'Maybe, the way I heard it, the old man's still the owner, but there's a new guy in charge of the day to days.'

'Old man?'

'Yeah… this old Romanian guy. Been there years. Kept a tight ship, so Billy used to say.

'Billy?'

'Yeah, Billy Harriman. He was on this beat for years. Hasn't long retired. Knew everything. Like someone wiped a hard drive when he finished.'

The briefing room was quiet: just a couple of older admin Peepos filing. Jamie settled at his desk. Scanning his emails he saw the SOCO's address and clicked.

Copies of official photos sent to your dropbox – As per.

The signature was an emoji of a steaming turd.

Jamie navigated to the photos. Studying the five amputation sites, he was struck by the cuts and their flat planes, neat and untorn. Staring at the perfect ellipses of white bone and maroon marrow: like legs of lamb in a supermarket freezer, cut so precisely because the carcasses were already frozen and as stiff as wood, before the butcher portioned them out with a power saw.

Jamie wrote his hypothesis on a notepad.

Next he looked at the neck. Close up, he could see impressions of thin, twisted strands. *Garrotte made from bike brake cable or similar?* He jotted in his notepad. Then he examined the shoulder and its tattoo – *Tikra Meilė* and the horseman with a sword logo, matching the photograph he already had on his phone.

Typing *Dr Jas* into the address bar of the email, it filled in the rest of the pathologist's name automatically. Dr Jason Cosgriff.

Cozza,

On one of the rare occasions you aren't pissed, please check out these thoughts.

Jamie outlined his ideas about the garrotte, then asked:

Does body show signs of being deep-frozen prior to dismemberment? Keep twitching.

He kept his thoughts about the tattoo to himself.

Jamie's eyes remained on the laptop screen, but were looking nowhere. A few minutes passed and, below the desk, Jamie's right hand was clamped onto his left wrist. He closed his eyes and she was still there: Cara, and he was holding her hand; his stubby, white fingers intertwined between hers, long, elegant and black. She was as she would always be, and he was younger, slimmer and still square-shouldered then. That was how they were in that final photograph; the image he kept in his mind to blot out the last picture he was shown; the one that flashed up on the inside of his eyelids in the dead hours of the night. He was bound to feel it today: this morning, talking to Baggage and his mother-in-law. He wanted the day bustling, tasks and conversations filling every corner of his consciousness. But, for the moment, he was alone at the distant empty end of the briefing room with pressure across his forehead and a sickly tension in his throat. It was there now. Guilt. Regret. The sense of his own stupidity and its destructive, unfounded jealousy

His phone vibrated.

Opening the door into the corridor, he walked past the gents' toilet and pushed the next door: a rarely used beige, windowless cube of an office. Fluorescent tube lighting stuttered and he sat and reached deep into an inside pocket for the cheap burner. The text was from Jephcott: a simple instruction to meet, but framed in cryptic words. Jamie read it and then cracked the phone open and inserted the next SIM card in the rotation.

Jephcott was Jamie's only link.

'Yeah, understood,' Jamie had said when he'd been recruited. 'Then if anything goes tits-up you only lose a few people, not a whole network.'

At 5:30 Jamie was in the canteen queue at B Division and Jephcott arrived behind him.

'How's it going, Jamie?' Jephcott's remark was deliberately bland.

'Yeah, fine.' Jamie was equally forgettable.

'Is this yours?' Jephcott bent down and seemingly picked up a piece of paper.

'Yeah, thanks. Shopping list. Sainsbury's on the way home. Life in the fast lane.'

'Well, you know what they say about Sainsbury's?' Jephcott grinned. 'Keeps the riff-raff out of Waitrose.'

And that was that. Jamie turned and placed his order and the two men moved to separate tables. Hovering above a Danish pastry, Jamie heard a voice at a *notice me* volume.

'No, Jaspal. It is our decision. Tell him. End of…'

'Bollocks. What's that prat doing here again? Fucking wannabe.'

Jamie looked down, so only the top of his head faced the man on the phone.

'Jamie. How are you my man?'

'Fine, Dunky, fine. Still nailing the bastards for us?' Jamie looked up and nailed on a smile.

'Holding back the tide, Jamie. Holding back the tide. Do more if it wasn't for all the spurious crap we have to put up with just to get through a front—'

The Ride of the Valkyries blared from Dunky's jacket.

'Sorry. Need to take this.' And his hand swept up to his ear. 'Lal. Enforcement. Yes, yes. Why are you even asking? You know what we do. Zero tolerance. He shouldn't have the satellite dish mounted that low.'

Jamie stared into his drink.

'Okay, okay. Tell him he's got a week, but if it's not done we'll hit him. Full force, fifty pound penalty.' As Lal finished and dropped the phone into the inside pocket of his suit, the lining flashed a bright red satin. 'Sorry, man, sorry. Jesus, it's not like I don't give these people clear instructions. Anyway. How's your day been? Heard you were in the precinct.'

Jamie looked bemused.

'Never underestimate the reach of the Housing Department.'

'Okay, yeah,' Jamie re-fixed his smile. 'Following a lead. Trying to track a girl.'

'Torso in the canal case. Yeah, yeah. Where are we with it now?' Dunky leaned forward. We? flashed across Jamie's mind.

'Trying to track some East European girls,' Jamie leaned forwards. 'Think it must be vice related.'

'What with there being a knocking shop down the road with the colloquial name Shag City…' Dunky assumed a knowing grin. 'Carters industrial estate, row G; been there a while. Discreet, low volume. But last few months it's moved up my alert board. More coming and going. No pun…' Dunky spread his arms and laughed. 'No, seriously man, not nice for the neighbourhood, 'specially if the punters start getting lairy with the local females.'

Jamie looked.

'We can't touch it. Not even with our powers.' Dunky's face was alive with dramatic incredulity.

'Don't want something worse to fill the vacuum,' Jamie repeated what the uniform in the precinct had said.

Dunky leaned back in his chair. 'More like they've got connections. Someone in the establishment with their nose in the trough. Did a random bin check a month back. Got the big Fuck Off when they saw me counting up. Used to be okay, low profile, when it was the old man in charge. Went in there once. He gave me a cup of coffee and a print-out of his payments, council tax, business rates, the lot. Now it's some big bloke always there. Foreign. Mind, so was the old man.'

'So, you reckon you can get me information? Identify some faces?'

'Well… now I know what to listen for. I can put out feelers. Make sure my network knows what you want.'

The Ride of the Valkyries blared out of Dunky's jacket again and, when he looked at the caller ID, he stood and began walking.

'Yes, yes Mum. I know. If Faizal's only has dried chillies, I'll pick up fresh from Malik's. See you at half past.'

And Dunky Lal was heading for the door.

Once in his car, Jamie took out the fake shopping list that Jephcott had slipped him.

Usual location. Check transport manifest: personnel criteria. Select best candidates. Timings etc. to follow. Trying to arrange extra operative to assist.

'More life and death decisions. No biggy,' Jamie put the paper back in his pocket. 'New operative? Wonder when he'll make an appearance?'

6

The bedroom was dark except for the random globules of green light drifting and morphing across every surface. Jamie always switched the lava lamp on when he wanted to feel her close. It was cheap tat: its cracked base held together with tape. Jamie knew it should've been bin fodder years ago, but she'd bought it. Bought it for its greenness and now, as he lay in his boxer shorts, its shapeless blobs washed over him, bringing a kind of comfort. Often she talked to him in the light, in the green that she loved. She talked to him because Jamie needed her to; her cajoling, her nagging, the sound of her voice when he needed to feel forgiven. So many thoughts, so many voices: his own, Cara's, Baggage's, Claudette's, faces with no names. Moments. Decisions. Words you wanted to drag back from the air and obliterate. The randomness of the words. The randomness of talking to Tony: never really even a mate. But he'd said it, in the hospital canteen. "You should give it go. Gets you out on the weekends. Travel. Time off with pay. The hospital like it. Doing their bit. Hitting a target."

When he'd told Mandy, Jacko had started singing some daft song about weekend soldiers and how one of his mates was in the TA. "Just another oil sump. Don't make it more exciting because it's on a tank instead of a hatchback," he'd said.

Tony? Jamie thought. *Where was he now?* He knew where he'd been six months later. Sitting in an African bio-hazard suit, sweating his bollocks off. Never saw the wind-surfing promised in the recruitment brochure.

Time passed. Jamie wasn't counting. Not tonight.

His phone buzzed and he pulled himself vertical. *Mandy*, a photo blinked on the screen: a woman, a man grinning inanely in the background and three kids and a dog squashed together at the front.

'Hiya Sis.'

'Hiya Jamie love. Thought I'd call tonight.'

'Thanks Mand. How are the kids?'

'Fine, all fine. Jacko's sitting with them while they drop off. He's on nights. Had a sleep this afternoon.'

'Have another tonight, if I know him.'

'Yeah, well. Says he prefers it when there's breakdown. Stops the night dragging. Anyway, how's your day been?'

Jamie missed the beat where his words should have come, so Mandy did what women do and saved him from the silence. 'I know, love, I know. Busy, but there's been moments, hasn't there? Bound to be today. Five years.'

Jamie swallowed.

'Five years... a lot of water... and it still feels like yesterday.' Mandy spoke his words for him.

'I can't get past the argument, Sis. The stupid bloody argument. She was so pig-headed and...'

'That's why you loved her. Two pig-headed buggers together.'

Jamie could feel the smile in his sister's words.

'Sums you up. Become a paramedic to save lives and meet cute Manchester nurses and finish up with the marines, married to an African doctor.'

'He was tall, built like a sprinter,' Jamie's thoughts just bubbled up. 'The army nurse girls used to fight to get on the same shift as him.'

'Like twins then, the pair of you,' the tease in her voice was gentle.

'Claudette saw through him. Wrong tribe, she said. Bunch of goat-stealers. She could tell what tribe just by looking. Not just tribes though. She could see it all – me, Cara, him. Knew Cara couldn't stand him, but I couldn't see it… Couldn't see it, but stupid enough to say it.'

Jamie's words came now, poring over old ground, like so many times before, but Mandy listened anyway. Listened about Jamie thinking the man was working at the same medical station. And the argument. Finding out after that he'd been in Geneva for three weeks; out of Africa for good, on the after-dinner speaking circuit for the UN in Europe.

'Christ. I made it worse,' Jamie seethed at himself. 'Cara would've hated him. Seen his type before. Forget they're doctors. Give it a few weeks to sound credible, then step over the bodies on their way up and out. Bastards. Sorry Mand.'

'It's okay love, the kids are upstairs.'

'If I hadn't said it. If I hadn't been such a nob. She wouldn't have gone. God, why did I think anyone was a threat? She never gave me cause, Sis. She did it because I was being a nob. They said there was none left in the country by then. Ebola was finished. Said it was Yellow Fever. Similar symptoms, less frightening for foreign investors. They were lying and I drove her towards it. There were flies on her lips, Mand – crawling on her eye-lids.'

Jamie tried to choke back his sobs, and delude himself that his sister couldn't hear the guttural gulps of air and the sniffling. All consumed, his emotional bandwidth was maxed out long before he might sense her silent tears, or the phone, muffled by her hand, as she let him repeat the details of death: of his beautiful Cara. She listened again how he'd heard the news; how her body was sprayed with disinfectant and hurried underground. Heard again how all he'd seen was a grave and a photograph of her face; flesh fallen close to bone – and the flies on her lips and eye-lids.

Jamie's words stopped. They always did when he reached the photograph.

Eventually, Mandy spoke. 'Saw our mam a couple of weeks back.'

'Still pissed in Gorton?' Jamie gave his expected response.

'Still in Gorton, but she wasn't too bad. She'd had a couple, but she wasn't slurring or swearing, so I got the kids out the car. She liked that. You should see her.'

Jamie exhaled.

'You should. I know she's a piss-head, but she's still our mam. You'll only feel guilty if something happens.'

'Maybe… for you. When's her birthday?'

'Months. June. You know that. What about Christmas? That's soon. Don't go Christmas Day, she'll be rat-arsed, that's why I can't have her round with the kids. But maybe a few days before. See her before the depression of the season kicks in.'

'Am I still invited for Christmas?'

'Course you are. Jacko gets maudlin watching the Queen without adult company.'

'Aren't you an adult?'

'Not at Christmas. I spend all day in a paper hat.'

For a couple of minutes Christmas arrangements went back and forth. Who'd be where and when, and what the kids wanted for presents. Then Mandy spoke again.

'We went to mass for her tonight, me and the kids. I know you won't go, Jamie. But we went for you. Said a few prayers. The kids lit candles.'

'Thanks, Sis. Love you.'

And he tapped *End Call* as 'Love you too,' became a tiny sound in his hand. Jamie dressed, put his phone in his pocket, then reached for his coat and boots. He had to get out. It didn't matter where he went. He just needed to stride out.

For two hours he walked, fast march, yomping pace, pushing the blood into the places where thoughts might form if he was still. And then he was home. He didn't wash. Just fell into bed and the darkness.

Eternal rest grant unto her, O Lord, came into his mind. Old words he thought he didn't want anymore, but they repeated on a loop. Then, from some distant school assembly, he heard himself whispering in the dark. 'Out of the depths, I have cried to thee, O Lord. Lord hear my voice. Let thine ears be attentive to the voice of my supplication. If thou, O Lord, shalt observe iniquities, Lord, who shall endure it?'

Jamie had observed iniquities, but he couldn't endure them. Not after Cara. And as he stared into the dark *Eternal Rest* went back on its loop, until he fell asleep. Another anniversary over.

7

The sullenness of the day stood on the sorrow of the previous night. Jamie looked at the briefing room door. As he entered, the small Peepo turned and his mouth opened.

'Fuck off,' Jamie mouthed and raised a middle finger. The man turned back into the macho huddle.

Jamie's mind embraced the paperwork on his desk, hoping it would leave no space for punishing thoughts. After a while the doors opened and the Peepos parted.

'Fucking Moonlight,' Jamie watched him cross to the raised platform.

A large screen lit up on the wall. Between the red bars of rolling news a cerise-jacketed woman berated journalists. Jamie had heard it before. Everyone had. He'd seen her first on his laptop in Sierra Leone: a short clip on the BBC News website. Strident, articulate, in a chrome yellow top, standing in front of a phalanx of skull-shaven men in t-shirts: washed-out blacks and charcoal greys.

'The first duty of government is protecting its citizens,' the woman was in full flow, her trade-mark bright colours shimmering in front of her dark followers. They'd upgraded too, from t-shirts to official uniforms and from a loose collection of mouthy activists to People's Police: Peepos – low-level migrant persecutors and kickers-in of doors.

Jamie ground his teeth.

'If Britain was a house and our neighbours were infested with cockroaches,' the loud woman leaned towards the camera. 'Our first duty would be to keep their grasping little jaws away from our foundations: to protect it from the hostile swarms bred by less developed nations.'

'That's our girl, gentleman. The magnificent Ms K.'

Jamie glowered as Moonlight began his rant.

'Yes, I know it's a bastard that she's a woman, but she's got bigger balls than any of the milksop men of the party. She tells it like it is. No to the self-serving bastards who profit from their pet, brain-drain back door migrants. But what do we say? Same as her.' Moonlight's hand swept towards the grinning woman on the screen. 'The people voted *Bollocks to your back doors*. We live here and you only get into our house through the front door.'

'Bitch,' Jamie held the words behind his teeth.

Moonlight was still pointing at the shrill, cerise woman. 'Yes, gentlemen. That's our girl.'

Jamie blew his nose loudly, then opened a large tissue and searched its contents as Moonlight glared from the front of the room.

'Sorry, sir,' Jamie semi-waved the tissue. 'My head's full of snot.'

Moonlight clicked a mouse and a PowerPoint replaced the rolling news. 'Back to business, gentlemen. I'm sure we'll all rush to call a paramedic if Sergeant Seagrief manages to blow his own brains into his handkerchief.'

The Peepos collected folding chairs from the room edge. Some passed near Jamie and he blew his nose again and arranged used tissues around his desktop in an unsanitary border of contempt. Sat in rows, Jamie looked above the thick necks and stubbled scalps as Moonlight's hand swept across a Google Earth image.

London Gateway. Jamie recognised the Thames coastline.

'Dead ground. No cover,' Moonlight pointed at the featureless land that surrounded the concrete and metal brutality of the docks. 'We know it's close to London and its potential for disappearance but,' Moonlight zoomed the map out. 'Control the Manorway, Ocean Boulevard and Rainbow Lane, and it is, as they say, a proverbial piece of piss. Even if a couple evade the initial dockside capture, you should pick them up faster than Sergeant Seagrief picks up a sausage sandwich.'

Moonlight smiled, but Jamie had dropped his gaze. London Gateway. Virtually all freight. His operations always used major ferry ports.

'We nail these bastards. I've gone out on a limb so you can do yourselves a bit of good, gentlemen.'

Jamie knew exactly who was aiming to do themselves a bit of good.

'Sometime in the next couple of weeks,' Moonlight looked into the room. 'Just awaiting confirmation.'

'Sir,' came a Peepo voice from the chairs. 'Thames estuary. Bit out of our area. How come?'

'Local knowledge. That's the case I made. Told them how most of the unit is South Essex. Said, if it turned into a chase, it'd give us an edge.' Moonlight paused for effect. 'In a world of captured illegals with virtually flawless papers and fake bio-data ID, we need to prove we're capable of more than kicking in doors.

'We've all heard the rumours of corruption among the country's liberal elite and their lackeys in the police and border authorities. And that's all good. It means when Miss K and her allies decide to flex their political muscles they'll know they've got an alternative ready to go. So, we nail them, gentlemen. Hard, fast. Sweet as… And any cocks-up?' Moonlight looked into the room, hands on his hips. 'I'll be ripping the offender's bollocks off and having them set in gilded clasps for the magnificent Ms K to wear as earrings.'

Moonlight collected his notes and memory cards and, turning for the door, had one last stab at rousing the troops. 'Chance to shine, gentleman. And keep your bollocks intact.'

As the door closed, the Peepos relaxed and began to shuffle the furniture back against the walls.

'Three vans.' One of them was saying. 'PowerPoint said only twenty in the consignment. Fit them in two vans, easy. So why the spare van, out on the edge?'

'Always too many vans when we do dockside snatches. Haven't you clocked it before? Anyway, bollocks for earrings,' a large hand was placed on the smallest man's shoulder. 'What'd you think of that short-arse?'

'No, problem, she wouldn't want mine,' the short Peepo grinned. 'My left bollock's twice as big as my right.'

'Yeah,' Jamie lifted his head. 'Wouldn't want anyone to think she was unbalanced.'

A few of the Peepo herd still grazed across the central plains of the briefing room as Jamie took a bite out of a post-lunch doughnut.

The door opened and a woman came in.

'Not bad.' An image from a CD case flashed across Jamie's mind, *The Eurythmics, Ultimate Collection* – a young Annie Lennox, all cheekbones and close-cut blonde hair and his mother playing the same track endlessly in her daily drink or drug induced stupor – *Sweet Dreams (Are Made of This)*.

As the woman crossed the room the grazers turned, like a synchronised leering team. Inevitably, it was the short one that spoke. His words were mumbled, but the woman's weren't.

'Not while there's dogs in the street.' She raised a middle finger. 'I'd rather sit on this. It's probably bigger.'

The other Peepos grinned.

Bit more Glasgow than Annie Lennox, Jamie thought. He enjoyed watching someone else take up the baton of resistance.

The woman crossed to the frosted glass offices and knocked on Clegg's door. Jamie went back to his doughnut. Then his desk phone rang.

'Get in here and don't bring that bloody doughnut.'

Jamie entered, brushing off sugar.

'And stop licking your fingers and messing up my carpet.' Inspector Clegg held out a hand. 'Sergeant Seagrief. Our Jamie,' Clegg spoke to the woman with Annie Lennox hair. 'He's better than he looks. He'd have to be.'

The woman suppressed a grin.

'Go and finish your doughnut. Wash your hands, tidy yourself up and come back in ten minutes.'

Jamie shambled through the door.

When he re-entered he was a sugar-free zone, his shirt and jacket were straightened and his tie was slid just shy of the still open top button.

'There, that's better,' Clegg said. 'Now you can play nicely.'

Jamie looked at the skirting board.

'Proper introductions. Jamie, this is Shona McCulloch; she's a sergeant, like you,' Clegg continued. 'I'd like you to outline our current concerns for her.'

'Like the headless torso?' Jamie's eyes lifted.

'Yes. I think that might qualify.'

Jamie was factually accurate, but said nothing about leads or theories, then sat, his eyes at right angles to the newcomer.

'And tell her about the people we work with.' Clegg continued.

'What, those out there?' Jamie indicated the briefing room. 'They're prats. Muscle, mouth and fuck all else.'

'Ladies present,' Clegg interrupted.

'Sorr—' Jamie stopped himself apologising, then continued. 'I'm not ascribed to a team, but I make links, work across departments.'

'Polite, better. That's the mood we want.' Clegg looked at him. 'So what's this lady's name again?'

'Sheena McTaggart.'

'Shona McCulloch,' Clegg's voice reminded Jamie of countless teachers from his teenage years. 'Try it again.'

'Shona McCulloch,' Jamie repeated.

'Yes. And, to help Sergeant McCulloch get a feel for the job, she'll be shadowing you over the next few days.'

'For fu—'

'Err…' Clegg lifted a finger. 'Like I said, ladies present. Now clear off back to your desk. I'll send her out when I've finished.'

Jamie was clearing his desk when Clegg's door opened and Shona McCulloch crossed towards him. The eyes of the herd were surreptitious this time. Sitting down, she placed her large shoulder bag on the desk. The zip was open, affording Jamie a glimpse of what appeared to be a document wallet inside.

'Secret plans?' Jamie nodded, as he tidied his desk.

'Yeah, the North Koreans don't like me leaving their missile blueprints lying about. Clegg says you should give me a lift to regional headquarters to collect my car. Said you could point out some of the city's more interesting areas on the way.'

'I've got all this to go over,' Jamie took a folder from his desk drawer.

'That's the one I just saw you putting away, right?'

Jamie sucked his teeth and pushed the folder back where it had come from.

'Any chance you'll tell me something useful over the next few days?' Shona said as they crossed the station's underground car park.

'I told you. Those Peepos are all prats.'

'Yeah, thanks. Like I'd never have worked that out for myself, you know, being a detective and all..'

Jamie arranged himself in the car; folding loose ripples of

jacket, taking his belt in a notch and pulling his trousers out of his crotch, then blowing his nose one more time.

'You could fart,' Shona said. 'If you wanted to take your disdain to the next level.'

'Look,' he clipped his words. 'I've got a headless torso. And maybe, just maybe, the clock's ticking till another body turns up.'

'So get on with it.' Shona replied. 'Just do what you'd do if I weren't here – except the farting in confined spaces.'

Jamie raised an eyebrow.

'Do your job. Don't fart in the car. That's all I ask.'

Jamie held in a smile.

Back home, Jamie balanced his laptop on a kitchen work surface as he washed up. Then, surprised by the beep of an incoming Skype, he pulled at his rubber gloves and dived towards the screen.

'Oh, bollocks,' a yellow finger end snapped off, but he used his naked index tip to manipulate the mouse.

'Daddy,' the voice was loud and cheerful.

'Baggage, you're—'

'Early. I know. School's started morning dance classes. Nanny's looking for my leotard.' Baggage smiled. A gap-toothed, clichéd cute kid smile. Her hair was bunched and the faultlessness of her copper skin was made even more perfect by the dense whiteness of the too-big towelling dressing gown.

Recognition. Melancholy. Jamie's thoughts were just there: memories of that dressing gown, that weekend, the illegal case cramming as they left the Rameses Hotel in Cairo. And his wife, on their last ever weekend trip together. The feel of that dressing gown on his cheek, her perfume, and her skin, dark against the white cotton.

'It's mummy's' Baggage broke in.

Jamie smiled. 'Bit big yet, treasure. But you look the part.'

Baggage tilted her head.

'Like a film star on a yacht,' Jamie smiled. 'Beautiful, like your mother.'

'Nanny,' Baggage called. 'Daddy's on the iPad. Is that my leotard?' As she walked away from the screen, she rolled her hips, trying to look the part.

'How's things?' Jamie spoke as the old woman eased herself into the chair. 'Moving well?'

'Probably hear my hip bones creaking over the internet.'

'Seriously Claudette, how are you?'

'Fine, fine. Just a bit of age. I'm not falling apart yet. Too much to do. Too much keeping me alive.'

'Baggage tiring you out?'

'Hours and moments, but weighing in the scale? You can catch being young. Keep being around them and they'll infect you with life. On balance, I'll take a bit of tiredness. Anyway, how about you? How you doing with the bad people?'

'Got this murder. Nothing by African standards.'

'All life Jamie. All sacred. You do good things.'

'But when you're getting nowhere and there's someone out there who needs stopping before...' Jamie could see the flash of white dressing gown across the back of the room as Baggage packed for school.

'You'll get them. You'll—'

'I'll keep getting nowhere and now they've given me a woman to drag around.'

'Given you a woman? Is that some sort of bonus payment.' Claudette rocked in her seat and chuckled.

'Bonus payment?'

'I've told you before, men aren't built to be alone. They need comfort and guidance.'

'Comfort and guidance?' Jamie exhaled. 'You've never met a woman from Glasgow.'

'What's her name, this Glasgow woman?'

'Shee – Shona McCulloch.'

'Shee-Shona? Nice name. Not heard it before.'

'No. Shona. Her name is Shona McCulloch. She's a policewoman. New to the area.'

'Is she pretty?'

'Haven't really noticed.'

'Pah,' Claudette exhaled. 'A man knows if a woman is pretty in a milli-second. First thought. Faster than thought. Always.'

Jamie's mouth opened, but only filled with fluster.

Claudette chuckled again. 'You and that child. You keep me alive. Her with her energy and you… you with your embarrassment. Grown man like you, bluster and blush whenever a woman is mentioned. You keep me laughing Jamie. Keep me laughing all day.'

'Nanny. Dancing.' Suddenly, Baggage was larger on the screen. Larger, with gingham; her school uniform replacing the white dressing gown.

'Daddy,' Baggage waved and blew a kiss. Jamie did the same. 'I've got my leotard on under my dress.' She pulled the shoulder strap where it was visible.

'Hope you don't need the toilet then,' Jamie teased.

Baggage popped out her tongue and walked away. Jamie watched as she shouldered her rucksack, then Claudette returned to the screen.

'Got to shut you down now, Jamie. Got a day ahead. Next time you call you can tell me if Miss Shona McCulloch is pretty. If you've noticed by then.'

And the screen faded.

Driving to work, Jamie's car was filled with talk-to-yourself words and thoughts more real than the uneventful streets.

Claudette and Baggage an internet presence, safe provided he kept himself a thousand kilometres from Freetown.

His wife? Photos and memories.

Precious videos lost.

'Fucking useless African cloud back-up and you. You bastard.'

A grinning border guard expressing his dissatisfaction with the bribe offered by grinding Jamie's phone under his boot. Hands and eyes on autopilot, random recollections filled his consciousness: the loss of Cara, his attempts to make amends providing safer exit routes for the desperate of Freetown. Falling foul of the local people-smugglers: fleeing the country: working his way to the Mediterranean via a succession of refugee camp jobs and then on the boats – pulling the poor bastards out of their sinking dinghies, sitting off-shore until one of the European states cracked under the pressure of world media and let them land. And eventually back to England – a very different England from the one he'd left. An England with tightly closed borders and tighter closed minds.

Then his cheap second phone buzzed.

8

Occasional Peepo night staff came in and out, dropping off and collecting documents. Jamie flicked through files.

'Me and my fucking shadow,' he was in work well before his shift started. 'See if I can get something done.'

Ninety minutes later, Shona McCulloch pushed open the briefing room door. The herd was in full throng. Jamie noticed the short Peepo – who'd been on the receiving end of her finger the previous day – open his mouth, but then close it in a rare moment of good judgement.

'Worried I wouldn't show up?' Shona settled on a chair. Jamie faked a smile.

'I've jotted down bullet points on the case, and an itinerary of people you should meet,' he slid a sheet of paper across the desk.

'You've gone to all this trouble,' Shona began to read. 'And there was me thinking you might try and get rid of me for a few hours.'

'No. Nothing further from my mind.' Jamie kept his eyes on a file.

'Love a good treasure hunt.' Shona picked up the paper. 'Chance to see our workplace at its best. Not sure I got the best first impression yesterday, what with those Peepos and then noticing the little bait boxes tucked under the S-bends in the ladies' toilets.'

'Yeah, perils of replacing quality components with cheap alternatives. Tends to encourage vermin.' Jamie's eyes flicked for a microsecond towards the Peepo sector of the room.

Shona reached for a pencil. 'Just rearranging these names. Be back and forth between rooms all morning if I went round in this order. And I know you wouldn't want me wasting time.'

'Be back before lunch. I've arranged a meeting.' Jamie's eyes stayed fixed on his papers.

'There,' Shona stood up. 'Everything organised. Maximum efficiency.'

As Jamie watched her cross the floor, Claudette was in the back of his mind laughing.

Then he lifted his phone and began typing.

Twenty minutes later it buzzed against his desk. He picked it up and de-selected speaker.

'Jamie, my man. Anything I can help with? Bit of joint enterprise?'

'Thanks for getting back to me. Appreciated. Look. I'm in the office now, but—'

'You need a meet?'

'Ahead of me, Dunky, ahead of me. Yeah, need a meet.'

It was just gone midday when Shona arrived back to the desk.

'Thanks for that. Probably clocked up my ten thousand steps and it's not even lunchtime,' and she sat.

'When you're ready,' Jamie stood and reached for his coat.

The pub wasn't far. Refurbished Victorian with a touch of wannabe modern. There was a gap at the bar, so Jamie dived in and ordered two lime and sodas. In a corner alcove he could see Dunky, phone in his right hand, clamped to his ear as ever, while his left waved around like Mussolini with the volume on mute. Dunky spotted Jamie and beckoned. He smiled at Shona; teeth and eyes, but kept talking.

'I told you what to do. Why are you asking again? If the satellite dish is still there, hit him with the fifty pound fine... No, no buts. Look, I've got another important meet.' Dunky dropped his phone in his pocket. 'Sorry, Jamie, sorry... Always the same. Can't take my foot off for a minute.' Again he smiled at Shona.

'Shona McCulloch,' Jamie made the introduction.

Dunky extended a hand. 'Hi, Shona. Good to have you on board. Dunky Lal - Enforcement.'

Jamie winced on the inside.

'Dunky Lal. Oh yes,' Shona smiled. 'You're one of my missing pair. Jamie sent me around the building this morning, so I could meet all the key people. Just you and one other I couldn't find.'

'Hiya, Nobhead.' A hand landed on Jamie's shoulder. When he turned, the man was holding a pint.

'Cozza,' Jamie said. 'Starting early aren't you?'

'What?' Cozza looked down. 'Calling you nobhead, or having a beer?'

'Both, you twat.'

Shona was grinning. 'Cozza?' she said. 'You're the other missing person.'

Cozza looked bemused.

'On her list.' Dunky joined in. 'She's been looking for the key players. Jamie sent her on a mission. We were the only two not polishing the office chairs with our arses.'

Cozza took a long sip of beer.

'Like I said,' Jamie commented. 'Starting early.'

'Started early.' Cozza took the glass from his lips. 'Called out before five this morning. Road accident. Load shifted on a lorry. Some poor bastard was hiding in the back. Two traffic officers threw up all over the hard shoulder. Pile of blood and bones when the packing case was lifted off. So yes. I'm starting early.' And he took another long swallow. 'On the plus side,' he continued, 'I saw a kestrel, two jays and a buzzard while the tow truck was pulling the lorry off the motorway.'

Jamie opened his mouth to speak, but Cozza leaned across him and placed his pint glass on the table. 'Keep this safe, while I go for a slash.'

'Night out with the pissed twitcher. One for the bucket list,' Shona whispered as he moved away.

'What?' Jamie said.

'Night out with a pissed twitcher. Dave Collins told me not to go for a drink with you or I'd finish up spending the night talking to a pissed twitcher – Cozza, I presume.'

Again, Jamie's brain missed its cue for words.

'Or is it both of you? Two pissed twitchers together?' Shona filled the gap.

'Heard you were keen on nature, Jamie. I'd heard that. But never heard anyone call you a pisshead,' Dunky joined in. 'Like a bit of nature myself. Hi-def and the surround sound on a big plasma. Like being there.'

Jamie shuffled in his seat.

'Saw this Attenborough thing once,' Dunky continued. 'Tigers in night-vision, strolling about in the middle of Mumbai. Bloody feet away from people. It was—'

Cozza leaned across Dunky, placed a fresh pint on the table, then drained the remainder from the glass he'd left.

'Just saying you and Jamie. Same interest. Two naturists.'

'*Naturalists*, you prat,' Cozza wiped his mouth on his shirt cuff.

'Oh, thanks for that,' Shona put her hands across her eyes. 'Christ. I may never sleep again.'

Dunky laughed, 'Oh, yeah, sorry. Wouldn't inflict that on you.'

'Like you'd be a bronze god in your pants,' Cozza pulled up a stool. 'So, who's been taking my name in vain?'

'Dave Collins called us a pair of pissed twitchers,' Jamie finally spoke.

'You, pissed? Be better company if you did get pissed,' Cozza snorted. 'Jesus. I thought he must have scurvy the first time I had a drink with him, amount of lime juice he got down him. No, Jamie's not pissed. Not even a twitcher. Just thinks he knows a bit. Delusional bastard.'

Jamie stood. 'Back in a minute. You can talk about me while I'm in the gents.'

'What'll we do the rest of the time? Your life isn't interesting enough to take up a whole piss.'

Jamie kept walking.

'Actually,' Cozza leaned into the table. 'The prat knows stuff. Species; habitat; slips in and out of Latin scientific names. Bloody encyclopaedic. Just normal life he says fuck all about.'

Once back on his seat, Jamie inhaled. 'Cozza, while you're here. How's the girl going?'

Cozza looked confused.

'Canal Girl.'

'Sorry. Tried a couple of times, but my boss keeps dropping other stuff on me. Two post-mortems. Urgent, he says.'

'Are they?'

'Not compared to a headless torso. Died in an old folks' home. Hardly unexpected and not even the same care home company, so God knows why they need investigating?'

'Cozza,' a voice called across the room. 'This is yours.' A hand held up a pint. 'And we're on next.'

'Two more urgent priorities for you,' Jamie's eyes angled away from Cozza. 'Beer and a game of darts.'

'Fuck off. I've seen enough for one day,' Cozza stood. 'Look, I'll give it a chase first thing in the morning.'

Cozza walked off towards the beer and darts. Jamie's gaze remained fixed.

'So, that wasn't much of a meeting,' Shona broke the silence.

'Wasn't with Cozza. He was just random. No, I thought Dunky

could take you around the area. Show you the hotspots.'

'Ooh, another treasure hunt,' Shona smiled. 'That'll mean I've been away from you nearly all day.'

'Love to Jamie. Love to,' Dunky was oblivious. 'But I'm in court this afternoon. Some bastard keeps nicking the lead off the depot roof. Nailed him with the CCTV. Should be open and shut, but I've got to be there. Anyway, the torso and brothel stuff? You know where all that is now, yourself.'

'So you could take me. Great. All is not lost,' Shona grinned. Jamie shied away from her eye-contact.

Dunky stood. 'Sorry about this afternoon, Jamie. Just a diary clash. It happens. Too many irons, too many fires. Like I say, you know the main sites yourself. And the precinct. It'll give Shona a sense of the locus. Shona, sorry. Some other time.' Dunky shuffled into his jacket. 'Oh, and that other thing. Leave it with me, Bro.' And he moved to the door.

'So,' Shona said as Jamie stared into his glass. 'Are you going to give me a tour? A sense of the locus.'

'Fucking locus,' Jamie almost smiled. 'It's an area – a place. Fucking locus.' And he stood and began walking.

Shona scrambled to pull her coat from the back of the chair and follow Jamie through the punters that crowded around the bar.

'Don't forget to write.' They turned to see Cozza blowing a kiss as he stood near the dartboard.

9

Shona jolted into the seatbelt as Jamie braked late for the zebra crossing. A mother with a pushchair mouthed fucking wanker, making sure that lip reading wasn't a problem. Behind her a child of about four was pedalling his bike expertly. He looked at Jamie and stuck out his tongue.

'He's right. You're driving like a prat,' Shona spoke the first words since Cozza had blown his goodbye kiss. Jamie made a low grunt. A minute later they were pulling onto the precinct car park, the car's tyres spluttering across the crumbling tarmac.

'It's a shit estate,' Jamie now spoke his first words.

'I know. I saw the kid on the bike.'

Jamie was about to speak again, but Shona went on. 'Stabilisers and safety helmets not part of the local parenting experience. That and the lack of skinny latte coffee shops.'

'If these bastards had skinny lattes they'd dunk their black pudding in it.'

Jamie walked over to a hardware shop, lifted the lid on a cardboard drum and let the little red-brown spheres run between his fingers.

'Pigeon peas. Good to see the old sports still clinging on. You don't see racing pigeons circling over people's houses like you used to.'

'No, the world's found new ways to shit on us all from a great height.' Shona looked at the hard, dried peas. 'Last job, the pubs used to call these grey peas and serve them boiled up with bacon. Bowl of these and a pint. Night on the town.'

'Where was that?' Jamie looked at her.

'Walsall,' Shona replied.

'They eat pigeon peas?'

'As a local delicacy.' Shona gave a slight shrug.

'In Walsall?'

'And the surrounding areas.'

'Fucking savages,' Jamie dropped the lid back down onto the drum.

Crossing towards the mini-mart in the corner, Jamie spoke again. 'So you worked in Walsall? Didn't it win *Britain's Fattest Arses* once?'

'Wouldn't know. I only used to go there on a tourist visa. I was based in Birmingham. Still, if Walsall wants to reclaim its crown I can negotiate your transfer fee.'

Jamie opened his coat. Underneath the cold weather bulk, layers of shirt crease met lines of trouser folds and a long tongue of leather showed a belt pulled tight. 'Half the man I used to be a couple of months ago.'

Shona's face asked the question.

'Price of upsetting Clegg,' Jamie went on. 'Bit of banter and the next thing the cow's put my name down for a compulsory fitness test.'

Shona tried to suppress a snigger.

A group of young women walked out of the mini-mart's door: their clothes short and more cheap nightclub sparkle than an afternoon at the shops. As they passed, Jamie and Shona heard their accents. Eastern European.

Jamie watched them cross the grey slabs. Then he and Shona walked into the shop. There were raised voices. One was an Asian male, the other local and vocal.

'So you'll owe me ten hours wages if I stay till five.'

'You fuck off now. I'm not paying a penny.'

'Ah, officer, good to see you again. Just in time to see me and my employer discussing the finer points of handing in your notice.' The woman had her pony-tail pulled back tightly, giving herself a council-house facelift.

'Officer?' The Asian man shifted from foot to foot.

'Legally a period of notice isn't mandatory, but paying for the hours worked is. Would you like me to show you the relevant paragraph in the law manual I keep at the station?'

The man opened the till and counted out fifty pounds. 'Here, ten hours pay. You stay till five then I get my nephew to take over.'

Jamie reached across and took two more twenty pound notes from the open till. 'And that gets us nearer to the level required by the minimum wage act.'

The shop owner cursed and retreated towards a storeroom door.

'I see you managed to get a substitute to help get you over the disappointment.' The woman smirked at Jamie. 'He came in here a couple of days ago telling me he was looking for a woman,' she turned her head to include Shona. 'But I told him I was unavailable.' She kept grinning, amused by Jamie's obvious unease. 'I know I should have let you down gently, but she's well above average for a bloke like you.'

'If we can get back on track,' Jamie shuffled from foot to foot. 'Those girls. The ones that just came out. Did they...?'

'Yeah. Well two of them did. Bought those cheap phone cards.'

'Are they...'

'Yeah. From the knocking shop on the industrial unit. Often in, this time in the afternoon.'

'And you haven't seen them anywhere else?' Shona asked this time

'Not really, no. Well, just in a taxi. Four of them; heading towards town. Sorry. Nothing else. I'd say if—'

'OK, thanks.' Shona looked towards Jamie. He nodded and they turned. Shona was already through the door when the woman spoke again.

'Thanks for that. The extra forty. Sorry I was a bit over the top with the teasing.'

Jamie smiled.

'I expect,' the woman continued. 'You'd need some kind of court order to demand details of the SIM cards we sell.' The woman began writing a post-it note.

'What happened to you?' Shona looked back as he emerged from the shop.

He held up a Mars bar. The wrapper was creased.

'Looks battered,' Shona commented.

'Glasgow delicacy, the battered Mars bar. No, didn't you see the cheap chocolates in the just-out-of-date bin?'

Shona began to walk.

'It's down that way,' Jamie spoke as they reached the edge of the car park. 'The industrial unit. Sign says it's self-storage.'

'Aye, well I suppose it'd be a give-away if it said brothel.'

'Actually one of the bigger units. around four hundred square metres, not counting the mezzanine floor.' Jamie flicked his key and the car lights and locks gave a synchronised blip.

'Mezzanine floor?' Shona opened her door.

'Dunky says it's on the business rates documents. Maximises the rent to profit ratio, apparently.'

'Outstanding,' Shona reached for her seatbelt. 'A brothel with a business plan.'

Easing off the car park and turning left, after a few hundred metres they saw the galvanised metal fence.

'About fifty yards down,' Jamie slowed the car as they passed through the gates. 'Row G.'

'Great,' Shona was looking at the corrugated metal building. 'Shagging on an industrial scale. You think the body from the canal is from here?'

'Don't know. But I think she's East European.'

Parking well short of the unit, Jamie pointed further down the service road to a huge building.

'That's the place that makes it feasible. All-night freight delivery. Lorries, workers in and out of here twenty-four hours a day.'

'So, there'll be CCTV,' Shona said. 'Car number plates for the knocking shop visitors.'

'Trouble is,' Jamie looked down the drive. 'The ones for the delivery depot are by their security gate. Brothel's punters don't have to go that far.'

'But the security guard might...'

'Yeah, might.' Jamie stared at the kiosk and the red and white barrier that marked the entrance.

Shona wound down her window as a young woman walked by about ten metres from the car. They both watched as she headed into the Shag City unit.

'Polish,' Shona said. 'See her carrier bag? *Moda Polska*. It's a fashion store. Probably online.'

Jamie didn't speak for a while, then said, 'You ought to see where we found her.'

Back in the car park beneath the police station, Jamie twisted to reach a document wallet on the back seat of his car. 'Should've shown you these before.'

Shona didn't flinch as she flicked through the photographs.

'Any thoughts?' he said when she was half way down the pile.

'Give us a second.' Eventually, she had three photos in her hand. 'Cuts are clean. Thought they'd look more hacked. There's a mark by the neck cut. Too thin to be rope. And that,' she flipped another photo to the top of the pile. 'That looks like a tattoo, but there's all sorts of other marks.'

Jamie nodded. 'Yeah. Got a blow-up back at the office. But the way the head and limbs—'

'Neat, like the frozen lamb at Iceland.' Shona finished his sentence.

'Yeah. That's what I've asked Cozza to check,' Jamie took the folder back. 'Clever place to do it though.' He took out a photo. 'Busy road, shops above, but down here…' his finger tapped the seemingly endless darkness beneath the bridge. 'Better put that out of sight.' Jamie nodded at the document wallet, then got out of the car.

Shona followed him towards the boot.

'Just drop it in,' Jamie clicked the lock.

'Phwor. Bloody hell,' Shona stepped back. When she steeled herself to return, she saw a bedraggled gym kit spilling out of a bag. 'Forgot it was there. Bloody compulsory fitness tests.'

'Only been there three days,' he smirked as she backed away. 'Think I've only worn it twice since the last wash.'

'My car's over there,' Shona clicked her key and her lights and locks reacted. 'I've got an induction interview in an hour, but I'll be back later. Some guy called Jephcott.'

Jamie didn't notice Shona crossing the briefing room.

'Nice to have a remark free passage.'

As he looked up Shona sniffed the air.

'What are—'

'Seeing if I can smell your running kit from here'

'Environmental health, said they'd sent a couple of blokes in bio-warfare suits to put it in the washer.'

An array of large envelopes lay on the desk in orderly rows.

'What's—'

'Just putting them away.' Jamie stood and opened a filing cabinet. His phone beeped and he extricated it from deep inside his jacket.

Pulling out his wallet first, it fell open on the desk.

'No, I don't want to sign a bloody petition,' and he turned back to the filing cabinet.

Shona leaned across the desk. Inside the wallet was a photo of a young girl, maybe two years old, copper skin and bright eyes. A hand was visible on the shoulder, female, much darker, elegant fingers.

Shona stared at Jamie's back. 'Saw that Jephcott, like I told you.'

Jamie grunted, locked the filing cabinet then sat down and began tidying various stationery. Shona was staring at the top of his head now.

His phone beeped again.

'Oh fuck off, Dunky you tosser.' He glared at the screen and stuffed it back in his pocket. The wallet followed. Then he grabbed his coat. 'Take this to Dave Collins and ask him what he can do with it.' He handed Shona a post-it note. 'And then I need a set of false number plates picking up from the maintenance unit. Ask Dave to phone ahead – and check they give you the ones with decent clips. Last lot slid about all over the place. I'll be back around five.'

Shona could feel her back teeth grinding as she watched his back cross the room. As the door closed behind him she took out her phone.

'Hi Dunky,' she began. 'Yes, used your business card. Nice design. Look, Jamie isn't here at the moment, but he said you'd messaged. Said it'd be important if it was off you … Yeah, yeah, just getting a pen now.

'Billy Harriman, Yes,' Shona was writing. 'And Jamie should ask him about the other old man. The friend: the poor one. Okay, got that… You say this Billy Harriman will be useful. Thanks, Dunky. I'll tell him as soon as I see him.'

About ten minutes later she was peering round Dave Collins' door. 'Hiya. Got something from Prince Charming for you.'

Dave Collins grinned.

'Unregistered SIM cards. Can they be traced?' Shona held out a post-it.

'Yeah, but better if I track them for a few days, see if they tell a story. So, you and Jamie—'

'Me and Jamie…' Shona's eyes closed involuntarily for a second. 'Words I will never speak in the same sentence.'

Dave Collins was still grinning. 'So?'

'Jesus. Where do I start? Thought there was a slight thaw when we were driving around, but since we got back to the station I've been back with my arse on an iceberg.'

'He is an enigma,' Dave Collins' lips and eyes held back any amusement. 'A paradox wrapped in a riddle.'

'He's a prat,' Shona cut in. 'And he wants some false number plates. Apparently I've got to check the clips are up to his exacting standards. He said could you ring ahead to make sure they're expecting me.'

'No problem. Look. I'll message him about the SIM cards. Tell him why a couple of days will tell us more. Save him quizzing you.'

'Thanks,' Shona turned to go.

'Here,' Dave Collins held out a post-it of his own. 'Postcode for maintenance. And he's right about checking the clips.'

10

Jamie was supposed to be back at the police station, but he wasn't. He was sat on a low wall beneath a sky of endless slate, looking into dark water. The canal was surprisingly clear. Not many tourist propellers churning up the silt at this time of year. His eyes shifted to the blue paving where she'd been laid, like a carcass in a butcher's cold store: no head, limbs sawn short, but in his mind he knew her for what she'd been. Alive and all that that meant. Her joys and pains and petty details; the ripples that moved those she touched.

His phone rang. He let it ring, let the weight of the place press on his shoulders: the inevitability, ticking like a metronome in the back of his skull. It felt like business is business, like nothing personal, like more to come.

A couple of dog walkers passed. Jamie was aware of his teeth chattering and his hands beginning to quiver. Weak sun reached the retail park roofs, bringing him back into real time. He started to walk while there was still light. A few minutes later he was driving. The thoughts of the afternoon no longer had words or form, but they were there; like the ponderous throb of his car's engine.

Jamie saw Shona from the doorway. As he reached her, she lifted a carrier bag off the floor and clunked it on the desk.

'Feel free to twang.'

Jamie was mystified.

'Number plates. Clips.'

'Just so long as they work when we need them.'

'Did you follow up that Dunky message?'

Jamie curled a lip.

'Thought you wouldn't, so I gave him a call,' Shona pushed a post-it across the desk. 'Said speak to this guy: ex-copper.'

'Yeah,' Jamie looked. 'Heard his name.'

'And…?'

Jamie straightened the post-it and began tapping the number into his phone.

'Billy?' Jamie had tapped speaker.

'Do I sound like an old man?' a woman's voice answered.

'No, just …'

'I'll get him. He leaves this phone all over the house. Billy,' the woman's voice was muffled as she began moving. 'Some young man wants to speak to a bitter and twisted old bugger.'

After the ritual introductions and exchange of who knows who and the comings and goings of mutual acquaintances, Jamie cut to the chase. 'The old Romanian. Seems significant, but…'

'Yeah, Neculai Morcanu. He had the unit.'

'Look,' Jamie's voice softened. 'You know that feeling when your boss wants to be seen as central if there's an arrest, but invisible if things don't work out?'

'I've got thirty-eight years' service.'

'Fair point, well made,' Jamie chuckled. 'Look, I really think you could help me out. Is there any way we could meet up?'

'I'll just check my time-management software. Hang on, it's Blu-Tacked to the fridge.' There was a sound of footsteps.

'So,' Billy had come to a stop. 'I've got the dentist on Tuesday.

When were you—'

'I was wondering about tomorrow.'

'Yeah, great,' Billy's voice quietened. 'Come here. Make it look random. If she suspects I'm going out I get the third degree on departure and return times and an in depth analysis of every item of clothing I might think of wearing.'

Jamie chuckled. 'I'll aim for ten. Any different, I'll ring.'

Across the desk Shona was shaking her head.

Next morning Billy Harriman was at the door before the bell rang. 'Saw you from the window,' he extended a hand. 'Follow me through. Jamie isn't it?'

At the back of the house was a conservatory. As the two men settled, Billy's wife came in with a tea-tray.

'I hope you've come to take him back,' she said as she placed two cups, a sugar bowl and a doily covered plate of biscuits on a low table. 'He's getting under my feet. I married him for life, not for lunchtimes.' At the door she stopped. 'I'm nipping up the shops, Bill.'

Jamie smiled and placed his car keys and phone next to the biscuit plate.

'See the cuts are biting,' Billy nodded towards the table.

'Wha—'

'That phone. Thought I was past my sell by date. Looks more suited to Morse code than the internet.'

After a minute or two of chat about shared colleagues, Jamie said: 'So, what are you expecting? That I'm investigating the possibility of clawing back your pension for consorting with call girls?'

Billy grinned. 'What, with my back? Pity the wife's gone out. She'd have told you there'd be insufficient evidence.'

'Nothing that'd stand up in court then?' Jamie grinned back.

'Nice to see you young ones still remember the old jokes. No,' Billy continued. 'I just did what I was told. Kept an eye. Made sure nothing crept up. Still got scans of my notebooks if anyone's painting a different picture. And emails. Used to report on email and apologise that I'd tried to ring.'

'BCC to your personal address?'

Billy nodded.

'Who told you to just keep a watching brief, Cleggy? Sounds like her style.'

'Couple of inspectors, Harris, Baldwin. They'd ask for the occasional update, make sure the status quo wasn't shifting. Not Clegg. Not really detective stuff, not her problem.'

'Not worried about…?'

'Me? No. Too small. Like the wife says, I'm a minor irritation. Covered my back and staggered to my pension and, like I said, copied & emailed everything.'

'Taking a chance talking like that to me, though. I might be part of our brave *New Britain for the British* world. I might be recording you, as we speak.'

'What, on that phone?' Harriman's grin widened. 'Nah, can't hide your inner surly. You don't have the look of a tool of the state. No offence.'

Jamie smiled back. 'None taken. That'd count as a compliment where I come from. Did you hear anything about—'

'The new bloke? Big Pole, Bak… something, it's in my notes. He was coming in just as I was winding down. Looked a nasty piece of work. Surprised at the old man. I asked him if he was training him up. He got shirty. Not like him. He always had time. We'd have some good chats. Real history buff he was. He'd have liked your phone.'

'Not like him, you say?' Jamie lifted his tea.

'No. He was always… measured, friendly. The girls liked him. I'd talk to them in the street. Said he treated them properly. Problems with their kids, or it was a school play or something. But then, as I was finishing, he always seemed irritated. Like he just wanted you out of the way. The girls said he was the same at the unit… when he was there.'

'And you say he's got kids?'

'Yeah. Grown up though. Boy and a girl. Both good universities. He was proud. The local stuff that he had? Shops, cash and carry, taxis… gradually moved it into other family hands. A sister, nephews, cousins. But his kids?' Billy shrugged. 'London, big operations, property, shipping, all sorts. Different world.'

'That unit. He was still the owner, not the big bloke?'

'Far as I know,' Harriman replied. 'But I was finishing, so… Give me a day and I'll have a read through my old notes. See what comes back.'

Jamie finished his tea. 'If I needed a native guide?' He picked the last biscuit off the doily. 'Could you?'

'Anytime. Just call. Anything to get me out of this bloody conservatory.'

Billy's wife was walking up the path pulling a shopping trolley as Jamie was turning away from the door.

'He had a pal,' Billy said. 'Another old Romanian. I'll make a couple of calls.'

Jamie held out a hand and shook. 'Thanks for renting him out to me,' he said as Billy's wife reached the door.

'Wouldn't like to make an outright purchase would you?' And she gave Billy a pat on the stomach as she went in.

Shona deliberately ignored the lime green Ford Focus and its boastful exhaust as it pulled into the police station car park.

She was kneeling on a newspaper, clipping false number plates onto Jamie's grey Toyota. 'One less thing for him to play the moany Manc about.'

'Gives you all the glamorous jobs.'

She turned around to see Dunky's teeth, displayed through a grin between the upturned collars of his ski-coat. The strip lighting in the police station's underground car park was dim, but Dunky was wearing sunglasses.

'I volunteered,' Shona continued clipping.

'That's what I do as well,' Dunky's teeth were undiminished. 'The old disguised number plate trick. Use insulation tape when I'm doing a bit of undercover.' He tapped the side of his nose with a single finger. 'Clocked the cameras on that unit. Get closer on foot sometimes: different coats, hats. You know, put them off the scent.'

'You should be careful,' Shona turned. 'Not a risk you should be taking.'

'Relax, sister. I'm fine. It's my patch.'

'Seriously, Dunky, if it was us, it'd be in a log, regular check-in times. And we'd go as a pair.'

'Okay. Okay.' Dunky shuffled from foot to foot. 'I'm covered. No way to trace me from my number plates and the old Focus RS has enough poke to pull me out of trouble.'

'Dunky...' Shona began to stand.

'Chill. Be a while before I can fit it in anyway.' Dunky zipped the ski-jacket as he turned away 'Places to be. People to see.'

It was mid-shift when Jamie walked back from checking a series of expensive bike thefts near Devonshire Green. Opening the briefing room door, he could see Shona's head bent over the desk.

'Christmas shopping on the firm's time,' Jamie pulled out a chair.

'Bus stops,' Shona turned an iPad towards him. 'If I knew where they live I could work out when they might be walking on their own.'

Jamie gave an almost imperceptible nod.

'Got the false plates on. I'll send you an invoice for a set of new nails.'

'Saw Billy Harriman earlier.'

Shona didn't speak.

'Might be useful,' Jamie continued. 'Says he'll do a bit of digging.'

'Another of your willing slaves.'

'More of a public service. The poor old bugger is going stir-crazy in his conservatory. Don't think retirement suits him.'

'Yeah, well I'm sure you'll find an angle to exploit.'

Shona re-focused on the iPad.

Jamie leaned back in the chair. 'Said he could see my inner surly.'

'Bloody hell, there's nothing inner about your surly.'

'Yeah, well. He said I didn't have the look of a tool of the state.'

'No, just a tool.'

Shona went back to her iPad, then, without looking up, she said. 'You need to be careful who you're using.'

Jamie stayed quiet.

'That Dunky.' Shona spoke again. 'He—'

'He sweats needy,' Jamie cut in. 'If he wants to play with the big boys, it's not my fault.'

Shona's mouth made to open, but Jamie was talking again.

'Leasehold, by the way; short-term, six-month renewables. So that old bastard Morcanu can't even blame falling commercial property prices. Anyway, all I asked Captain Wannabe to do was to look at a few bits of paper. Move a couple of possibles into the probables column.'

'And no hints, no macho challenge. No poor me, I can't find this out, Dunky? No wind him up and watch him go?'

'What can I say? The boy's keen. Why so concerned?'

'Why so...? Because the silly bugger's freelancing. Pulling his hat low, turning up his collar and walking around that industrial unit like he's in a nineteen-forties thriller. Jesus, he saw me with the false number plates and told me he does the same thing with bloody insulation tape.'

Jamie grinned. 'I must be an inspiration,' he stood. 'Anyway, canteen time. All this motivational speaking lark puts an edge on the appetite.'

Shona remained seated. Jamie went to speak, but he saw her eyes and he turned away.

'Did you get Dave's text?' Shona was still on the iPad as Jamie got back from the canteen.

'Oh yeah,' he mumbled. 'That's fine. Makes sense,' he reached his phone out of a pocket.

'You're okay with him doing a few days tracking?'

'We've got fuck all else.' His eyes stayed on the phone when it buzzed again. 'Shit…Cozza,' Jamie twitched from foot to foot as the dial tone kept beeping. 'C'mon, c'mon.' Then he inhaled and, 'at last, you prat. Is it?... Right. Stay there. We'll be down.'

Shona looked up at the word *we'll*. Then she was chasing Jamie across the briefing space and out towards the lift. It went past them.

'You bastard…' Jamie punched the down button and turned for the stairs. Crossing the reception area, Jephcott was coming in through the main entrance.

'Can we have—' he began.

'Sorry, not now,' Jamie kept moving.

'And Miss McCulloch. Perhaps another day?'

Jamie didn't register Jephcott's handshake to Shona. His only focus was the car park. Then they were driving. Neither spoke, except for Jamie swearing at traffic lights.

11

The first hospital buildings they passed were ornate Edwardian: ochre stone and terracotta brick. But then the bulk of the facility grew and loomed over like a concrete tumour. From its central mass, smaller cuboids tumbled, some stacked, some sprawling in cancerous grey tentacles.

'Shit, shit, shit,' Jamie hit the steering wheel as they passed yet another full car park. 'Fuck sake, shift yourself,' he gritted his teeth as he spotted a woman getting into a red Citroen. Then, swinging into the vacated space, he was out of the car and moving. Only the bleak cuboid and its distant blue door registered in his senses as Shona semi-jogged to keep up.

'At bloody last.' Jamie pushed as an electronic lock buzzed. Scribbling a signature at the Forensic Pathology reception desk, he was striding off again, oblivious to Shona still rushing to sign in and follow. 'About bleeding time,' Jamie was speaking before he was through the office door.

'Blame my manager, not me. He keeps filling my days with crap and courses.' Cozza's white lab coat looked like he'd slept in it.

'And those urgent care home jobs?'

'Weren't. Just wanted evidence for his pet research project.'

'And that takes priority?'

'No, not usually. But I am a simple servant of institutional hierarchy.'

'Bloody simple, that's for sure. So…?' Jamie's jaw clenched.

Cosgriff handed over a folder.

'No conclusion on cause of death,' Jamie read, skimming over a page.

'Initially, I thought wire garrotte, but there's insufficient evidence. Can't establish a definite order.' Cosgriff pushed his hands into his pockets. 'But cutting off the head and limbs? You were right. Must've been frozen solid when they sawed her into bits. Wounds would've been more ragged else.'

Jamie nodded. He was easing into work mode as he read the tox screen.

'User, but casual, like half the twenty-somethings in the city. Nothing to indicate overdose.' Cosgriff's tone adjusted.

Digestive Tract and DNA of Vaginal Contents. Jamie exhaled as he turned a page.

'Yeah, surprisingly low level of DNA degradation,' Cosgriff went on.

Degradation. Jamie felt the irony of the word.

'Can't identify an individual, but there's clear indication of recent sex with a wide variation of—'

'Could've been a gang-bang at the United Nations.' Jamie took in the rainbow of racial possibilities, then shut his eyes, suddenly aware of the detachment in Cozza's voice in comparison to its subject matter: the pain and terror of one girl's journey from life to butchered oblivion.

'Could be multiple assaults. More likely died at the end of a busy shift,' Cozza plodded on. 'Couple of weeks in the canal. Lucky to get anything. That wrapping must've stayed watertight for ages. The remnants of plastic and duct tape indicate it was eventually ripped by propellers, or bouncing off the lock wall.'

'Professional,' Jamie looked to Cozza. 'Like they wanted her found. So she could be a warning – the price of non-compliance.'

'Fits the evidence,' Cosgriff agreed.

'So, take me through the headlines.' Jamie put the folder down on the desk and began messing around with his phone.

'Headlines? No head, so no facials. No hands, no fingerprints. If you've got a shed load of money, you could analyse bone chemicals to tell you where she grew up.'

'Lithuania,' Jamie held up his phone.

Cosgriff looked.

'True Love. *Tikra Meilė*. The tattoo on her shoulder. And the stick man and his horse,' Jamie explained. 'Google translate. Google images. Police budgets just love Google.'

'Hi ya Jamie,' the lab door opened and Cosgriff's admin assistant, Lauren Luckhurst, came in carrying a print-out. 'I see you've mastered the *I'm a smug bastard* look.'

'Yeah, Sherlock's worked out where she's from and saved the department a fortune,' Cosgriff added.

'Didn't know emails cost that much,' Lauren passed Cosgriff the print-out. 'That sample you took the first day. I sent the results to Europol and they've finally got their fingers out their arses. Seems she had prior, so we've got a DNA match.'

Cozza had a brief scan, then handed over the print-out. Cozza kept talking while Jamie read.

'Pretty girl, well was… Not exactly career criminal was she? Proper qualifications, engineering. Tempted to say had a good head on her shoulders, once. And you can carry on being a smug bastard. She was Lithuanian, from Vilnius.'

Then Cozza's voice and the world fell away and all Seagrief felt was his fingers fastened across his mouth, holding back a silent scream.

'Nice shade of grey,' Cosgriff was behind him now. 'They usually go that colour when they see me open a chest cavity, not an email.'

But Jamie didn't hear him. He was at the door before the paper spiralled to the floor.

Staggering into a corridor where flat walls and geometric signage rippled jagged beyond his tear-blurred eyes, Jamie searched for the toilet. Pushing the door open, he stumbled into a cubicle just as the damburst of vomit broke. He retched and retched until stomach cramps signalled that he was void. Across his clamped-shut eyes was one grainy image and across his mind one phrase.

All over for Normova.

It had been over a year since Jamie had given the instruction. He soon forgot the names of those who made it; those where he said *Yes*. But he never forgot the *Nos*. Never forgot their names. Never forgot their faces. Liliana Normova. Baltic Babe. Engineer. Some specialism in plastics.

12

'You drive,' the pathology unit's door closed behind them.

Shona watched Jamie stride ahead and open the passenger door. As she drove, she glanced across. His eyes were staring nowhere, hands were clamped together and shaking. Shona turned left out of the hospital, towards the police station.

'Drop me home, please,' Jamie reached across to the satnav and let it do the talking for him. His phone buzzed. He stayed leaning on his hand, staring out the car's side window.

You have reached your destination.

'Surprised you've got a woman's voice on your satnav. Do you go left every time she says *Turn Right*?' Shona spoke for the first time as she stood on the pavement and handed Jamie his keys.

He gave a weak smile. 'Thanks, I'll give you the taxi money to get home,' and he reached into his jacket.

'No, it's fine. I'm not far from here. Walk'll do me good.'

Shona didn't mention that her car was still at the police station, so she had a bit further to go than a stroll across the park and home. On the other side of the road, she turned and looked back. Jamie's keys were hanging from the lock and he was holding a piece of paper. As she watched, he ripped it up and shoved the bits back in his coat pocket. So many questions she wanted to ask, but not today. Not if she was going to get an answer that meant anything.

Once inside his flat, Jamie sat on the sofa. His eyes were wide open, but saw nothing. His calf muscles began to twitch, his fingers flexed of their own accord. He stood and began to pace, round in circles like a zoo animal driven insane by the confines of its cage. He lay on the bed and let winter's early evening dark creep over him. In time he became aware of his rigid legs moving in arcs and his fingers digging into the bedding, repeatedly clenching and unclenching. He wanted to sleep, but not because he was tired. He craved its release from his racing mind. There was rain. He could hear it now; imagine its December ice-sting.

'Good,' he spoke aloud. 'Serves you right. Better than you deserve.'

In the dim flat, he smelt his kit before he saw it, as it still lay in a sweaty pile after the previous night's exercise. Lifting a t-shirt and sliding in his arms, he flinched as the moist cold fell against his shoulders. He left the sweat-top and jogging bottoms on the floor; he didn't deserve them.

Leaning on a low wall outside his flat, he began to stretch calf muscles and hamstrings while the wind-driven rain pinged in points of pain across his body. As the storm intensified it clamped his skull in a vice. He smiled. It hurt, as it should. He began to walk, crinkled football socks flopped over his trainers. From a walk, he eased into a jog. The cold air stung his mouth, but his snot-clogged nose gave him no access to oxygen.

'Hold, hold,' he told himself as he jogged level with the second lamppost. Same as last time, he was alternating, two lampposts, jog, two lampposts, half-pace. 'Might try a three when my chest clears,' he told himself.

After fifteen minutes, oxygen debt and aching muscles pushed back the army of despair. He drove on and managed a four lamppost sequence. For the next forty-five minutes he alternated jogging with one, two and three lamppost bursts, finally turning the corner by his flat. The warmth of exercise had blunted the edge of the cold, but his fingers still fumbled to grip his keys when he reached the door.

He stripped, leaving a pile of wet kit leaking across the tiles. Low-level nausea reminded him that he didn't deserve the comfort of food. He boiled a kettle, poured a cup of hot water and groaned into bed, clicking off the light.

'Bout time you made an effort,' Cara came alive as he crossed the edgeland between awake and asleep. 'Covered a few miles tonight, Fatboy. Need to. Long road back from your doughnuts and cola life.'

'You're a doctor,' he heard himself saying. 'You're supposed to raise the tone, not start talking squaddie lingo,' he was smiling in fake indignation. She was laughing, but then he felt the need to fight; fight to stay sleeping, to stay with Cara. But then he could hear his own voice. 'No, no...' out loud. And it continued as his eyes opened, staring into the dark. Eventually he sat up in bed; knees raised, head bowed and he began to rock. Talking to Cara and her words coming back. Not the vivid, living breathing dream of Cara, but her voice in his head, bringing comfort as he pulled his arms around his knees.

'Put my light on.'

He stretched out a hand for the switch on the lead. The soft green lava light bathed the room, shadows of slowly morphing shapelessness. He continued to rock. Time lost its shape. He might have slept, unconscious moments, but nothing of substance. After a while he swung his feet onto the floor and stood. Early shift, six o'clock start, but that was still a couple of hours away. He began pacing again; circling until the clock ticked to work time.

Even from a distance Jamie looked rough.

'Morning,' Shona reached the desk and pulled a chair over. 'Anything happening?'

Jamie shrugged and gave a weak smile. 'Text from Billy. He's gone through his notes; had a think.'

'So you're meeting him?'

'Suppose so.'

Shona watched him shuffle papers aimlessly. Then his phone buzzed.

'Yes… okay. See you in a bit.'

'Anybody important?' Shona scanned the void of his face.

'Dave. Maps and bollocks. He wants to get his face out that screen once in a while.'

Shona's mouth opened, but Jamie carried on. 'Fucking techy crap. Jesus. Maybe later I'll have a—'

His phone buzzed again, echoing against the desk. The name Cozza flashed on the screen, then a text.

Fucking get here and a postcode.

Jamie was striding, pulling his coat on, and Shona was in his wake, again.

In the car Shona had Google Earth on her phone. It was just bobbly green.

'Zoom out,' Jamie pressed the ignition and leaned over to look. 'Woods.'

'Just off Manchester Road. Near the golf club,' Shona was reading.

'Yeah, got it. Black Brook.'

Ten minutes later he parked behind three patrol cars and the SOCO van. Cozza was leaning against it. 'Waiting for Tommo to get his gear rigged.'

'Tommo?'

'Yeah, he's the only one who's been on the course.'

'This way,' Jamie began following a stream.

'How d'ya—' Shona began.

'Easiest way to find your way in and out in the dark.'

After about two hundred metres the stream ran under a line of *Scene Of Crime* tape.

A uniformed officer took their details. 'Reckon it's been there ages.' He handed them elasticated shoe covers.

At the centre of the area, ropes were hanging from one tree and secured with straps and various clips to its neighbour. Tommo was leaning back, taking the strain on the untied end of the rope. He was wearing a red plastic helmet and a harness covered in carabiners. They looked up, but the angle of the sun obscured detail as the object hung about thirty feet above their heads.

'I can get something if I move around and use a lens filter.' A young woman in the forensics suit was circling with a camera and telephoto lens. She had another camera around her neck.

'Didn't let your missus choose the rope, did they Tommo?' Cozza called across to the man in the climbing harness.

'Nah,' Tommo grinned. 'My boss told her it'd cost a thousand quid to put someone else on the tree climbing course.'

The young woman with cameras moved towards Tommo. 'When you're up there take some pictures, before you touch anything.'

Tommo began sliding the specialist rope ascenders, hand over gloved hand, reach, lock, pull; each time rising an arm's length towards the silhouette hanging close to the trunk. As well as the taut rope that carried his weight, another was trailing loose from the back of his harness.

On a flat bit of ground, a little away from the tree, a white tent was already erected and a SOCO in a forensic suit was kneeling on a plastic sheet arranging tweezers and evidence bags.

Cozza called across. 'If it was my decision, I'd make you put the tent up around the body while it was still in the tree.'

A head in a paper hood turned. The turkey-like SOCO looked

at Cozza and raised his hand in his well-practised middle finger salute. 'Bellend,' his lips were easy to read.

Tommo was into the branches now and taking a breather, sitting back in his harness and rubbing his arms. Below there was time-filling chatter and general shuffling about. The sun made looking up difficult.

'So, you think it's linked?' Cozza's voice was most active. 'Hidden then—'

'Fucking shit!'

High above, Tommo was flapping his arms and swaying as a cluster of black birds exploded past his face.

'Murder of crows,' Cozza grinned.

No one grinned back.

Drawing level with the suspended bundle, Tommo swung towards the trunk. Then, pulling himself close, he had his feet on a branch and secured a safety line. Thirty feet above his head, Jamie watched Tommo twist and shuffle around, taking photos from numerous angles. Then, clipping the camera to his harness again, he reached above his head. Looping a pulley over a branch and threading the trailing rope through, he began tying it onto the object.

'It's thick, nylon netting,' Tommo shouted into the wind. 'With metal eyelets. Pretty solid. But I wouldn't stand underneath.'

Everyone shuffled well away from a direct line.

Two uniformed officers picked up the loose end of the trailing rope and made a turn around a thin birch trunk. Tommo was sawing now. His arm moving back and forth. There was a low screech as the pulley took the weight. Below, the rope tightened. Tommo raised a hand, then lowered it, palm down. The two uniformed officers held the rope taut around the birch and began a slow walk, easing the object towards the ground.

Out of the angle of the sun, the blue nylon net became visible. The bottom was lined with a thick blanket and inside was a crouched form, in an upright, foetal position similar to the mummy bundles that are carried around on Mexico's Day of the Dead. Jamie stared, oblivious to the camera girl, clicking away behind her telephoto lens.

'Wait,' the SOCO called as the bundle came lower. 'Let me get a forensic sheet underneath. Don't want that incompetent bastard blaming me when he can't find anything.' He was looking at Cozza.

Bit by bit, the contents of the net revealed themselves: blackened flesh, an eyeless, picked-clean face and the last remnants of scalp where a knotted plait of hair remained: bleached blonde, still flaunting itself through the accumulated dirt of death. It was the classic, grinning skull from a cheap horror film, courtesy of the crows and other tree-top scavengers. An elbow bone protruded and a knee; feet and arse were shrouded by the blanket. Shadows of rotten organs lurked behind a window of rib bone. The younger of the two uniformed officers was leaning back against the rope, retching.

'Go on, son, I can manage,' the older man said. 'Not much weight left in it.' Staggering away, the younger officer bent double as his vomit came in repeated spasms.

The sheet was in place and the remaining officer began walking again, until the net was almost on the ground. Then he slowed, and slackened the rope its last few inches. Even so, there was a sickly creak as gravity and the ground proved too much for bones with decay-weakened joints and the body eased onto its side.

Cozza gave the thick blanket in the bottom of the net a poke. 'Suppose this was to stop body fluids dripping onto random dog walkers.'

Shona and Jamie stayed quiet and stared. Insect larvae had mined the eye-sockets and, wriggling in a cavity behind the exposed ribs, there were occasional flies, crawling jewels of iridescent green, but Jamie knew this was the tail end of the feast.

The open net had allowed air and nature to get on with the job. Much of the remaining flesh was wind-dried and the time for crow and insect pickings was almost passed.

'I expected a real stench,' Shona spoke at last.

'Leaving it so open to the elements speeds things up,' Cozza was mercifully factual. 'But I wouldn't want to have been standing here a couple of months ago. Christ, it'd have been an olfactory treat then. Flies are winding down now, but it's been a mild winter. Not many frosts.'

'Yeah, my guess, she was supposed to be found a while back, before canal girl. They just got unlucky with the tree. But it's professional.' Jamie wasn't asking a question.

'Looks it,' Cozza agreed. 'And, like you say, meant to be found, otherwise she'd be under some road, or in a landfill or, if they were into retro, pooping out the back of some little piggy.'

Shona's look of disgust encouraged Cozza.

'East End fashion in the sixties. Use an Essex pig farm for body disposal. Pigs'll eat anything; even bones, 'specially if you give them a start with a sledge hammer. Crunch their way through a skull like a little piggy Easter egg.' Once again Cozza was smiling on his own.

Tommo knelt down and began unhooking his rope. Shona, Jamie and Cozza walked around, taking in the sight from different angles. The forensic camera girl did the same, snapping away. Comments were short; factual, professional. Then the SOCO asked for help sliding a board under the plastic sheeting so the remains could be moved inside the tent, without any bending.

'Thanks,' the SOCO was uncharacteristically polite. 'Always pleased when I've got the evidence undercover. Flies, maggots and journalists with long lenses. Three things that always arrive early when there's a dead body.'

Jamie and Shona looked up. The remaining autumn leaf cover

was sparse and a rising wind sent a few more remnant leaves twisting through the air.

'Same as the canal.' Jamie shielded his eyes. 'Hide it so it shows up after a few weeks. Dense leaf cover when they strung her up close to the trunk. You'd have needed to have been up the tree yourself to spot her.'

Shona nodded. 'Clever bastards. Knew they'd get a double hit, first when she disappeared and again when the leaves fell.'

'Except they chose a sycamore.'

Shona waited.

'Sycamores can have a long leaf fall, especially if they've got their roots in water like that one. Most species? Pretty sparse by mid-November. But this one's pretty sheltered from the wind, what with the short days and crappy walking conditions. And sycamore leaves? They're big, so even if most fall off, a few, say ten or fifteen percent, dotted around the twigs. Wouldn't exactly hide it, but...'

'Like camouflage netting,' Shona understood what he was saying. 'Breaks up the outline.'

'Bout the size of it,' Jamie said. 'If they'd strung her up an ash tree she'd have been found weeks ago.'

At the gap in the crime scene tape, they handed back their shoe covers.

'Female again,' Shona commented as they sat in the car.

'Blonde again,' Jamie added. 'Wonder if any of her clothes are Moda Polska?'

13

Jamie's tea had been chips and curry sauce and it wouldn't settle, so he'd gone out, trying to walk his way towards digestive calm. There was nothing winter crisp about the night. Clouds had stalked in from the Pennines and sealed the city's horizons within a bleak dome. Jamie felt their weight.

'Another one?'

Her voice broke in his mind. The road was empty, except for occasional tunnels of orange light where beams of streetlamps reflected off the misty air.

'Nothing you weren't expecting though,' the voice was composed.

'No, nothing,' Jamie answered. 'Well, we didn't know the method but—'

'Motive and purpose?'

'Yes, love, motive and purpose.' Jamie found a bench near an overhanging bush. 'And all I can hear is a ticking clock.'

'You can hear me, Jamie.'

'Yes Cara. I can always hear you if I sit in the dark.'

'You spend too much time in the dark. That's why it infects you. You have to stop blaming. Get back to yourself. Back to my Jamie. Back to your medic mentality. These girls deserve your best, not your self-pity. Don't look back. That's what we used to say. Become a robot: professional. Black and white. Life, death. Breathing, pulse – save or move on. Emotion wastes time. Kills more. No backsliding now Fatboy: heart and mind and fitness. You were never a quitter, not my Jamie.'

'But...'

'But why are you blaming? You aren't to blame.'

'If I'd said yes to that other girl, Liliana Normova.'

'And if she'd been stopped enroute you could've lost dozens. And this one. Tree girl. Nothing down to you.'

'They're all down to me, if I miss something, if I can't stop the clock that's ticking.'

'Jamie, Jamie,' her voice was in the centre of his mind. 'It's not all down to you.'

He closed his eyes and felt the tears push against the line where his lids met. 'But that's how it feels Cara. That's just how it feels'

When he opened his eyes the streetlights were blurred, but it was quiet. Cara had said her piece. Jamie stood. His stomach felt less congested.

'Might as well make an effort,' he told himself. 'That fitness test won't pass itself.'

And he began to jog.

Two street lights on, he wound up the pace. He repeated the slow rotation, walk, jog, accelerate and, by the time he was home, a patch of cold sweat had formed in the small of his back.

A text appeared on his phone at 07:03. Jamie was already in the office.

Dropping car off for service. In by 9:30 – S

He pushed his phone to the far side of the desk and began reading the contents of a buff folder. It said *Position so far* in pencil on the outside. There were photocopies of maps with a cluster of Xs on a street a couple of miles from the unit. Jamie glanced for a few seconds, then folded it shut and began walking to the canteen.

His coffee was black and bitter, so he bought two Danish pastries to take the edge off.

'How's the push for fitness going?' Dave Collins walked over and looked at Jamie's plate. 'Did you—'

'Not properly,' Jamie sucked pastry debris off his fingers. 'See if I've got time later.'

'Let me know when,' Dave held up a take-away cup. 'Expecting a call. I'll drink this in the office.'

Shona watched Jamie's eventual return to their desk.

'Dave's doing good work on the SIM cards, you should…' she held up the buff folder as he sat down.

Jamie took out his phone, oblivious to everything but the contents of its screen. Shona leaned over. A snake appeared to be chasing a blue hedgehog.

'Busy then?' Shona didn't bother to cover her irritation.

'Been waiting for Cozza to reply to my—' there was a buzz. 'And there he is.' Jamie stood and began pulling on his coat. 'You coming?'

'Didn't you read the text?' Cozza ignored any conversational niceties as Shona trailed Jamie through his door. 'I've had a quick look, but I'm all over the place today.' Cozza's desk was stacked papers.

'But what did—' Shona began, then noticed the ID photograph of Liliana Normova sitting on an envelope. She looked at Jamie and knew he wasn't listening.

'Okay, Tree Girl,' Cozza began, as Shona tapped record on her phone and opened her notebook. 'Just an external and the non-invasive samples, so far: swabs, blood. But I'll push on with the full post-mortem ASAP.'

'Said your boss kept slowing you down with the Canal Girl?'

Shona was writing.

'Yeah. I'll find a way to bypass him with this one. Bit of sleight of hand,' Cozza tapped his nose. 'Freezer and canal water makes time of death on the first one a bugger.' Cozza looked, but Jamie's eyes remained disengaged. 'Bit easier with Tree Girl. She's into the dry decay phase, so I reckon the bug man will get it pretty close when he's finished tracking back the insect life.'

Bit easier. As she wrote, the words sat in her mind. Tree Girl's last minutes on Earth: pain, terror, loneliness, the sense of worthlessness. Bit easier. Jesus wept.

'Tissue sample results, DNA? It's murder and I've fast-tracked it,' Cozza walked to a filing cabinet.

'But?' Shona pressed.

'Everything so far,' and he pushed an envelope towards her. 'And I'm due in a budget meeting ten minutes ago. My guess,' Cozza kept grabbing papers. 'Looks like they froze her so there'd be less fluids slopping about and to make her easier to haul up the tree. Imagine trying to get a floppy body in that net.' Cozza's head and arms lolloped about in a bizarre imitation of a flaccid corpse.

'And the garrotte,' Cozza was talking again. 'First impressions; same as before. Like piano wire. Classic. But there's some indentations need looking at.'

Shona looked up from her notebook, Jamie was still staring, like someone looking through a window and thinking of another place.

Cozza didn't pause. 'I've photocopied everything. Some interesting snippets.' And lifting his rucksack onto his shoulder he was walking. Reaching the door he raised a hand. 'The snippets?' Cozza made scissor movements with two fingers. 'And the face. Not just the decomposition and scavengers…'

The afternoon was fading as Shona pulled up in a multi-storey car park. Constant vandalism to the CCTV had led to the owners adopting the cheaper option of wall signs that read *The company accepts no liability*. Stepping from the stairwell, she moved into the foot-level lighting of the roofless top floor. 'Hope they haven't got my shoes on a database,' she muttered to herself. 'There's fuck all else visible up here.'

He didn't flash his lights. She knew where he'd be.

'He's on the edge,' Shona sat in Jephcott's car. 'Thousand yard stare. All the bluster and bullshit, it's nowhere. He won't last like this.'

'So, what are you saying?'

'He needs help. Pulling into a world beyond his own…'

'Own what?'

'Head – guilt probably. Like the rest of us.'

Shona watched as Jephcott searched for a response.

'So, any ideas?' he broke his silence. 'Is it general guilt, or has something more specific raised its head?'

'Something that hasn't got a head, more like,' Shona replied. 'We were discussing that first body. Torso in the canal. Cozza had some results back. He was chipper then. Cocky. He'd worked out the girl's nationality from a tattoo. Then this forensic girl, Lauren, came in with an email from Europol.'

Jephcott didn't speak.

'It kicked the legs from under him.'

'The email?'

'Must've been. He'd been grinning with Cozza about getting the nationality right. Went from smart-arse smug to staggering for the toilet in a couple of seconds. Cozza was saying something about the dead girl's qualifications and being pretty. Jamie was reading and grinning. Then his face… Dropped the email and out the door. Came back stinking of vomit. Grey. Christ, he was grey.'

'Take me through it,' Jephcott said. 'See if we can pin it down.'

'Oh, I can pin it down,' Shona replied. 'It was the name… On the email.' Shona took a crumpled piece of paper from her pocket.

'Picked it off the floor.' She smoothed the paper and handed it across. 'Europol.'

'Fucking shit.'

Shona was taken aback by Jephcott's language.

'Liliana Normova...' he leaned back and closed his eyes.

Shona waited in his silence.

'You're right. The name,' Jephcott looked ahead. 'You'd think we'd never remember... Jamie had the final call, but, you know – the names stick, maybe not the reasons, but the names.'

Shona took the paper back. 'Cozza was right. She was pretty... and qualified. Jesus. Nicking a few sweets when you're a kid and being a bit of a prat when you're pissed one night in a bar. Not much to lose your life over'

'But,' Jephcott said. 'She was a risk.'

'Aye... he made the right call. This proves it. Any random checkpoint, she'd've shown up. Not just her then... all the others, the driver. They'd all have been arrested... then God knows how far up the chain.' She looked again at the small creased face. 'But that's not how it feels, is it? The right call. Not how it feels when you're staring at a name and knowing you haven't even found all her body parts.'

'He'll need time,' Jephcott said as they both stared into the blackness beyond the windscreen. 'But we need him back on track. You'll need to look... wait till he's able to listen.'

'Could be a bit.'

'Maybe. Maybe not. He's dealt with stuff you and I... He'll man up again. He's got to...'

'Aye. Man up. Fuck sake,' Shona shook her head. 'I'll remember that in case anyone asks me to define an oxymoron.'

Jephcott smiled. 'You'll know when. Maybe use the Hitler's train timetable argument.'

'Your training session party piece?'

'Okay. You'll know when,' Jephcott repeated. 'And at least he knows he's not alone now.' He looked at Shona. 'You have told him?'

'It's on my To Do list,' she took a breath. 'Every time I seem to be getting somewhere with him, he reverts back to prat mode.'

'So you—'

'So I'll tell him. I know… Might work to our advantage. Tell him. Let it sink in. Then talk him round.'

'I'll leave it with you, Shona. But remember. He's one of our top operatives. That doesn't happen by accident.'

'Thanks for that.' Shona began adjusting her scarf. 'Give me something to ponder on the way home.'

As she zipped up her coat, Jephcott opened the glove compartment. 'The list. Another copy. I'm guessing his last one might be beyond reading.'

14

Shona yawned as she stepped from the police station lift. She'd been turning Jephcott's words over in her mind half the night.

'Tell the twat,' she told herself. 'Never be a right time. Maybe drive to the crosses on Dave's map. Trace the bus routes. Get a sense of where the girls might be walking on their own.'

She was at the briefing room door now.

'Get him in the car and tell him.'

As she approached, Jamie had his phone to his ear. Seeing her, he jotted *Coffee? I'll pay* on a post-it, then opened his wallet one-handed and took out a ten pound note.

The woman on the till was pushing the lids on the coffee cups.

'Jamie says we need to talk.'

Shona turned to see Dunky. He already had a drink.

'He'll be waiting,' she held up the cups. 'You know what a grumpy sod he is.'

'No, look, he's just said,' Dunky lifted his phone.

'This'll be cold then.' Shona made her way to the table as Dunky pulled out a seat.

'Nah, not with the lid on. And a bit of insulation.' Dunky took off his scarf and wrapped it around one of the cups.

'What's so important?'

'Jamie says it'd be helpful if I explained my role.'

An image of Jamie grinning flashed across Shona's mind.

'So, housing department,' Shona took the lid off her coffee and took a sip.

'Yes, well, no. Not as such. More the wider implications. The... what do they call it? The soft power.'

Shona looked at the cup on the table and thought it might need a thicker scarf.

'So,' Shona stretched into a smile. 'Soft power.'

'Yeah, yeah. I know some of the stuff is... well, not strictly in my jurisdiction, but we're all on the same side, right?'

Shona held her smile.

'You see, the housing department, what most people don't realise, is that we're a kind of a canary in the coal mine for crime and social problems.'

Shona was nodding now.

'Fly-tipping, sofas in gardens, bricks on cars in drives. They're the clues. Ignore those and next thing you know you've got a sink estate – a no-go area. That's what I'm always telling my agents. Today it might be a couple of mattresses dumped in a back alley, but let it slip, give it six months and the gangs move in; drug dealers setting up shop behind steel doors, young kids biking cocaine round the streets like Deliveroo riders. So that's why we keep them open.' Dunky lifted his sunglasses and pulled an earlobe.

'See it now, Dunky. The big picture.' Shona reached in her pocket. 'Sorry, felt it buzz,' and she took out her phone. 'Jamie. Wants to know what's happened to his coffee.' Shona began unwinding the scarf from around the cup.

'You took your time,' Jamie didn't make eye-contact.

'Tosser,' Shona plonked the coffee on the desk and slid his change in an arc of displeasure. 'He showed me your text.'

'Is it sugared?'

'What was that bollocks about a clock ticking?' Shona threw four sugar sachets towards him. 'Can't be ticking that fast if you've got time to act like an arse.'

'Needed a bit of time to weigh this up,' Jamie rotated a piece of paper on the desk and Shona looked down. Jamie flipped it back then folded it into an envelope. 'For all the bullshit, he does have access to property records that we'd have to faff around to get.'

'You're just like those bald-headed bastards. Take the piss. Exploit. Hoped it was just front.' Shona leaned into Jamie's face and her voice dropped to a low hiss. 'Considering all the other stuff Jephcott says you've done.'

Jamie's eyes shot up.

Shona leaned even closer. 'My car. Give it a couple of minutes then follow me out. You need to do some fucking listening.'

15

'Jephcott,' the moment Jamie's back touched the passenger seat, Shona stared into his face. 'Guess what comes next Mr Detective.'

'So you do what I do?' Jamie's head dropped.

'Not as productively, according to Jephcott, but I try.'

'And Jephcott thinks I need a motivational speech?'

'Yeah, but I favour a kick up the arse… look, I know you've seen stuff—'

'Jephcott been giving you my life story?' Jamie's voice hardened.

'No. Just you've done stuff. Lot of good for a lot of people.'

Jamie's eyes narrowed.

'Yeah, I couldn't believe it either. Given that I've only ever seen you act like a tosser.'

Jamie looked away, through the car's side window. There was a concrete pillar.

'Look,' Shona continued. 'I can understand how it pulls you down. Days when things go wrong and you think about the people.'

'And you're going to give me the whole Jephcott's Christmas cracker philosophy bit? If a tree falls in a forest and there's no one to hear, is there a sound?'

'I can't lie, he did fall back on the management-speak bollocks, but I think he was trying to get his head round what I told him.'

'Told him?'

'Yeah, about you. The bloody state you've been in since Liliana Normova.'

Jamie turned his gaze from the pillar and looked Shona in the eye. 'You need to mind your own business.'

'Yeah, well. I think it is my business if I'm stuck with a partner whose state of mind threatens us all. Jephcott,' Shona's voice softened a little. 'He recognised the name as well.'

Jamie was looking at his hands, fingers linked, thumbs crossed.

'It might be Christmas cracker philosophy,' Shona's voice was still soft, 'but it's true. Those people are still there, just like the noise of the falling tree. Just because you can't hear them doesn't mean they're not there. Just means they're in less safe hands than yours. You might feel better not knowing, but those poor sods on the transport don't.' And she reached into a pocket. 'Jephcott wondered about the original?'

'Keep it.'

'But I saw you ripping—'

'Already scanned onto an encrypted email, and I've got a printer.'

'Jephcott—'

'Jephcott wanted you to talk me round. Pick your moment.'

'Use my charm,' Shona smiled. Jamie still stared at his hands.

'Thanks for missing out Jephcott's party piece,' he eventually broke the silence. 'If you were timetabling the trains to Hitler's death camps… thanks for sparing me that.'

'I guessed you'd probably join in with me. Jephcott recites it like the Our Father whenever there's a bump in the road… anyway, now you don't need to worry about me noticing you do something that doesn't fit with the day job.' Shona lightened her voice. 'And it'll be Christmas soon. Maybe Jephcott will get a new box of crackers.' After a pause, Shona looked across to Jamie. 'You can't carry it around. The guilt. Liliana Normova. You don't deserve to.'

'What do you know about what I deserve?' Jamie's eyes made momentary contact.

'I know you did your best. Made the right call. A lot of people could've been lost.' She faced him now. 'You can't fill yourself up with guilt over Liliana Normova.'

'Jesus. I wish. Guilt? Yeah, but Liliana Normova? Tip of the fucking iceberg.'

'Would it help if—'

'We work together.' Jamie cut across. 'You don't know me. All this confession is good for the soul bollocks. I'm a long way from a confessional. And you're a long way from being my priest.'

'Maybe so, Jamie,' Shona kept her voice calm. 'But we've all got something. Guilt? It's a great motivator, if it doesn't break your heart.'

Jamie remained mute as he reached for the door handle.

'So, no… I'm not your priest,' Shona started the engine. 'But I might be your best hope.'

Jamie's hands were clamped, so were his teeth, as he eased his car into the traffic. Driving on autopilot, he reached his flat and went inside.

The lava lamp was on his bedroom windowsill. He felt for its rocker switch then drew the blind and watched amoebas of green light grow and multiply until they swam over every surface in the room. He lay on the bed and, bathed in the bizarre glow, closed his eyes. He deserved to see nothing but his own, personal iceberg and its hidden mass. His mind flooded with Africa: mass graves, traffickers, the refugee boats, the camps and Cara. Always Cara with the flies on her eyelids.

16

Moda Polska: Jamie kept seeing the logo in his mind. Driving into work he scoured the pavements, looking at shopping bags. The Polish girl was a way in, he knew that, and he needed to feel he was doing something.

Shona was already at the desk when he opened the briefing space door.

His morning was minimal as he sat. She looked up from sticking neon place markers on pages in a ringbinder and acknowledged him with a nod. He took a file from a drawer, spread its contents across the desk and ignored them. Then his chair shot backwards and he stood, propelling himself upwards, fingers splayed on the desk.

Shona flinched. Her mouth opened, but Jamie was speaking again.

'Use your initiative.' And he was striding across the central space. A couple of Peepos turned as he passed.

'Did Jamie ask—'

'No, I used my initiative,' Shona walked towards Dave Collins' desk and he beckoned her to sit.

'You should see this,' he had maps spread across his workspace;

various streets picked out with fluorescent highlighter. 'Each colour is one of those SIM cards you gave me.'

'Routes and routines,' Shona traced her finger along the lines.

'I've labelled everything with dates and times,' Dave indicated to small, black numbers.

'So, that must be where they live. Brilliant.' Shona found the parallel map on Google Earth while Dave went to the kettle. By the time they'd drunk their coffee, Shona had worked out significant points between the girls' accommodation and their workplace.

'This is interesting,' Dave tapped his pen on the paper. 'There's an occasional arrival here some nights. You can see them leaving the unit around ten.'

'Early finish for their line of work,' Shona commented. 'Maybe a bit of private enterprise?'

'More likely a premium off-site service for its more valued clientele… only ever seems to be one girl there at a time.'

Shona took in the times and locations, then Dave spoke again. 'This one seems to go here a lot, late morning, early afternoons. So, maybe a bit of retail therapy before her shift starts?'

'Think I know the shop…' Shona had dragged the little figure onto the map and was scanning Street View.

Jamie was driving. He hadn't seen Dave's map yet, but the daily destination was obvious and so was the nearest bus stop. A couple of hundred metres from the industrial estate, a tarmac path ran across a grass verge that widened out to accommodate a bench. Jamie parked and waited. The day was cool but bright, so the sun made the car warm through the glass and his head sunk into his coat collar. Long, black blinks punctuated his vision as he fought the urge to doze. And then he saw her in the car's wing mirror, silhouetted against a low winter light and hurrying on unsteady heels. He didn't need to see the Moda Polska bag, he recognised her hair, black and bobbed. Opening the passenger side window, as the girl drew level, he stretched across towards the door handle. The girl stopped and looked with hard eyes.

'I only get in car for money.'

'Just a word, I—'

'Don't do chat. You want chat use phone. I got sex, you got money. Simple. Money, sex, or piss off.'

'But—'

'Sex, money or piss off. What you expect, Nectar Points?'

'I'm police.'

'Role play extra. And don't do handcuffs.'

'I'm trying to help.'

The girl began walking again. Jamie started the engine and, trying to stay level, leaned towards the open window holding out his warrant card.

'Could be test.' The girl kept walking. 'See if I good slut who keeps mouth shut.'

'No, look. Police ID. Look at the holograph. I'm here to protect you.'

She laughed. 'Photoshop. Or maybe you boss's pet policeman. Poland full of pet policemen. Piss off now. Go.'

'*Tikra Meilė*,' Jamie said. 'The horseman with a sword.'

The girl glared, then pulled her phone from her pocket. 'I take picture. Show boss. Show him so he know. Show him I good slut.'

'Sorry,' Jamie held up an open hand. 'Sorry. I didn't mean to... sorry,' and he put the car into reverse. The girl tottered on as fast as her stiletto boots would let her. At the galvanised gates she turned and looked back.

'Fucking shit,' Jamie was cursing as he drove. 'Christ... do something. I had to do something, just so I could feel... twat.'

Shona was sitting at the desk as Jamie hunched across the briefing space.

'Been busy?' she asked.

He folded into the chair with a grunt.

'That's a no then?' Shona didn't speak for a minute or so, then: 'If you do get a spare moment,' she slid a folder across the desk. 'Dave's stuff. Could be a real breakthrough.'

Jamie stared at the folder. Breakthrough. It seemed to make it worse. Someone else's calm, methodical success. Useless didn't cover it. He'd achieved nothing. Worse than nothing if Bakula was staring at his picture on a whore's phone.

Shona stood. He felt her eyes on him.

'Got a couple of odds and ends to sort,' and she left him to himself, eventually coming back with two coffees and a selection of nutri-bars.

The room was quiet now the day shift had gone home.

'So?' she placed one of the coffees by Jamie.

Jamie nodded, indicating the map and where he'd added his own notes to the highlighter lines and labels.

'Yeah, good old Dave. Might be a chance to shovel up some shit of my own making,' Jamie nearly smiled.

'Shit of your own making? What do you—'

'That girl,' Jamie didn't make eye contact. 'Black hair. Made a bit of a…'

17

When Shona arrived the following morning Jamie already had notes spread across the desk, sticking post-its onto pages.

'Early start?' Shona reached the desk.

'Court case; routine housebreaking from months back. Quick refresher,' Jamie picked up some postcards. 'Don't want the defence barrister making a prat of me.' And he lifted his coat from the back of his chair.

Around ten o'clock Shona had a photocopy of Dave's map on her passenger seat and she tapped a postcode into the satnav. Jamie's cock-up had done some good. Time, location and Dave knew whose phone to track.

Parking a little away from a junction, Shona made sure she had a line of sight. *Probably a waste of time*, she thought. *Not like she's here every day.* But just turned eleven, she saw her cross the road towards a clothes shop.

Shona waited a minute then followed. The girl with black hair was browsing along the rails of coats. On the back wall was a sign that read *Witamy* and lines of bunting, each flag half white, half red. Shona began looking on a rack some distance away and, gradually, trying to seem random, moved nearer. Eventually she reached across to look at a nearby blouse and the girl looked up.

'Dzien dobry,' Shona smiled.

'Dzien dobry,' the girl looked unsure. 'How you know I'm Polish?'

Shona looked at the shop's bunting. 'And kurtka – your jacket, Warmia... How'd you know I wasn't?'

'Accent. Clothes style; English.'

English. Shona glossed over the word. 'Yeah, maybe, but East European designs are on the up. 'Specially winter stuff.'

'Polskie understand winter,' the girl kept looking along the rail.

'When I was a teenager.' Shona said.

The girl looked up.

'My mum was ill. Had to live with my auntie for a couple years. Her husband was Polish. The grandfather lived with them. Her husband spoke Polish to him. And my auntie, a bit.'

'So you live with Polish family?'

'Well, Polish-British. The old man came for work. Always thought he'd go back. Hardly bothered learning English, stuck with his friends at the Polish Club. But then the Russians... and by then his children knew Britain.'

'They want us in war. Want us after. Make buildings, sweat in factories.' The girl held up a skirt, but so that Shona could see.

'Like it,' Shona smiled. 'The old man was a welder. Hard life. Bloody cold life on the Clyde.'

'Clyde?'

'River Clyde. Glasgow. Where I'm from – Scotland.' Shona felt the fabric of the skirt the girl was holding. 'Moda Polska,' she continued. 'They do some nice stuff. More of it coming in now.'

'Kate Moss,' the girl pointed at a poster on the wall. '*Reserved*. Number one in Poland. Got shop in London now. And online.'

'Big launch,' Shona tilted a blouse for the girl to look at. 'In the papers. Big money; Oxford Street. Used to be British Home Stores.'

The girl grinned.

'I'm Shona,' she held out her hand.

'Katya,' the girl said, making the lightest touch.

'No, I like this stuff because it's different,' Shona stayed chatty. 'Moda Polska; Reserved's own brand stuff, I can afford that, but the real high end stuff? Out of my price range. Non, Robert Kupisz, Kaaskas. Next big thing.'

'Good to see Polski high-end somewhere,' Katya was deadpan.

'Always like quilted for winter,' Shona held a hip-length parka against herself. 'Ah well, need to be back at work. Na razie. See you,' Shona smiled and walked towards the door.

No one followed her to her car. She checked. It was progress, but a long way from trust. *Shop worked well*, Shona thought. *Clothes break the ice.*

'Need a bit of your Buddha-like wisdom,' Shona slid half a dozen squares of chocolate across the desk towards Dave Collins, then unfolded the highlighted map.

'Could just keep a focus on her real-time track.'

Shona waited for him to go on.

'Give you a handle on where you might find her.'

'So, that's today,' Shona was scouring across the maps. 'Or here would be good. She uses this café.' Shona tapped a finger on a street that ran at right-angles to the Polish clothes shop.

It was just after one when Shona read Jamie's text. He was in the canteen. She was surprised he'd bothered to let her know. When she arrived he was in the queue.

'C'mon,' he beckoned. 'Saved you a place.'

'Christ, like being back at school?' Shona squeezed in. Jamie indicated towards the Peepos just ahead.

'So, we've got to be back by quarter to?' Hobbes was saying. 'That's less than we're entitled. Nowhere near the full hour for lunch.'

'Yeah, well maybe you can tell him when the meeting starts,' another cropped head sneered back.

'Anyway, it'll just be more of that rumour crap that's been going around,' Hobbes was trying to be the centre of attention. 'All that bollocks about the government wanting the clever illegals to slip through.'

The sneering Peepo turned and noticed the narrowed distance between Hobbes and the detectives. 'Why don't you just put your head on his shoulder?' The man straightened and squared his shoulders.

'Bloody right. Too bloody close,' Shona didn't miss a beat. 'Don't know if it's his breath or his armpits I'm smelling. Christ, if you stood him on the white cliffs of Dover any migrants would take one whiff and paddle back to France.'

'You... you Manc bastard,' Hobbes was twitching from foot to foot. 'You're saying nothing.'

'Yeah, I was worried you'd turn your razor tongue on me. You always do so well with my Celtic colleague.'

'Wouldn't be surprised if you pair of lackeys aren't in on it,' Hobbes twitched and leaned towards them.

Shona didn't move back. 'That rumour? You can see why it started, mind.' She smiled her contempt. 'Apparently some politicians think we need migrants to counterbalance the high percentage of English-born morons in the population.'

'Boys,' Hobbes was rocking, looking for a reaction. 'She said the British are thick.'

'No, I didn't,' Shona held her gaze until he looked uncomfortable. 'I said English.'

Jamie sniggered and the Peepos behind Hobbes turned away chuckling as the natural order reasserted itself.

'Good work,' Jamie looked across the canteen table. 'Put the bastard in his place. Enjoyed that.'

'Rather not draw attention though,' Shona stirred her tea.

'Keeping under the radar is good,' Jamie lowered his voice. 'But sometimes it's when you shrink back they start to suspect.'

As they left the canteen, a group of Peepos went into the gents. 'Listen,' Jamie nodded towards the door. 'I'm going in there. Give it thirty seconds then call my phone.'

Inside, he saw three Peepos' backs as they stood at the urinals. 'I heard this was the place where the big nobs come to hang out,' Jamie's voice was loud. 'Obviously, I was misinformed.' And he went into a cubicle and locked the door.

His phone rang.

'Yes boss, I know. Those bald-headed bastards have been talking about it,' Jamie could hear feet and low chuntering beyond the door. 'I know. Me and Shona have just been taking the piss out of them but... yes, boss I know it's not a joke, Christ that's the last thing we need, some of our own deliberately aiding and abetting... yes, I know. Laws need enforcing. Not our job to turn a blind eye just because some two-faced politician wants to cheat the system. Like you said before, boss, there's no brackets that say *unless you're a clever twat*.'

Jamie went through a series of pauses and yeses and nos and more I knows then: 'But we're already on it. You know that. If we get a whiff... a whisper of any names... yes, ma'am, even if it's just a hint. I've got the message.'

When Jamie unlocked the cubicle and moved to the sink, the Peepos hurried to the hand-dryers.

'That's it lads, leave your zips open, get some warm air on it. Might become visible to the naked eye.' And he made his way into the corridor, shaking his hands and wiping them on his trousers.

Shona was already at the desk when Jamie ambled back. The last of the Peepos trailed in as Moonlight was arranging his PowerPoint.

'You missed the fun,' Shona looked towards Moonlight. 'Prat

caught his finger in the stapler. Should've seen the arse-lickers running around.'

'Closest the twat's been to giving blood for the cause.'

'Anyway what was—' Shona turned back.

'It'll filter back,' Jamie winked. 'Cleggy using us to sniff out any subversives in the ranks.'

After a couple of minutes Moonlight's eyes lifted towards the Peepo herd. 'Gentlemen, thank you,' and he held out both hands, palms down. There was a plaster on his index finger. 'Britain voted to be British,' he tapped his laptop and images of sad humanity carouseled behind him. 'And today we begin the fight-back against the dogs of the anti-state. Those, hummus-eating, we-know-better-than-you bastards who are sneaking their smart-arse overseas pals into our green and pleasant land. But we're not having it.' Moonlight pushed both fists onto his hips. 'Tough shit, I say. That's how democracy works. This is our country. Ours by the will of the people. Ours by the law of the land.'

Shona and Jamie looked. The herd had their backs turned, but their shoulders were squared and risen. Beyond, on Moonlight's screen, images flipped between refugee lines and multi-skinned criminal types in everything from hoodies to limousines.

'Love a good motivational speech,' Shona whispered. 'Makes me feel all community spirited.'

Jamie looked back at her and put his fingers in his ears. 'You remember that bollocks about the tree in the forest. Do you think if I can't hear Moonlight he'll fuck off and cease to exist?' He closed his eyes for a few seconds. 'Nah,' he said as his eyes blinked back open. 'I can still see the twat.'

Over in the enclosed offices Clegg was visible above the line of frosted glass, peering into the room.

When Moonlight clicked his laptop, the screen darkened and the Peepo herd dissipated. Clegg beckoned at Jamie.

'Just because he isn't as clever as he thinks he is, doesn't mean he's not a danger,' Clegg began as her door closed.

'Irritant more than danger, surely boss,' Jamie shrugged slightly.

'No, dangerous. Twats like Moonlight are looking to eat into our jurisdiction. They're cheap. They've got muscle. And some of our smarmy, Category B politicians see them as a way to big themselves up... Can't let those bald-headed bastards be seen as an alternative.'

'Gives us an idea of their routes, working hours,' Shona had already spread a highlighter-lined map across the desk when Jamie began his morning shift. Again, she was cross-referencing with Google Maps. 'And the occasional place where they spend time besides.' She turned her laptop. 'Where they live and...' clicking a different tab. 'And this seems to be the preferred location for premium clients.' There was a view of a hotel.

'So,' an hour later and Shona suggested a breakfast boost. 'What was Clegg saying last night?'

'Low-profile. Under the radar.' Jamie grinned, then pushed open the canteen door. 'Fuck sake. Thought these bastards were on the street now.'

Ahead, a line of Peepos snaked towards the counter.

'Jesus,' Shona looked along the line. 'There'll be nothing left after these cuddly boys have had their noses in the trough.'

'Yes, love,' Hobbes emerged from a knot of dark shirts. 'I'm a man of vast appetites – and afterwards,' he rubbed his stomach. 'I like a full English.'

'Well,' Shona stepped forward a little. 'Remember, you are what you eat.'

Hobbes leered and struck a body-builder's pose. 'Yeah. Full English.'

Shona nodded. 'Aye... mostly pork and covered in grease.'

Hobbes' mouth fell open, but his stammering was swamped by the sniggering of the nearby Peepos.

'Think I might need to work on that *under the radar* thing,' Shona moved behind Jamie's shoulder and smirked.

As they finished up their tea and toast, Jamie said: 'Around ten, could you—'

'Sorry, already booked. Need to be gone in a few minutes.'

Shona parked and began her wait. Around eleven, her phone buzzed.

'She's on the move. Coming your way.'

Shona was out of the car, listening and walking.

'And, she's in.'

'Thanks, Dave. Just coming round the corner.'

18

In the café, Shona deliberately walked to the counter, pretending she hadn't seen the girl. Then, turning with a coffee in her hand, she feigned surprised recognition.

'Katya, isn't it? Mind if I?' She was already pulling the chair from under the table. Acquiescence passed across the girl's face.

'Kawa,' Shona lifted her cup. 'Coffee.'

'Bloody Scotland accent,' Katya smiled.

After some bland social wittering, Shona said: 'Look, got this last week,' and reached into her bag. 'Been on their mailing list since I bought a jacket and boots.'

She placed a glossy magazine on the table. On the cover, above the pouting model in her swirling clothes, was the title RESERVED. After a minute or two rotating the magazine between them, Shona continued: 'Mind if I? So we can see better.'

She came to sit alongside Katya. Two more coffees, Shona insisted on paying; half an hour passed. Nothing mentioned but fashion and it was Katya who moved her chair backwards and began to stand.

'Bloody time. Thanks. Need go to work.'

'Here,' Shona shut the magazine. 'You have it.'

Katya hesitated.

'Go on. I'll email. They'll send me another one.'

'Thank you. I will read.' Katya put the magazine in her bag, then smiled as she moved away.

Shona finished her coffee. Back in the car she took out her phone. 'Dave, thanks. Went as well as—'

'She's on the bus now,' Dave Collins was following the phone app on his office computer. 'So, what did she tell you?'

'Nothing,' Shona said. 'Didn't ask. Just laid a bit of groundwork. Maybe next time, or the time after.'

'Time pressing.' Dave told her what was already at the front of her mind. 'If it's not just the two…'

'Aye, I know. But, if I push too soon… do me a favour. Don't mention this to Jamie. Not just yet.'

It was just after lunch when she arrived back in the briefing room. On the desk were two manila folders. One said *Liliana Normova*, the other had a case number and *Tree Girl* written on it. Shona began reading. She didn't notice Clegg had left her office until she was alongside the desk.

'Told him to have a couple of hours physical. Got that compulsory fitness test coming up and he looks like a sack of shit,' Clegg sat, trying not to smirk. 'So, how are you two hitting it off?'

'Roller-coaster of emotions,' Shona inhaled. 'With tolerable as the high point.'

'It's a shit case,' Clegg's eyes fixed for a moment. 'And it's easier to be aggressive than admit you're feeling the pressure.'

'I know, but there's no predicting. Sometimes he's okay, then… but you don't see why the change.'

'No, I've never been able to get to the bottom of him…' Clegg rotated a random paperclip. 'My advice? Enjoy the quiet. Tomorrow, and our Jamie will be here soon enough.'

19

As Jamie drove onto the main road, Shona guessed where they were going. 'So, we've got something to look at?'

'We've got fuck all,' Jamie ground his teeth, scanning the traffic for a gap. 'Fuck all but a murdering bastard and a ticking clock.'

'So?'

'So we look. Ask more questions. Walk about. Fucking pray if you like.'

Shona didn't bite back. She knew where his words were coming from; where their anger was aimed. After a pause, she said: 'Maybe something'll drop: a face, or a car round by the unit?'

The quiet wasn't hostile as they drove. Shona looked along the streets at the shop fronts. 'We're early,' she eventually said. 'There's a drive-in coming up. Do you want a coffee? I'll pay.'

'Early?' Jamie looked at her.

'If we're looking at the unit. The girls won't be arriving yet.'

Seeing the lane to the serving hatch, Jamie pulled up alongside the microphone. 'Large flat white, black Americano and a Custard Danish.'

'What happened to the fitness test? And I only offered to pay for coffee,' Shona faked indignation.

'Just the coffees,' Jamie interrupted the voice repeating his order. 'Not the Danish.'

'Thought Cleggy gave you yesterday afternoon to hone your physical prowess.'

'I did. An hour in the gym, then went for a swim.'

Shona checked the lids on the coffees and held them both until they reached the street that linked the main road to the industrial estate and the unit. On the opposite side there was a footpath and grass verge.

When the coffees were finished, Shona slotted the cups together. 'I'll just dump these.' She got out of the car.

Jamie watched her cross to a waste bin next to a bench. She was nearly there when Jamie waved his hand out of the window and pointed behind.

Shona turned and saw.

Jamie's car door began opening, but she gestured for him to get back. In the corner of her eye, she saw a familiar silhouette, walking on unsteady stiletto boots.

Shona threw one of the coffee cups in the bin and pretended to drain the dregs from the other in between checking her phone. Feigning surprise, Shona looked up and smiled.

'Dzien dobry,' then she stood and spread her arms. 'Nowa kurta,' and she extended a foot, 'i buty.'

Katya smiled. 'New jacket and boots. Reserved?'

Shona shuffled along and patted the bench. 'Another coincidence.'

'Coincidence?' Katya hovered.

'Strange we're in the same place as each other again.' Shona touched Katya's arm and patted the bench.

'Not so much. Walk this way most days on way to work.'

'But I don't. The office misplaced a parcel. Boss told me to taxi it over to that lorry place on the industrial estate.'

'Taxi, that was kind.'

'Not that kind. He told me to get the bus back. Still, excuse to wear my new jacket and boots.'

'Need be at work,' Katya said. 'Not happy if I late.'

'Boss a bit of bastard?' Shona sensed her slipping away and touched Katya's hand. 'Know the feeling.'

Then Shona slid open a zip, reached into an inside pocket and slipped a folded piece of paper under her thigh. It wasn't a decision. Just an instinct: a now or never.

Jamie was aware of the girl going to stand, then Shona reaching out, holding both hands, to form a circle of reassurance. But then he saw a hand break free and Katya on her feet. Shona remained seated, her mouth moving, still clinging on. There was a half turn away, then Shona was holding a paper, shaking out its folds and lifting it up. Jamie watched the instantaneous shift, the slow fall back onto the bench, the girl's eyes locked on the paper and Shona still talking. A few seconds passed, Shona eased the paper back as their bodies turned together, the rigid reluctance and anger fallen away. Eventually, Katya gave a slight nod and stood. Parting words were exchanged and she began her slow walk on her unsteady heels.

Shona remained on the bench until Katya had disappeared through the galvanised gates. Then, looking around, she walked back. Jamie started the car and began to drive. For a few seconds he didn't say anything, then: 'So, what was that?'

'Shit or bust,' Shona leaned her head on the window.

As Jamie drove, Shona assessed his face. Dead blank while his mind and emotions fought to process what he'd just seen. Shona watched until, finally, as he turned into the police station, he went to break his silence.

'Dave's office,' she cut him off. 'It'll make more sense.'

And she was out of the car and walking.

Dave boiled the inevitable kettle and spread the maps over his desk.

'I've already seen these. It's good, but—' Jamie began.

'Dave's took it further,' Shona traced a hand along the neat lettering. 'Real-time tracking.' She explained about the clothes shop, then Dave noticing the café and engineering another meeting. Jamie listened, but didn't speak.

Maybe acknowledging a woman doing better than him, went through Shona's mind. As they left the office, she asked: 'So?'

'So?' Jamie's eyes were still and empty. Then, after a few seconds, he said: 'Yeah. Could have legs. Better than my attempt anyway. Oscar Pistorius got more legs than anything I've turned up lately.'

Shona watched him walk on ahead, shrunk into his collar and scarf.

Another silent session embarked across the desk, but Shona didn't feel the expected anger radiating, more a gradual coming to terms.

After a while, she whispered. 'The organisation needs to know. Jephcott needs a call.'

Jamie nodded.

'And you need to know what was said on that bench.'

20

Jamie drove west out of the city centre, pulling up on the edge of a park with a reservoir. Shona took out a cheap mobile and texted.

Call ASAP.

'So?' Jamie flexed his fingers. 'While we're waiting for Jephcott…'

'On the bench, Moda Polska girl,' Shona began. 'Name's Katya, and I think she might find a way to talk to us.'

'Or she might just blow us out and carry on whoring.'

'She might,' Shona said. 'But if she was going to do that she'd have done a runner. Especially after I showed her my police ID.'

'Wasn't just police ID though, was it? You unfolded a sheet of paper.'

'Photograph: print-out of Liliana.'

Jamie's head turned and his eyes blinked. 'Not one of those from…'

'No, Christ no. Head and shoulders from the file. When she was still alive – and beautiful.' Shona's phone beeped.

'Not like you call every day,' Jephcott's voice was metallic.

'There's been a development.' Jamie's cut in, then read out their postcode.

Jephcott sat on the rear seat of Jamie's car and leaned forward as Shona began delivering the agreed narrative. When she paused, Jephcott spoke.

'That could suit us; use the murder operation as cover to keep tabs on anti-migrant operations. Hell'uva gamble though, showing her your police ID. Surprised she didn't run a mile.'

'She was close,' Shona said. 'Bloody close. Wasn't sure if I'd made enough of a connection. If I hadn't put my hands on hers, she'd've walked. If I hadn't kept saying Zaufaj mi. Zaufaj mi.'

'Zau…?' Jephcott tried to echo.

'*Zaufaj mi* – Trust me. Speaking Polish helped. Dzien dobry drew in her in.'

'Jin what?' Jamie finally spoke.

'*Dzien dobry*. Good morning.'

'But she agreed to?' Jephcott pressed on.

'Yeah. Clincher was the photo. I'm confident she'll come good. If we could just set up some covert communications.'

Jephcott absorbed what he'd been told, then: 'How did you manage to—'

'All stems from Dave Collins,' Shona continued. 'He zeroed in on some phone card numbers that Jamie got at the precinct.'

She explained about maps, highlighter lines, times and frequent locations, but didn't mention that she'd already used the shop and caffé Dave had pinpointed.

'Pity he's not one of us,' Shona said. 'We were banging our heads on a wall till he came up with this.'

'Impressive,' Jephcott said. 'But, like you say, he's not one of us. Just be careful. Have you…'

'Normal procedure,' Jamie blew mist on the window.

'That's right,' Shona agreed. 'I do trust Dave, but it's irrelevant. Nothing he's touched goes beyond the murder investigation.'

Jephcott looked as if he were about to speak.

'There's nothing,' Jamie cut across.

'Alright, I know… just saying,' Jephcott opened the car door. 'You did right to fill me in. Good work both.'

Driving back to the police station, Jamie pulled into the drive-through and ordered a flat white and another large Americano.

'My turn,' he said and tapped his bank card.

Sat in the car park, Jamie held the cup against his lip. 'Might've been different if you hadn't talked to the girl in her own language.'

'Katya,' Shona said.

'Yeah, Katya… that Dzien stuff…'

'Dzien Dobry. And Buty. Boots... Nowa kurta i buty. I was showing her "New jacket and boots".'

'And she cared, why?' A cog slotted into gear in Jamie's head. 'Random woman leaps off bench and shows complete stranger new clothes? Like Jephcott said, Hell 'uva gamble.'

'Yeah. But maybe not quite that much of a gamble,' her eyes lifted and looked at Jamie. 'I wasn't exactly a stranger. We've met before. Twice. Once in a shop and then in a café.'

'When was this?' Jamie let the edge slip back into his voice.

'Past few days. Saw her in the café and a day earlier in the shop. But I wasn't planning for this today. Rushing it could be more dangerous in the long run.'

'So, it looks like we've got some bastard knocking out murders one a month like a fucking metronome and you're playing the long game? Jesus. What the fuck did you talk about?'

'Girly stuff. Talked about me a bit – why I've picked up a few words of Polish.'

'Not her? Not any background, or anything useful?' Jamie's tone hardened with every phrase.

Shona glared. 'Clothes. We talked about clothes a lot.'

'Clothes? You talked about clothes. For fu—'

'Yes. Clothes. And strangely, it was the clothes, the *Nowa kurta i buty*, that got her to sit on the bench. The clothes and the opening up and the few words in her own language. How the fuck do you think she'd of reacted if some random fucking moron, to use your words, asked her to sit down and trust me?'

'But clothes. Wasting time on—'

'Christ, no wonder you're on your own. You probably know more about quantum physics than you do about women. Clothes. Women like clothes. Women like talking about clothes. Clothes are neutral. Clothes aren't "let me pump you for information". Clothes are let's talk. Let's see if we like each other. Clothes are connections.'

Shona took a breath, but Jamie had stopped listening and was staring into a void, where a scene was replaying of a girl in stiletto boots walking away from a man saying *Tikra Meilė* and holding up his police ID.

'Soft skills. Ever heard of them? Soft skills.'

And Jamie was shrinking again; slowly imploding.

Shona opened the fridge. No milk and the only place open was the all-night garage. Driving past the park she saw a figure she recognised and pulled up in the shadow of the tree-lined pavement. The figure jogged to a lamppost, then upped the pace to the next, then jogged again. Shona watched the sequence repeat three times, before the runner flopped onto a bench. She opened her car door and began to walk. As she got closer she could see the rise and fall of the chest and clouds of misty breath that spiralled and dissipated around the bent-over form.

'Is that the official Olympic tracksuit?'

Jamie's eyes rolled up, but his head remained suspended above his knees. His kit was a hotchpotch of random brushed cotton and crumpled nylon football gear.

'I'll just enjoy this moment,' she was smiling. 'While you're too oxygen starved to speak.'

Jamie's head rocked and she thought he nearly joined her in

a smile, but then he blinked and wiped away the stinging sweat with his sleeve. He continued blinking and wiping as Shona sat on the bench.

'Movement's good,' she said. 'Helps burn away the anxiety and sense of inadequacy. Gym bunny, myself. It's warmer.' She looked at Jamie. The clouds of breath were slowing a little.

'Guilt,' Jamie slid words between breaths. 'You forgot guilt.'

'No, I never forget guilt,' Shona brought her hands together as her elbows came to rest on her knees.

'So,' Jamie's chest was slowing now. 'What's next? You tell me what I already know? How I've been pig-headed and we'd be arse-deep in shit if it wasn't for you and Dave?'

'You know what happens if I moan about you to Jephcott?' Shona straightened.

Jamie wiped his mouth on the back of his hand.

'He just says you're one of his best operatives. Says you've seen stuff.' She paused. 'It's like he said. You remember the names of the ones that don't make it,' and she closed her eyes for a few seconds. 'You're the one they trust: the drivers, the safe house keepers, the document forgers. You need to get back in the saddle – a lorry load of young Baltics need what you know.'

'Christ,' Jamie rolled his eyes. 'Jephcott been helping you perfect your effortless patronising?.'

'You're a bastard at times,' Shona's gaze remained at right angles. 'Most of the fucking time actually. Do you think you're the only one who's seen stuff? The only one who's asked themselves *what if?* Maybe you've seen more, but you haven't got a monopoly, you sanctimonious prick. First job,' and she swallowed. 'First job... wasn't my fault... this girl, in Birmingham, all she had to do was get on a train, but going into New Street station she gets spooked. Sees something. Imagines it probably. But she panics. Tries to cross the rails. I was at the top of the escalators. It was all over before I got trackside. But I saw her.' A film of water hung across Shona's eyes but didn't fall and, as her breathing steadied. 'So, yeah, I've seen stuff. I've seen a poor girl's innards wrapped around railway tracks.'

'But it wasn't down to you.'

'No. Thanks. You saying that makes it all better. Can you do the same trick with something that was my fault?'

Jamie began to speak.

'Don't ask. You don't know me well enough.'

And she stood and strode off. After a few yards she stopped and came back for the plastic milk carton she'd left on the bench.

Jamie's mouth opened. 'I'm sor—'

'Not even close.' She cut him dead and she turned away.

21

'I am sorry,' Jamie spoke quietly, his eyes focused on the desk.

'New day,' Shona's voice was clipped. But a few seconds later she said: 'So, using the lampposts for intervals?'

'Fifty metres. One jog, one sprint, then double it up to hundreds. Done fifteen reps when you turned up.'

'Well on course for the fitness test then.'

'Yeah. Thought I might push on and get a bit back.'

'Back?'

'Yeah, bit nearer to what I was when the army wanted me. Proper fit then.' He looked up. 'Top ten in the North-West regional cross-country once.'

'Impressive.' Shona was conversational now. 'Did you never want to…'

'Wrong build,' Jamie was grinning a little now. 'Legs too short, body too long for a real runner… okay for the army though, yomping around with a backpack.' He paused as the memory formed in his head. 'Sometimes, they had so much weight in them, you'd have to lie on your back, slip your arms through the straps and get your mates to pull you onto your feet.' He paused and looked at Shona. 'Amazing the weight you can carry, if you've got someone to help you get upright.'

'Aye, well. You know that sorry bit, you started with? For your penance, it's your turn to fetch the tea.' And she spread a handful of coins across the desk.

'Don't push your luck,' Jamie grinned as he scooped the money into his hand.

'Dodgy if we're always hanging around in the same places,' Jamie pulled the car into a petrol station. 'Just needs one of her minders to drive past and she's in the shit.'

'I know. I told her I'd leave her a message in a newspaper.'

'What? A want ad? Respectable policewoman requires skanky whore to betray murdering boss. GSOH preferred.'

'No, you prat. Like a dead-drop. I'll leave a paper and she'll pick it up and the message will be in there.'

'Dead-drop? Jesus, did you get a John Le Carre box set for Christmas? Where are you leaving it?'

'Told her on the bench.'

'Shit. With our luck somebody'll sit down before she gets there and go "look, a free newspaper".'

'Thanks Einstein. I'll use a Polish paper. Who's gonna want that?'

'Where'll you get one of those? Easier just to use an old paper no one wants.'

'There's Polish shops... and there's that big Polish church with a club by the park – soft skills. Her own language. Trust.'

Jamie grunted. He knew she was right. In his mind he saw newspapers at the back of church. Him and Mandy with their nan after mass; papers in the piety store, *Catholic Herald*, *The Universe*, *Ireland's Own*. The old biddies buying them, clinging onto who they used to be. He remembered his nan getting them dressed, best clothes, clean faces then her shouting, "And if you're not up and dressed by the time we get back from holy mass, I'll introduce you to the back of my hand, big as you are." Shouting at his mam, like she was the child. He'd liked that.

Jamie drove along, then parked in the street. He wasn't there yet, but he wanted to feel it: their locus. Shona was silent as Jamie's eyes focused out into the dirty terraces that stood, or crumbled, like decayed teeth in the marked for demolition streets.

Winter sat below the clear sky. If he'd been on grass or between trees, Jamie would have enjoyed the cold morning. But not here, where life was sparse and barking dogs echoed from hard brick yards. He began to drive again, slowly. Outside a shop, a group of thin youths eyed them suspiciously, heads bent in hoodies. Jamie returned eye-contact and they turned away. Beyond the next corner, the street and numbers tallied. Three adjoining terraces; home to the Shag City workforce and an occasional child.

'The land of opportunity,' Jamie sucked his teeth. Opportunity to lie in a metal box, sweating under a grunting stranger, ran through his mind.

Shona pointed at Katya's house number and Jamie parked their innocuous car. After a while a door opened. He could see in. It looked warm and homely. Katya and her dark hair; she turned back, adjusting clothes, talking to someone unseen in the hallway. Then the door was shut and she was walking towards the bus stop. When she'd turned the corner, Jamie started the car.

Shona took a pad of post-its out of her bag and wrote on the top one – a telephone number and a message: *Bądź silny*.

'What's that mean?' Jamie nodded towards the post-it.

'Stay strong.'

Shona tried to remain silent on the drive, but as he shot across the traffic light just after the amber had slipped to red, she hissed between her teeth.

'Christ Jamie, why don't you just stick the blues and twos on, if you really want to attract attention? We've got loads of time.'

Jamie didn't speak, but he did ease down.

When he pulled off the road between the bus stop and the

industrial estate, Shona got out and walked to sit on the bench while he crawled into a side street that had a clear view. Shona pretended to read. In the distance he saw the bus pull up and Katya get off. A second later another girl, dressed for business, was alongside and the two were talking. Jamie cursed under his breath and slid lower in his car seat. As Katya got nearer, she saw Shona on the bench holding the newspaper. Shona watched her slow and look around. Then Katya's shoulders straightened and she strode out. Shona stood, held the paper up, folded it carefully – making sure the paper's name banner was clearly visible – then jammed it into the armrest of the bench and walked off towards a narrow alleyway that disappeared between wooden panels. Before she reached the walkway, she took out her phone, turned in the direction from which Katya was approaching and made a call. Jamie wanted to shout, but had to remain low in the car and seethe quietly. After a few seconds, Shona put the phone in her pocket, walked beyond the fencing and disappeared.

Reaching the bench, Katya stopped, picked up the newspaper and showed the headlines to the other girl. Jamie's senses focused on Katya and her companion and he saw a split-second of fluorescent protruding between pages as the newspaper was folded and dropped into her bag. Then the two young women carried on chatting until they disappeared into the industrial estate. Jamie was still staring at the galvanised gates as Shona opened the car door.

'Who the fucking hell were you calling? Jesus, what if you were seen?'

'What if?' she shrugged. 'I wanted to be. That's why I pretended to be on the phone. I wanted Katya to see me. I wanted her to know we were on.'

'But the other one?'

'The other one probably noticed nothing, but if she did it was just a woman, in no hurry, making a casual phone call.'

Jamie knew she was right, but still needed to seethe at something. They were walking across the station car park when he spoke.

'So, she's got a number to call, if she doesn't bottle it.'

'It'll be tomorrow before we hear anything,' Shona pressed the button of the lift. 'She'll need a pay phone. She won't use her own. I bet her boss keeps tabs. Be tomorrow before she gets a chance.'

Shona kept glancing at Jamie for the rest of the afternoon. His movements were twitchy, as if his body was fighting not to unravel. She kept words to a minimum and looked for jobs that took her away from the desk and his exhausting tension. Eventually the shift ended and she headed for the gym.

Jamie went straight home and ate. He tried to read, but couldn't focus. After a few minutes he went to the kitchen, pulled on some rubber gloves and looked in the cupboard. He began cleaning window frames, doors, toilet, shower: anything to fill the time with distraction until his dinner was digested enough for him to risk a run and hope exhaustion would lead to sleep.

It was around ten when he pulled on his jumble of mismatched sports gear, closed the door behind him and gave himself to the lamppost markers. Forty minutes later he was bent over a bench gasping, sweat tumbling onto the tarmac again.

'Shaping up, soldier,' he heard her voice between breaths. 'Where's those abs I used to love?' She was laughing at him: Cara, in his head.

'Give it time,' Jamie heard his own voice. 'Take a bit of time to get from Captain Doughnut back to world class athlete.'

'World class,' Cara laughed.

'Well, North Manchester under-14s cross-country. You saw the medal.'

'Jamie, Jamie, we don't have time to list your vast haul of athletic honours.'

'Any reason you're here?'

'Just checking you're okay. You seem in a better mood. Anything happened to cheer you up.'

'Well, me and Shona—'

'Shona? You and a woman?'

'Come on. You live in my head. You know…'

'Yeah, but I still like to see you squirm.'

'Anyway,' Jamie moved on. 'The case, might be taking a step in the right direction if…'

'If?'

'If we get a phone call. Anyway, you know all this. You know everything I do.'

'But if I make you say it, maybe it—'

'Helps, I know.'

'So, this woman. You told her about me?'

Jamie's inner eye stared at Cara in his mind. 'Tell her about you? Tell her my dead wife talks to me? Christ, she already thinks I'm mental.' Jamie straightened. 'Anyway, we both know you're not really there. Just sometimes it gets clearer, makes more sense if it's your…'

'Okay, Fatboy,' Cara's voice was lighter. 'Bit of a warm down then home. Try to sleep.'

Shona's burner phone almost vibrated itself off her bedside table before she was awake enough to grab it.

4:38 am.

She didn't use her name or any police reference.

'Dzien dobry,' the voice began.

22

Sorting through his running gear, ready for the washer, Jamie felt a weight in the pocket of his jogging bottoms. It was his phone: missed call at 4:51am. He clicked voicemail. It began to dial, then died. Frustration shot to max as he saw the red zero for power. Work. He needed to be gone. His charger was always by the bed, except it wasn't. So, choice? Waste time scouring the flat and be late, or be on time and use the spare charger he kept in his desk?

The drive to work was a succession of swearing, hand gestures and playing chicken with the traffic lights. 'For fuck's sake,' echoed off the roof the station's underground car park as he dropped his car keys and they slid under a van. One of the civilian admin women tutted and, as he raced for the lift, she closed the doors.

Swearing his way through his desk, the charger was in the third drawer he'd emptied. He plugged it in, despite the fact that the chord was jammed around a hole-punch.

'Jesus, God. Why does the whole world hate me?' The phone screen stayed dead. Last time he'd completely flattened the battery it'd taken ten minutes to boot back up.

Six minutes. He sucked in air and the phone screen lit up. Still plugged in, he scrolled through voicemails, then eventually...

'Jamie, Sorry this is so late, eh early. Thought you'd pick up.

News from the paper was good. You know, the big story. Tell you more when I get in.'

'It's good,' Jamie kept saying to himself, tapping his pencil against the desk. 'It'll be good.'

He was still tapping an hour later, when the door opened and Shona crossed the briefing space.

'You didn't rush,' his eyes narrowed. 'So…?'

'Not here,' Shona whispered. 'Give it a couple of minutes. Canteen should be quieter by now.'

Shona pretended to organise papers. She sat and consulted her notebook. Jamie just sat. When she stood, so did he.

The breakfast rush had passed and there was a table in the corner.

'So, what the—'

'If you shut up I'll tell you.' Shona leaned over her tea. 'She was waiting for her taxi. There was a pay phone.'

'No pay phones near Shag City.'

'No, but every week she says she gets hotel bookings. More, lately, with it being Christmas.'

'So she's sure to have something coming in her stocking.'

Shona carried on as if he'd never spoken. 'Means she's away from prying eyes for a bit. Says she'll be there again on Wednesday. Said if we book a room near hers, wait till the last punter's gone. Same hotel Dave tracked on Google Maps.'

'Clean,' Jamie had Tripadvisor on his phone 'Kettle in your room and a decent breakfast.'

Shona didn't react. 'If we're there by nine she'll find a way to let us know her room number.'

Parked with the hotel reception in the rear view mirror, Shona plugged in earphones and flicked through her podcasts. Jamie held a small, palm-sized book low on his knees: a weak light from the instrument panel leaked across the pages. Occasional drivers parked and towed suitcases towards the door. Just before nine, a tangle of unsteady men in suits and low-slung ties spilled out of a black cab.

'Joys of the expense account life,' Shona slumped back in her seat, but then Jamie tapped her shoulder. Silhouetted against a streetlight, a short-skirted figure was tottering nearer on high heels. Shona held her phone under her chin, letting its light wash across her face. The figure changed her line.

'Good girl,' Shona whispered as the figure passed close-by.

There was a soft thud and a paper under the rear wiper blade. Jamie reached for the door handle, but Shona grabbed his hand. Katya continued to walk. Shona's hand remained on Jamie's until she'd reached the hotel entrance.

Beyond the plate glass, Katya talked to the receptionist, then walked out of sight. Shona's hand released Jamie's and he was out and striding towards the wiper. Getting back in, Jamie held out the note:

Room 211 – Finish about 2:30

'Look authentic.' Shona linked her arm through his as they approached the front door. Inside, they made their way to the bar, where the expense account taxi boys were having a night-cap. Every now and again one would leer towards Shona, then turn back to the group and laughter would erupt, followed by other eyes surreptitiously taking a glance. Shona resisted the temptation to raise a middle finger.

'Going for a recce,' Jamie stood.

'Thanks, I'll just sit here and put on a show for the boys who put the reptile into sales rep.'

A few seconds later, Jamie was back. 'Found this on a table by the reception desk.'

He plonked down a copy of *Woman and Home*. Shona let her eyes speak for her as he walked away.

It was nearly ten minutes later when Jamie returned. 'Yeah, it's on the floor we thought. Made a note of nearby rooms.'

Huddling together, they talked about next moves as the cluster of expense account boys slowly fragmented, swaying off towards their rooms.

'Just those last two finishing their drinks.'

'Great,' Shona picked up *Woman and Home* again. 'Maybe there's a new Pilates pose for me to master.'

'Bollocks,' Jamie hissed a few seconds later. Instead of leaving, one of the last two expense account boys was buying more whisky at the bar. When the man sat, he placed two drinks on a low table.

'Bloody hell,' Shona leaned into Jamie. Earlier in the evening one of the men had been the chief leerer, but now he reached across and was stroking the back of the other man's hand. The man was smiling back.

'Come on,' Jamie stood. 'While it's quiet.' And he began walking back towards the entrance.

As the receptionist reached for a key fob, Jamie said 'What have you got on the second floor?'

'The rooms are all pretty similar,' the receptionist began checking numbers.

Jamie leaned to look at her computer screen. 'Great, sweetie, our special room's free,' he wrapped an arm around Shona. '227, please. Bit of an anniversary.'

Shona felt her mouth drop open.

Reaching 227, Jamie pointed a couple of doors down to 221 then swiped the key card. Shona looked in the bathroom, then filled the kettle and sorted through the teabags.

'I could listen for the door, tell her where we are between punters,' Jamie said.

Shona was already unfolding sheets of A4 paper. Each was a photocopy of a magazine cover, except a piece of paper must have been taped to the middle to leave a white expanse. The title read

Reserved in bold letters. Shona opened her handbag, took out a felt pen and wrote 227 in large black numbers.

'Fashion magazine. Gave her a copy last week. We talked about their new store in Oxford Street.'

Then she walked into the corridor. Opposite 221, and Katya, was a small emergency evacuation poster. Shona blu-tacked one of the Reserved 227 photocopies next to it – right in the eye-line of anyone leaving the room.

Jamie took off his shoes, then slid onto the bed and began reading the palm-sized book again. Shona returned to the room, turned a pillow vertical, took out her phone and began to untangle earphones.

'Getting comfortable?' Jamie loosened his belt.

'Taking one for the team.'

After about twenty minutes, Jamie went to the bathroom.

'I hope you've washed your hands,' she was holding his small book.

'Observer's Book of Birds,'

'Aye, my brother had a couple,' Shona said. 'But not nature, aircraft and astronomy.'

'I've got a few,' he eased back onto the bed. 'Trees, Eggs, Insects. Only the old ones, nineteen-fifties and sixties. Illustrations are brilliant. Much clearer than the crappy photos in the later versions.'

Shona plugged herself back into her earphones.

Around four hours passed and there was a quiet tap on the door. Shona roused from a nodding sleep. Jamie was already turning the latch.

'Quick,' Shona beckoned as the door opened.

Once inside the girl sat on the bed. Shona was alongside, but Jamie was leaning on the wall.

'Last bastard of night,' Katya pulled at the hem of her skirt.

'Last?' Jamie asked. Shona sucked her teeth.

'Third,' Katya was flat. 'Pre-book and pay for bit of comfort. Not like unit.'

Jamie lifted the kettle and walked towards the bathroom.

'Tea or coffee?' Shona asked.

'Tea, weak, black with sugar. Is Earl Grey? Sometimes they have Earl Grey. Like better if no lemon.'

'At my auntie's,' Shona said. 'They bought good tea for the old man.'

Katya smiled and took a thin neck chain from her bag and fixed it around her neck. A finely enamelled rectangle fell a little below her collar-bone.

'Black Madonna of Częstochowa,' Shona recognised the Byzantine-style icon of a virgin and child, dark-fleshed against gold halos.

'My grandmother say Holy Mary, keep you pure,' and she grinned. 'Always wear it. For grandmother. But not for punters.' She looked down, holding the image between her fingers, lost for a moment.

'So, how long have you got?' Jamie blustered back to business.

'No time,' Katya replied. 'Suppose call taxi. Go back. But say fall asleep.'

'Won't you…?'

'Not week-end. Plenty girls at unit. Small bollocking, for show.'

Shona passed her the Earl Grey tea, her eyes dwelling on Katya's nail varnish.

'Scarlet Harlot,' Katya looked back. 'Good colour. Does what say on tin.'

'I was there when Liliana was found.' Jamie spoke into the pause.

'And both of us when the other girl…'

'We think the other girl might have been first,' Jamie was quieter. 'From the…'

Katya nodded. 'One a month. First September. Not know

others. Bakula show us photos. Only Liliana, Nadia four, our unit, end October.'

'Four?' Shona picked up.

'Our working names. All Poles Katya. I am number two. Liliana Lithuanian, so Nadia four... Olgas are Belarus, Tatianas Russia. I lucky girl.' Her smile was deadpan. 'Kasia my real name. Sound same nearly.'

'Numbers,' Jamie was staring at his hands.

'Was joke. Old man, Mr Morcanu, say not remember all names, so say, "Poland – I call you Katya. Lithuania – Nadia". Then mafia man, Bakula, say "Good idea, use at other units". Then not joke. Give him time, he tattoo bar code on our arses.' Katya drained the last of her tea.

'So a girl disappears every month?' Jamie looked up.

'He show us faces, show excel sheets. Incentive, Bakula say.'

'Excel?' Shona seized the word.

'Keep count. Bonus scheme... bonus is not last, not disappear.' Katya stared into her empty cup.

Eventually, Shona said: 'When did it start?'

'Bakula arrive May. Nothing then, or June. Then old man stop coming. Was August he talk about score sheets and projector. He paint big wall white. Beginning October first photo.'

'And he projects excel sheets?' Jamie asked.

Shona and Jamie exchanged glances.

'When quiet,' Katya continued. 'He project girls' faces, like cheap disco. Bottom three girls spinning across wall, coloured red. Rest of us normal pictures, but with znak...' Katya traced a shape in the air.

'Question mark,' Shona said.

Katya nodded. 'First one, he say from Rotherham unit. Next month, Doncaster.'

'So you're saying Bakula scores you all and at the end of the month?' Shona asked.

'Bakula say big boss keep score. Spreadsheets all go back to Katowice.'

'Katowice?' Jamie straightened a little.

'Big boss there,' Katya mimed hands controlling puppet strings. 'Bakula has excel sheets. Sometimes blanks out names. Only show numbers. Say, "Don't rest. Might be you".'

'So, total shags?' Jamie's words made Shona shudder.

'Not shags,' Katya was unflinching. 'More like accounts. Shags multiplied by price. Some can charge more. Girls at bottom end start scrambling in last week. See if price drop bring more punters.'

'Pile 'em high—'

Shona stopped him with her eyes and the room became still, as if everyone was dwelling on their own mental picture of those end-of-month days.

'If we could…' Jamie spoke again. 'Could get some evidence, maybe then we could nail him before the next…'

'Nearly Christmas,' Katya said. 'You think?'

'I think December might be too soon,' Shona's knees were angled towards Katya's, holding her hands as they sat on the end of the bed. 'Honestly? December is soon, unless we get really lucky. But before the end of January, that could be…'

'If we can get definite evidence,' Jamie's voice stayed low.

'Of murder?' Katya looked.

Jamie nodded a yes.

'More likely the people trafficking,' Shona cut in. 'As a first step, then dig for the murder.'

'People trafficking would shut them down,' Jamie moved closer. 'Get them locked up for years.'

Shona felt Katya's eyes on her, until she nodded a confirmation. 'We think he has help. Someone organising vans when the ships unload.'

Katya nodded. 'Yes. Vans, then house. Girls tell me that.'

'Tell you?' Shona asked.

'Yes, girls Bakula bring. I here two years. But scumbag husband piss off. We have business. I work in shop in day, organise accounts, bookings at night,' Katya's eyes narrowed. 'Then, when government stop foreigners' benefits, he empty bank, take passport, everything. Shop money shit, not even pay rent. Sleep in doorways. At least was in summer. Then friend bring me to old man Morcanu. Offer me another shop job, but I say no need more money, so...'

Shona squeezed Katya's hand.

'But at the docks, when?' Jamie breathed.

'Say before they change van. Man in long coat. Have ski mask, like men at docks. Maybe uniform underneath.' Katya shrugged. 'In front of van with Bakula. Girls hear.'

'And they think it was one of the uniformed men from the docks?'

'Tall. Same voice maybe, but at docks all panicking, running everywhere, ski-mask men splitting them off, *The Beautifuls*. Girls say they yell, "Sort out the Beautifuls. Get them in Glamour Waggon".'

'Glamour Waggon?' Shona echoed.

'What they call van they trick the girls into. Others in police vans. Proper ones. Like minibuses.'

'If we could find this uniformed man,' Shona was holding both Katya's hands in hers again. 'Tie him in the trafficking. Prove Bakula's not just an employee. That he can't hide behind one of how many businesses the Morcanu's own.'

'Old man, he tell us, he had lots. Say, he old now. Only unit left. Everything else? Nephews, nieces own: shops, cash and carry, taxis we use.'

'And his own children?' Shona asked.

'Oh yes. Very proud. Son, daughter, but they in big city deals; offices London,' Katya paused. 'But we not see old man since summer.'

'So, if you could help?' Jamie was measured. 'Nail Bakula and this uniform bastard: people trafficking, illegal money. Years in jail.'

'Tonight has really helped,' Shona was still knee to knee with Katya, cradling her hands. 'Things we didn't know. When it started. Bakula taking over. Maybe one of the little things that seems like nothing tonight, but then we give it pull and...'

'Like bad knitting,' Katya spoke to herself.

'Like bad knitting,' Shona gave her hands another squeeze.

'I've set this up with Shona's number,' Jamie took a phone from his pocket. 'But it won't ring, so texts, and you can call us.'

'You confident I say yes,' Katya looked at him.

'Not really,' Jamie held the phone out. 'Twelve-ninety-nine from Tesco. I could take the loss.'

Katya smiled. 'Not here. Get searched when I go back.'

'They search you often?' Shona asked.

'Bags most days. Tonight late. Check for cash. Check phone, see I not go off route. Not doing private business.'

'So?' Shona was still holding her hands, but Katya slid them away and stood.

'In morning, eleven o'clock. Corner near my house. I go in shop. Can get it straight back to house then.'

'And you'll be there?' Shona said.

Katya had her own phone by her ear as she reached the door. 'Pick up please. Usual run. Sorry I bit late.' She looked back at Shona. 'Eleven o'clock. I get things now, ready for taxi.'

23

After a couple of hours paperwork, Jamie and Shona made their way to the car park. Shona paused by Moonlight's black Merc.

'Thought the Chief Constable was visiting first time I saw that.'

'Third in a row,' Jamie carried on walking, 'All pretty identical except for the look-at-me new car number plate.'

'Way above any Peepo payscale,' Shona caught up.

'Yeah, that's what I thought. Had a dig. There's a house as well. Big drive, electric gates. Bank of Mum and Dad, apparently. Couple of Peepos told me in the dim and distant past, before I'd pissed them all off.'

'So what's he…?'

Jamie shrugged.

Jamie parked where they had a good line of sight. Twenty minutes, less words, Shona's hand constantly poised on the door handle and then Katya was walking along the street. Shona saw her face, but little else. Her parka hood was low and from shoulders to Ugg boots she was submerged in its quilts. Katya entered the shop and Shona was up and out.

Jamie stared into the space between his car and the shop door. Three or four minutes passed. Katya came out first and turned away carrying a thin plastic bag. The weight and outline suggested a two litre milk carton. Another couple of minutes and Shona emerged, carrying a bottled water.

'Well? Did you?'

'Fine. All fine,' Shona hadn't even lowered herself onto the car seat.

'What did she say?'

'Nothing. Just stood alongside her at the magazine rack for a few seconds and dropped the phone into her plastic bag.'

'And she looked fine?'

'Well tired, like all of us. But no marks and she turned up, so I'm guessing they believed her story about dozing off.'

After lunch Jamie, took out his phone and tapped Cozza.

'The post-mor—'

'I'm on it,' Cozza cut across him. 'Told you, now the prat's left for his conference. Supposed to be talking to some uni research twat now, but I've cancelled. I cancelled, so I'm on it. Soon as I've finished my sandwich.'

Jamie inhaled, words forming, but Cozza spoke again.

'Cheese and pickle. Leave it with me. I'll get back.'

An afternoon of fragments: straws within clutching distance. Shona was slotting the last files of the day into precise drawers, ignoring Jamie as he leaned back in his chair. Then his phone beeped and he held it up for her to read.

Finished. Pie and pint.

Shona knew the pub. Dirty white exterior with doors and windows picked out in chipped green gloss.

'Fucking luxury,' she said as Jamie held open the door.

Across the bar, Cozza had an almost empty pint and a plate smeared with gravy and a skidmark of mushy peas.

'I'm on my fourth,' he announced as they reached his table.

'What, pie?' Jamie went for the easy banter.

'No pint, you prat. Five's on the way and my second pie. Need a bit more lining. And I've ordered supper for you pair.'

A barmaid arrived with drinks and three pies. Cozza lined the new pint up alongside the one he was drinking, then slid a large lime and soda towards Jamie and placed a whisky with a small water jug in front of Shona.

'Took a forensic guess, darling,' Cozza grinned. 'Based on your racial profile.'

'I hope you're as accurate with the autopsy,' Shona poured water into the whisky.

Cozza launched into his pie, but then put his knife and fork down. 'So, you know there's tissue samples, tox screens, DNA shit and the bug man's report, all need to run their course. That said, what I found? Yes, frozen. Same MO as canal girl, just different method to obscure ID. So, no fingers, no prints. The face? Severe acid burns. Teeth were intact, so we could try records, but my guess is she's never seen a UK dentist. The garrotte? Window dressing. Close up you can see strand patterns from a rope. Also, the piano wire hadn't cut in too much, so it was probably put there when she was frozen solid. Makes sense, otherwise it'd have sliced through the carotids and jugulars: blood everywhere. She had tattoos as well, but they seem pretty standard: hearts and roses, skulls and Celtic knots, like half the under-thirty world. No words or names. Hair was bleached, surprise, surprise.'

'So assumption,' Shona kept adding water to the whisky before taking gesture sips. 'Same killer, same motive, same victim profile; but without any ID or racial origin. Any clothes labels?'

'Moda Polska? Reserved?' Jamie chipped in.

'Jesus, you been reading Marie Claire again?' Cozza shook his head. 'No. She was stripped. Heavy duty bin bag under her arse and that big blanket.'

'So we're...' Shona paused.

'Working assumptions? Guessing September because of the leaf cover and the drying out. Tox and bugs? Awaiting results. DNA? Needs a bit of to and fro with our continental cousins and a lot of luck. Corrosive substance? Paint stripper, drain unblocker; loads of over the counter shit would do the job. Fingers? My cheap garden loppers will go through inch thick branches, easy-peasy.'

Cozza stabbed a fork into the middle of his pie and gravy bled out. Then Jamie's phone buzzed. Shona watched him check the caller ID.

'Got to take this.' And he was pushing through the crowd, heading for the door.

'He does a lot of that,' Cozza swallowed another clump of pastry.

'Always something setting him off,' Shona swirled her drink. 'Good job you're happy in your work.'

'Yeah, I think it's the creative fulfilment that makes me celebrate at the end of every working day,' he drained his beer, then reached for the new glass. 'Always ahead of the game.'

Shona focused on her pie.

'Compartments,' Cozza whispered the single word.

Shona looked up.

'Like on a ship,' he went on. 'Walls and watertight doors shutting things off.'

'And that's why your life is banter and beer? God forbid you could ever communicate.'

'Communicate?' Cozza was looking away now. 'Communion. That's my speciality. Like the best psychic you've ever seen. Communion with the dead. I'm the last person they talk to in this world.'

Shona took another sip of whisky.

'I'm a good listener,' Cozza's words slowed. 'I listen to wounds screaming their stories: the drugs tiptoeing through blood vessels.

Sometimes I hear bacteria whispering, hoping I won't notice them hiding in septic organs. Oh, I'm a good listener. I listen for hours some days. And I've listened enough for today. Conversation, communion, tell me your last story and then I'll seal it in the appropriate compartment. Two more pints, I reckon I'll have that watertight door locked. Pissed enough to ignore their chatter.'

'And then you'll go out and watch baby birdies in their nests.'

'Maybe when you spend your days picking through offal, you need to remind yourself that there's life in the world beyond your stainless steel table.'

'New life and the occasional truth,' Shona lifted her whisky glass in salutation.

'Yeah, and if that's not an option,' Cozza clinked his pint against her tumbler. 'Have another pint. At least I can get off to sleep when I'm rat-arsed.'

Cozza's hands surrounded his glass and Shona watched him stare into its distorted reflections. After a few seconds he spoke again. 'Got to be something wrong when the aim of your day is to slip into pissed oblivion?'

'Aye, well,' Shona reached out and held his hands around the glass. 'I was born in the city of oblivion.'

The movement of the bar door caught Shona's eye and Jamie was pushing his way back across the room.

'Oh good, we could do with someone to cheer us up,' she released Cozza's hands. 'You look flustered,' she said as Jamie plonked himself on the chair. But before he could speak a face squeezed through the crowd.

'So… found you. Okay if I join the Holy Trinity? Make a bit of a quadrangle.'

'Bloody hell, Dunky,' Jamie looked surprised. 'Where'd you spring from?'

'You walk on my manor, I hear your footsteps. Contacts everywhere.' Dunky held up a high-five. Cozza missed.

Dunky sat and Shona bought into his harmless self-aggrandisement. Jamie radiated scorn. Then Dunky reached inside his jacket pocket.

'Only on my pass,' he beamed. 'You'd have to get clearance,' he unfolded a pencil-written list. 'Connections to Shag City, as the natives call it.'

'So the owner's got—'

'Steady tiger,' Dunky extended a palm towards Jamie. 'Shag City is a leasehold. Short-term, six months, renewable. Been that way a while. Like I told you before.'

'So you've got a name?' Shona spoke before Jamie could react.

'Well, thereby hangs a tale, so the saying goes. But, yeah, there's a name.' Dunky looked pleased with himself. 'But you know my motto, "above and beyond"…'

Shona smiled encouragement.

'Had a look at the paperwork behind those addresses where the girls live. Dig past the letting agents and they're all owned by Vulpes Properties. Big operation.'

'And it's all the same owner?' Jamie was first to respond.

'No, not that simple. But the name on the Shag City lease has connections. Shows up on a lot of local firms: Morcanu. Took me a few visits to the record office to bottom it out. That Peepos' boss, Moonlight, saw me trying to get in. Waved my pass at him. Told him he needed to get some real powers. Didn't crack his face. Boring twat. My auntie says he's been in and out, sniffing around the girl on the front desk, bringing her coffees.'

'Your auntie?'

'Indian thing. Auntie Ji, just what you say if it's a close family friend. Anyway, she says he's a smarmy git.'

'But does she know what he's looking for?' Shona looked at him

'Ain't looking for anything at the moment,' Dunky grinned. 'But if he was, she'd know. Council system. Every pass got a chip. You open a door. It knows. Even knows which drawers in the record office. Have to swipe your pass every time.'

'So, if you wanted to know what someone was looking at, you'd just…'

'Ask auntie. She's the supervisor. All registers on her computer.'

'And Moonlight?' Shona was aware of Jamie stiffening.

'Like I say, she thinks he's a smarmy git. Every time the girl brings her his request card, she puts it on the bottom of the pile,' Dunky laughed and looked from Shona to Jamie. 'And as long as she's on duty, ain't no one looking at her computer, or messing around with her cards. Especially, after she's seen me put the twat in his place.'

'But you, Dunky, with your enhanced access…' Jamie leaned forwards, fake smiling. Shona felt the back of her tongue tighten.

'Yeah, so the Shag City lease is old man Morcanu, but all his old business interests? In the hands of various family members.'

'Like Billy told us, first time we met him,' Jamie exhaled.

Shona watched his eyes drift into a disdainful dead zone. 'But Vulpes,' she said, covering Jamie's contempt. 'Vulpes gets all the money?'

'Like I say,' Dunky was in full flow. 'Not that simple. Got to know your way round the system. No, Vulpes are the property owners, but there's letting agents and sub-agents in between, all taking a cut.'

'Taking a cut and taking the piss.' Jamie was staring into his lime and soda.

'Done a bit of drilling down,' Dunky went on. 'Tapped my network in the key places: cafes, shops, even had a walk past Shag City myself. That overnight lorry depot down the far end, had a word with the security guard on the barrier.'

'You went past?' Shona felt her words catch.

'Chill,' Dunky gestured, both palms facing down. 'Left the Focus at the back of a warehouse and I was in my ski-coat with the big collar. Anyway, no one's seen him for months, old man

Morcanu. Barrier man says it's just this big bloke; says he drives a van with Polish number plates and every now and again turns up in a German registered Merc.' Dunky reached across the table for his drink.

Shona's mind scrambled for words that might say, 'keep yourself safe,' without sounding like 'leave it to the grown-ups.'

But then Dunky was off again. 'So, it's Vulpes that owns the properties, but then there's this sub-agent. Name on the tenancy agreements, Solar Properties. Tried loads of the other agents around town, nobody's heard of them, so they must be small, maybe just starting up.'

'Not a dead end, though: not to you,' Jamie was leaning forwards. Shona glared hate at his faux encouragement.

'No, no. Temporary delay. Give it another go in the records office. Could try Companies House. I'll keep asking around. Maybe if you could identify a couple of tenants, you could ask them if they get visits from a rent man, or the like.'

Once back in the car, Shona's eyes narrowed on Jamie.

'God, you're an effortless arsehole.'

'What?' Jamie was blank.

'With Dunky.'

'No one asked him to get involved.'

'No, *you* didn't ask,' Shona looked away. 'Just tell yourself that.'

Jamie pulled into the traffic and, after a couple of miles, Shona spoke again.

'So who was on the phone that was so important?'

'Our Mandy. Fucking badgering me again. I've told her already, but she keeps going on.'

'Mandy?'

'My sister. Just family shit.'

24

Exercise helped, but he didn't deserve help. He deserved penance. He'd given up on logic. Shit happens. Some days more than others. A random word, a shift of chemicals in the brain and the world was a film playing in the background of his depression.

Jamie walked over to a pile of kit on the floor. His phone was set for time and distance, graphing his speed. At least the peaks were outnumbering the troughs now. A fortnight ago that pattern was inverted.

After forty-five minutes, Jamie was back home, aiming for a shower, then bed. Sleep came easily, but then he'd woken, the edge taken off his tiredness. After an hour in the dark he was awash with thoughts and no prospect of sleep. He got up and unfolded a clean t-shirt. Ten minutes later he was edgeland ready: coat, boots, rucksack, torches.

He drove towards Manchester Road and parked in a drive that cut through the cemetery and led on to the allotments and fields beyond. The level of light spillage was low and a full moon picked out the line of tarmac as he walked between rows of headstones. Eventually he passed a children's playing field, now the footpath snaked to a stream where slow water sounds merged with the bass note scent of dead winter leaves. Jamie huddled near the treeline, observing a rough-clumped grass slope. Settled and silent, he could hear the occasional scuttering of mice and voles. Still, he was able to concentrate, focusing his mind away from inner thoughts, letting his muscles relax.

'You're too hard on yourself, Jamie. This is the world of *shit happens*. It's not all down to you.'

Cara's voice was soft in his mind, saying things he could never tell himself. His coat was warm and he dozed between dreams, Cara's voice tuning in and out. Tonight she was gentle, not in her *pull-yourself-together* mode.

Then the screeching started.

Jamie jolted, eyes unable to focus at first. Then, in a moment, he was aware of a patch of white tumbling upwards. He blinked. It was a barn owl. A young rat was dangling from its talon, flailing away, then free and spiralling towards the ground. The owl eased into a hover, positioning its radar hearing, but its prey was beyond sound. Jamie swept a torch beam across the area of final impact. LED light fell across the rat, white belly, brown fur washed with blood. It was dead. Jamie knew death and it released itself across his mind in its many forms. Disease victims, fallen soldiers, desert vehicle crashes and Cara – with the flies on her eyelids. Again there was a flash of white: luminous in the torchlight. A moment later the barn owl was arcing up again, duller now, and only moonlit. This time the rat was motionless in the talons.

Jamie stood, felt a tightness in his chest and began to jog. He felt like the rat, moving beneath some unseen predator, constantly in fear of death from above. Tomorrow this would be depression, but tonight it was anxiety; an illogical fear that gained momentum as he crossed into the open ground of the playing field. Cara's voice was lost in the sound of his own breathing as he ran.

Reaching the tarmac, he became aware of moonlit headstones, row on row and all around, flowing across the undulating ground like bodies on a gentle sea.

South of Lampedusa, just outside Italian territorial waters, he'd seen the bodies lain on waves in the moonlight, rising and falling in rows, tranquil until you got close and saw where the fish had eaten out their eyes and nibbled the flesh from finger bones.

Jamie ran until he was back at his car, gasping, waiting for his eyes to clear, for his breathing to regulate and for the ticking pulse in his temple to ease.

Back home, he closed the door behind him, sealing out the world. The clean t-shirt was sweaty now, as he climbed into bed. Edgelands and walking; movement and thought, sometimes head-clearing, sometimes replaying images and words. Cara was there more now; since Liliana. Clearer in his mind, her presence, her words, bringing him comfort, chiding, straightening him out. Dead Cara's mirage words and Baggage and Claudette, brief facetime interludes; imagination and the iPad were the most real parts of his life.

In three hours his alarm would be blaring. He reached out and switched on the battered lava lamp and random green globules of light and shadow rolled across the room. 'Green. It's my colour,' Cara used to say. 'Bright, emerald green. None better with my skin.' Her best dress had been green, that bright emerald. And she was right. Jamie remembered her in his mind's eye, remembered how the brightness of the green lit up the beauty of her blackness.

25

Shona woke and checked her phone. There was one text:
Clothes shop 12:15
After a shower, she found a small bag and zipped it into a coat pocket. As she grabbed keys, her phone beeped. A second text:
Fucking Clegg. Not in today.
As she reached her car, there was a third:
Nor tomorrow a.m. Meeting Billy.

'I know it's childish,' Clegg was chuckling as Shona entered her office. 'But I couldn't resist. Rudy's phoned in sick and I had to send someone to the PACT conference.'

'Aye well seems a shame not to make the most of his people skills.' Shona smirked as she imagined Jamie trying to be polite in a room full of Neighbourhood Watch co-ordinators. 'Maybe I could text to see if he's free for a photoshoot? The face of Police and Community Together. Maybe a poster campaign?'

'Go on, bugger off,' Clegg was still grinning. 'Enjoy. And remember, as your peaceful day passes, it was me that made it all possible.'

Shona wanted to work through the backlog of reports peacefully, but Katya was on her mind. When the Peepos had dispersed after their morning briefing, she headed for a coffee. Moonlight was walking slowly ahead of her, zig-zagging along the corridor on his phone.

'Flash twat,' were the first words she heard, then: 'I'm not having him taking the piss.'

Shona slowed her walk.

'I know… yes, leave it with me… the girl's on the supervisor's desk for a couple of days. I'll get her to look up—' were the last words she could hear without making eavesdropping obvious.

Twitching her way through a coffee, Shona couldn't stand the inertia any longer and made for the car park. A familiar figure was walking ahead of her.

'Morning. Have you…' her voice echoed off the concrete ceiling.

'What?' Dunky turned and waved.

'Moonlight—'

'Yeah, rattled his cage a bit,' Dunky opened his car door. 'Like I said, pointed out a couple of his limitations.'

'But—'

'Sorry, tight schedule. People to see. Laters,' and Dunky slid into the driver's seat.

Shona turned away from the lime green Ford. Then flinched back as Dunky dropped the clutch and his sports exhaust echoed around the callous box of a car park.

Katya was on time. Shona stopped scrolling on her phone, gave the street a last sweep then locked her car. Inside the shop a woman was near Katya. Shona browsed at a distance. As the woman moved away, she and Katya began their slow approach along the clothes rails. Shona unzipped a coat pocket and slipped a small bag onto a hanger.

Katya nodded and edged towards it.

The woman reached the front of the shop, paid and left. The

girl on the till pushed a set of earphones in and began humming to herself. Casually, Katya browsed within range, then lifted a blouse towards a window and turned.

'Spare battery and charger,' Shona was at right-angles to Katya's back. 'Hide the phone somewhere general in the house. Then, if it's found, they won't know who it belongs to.'

'Bakula's wife come,' as Katya swapped the blouse, she slipped the battery and charger inside her coat, then she lifted another blouse into the light. 'She talk to us when here.'

'Here?' Shona asked.

'Home most of time, Poland, Germany. But come often. Keep eye on him. Keep his ball sack empty. "Oh darling", she say one day. "I make sure this not get too heavy for you", and she spread her hand over his zip, God, he go so red. "Keep it light", she say… "so you not need tamper with stock".' Katya glanced to check the till girl, then made eye contact. 'That's what bitch said, when she in the unit other day, in her Jimmy Choo shoes.'

'Expensive tastes?'

'Her, yes. He peasant. When she not here he drive old van. Tools in back… sometimes dead pig.'

For a second, the image of a pink carcase bouncing in the back of a van filled Shona's imagination, but Katya was still talking, telling how Bakula went from family farm to a mafia marriage. How he'd made himself useful following orders and caught the eye of a niece of the local Mr Big.

'Lucky boy,' Katya said.

'Fell on his feet,' Shona replied.

Katya looked puzzled then grasped the phrase. 'Yes, on feet. Katowice bad town. Dog eat dog in Katowice.' Katya's eyes looked straight at Shona. 'And father of wife biggest dog in town.'

'So—'

'Bakula muscle. Wife family brains. Smart. Not like old days.'

'Grupa Pruzkowska, Wolomin gang.'

Katya looked surprised. 'No. Pruzkowska, Wolomin – most dead or prison. Vendetta, like in Godfather. Now Russian mafia, South American drug gangs try take over. Poliski know if fight each other, get eat up. Bribes and business and keep out of newspapers. Smart now. Like rats – do everything in dark.'

'So how do you know...'

'Zofia, one of girls, from Katowice. Says wife's father have lorry business, then bar, then few more, then lots more: lorries bars and big house out of town with wall, electric gate. And she remember Bakula family. Shit-heap farm with little abattoir. He work there from when boy. Zofia say make sausages, smoked ham.'

'Krakowska?'

'Kabanos. Good. Lots of caraway.'

'Gets it sent from Poland?'

'Makes own here. Told you, he peasant. And kaszanka. He bring in sometimes.'

Shona scrunched her lips.

'Not like pig's blood?' Katya grinned. 'Kaszanka better than English black pudding. More herbs and spice.'

'Aye well, I'm not keen on English black pudding either... but Bakula,' Shona continued. 'You say is just muscle.'

'Lucky muscle. Lucky peasant in old van. Stay lucky if not upset wife. Not make boss daughter look bad.'

'But Mrs Bakula's different?'

'Oh yes. Make him drive Merc, wear designer clothes when she here. Must have car in garage somewhere. Only drives when she here. She chat like she thinks she's friend, but she just brag. Mercedes this, Dolce and Gabbana that. Shows us pictures of chandeliers in house they buy in Black Forest. Suka... bitch.'

Shona didn't need the translation.

'She go to London shopping,' Katya looked towards the till girl.

She was browsing her phone now and giggling. Shona moved out of sight, behind a changing room.

'Say she going drag Loobie home for Christmas.'

'Loobie?'

'Lubomir. She call him Loobie. Bakula's name.'

'And you call him Loobie?'

'No, no one call him Loobie. One of girls say it once. He slap her hard. Anyway, if he go home Christmas we all get break.'

'Is he likely to?'

'If wife say. Buy presents,' Katya shrugged. 'And fuck off back Katowice for few days.'

'Christmas. Family,' Shona picked up a light-up reindeer headband. 'Does your heart good to see a few old-fashioned virtues.'

'Oh yes,' Katya's face didn't flicker. 'Family, religion. Very Polish. Like Italians – all popes and hitmen.'

'He collects your rent?'

'No, other man. Buzzard collect cash. Rest standing orders to bank.'

'Buzzard?'

'His nose, hooked like a bird, and skinny, long,' Katya glanced around to check the girl was still focused on her phone, then lifted and hunched both arms out like wings. 'Buzzard, feed on dead meat.'

In Shona's mind's eye an image flickered for a second. When she re-focused, Katya was edging along the clothes rail. Shona sensed a conclusion and stepped away. There was one, final moment of eye-contact as she mouthed *thank you, dzieki*, and Katya browsed away.

Shona carried on looking at random items until she deemed enough time had passed to make them seem unconnected, then she made for the till, paid for a cheap t-shirt she didn't want and walked out.

26

Finding the Buzzard? Bit of surveillance. The simplicity of that step made Shona feel as if, at last, a fragment of control was shifting. It wasn't until she was driving back that it hit her.

'Fucking bollocks,' and she hit the steering wheel with both hands. An old lady who was half-way across a pedestrian-controlled crossing mouthed something obscene as she peered through the windscreen. Shona was annoyed with herself for not asking the question. It was the logical follow-on from what Dunky had said about agents and sub-agents. Taking a breath, she moved on. It would just need a text and a bit of a wait and she'd be back where she wanted to be.

At lunchtime Jamie took his paper plate buffet outside, preferring wind-chill to the earnest notables of Neighbourhood Watch. Behind a bank of shrubs, he took out his phone.

'Billy,' he began. 'Sorry it's been a few days I've—'

'It was on telly: South Yorkshire News. They had the Assistant Chief Constable being reassuring.'

It was half-past nine the following morning when Jamie rang the doorbell. Fragmented by frosted glass, Billy was already in the hall, wearing his coat.

'Hope this bloke has gone into hiding,' Billy's wife called as Jamie was standing at the door. 'Longer you're out from under my feet the better.'

Billy rolled his eyes. 'Usually about half ten when Morcanu's pal gets in,' and he shut the door.

The café wasn't far from the bus stop that Katya and the girls used. As they walked around, Billy was recognised by a few people; conversations were light and affable. After a while they ambled into the café, about twenty-five minutes ahead of the old man's estimated ETA.

'Your notes and stuff?' Jamie sat down with two mugs of tea.

'Yeah, checked through, made a few calls. Old man Morcanu hasn't been seen for a while. Went into one of the nephew's shops. Seems he's been ill.'

'With?'

'Don't know exactly. They're tight-lipped on family stuff.'

Jamie took a sip of tea.

'From their manner, I'm thinking not trivial. They confirmed the Pole,' Billy consulted his notebook, 'Bakula, was acting as manager.'

'The nephew told you this?'

'Yeah, and a couple of the girls were at a bus stop. One of them muttered *bastard* when I said his name.'

'Swearing in English, nice to see they're fitting in.' Jamie dunked a biscuit.

'Maybe… mind you, it's the same word in Lithuanian.'

Jamie looked at Billy.

'I get bored. Google translate.'

'What's it like inside the unit?' Jamie changed tack.

'Only know what I've been told… and I've seen the containers through the door.'

'But…' Jamie waited.

'But I've never actually been in. Bad optics as the politicians say. Imagine if anyone clocked me in there... and there's CCTV staring down from half the buildings on that trading estate. Last thing I'd have needed was someone checking the time signals. Might just be a cup of tea, but you can do a lot of other things in the time it takes to drink a cuppa. No, I talked to the old man a lot, but in the street, or shops, or in here. That's why I know about his pal, Michael.'

Jamie was grinning.

'What's rung your bell?' Billy asked.

'Nothing,' Jamie stood up. 'Just imaging your missus getting a video of you going into Shag City. You might never have had your biscuit on her doilies ever again... I'm getting another tea ... do you want anything else?

'Just a tea thanks.'

Jamie brought a tray back to the table: two teas and there was already a bite out of the greasy lump on his plate.

'You get your five a day then,' Billy said as Jamie licked the sugar granules that had clung around his lips.

'Only if they've reclassified doughnuts as fruit. Actually, first I've had for days.'

'Anyway, the unit. Had a bit of a transformation just as I was finishing. When it was the old man, the downstairs was mainly wholesale storage. Most of the containers where the girls worked were upstairs. So—'

'Front was holding stock for the various family shops. But then...'

'But then, after that Bakula had his feet under the table, seems the employee numbers multiplied and it morphed into a gym. Called it a Man Spa.'

'Man Spa?'

'Yeah. Couple of exercise bikes and a treadmill and some girls dressed in lycra. Cover story I heard was they were either classified as personal trainers, or the more traditional masseuse role.'

'Specialising in horizontal jogging?' Jamie was dabbing the jam on his plate when Billy tapped his hand. The café door opened and a sparse old man in an overcoat and woolly hat shuffled towards the counter. Jamie was up and, as the old man reached for his tea, he dropped coins onto the counter. 'I'll get that.'

The old man looked bemused but followed Jamie to the table.

'It's Michael, isn't it?' Billy was smiling.

'Mihai,' the old man sat down.

'I remember, you were often in here with Neculai. Always drinking Earl Grey.' Billy nodded towards Mihai's cup.

'Always speak,' Mihai took a sip. 'Not like young police. In cars, rush about.'

'Yeah, way of the world. No one's got a minute. I remember one time, years ago, Neculai telling me how he got here. Talked about back home. Everything slow. Donkeys, not cars and tractors. Said he escaped a year before Ceausescu fell, so that was…?'

'1989. December 25th. Machine-gunned, on television. Romania's Christmas present.' Mihai wrapped his hands around his cup.

'I thought Romania was pretty well sealed off in those days,' Jamie joined in.

'Neculai buy Aussiedler papers,' Mihai pulled at his fingerless gloves.

'Aussiedler?' Jamie asked.

'Ethnic Germans,' Billy said. 'I remember him telling me. Communities in Romania; spoke German. The government wanted them out.'

'He spoke German?' Jamie looked to Mihai.

'Little bit.' Mihai stirred his tea. 'There was security guard at airport. Liked bribe. Neculai and his wife, sell everything: farm, all animals. All his money. Shit or bust, Neculai say.'

'So he paid all that money and next year Ceausescu was gone and he could have just caught a train to the Channel Tunnel.'

'Ferry,' Billy chipped in. 'Channel Tunnel didn't open till the mid-90s.'

'And Romania not EU, so not easy to get UK.' Mihai looked Jamie in the face. 'Neculai and wife use papers at British Consulate. Papers say he ethnic cleansed, so they get visa.'

'And you came at the same time?' Jamie asked.

'No, later,' Mihai's gaze dropped back into his cup.

'But when you first knew him?' Jamie asked.

'Three shops, already. Meet at cash and carry.'

'And?' Jamie looked.

'More shops, then taxis.'

'So—' Jamie waited.

Mihai shrugged. 'I have market stall… twenty years.'

'And he got rich and moved out to the Peaks.' Jamie stared into his tea.

Mihai narrowed his eyes. 'But he stay my friend. Send taxis, take me his house.'

'Out Hathersage, Bamford way, he told me,' Billy waited for confirmation.

'By golf course. Big drive from road.' Mihai sipped his tea. 'You see Neculai, tell him I want see him. Worried in case done something to upset him.

'Why would you think you'd upset him?' Billy's voice was low.

'Don't know. For a while seem… angry, little things. Not like himself. I make joke about us getting old, he go quiet. He always brave, strong. Sixty years old, still built like bear, but last year he limp, complain fingers tingled sometime. Last time saw him, was dabbing corner of lip with handkerchief, like spit leaking.'

Mihai breathed out and Billy patted the old man's hands and he and Jamie stood.

At the till Jamie handed some cash to the waitress. 'Take him a jacket potato and cheesy beans.' And he looked back at the figure hunched over his tea.

Leaving Mihai to his lunch, Jamie guessed both Billy and his wife would be disappointed if he went home straight away.

'Fancy a coffee in the old place?' Jamie turned into the police station. Billy had his seatbelt unclipped before they'd found a parking space.

Going through reception the sergeant called across: 'Bloody hell Billy, I thought we'd got an injunction to keep you out.'

'Got a call from public health,' Billy leaned on the desk. 'Problem with the toilets. Apparently no one can find their arses to wipe them, since I left.'

'Bloody closer to the truth than you know,' the sergeant pressed a button and an electronic door lock buzzed open.

'Still remember the way to the canteen?' Jamie asked, then texted up to Shona.

Jamie tapped Billy's hand as Shona came through the canteen door. Reaching the table, introductions were made. She sat and took the lid off the waiting cup.

'Word on the street, as the saying goes,' Billy tasted his tea, 'is old man Morcanu treated the girls well.'

'Yeah, Ka—' Shona stopped. 'Backs up what we've been hearing. Didn't squeeze every last drop. That's why vice tolerated him.'

'Nature abhors a vacuum,' Billy dipped a biscuit. 'That's why she fills them with shit.'

'Jesus, listen to you pair,' Jamie's eyes swept around the table. 'Surprised anyone got a shag last Christmas. What with Morcanu's whores spending all their time at Nativity Plays watching their kids dressed as angels and camels' humps... but this year's different,' his jaw tensed. 'He turned a blind eye to Bakula and his methods. Pissed off with his money and fed those poor cows to a mafia psycho... So don't tell me you're nominating him for Pimp of the Year.'

'Yeah, well,' Billy held his cup on his bottom lip. 'Haven't nailed down the illness angle yet. Dribbling, unpredictable, angry moods...'

Shona looked at Jamie. 'Sounds like he's got the same as you.'

When Jamie got back from dropping Billy home, Shona was in the car park. She opened his passenger door and got in.

'Saw Katya. Let's have a drive.'

'What did you talk about?' Jamie turned west, towards the more affluent suburbs.

'Life, death, sausages…' and she outlined Bakula's rise to power.

'But this Buzzard?' Jamie seized on what they both knew. A face. Someone to follow. Someone who might meet other faces.

'Gives them a couple of days to organise cash, then comes to the house to collect.'

Jamie waited.

'They're paying twice as much in cash than the official bank transfers for their rent.'

'Bank transfers?'

'Yeah. So Katya must have a sort code and account numbers to pay the legit part of her rent. That's my next task… then the bank and eyes on this Buzzard.'

27

'I knew you'd run it down to the wire. I told her by eleven in the text.'

'Sorry Mand. Roads were crap over The Peaks.'

Jamie stepped away from the front door and the kids ran out and hugged him.

'Oi,' Mandy yelled. 'Get back here.' The kids trooped back and picked up car seats and bags. Mandy fixed seatbelt straps and, before getting in, turned to Jamie. 'I know you hate it. But she's our mam and yes she is shit, but the kids have got to give her Christmas presents.'

'Like she'll have a tree to put them under.'

'Yeah, well. Today'll be okay, if we're early she won't be too pissed.' Mandy banged the car window and the squabbling stopped. 'Can't have her for Christmas, not all day with the kids, but today, Jamie… one day, we won't be there long… now, no swearing in front of the kids and pretend you're—'

'Happy?'

'Normal,' Mandy said and reached for the car door.

It was the kind of street Jamie only ever wanted to drive through now: deep red Manchester brick, every other house even redder because someone had thought it looked classier with a coat of paint. Classier had flaked off long ago. It reminded him of chronic psoriasis. Some of the windows were blanked out with brown metal plating. Mandy checked the numbers and they parked. There was a sofa on the footpath.

Mandy released the kids and they huddled behind her as she knocked on the front door. Jamie watched from the car. Mandy stepped across the footpath and knocked his window. Her eyes narrowed and her finger pointed. Jamie unclipped his seatbelt.

'Just resetting the satnav,' the car beeped as he locked it. Mandy's mouth stretched into a smile, but nothing else moved on her face. Behind her the front door opened.

'See, that wasn't so bad,' Mandy brought in tea and cake and sat next to Jamie. The winter sun was warm in the conservatory. 'Could've been much worse.'

'At least she didn't smell like she'd pissed her pants today… But I noticed you put carrier bags under you and the kids when you sat on the sofa.'

'Stop it,' Mandy laughed and gave him a push. 'Look, we've done our duty. Now we can enjoy Christmas with a clear conscience.'

'You okay with me coming Boxing Day? I'm on shift Christmas Eve, then long shift Christmas Day.' Jamie stroked the dog as it sprawled across his lap.

'Brill. All that overtime means I can expect really expensive presents.'

Jamie got back from Mandy's around ten. 'Early night. Set me up for the day.'

Seven hours sleep, a decent breakfast and he was still in work before seven. Moonlight was early as well. They didn't acknowledge each other. Moonlight's phone vibrated on his desk, but he ignored it. A couple of minutes later it buzzed again. This time Jamie watched him lift it and tap the fingerprint recognition, but the plaster from the staple wound meant he had to use the pin number. It was a drag screen.

'Bloody obvious, you arrogant bastard.' Jamie whispered behind clenched teeth. Then he heard Moonlight speak to whoever was calling.

'If you can't find an alternative, but it won't be today. Got too much on to be checking car numbers, and you know where I'll be tonight.'

After watching him end the call and go back to a folder of notes, Jamie moved anonymously towards the canteen.

Moonlight's second-in-command was leaning on the door as Jamie tried to re-enter the briefing room. The door eased open and a long bony finger sat below his long bony nose as he silently indicated *shhh*. Then he pointed to a route around the edge of the semi-dark space. Moonlight clicked off the last slide on his PowerPoint and the lights came on before Jamie reached his desk, but he'd already clocked the Google Maps image. At the edge of the Peepo tribe were two men in immigration force uniforms: high-ranking, Jamie guessed from the braid and badges. They were speaking to a man in a suit and their manner was deferential. Two further men in suits flanked the group, but didn't speak. Close protection security; Jamie knew the body language.

'So, any questions?' Moonlight didn't wait. 'No? Good, go and get kitted out. Have you dealt with the paperwork, Hobbes?' Jamie followed Moonlight's focus. 'We all know the drill, don't we Hobbes? Hit 'em hard. Nasty, brutish and short.' Then addressing the room. 'Back in twenty. Don't fanny about down there. It's a raid, not London Fashion Week.'

The Peepos trooped out. The lanky guardian of the door came across to Moonlight and the VIP group. Jamie watched as the handshaking and *pleasure-is-all-mine* comments were exchanged. The guardian moved ahead and held the door open with one hand and saluted with the other. When all were safely out in the corridor he looked towards Moonlight then followed the visitors. Jamie watched Moonlight as he adjusted the leather strap that ran diagonally across his chest, then he clicked on a holster. He pulled on a stab vest and secured a body-cam near the shoulder. As he checked it was operational, he laughed to himself. 'Nasty, brutish and short.'

'Yes sir, he is.'

Moonlight looked up.

'Nasty, brutish and short, sir. Pity his name's Dormston, not Hobbes.'

It took a second for Moonlight to focus on Jamie's position, but then: 'My small joke. Naming him after a philosopher. Compliment really. Hobbes is my lion, detective. He's employed for action, not stimulating conversation. Wittgenstein said: "If a lion could talk, we could not understand him." You know Wittgenstein?'

'Course, sir… is he still playing midfield for Bayern Munich?'

Moonlight took the pistol from its holster and checked its movement. 'There now.'

Jamie was amused by Moonlight's contrived calm.

'Ready to go and exert some moral authority. The condition of man is a condition of war of everyone with everyone.'

Jamie made no eye-contact. 'Hobbes again, sir. Lived through the English Civil War, bound to have coloured his opinions.' Jamie put a case file under his arm and began walking. He could feel Moonlight staring at his back until the frosted glass door closed behind him.

Once outside, Jamie scanned the corridor, then ducked into an office where the lights were off.

That short-notice job. It's a go. Pulling an all-nighter. Keep you posted.

Jamie clicked send.

Jamie clipped on false number plates and began driving early. He wanted to be in place, with a view of the entry point, before the official vehicles arrived on site.

28

The office was quiet. Just a couple of low-level Peepos monitoring phones and emails. Shona passed across the central space. Upon reaching the desk, she took in the navy suit jacket as Jamie yawned. His red tie had been visible from across the office against its background of white, crisply ironed shirt.

'Thought you'd at least be in late. London Gateway and back,' Shona whispered. 'How much sleep?'

'Didn't bother. Just showered and changed.'

Shona went to speak, but Jamie went on.

'Needed to be in. So they can say they saw me at the normal time.'

'And hence the pimp at a wedding fashion statement and… bloody hell, deodorant.'

'Need to see Clegg,' Jamie moved on.

'Why? Nothing new to report.'

'Establishing a presence. If she remembers me looking smart this morning…'

'Traffic cameras,' Shona thought aloud. 'If your car was…'

'Nah,' Jamie grinned. 'Exemplary clip tightness on the plates.'

Shona leaned forwards. 'Keep thinking about Katya's rent: the cash. If we—' a figure moved through a frosted glass door.

'Ma'am,' Jamie put his head around Clegg's office door and Shona shuffled in behind him. 'Just wanted to say, ma'am.'

Clegg remained seated.

'Wanted to say, Cozza's findings don't undermine our working supposition that the murders are linked.'

'So, nothing's changed since the last time then,' Clegg's eyes came up. 'Bloody hell, Jamie. You on a disciplinary?'

'Tie up to the collar, every shirt button fastened...' Shona grinned.

Clegg's head tilted to one side. 'Go on, fuck off and do some work. Come back when there's something to tell.' Then she sniffed. 'And don't let that deodorant lull you into a false sense of security, Ms McCulloch. He can still fart.'

'Ma'am,' And Shona closed the door.

The day came and went, cross-referencing paper and computer documents. The boring crap that nails more bastards than all the flash and crash. Every time leg-work was needed, Shona sent Jamie to keep him awake. She collated information onto the database on her laptop while Jamie's yawn rate multiplied into the afternoon.

'Go on, bugger off,' Shona shook his shoulder. 'It's nearly shift end, I'll tie up the loose ends. Your brain's been having an out of body experience since lunchtime anyway.'

Jamie wound down his car windows and used the December air to fend off sleep as he drove home. Once through the door, he hung up his coat, kicked off his shoes and, walking into the kitchen, stood over the toaster. Soon, he was on the sofa with a plate: a cluster of beans tumbled off a fork and slid down his tie.

When he'd finished eating he dragged himself to the bedroom and stepped out of his clothes. The pimp-at-wedding jacket would need pressing when he eventually picked it off the floor.

It was early when he woke up, but he felt much better. After dealing with last night's washing up, he made more toast.

Shona was pleased with yesterday's efforts, everything time ordered and annotated, so sequences and connections were more explicit. Taking it all in, Jamie suggested tasks they might cover over the coming days. Shona was surprised when, after twenty minutes, he stood and offered to get a couple of coffees.

As the briefing room door closed behind Jamie, Clegg peered over the frosted glass line and beckoned to Shona.

'So, you and laughing boy. Any leads?' Clegg motioned Shona to pull up a chair.

'Just circumstantial, boss. Leases and rentals. But we can't tie property owners in with anything illegal their tenants might be doing.

'Names?'

'There's an old guy, Morcanu, who still holds the lease for Shag City, but he hasn't been seen for ages. Got this Polish gorilla managing it for him. And there's rented houses used by the working girls, but nothing to connect the rentals to the old man.'

'So, who...?'

'There's a company called Vulpes.'

'So Vulpes is running whores?'

Shona inhaled. 'Unlikely. Vulpes is big. Property nationwide. So, best guess, some local operation is subletting at a profit.'

Clegg had her hand on her laptop: the search bar was open on Companies House. 'Fuck sake, you're right about Vulpes. Don't piss about with these unless you've got something copper-bottomed and gold-plated. In fact don't piss about with these unless you've cleared it with me. Christ, have you seen whose CEO?'

'I know,' Shona said. 'But, if there's a lead it'll be the sub-agent.'

'Name?' Clegg had the cursor in the search bar again.

'Solar Properties,' Shona said. 'But we haven't turned up anything locally. Registered offices are near Marble Arch, so…'

'So, dummy company renting a post-box somewhere flash.'

'And the names, addresses and dates of birth of the directors don't tie together.'

'What did Jamie say?'

'Don't put out feelers that might mean whoever set this up gets wind of an investigation.'

'See, he might be a fat bastard, but he's not daft.'

'Not so fat now, ma'am. I think police fitness test fever might be kicking in.'

Clegg leaned back and grinned.

Shona stood and, as she reached the door, Clegg made her parting shot. 'I'm relying on you to keep me up to speed. And I mean what I said about pissing about with Vulpes – don't.'

Shona was crossing back to the desk as Jamie entered with the coffees.

'What's Clegg want?'

'Just enough information to tell her bosses she's across the investigation and not so much that she can't shift the blame if it goes tits up.'

'As per,' Jamie placed the coffees on the desk.

'And Vulpes is off limits, unless she gives the okay.'

While they finished their drinks, Moonlight came in carrying a portable hard drive and began setting up connections to the large wall-mounted screen. Video, still image, maps and texts raced across the screen in fast-forward echoes of scenes Jamie had witnessed on his overnight sortie.

After a while, the briefing room door swung open and Shona and Jamie concentrated on fading into the office background as a succession of Peepo clusters jostled into the open space.

Eventually Moonlight straightened. 'Gentlemen. Thank you… for your attention and for the other night – a job well done,' and his hands began a loud, rhythmic, wide-spaced clap. The herd took it up and accelerated it. 'A good night, gentlemen.' Moonlight raised a hand. 'And we're on the road to more.'

The screen filled with images. At first they were steady, panning from a single point with Moonlight commentating, his words like a corporate promo, but then shuddering images with breathless voices cut in and, as the film went on, the controlled, fixed viewpoint became interspersed with a juddering immediacy.

'Be a winner on YouTube,' Jamie leaned towards Shona. 'Way the body-cam shots make it feel fly-on-the-wall.'

'Not only well done, gentlemen, but filmed to look even better.' Moonlight's hands were on his hips now. 'As we speak copies are being viewed in high places. Who knows, one of them might accidentally leak to Sky News.' He laughed at his own joke.

'What's that?' Shona whispered and pointed. 'A cuboid shadow flickered in and out on the edge for a second.'

The video cut back to the professional filming, an arc of vans blocked the ferry traffic's exit route, then Peepos were up on lorries with pick-axe handles and baseball bats, thrashing the metal containers like drummers in some immense, tuneless gong orchestra.

'Jesus,' Shona was flinching at the audio. 'God help the poor bastards inside. Christ, it must be like…' she shook her head.

Cutting to body-cam close-ups, a set of container doors were flung open and a dozen young immigrants, hands clamped over their ears, staggered into a floodlight beam. Disorientated, two of them fell the metre or so from the back of the lorry to the ground. One stood quickly, but doubled over, obviously winded, the other squirmed on the ground, groaning with pain. Jamie was fixed on the action, but Shona was writing.

'Look at the angle of her foot,' Jamie hissed. 'That ankle's broken.'

'Corner of the film,' she indicated with her biro. There was an

ID number for the body-cam etched into the top corner of the image, along with a date and running timer.

The fixed viewpoint camera cut back in and the soundtrack faded as Moonlight's corporate commentary described another container opening and the spillage of more human cargo. As different body-cam viewpoints cut in and out, Shona scribbled down the succession of ID numbers and time data. The multi-images moved close in and steadied: balaclavaed figures cajoling pale faces into groups, pushing, shouting, the occasional slap. Then a new viewpoint, further back and the time signal showed events had jumped forwards about twelve minutes. An arc of transit vans dominated the frame, with huddles of migrants shoved together as the Peepos funnelled them towards the prisoner transport.

'Bloody hire vans,' Jamie shook his head and the film continued: more human flotsam, more estate agent-esque description from Moonlight.

But then, as the first van of misery pulled along the road, a brief clip of a body-cam shot was used for perspective. The cluster of vehicles could be seen in the right of the shot and a distant, but just visible, small knot of shadows and twinkling lights tracked left across a field and, for split second, as the body-cam bounced, in the bottom corner of the frame, what had been a brief, cuboid shadow came into focus.

The film ended with the official convoy rolling along the road, dock gates receding behind them. Moonlight began the slow clap again and the ritual was repeated for a final hurrah. Shona stood, but Jamie was writing as the bald heads and bulky bodies dispersed towards the morning's tasks, or the canteen.

'If we could just get that hard drive,' Shona hissed between her teeth when Moonlight finally made his way to the corridor. 'Bastard and fuck.' And she took a half-hearted kick at a chair. The solitary Peepo who was seated in the far corner turned and shook his head.

'Might not need it,' Jamie pushed across a piece of paper. He'd copied the contents of the address bar that had appeared on the computer during Moonlight's final speech.

'That's our server,' Jamie said. 'Must've copied his files across before he started. Portable drive's slower, more prone to problems.'

Shona was rooting through desk drawers. 'You beauty,' she pulled out a high capacity memory stick, still in its see-through packaging, then she began strolling around the briefing room brushing her hand across a mouse or tapping a random key.

'What are you…' Jamie mouthed towards Shona, but then it registered.

Shona was moving diagonally across the room, staying distant from the solitary Peepo. Then she made eye contact with Jamie. He stood and moved into a line that blocked the man's view, then Shona squatted behind a computer that had woken up when she'd touched it.

'Not hungry?' Jamie said, standing at the man's shoulder now. 'Just thought the Hollywood epic might've fired up your appetite, like your pals that headed for the canteen.'

'Hollywood?' the man mumbled.

'Moonlight's film,' Jamie pushed on. 'The prat-on-the-wall documentary you've all just sat through.'

'Fuck off.'

Shona heard the man shut Jamie down but, by then, she was back in her seat.

Jamie was a witness in a shop theft case in the afternoon and while he was at court Shona headed for the white monolith of the central library and lost herself behind a regiment of shelves with her laptop and a memory stick. After an hour she took out her phone.

After his brief visit to the witness box, Jamie was drawing breath over a cup of tea when there was a buzz in his pocket.

When you're free, can we meet? S
The reply was immediate.
Already done. M&S cafe 30 mins.

'Got some stuff to clarify' Shona slid her tray onto Jamie's table. 'M&S? Bit out your comfort zone.'

'Bought some pants,' Jamie answered.

'Pants, bloody hell. Going up market, buying a second pair.'

Jamie stirred his tea. 'So…?'

'Had a quick scan. It's all we could've hoped for. It's a folder. The film we watched, but all the uncut body-cam footage as well; separate file for each camera.'

'So?'

'So, the cameras are running all the time. Over forty hours when you add all the individual camera files together… and if we can get the sign-out list—'

'Match each camera to a name, you've got whose where and when, second by second,' Jamie finished the sentence for her. 'Brilliant… potentially.'

'That van,' Shona continued. 'I'll give it some time at home, but those lights, people moving over that field. Match the body-cams, find the herders.'

Jamie nodded.

For a moment they were both staring into their tea as the significance weighed in the air around them.

Eventually, Shona said, 'Anyway, your afternoon?'

'Open and shut. Never called.'

'So, waste of time?'

'Kept myself amused with Dunky.'

Shona felt her teeth grate.

'He had these bloody diagrams to present at court, about somebody on a fly-tipping charge. Told him how I wished I'd got his security clearance for the council's property records, how it'd speed us up on the lettings and ownership backgrounds, blah, blah…'

'Jesus, you just have to spoil it, don't you.'

'What?' Jamie shrugged. 'Just told him how we're struggling for resources. Can't get enough surveillance. Not got anybody with your knowledge of the locus. Oh, and I saw the insulation tape making P an R and F into E. I said to him "bloody hell Dunk, if I run that through number plate recognition will it come up as James Bond?" He liked that one. His little shoulders went all proud.'

'Christ, and I was thinking you'd beat your personal best for not being a prat. What's that standing at now? About thirty-two minutes?' Shona stood.

'Want to see my pants?' Jamie reached into a carrier bag and held up a pair of blue boxer shorts.

29

Shona balanced her laptop on any nearby surface, as she moved around her flat. She cooked and ate a stir-fry, hardly taking her eyes off the screen: body-cam video, watching, getting a feel, trying to match clips to camera numbers, working out times and positions, straining to pick out voices. Hour upon hour she tracked, noted and slotted into tables until, deep into the early hours, intervals of involuntary dozing overwhelmed her. Four hours later, her alarm exhumed her from sleep and she staggered towards the shower.

At their desk, yesterday's M&S spat with Jamie was stacked in the dustbin of past conflicts, as the pair huddled around the laptop, hiding it from accidental eyes and sharing an earplug. Initially an arc of Peepo vehicles was hidden behind stacked containers, then Shona pointed to the edge of a frame.

'There's that other van.' She paused an image of semi-derelict land on the far side of the main dockside drive.

'Local,' Jamie pointed a pen at the company logo. 'Decent van as well. Merc Sprinter. But these?' He indicated to the main Peepo fleet. 'National. Got hire centres everywhere. Mind, their vans are French crap. But that Merc van... might have a wander down to admin, see if the paperwork matches.'

With the previous night etched in grit on the inside of her eyelids, Shona nodded and blinked her way through another hour of screen time.

'And Clegg was in the corridor,' Jamie was carrying two coffees when he came back from admin and confirmed the expected. 'Had one of her random thoughts about collating burglary statistics.'

'Jesus, this is a murder. Why just us? Couldn't she farm out the crappy distractions to someone else? What's Tommo doing when he's not up a tree?'

'Pretty much what I told her,' Jamie sat back a little.

An image of Clegg formed in Shona's mind as Jamie eased into direct quotes. ' "I go home, turn up the central heating and care about what the powers that be tell me to care about. One more prozzie, or druggie?" Then she said she wasn't taking the flak for rewriting the Christmas holiday roster.'

Shona closed her eyes and sucked in a breath.

As the afternoon moved on, staff numbers in the briefing room declined. Eventually, it was just Jamie and Shona huddled over their computer screen.

'Like bloody fire-flies,' Jamie pointed to a cluster of flickering lights moving across the semi-derelict expanse that lay between the dockside and the mystery van.

Shona nodded. She had a sense of dark forms moving between the shadows of broken walls and formless bushes that littered the scrubland.

The next morning's shift began as yesterday's had finished, with them scouring the now familiar video. As the Peepo herd loitered in the central space, Moonlight's lanky deputy began filling in a flip-chart.

'We could mention it without giving away that we've seen all the other stuff,' Jamie leaned close. 'Drop out a couple of details, look for a reaction.'

Shona nodded, but didn't understand what he was saying.

When the debrief broke up, Jamie gave Shona a nudge, and he was up, heading for the corridor, dodging between bodies until he was alongside Hobbes. As Shona caught up, Jamie was saying: 'Bet there's a bit of aggro about who gets the Merc Sprinter.'

Hobbes looked bemused.

'All those shit French vans and there's just one Merc van parked on its own. Bit of luxury for the fit birds is it? Off trailing perfume into the night, while the rest of you are stuffing the slappers into the crap Peugeots.'

Shona leaned on the corridor wall, just out of Hobbes' eye-line.

'Yeah,' Jamie was saying. 'Who gets to drive it, the Merc, the old Glamour Waggon?'

Jamie and Shona's eyes met for a second and they both knew. Glamour Waggon. No flicker. It wasn't a phrase Hobbes had ever heard before.

'So who does drive it – the Merc? Somebody with a bit of clout. Somebody from another city? Obviously, not you, Cheeky Chops.' And Jamie pinched Hobbes cheek.

'Fuck off, twat,' Hobbes shoved a hand into Jamie's shoulder. Jamie grinned and walked off.

'He goes over the top sometimes,' Shona pushed herself off the wall. 'This latest case is a bastard.' Hobbes glared at her. 'He's getting nowhere and he knows it, so he's got to have a go at someone.'

'Sympathy? From you?' The little Peepo began turning away.

'Sympathy? No. Just glad it was you instead of me. It's alright for you. I've got him all day.'

'Tough shit.'

'Yeah, well,' Shona zipped her jacket. 'Bet he's right about you all being pissed off not getting a ride in the Merc full of Euro-totty.'

'Nah,' Hobbes was walking away as he spoke again. 'Not if it means mixing with the bosses. Transits, unmarked vehicles, all sorts. Bloody Moonlight and his mate commandeered a BMW pursuit car one time.'

Shona lengthened her stride and went to speak again, but he grinned at her and pushed on the Gents toilet door.

Feeding the girls to a mafia psycho.

The phrase constantly echoed around in Jamie's mind and knotted itself between his shoulder blades. When he got home he didn't bother with food. He knew that oxygen debt was the only prescription for his disease.

An hour, alternating three-quarter pace and jogging. Work to do: leaden compared to years past. How much was lack of training? How much psychological: holding back from long-dormant hamstrings and calf muscles that he feared were breakable? Whatever, he'd hit a limit of sorts, steam rising from his gasping body, bent double in the winter night.

Watching his sweat fall onto the flagstones in spattering circles, he heard a car. As his breathing steadied, a door opened and shut and he became aware of a neat beat; hard heels on limestone slabs, but he remained bowed and breathless as the sound neared and stopped. He wiped a sleeve across his eyes and turned his head a little. Shoes, business-bright, black patent.

He straightened, still steaming.

Beyond the woman was a Land Rover. He recognised it was the latest eco-model, with all the bells and whistles.

'Electric,' he said. 'Good for the planet.'

'I can afford to be ethical,' the woman's voice matched her shoes.

Shifting his focus from the car, Jamie took in the woman; dark hair, mid-thirties, slim. Tailored overcoat, open over a wrap-around dress. Shona would have registered the significance of the hip-buckle logo. Jamie just recognised expensive.

'Sergeant Seagrief,' the woman went on. 'My name is Marika Morcanu. I think we share the same problem.'

'If we do,' Jamie's voice slid deeper into clipped Manc. 'I doubt we'd share the same solution.'

'No, not at the moment,' the woman's words were unhurried, middle-class, accentless anywhere. 'But discussion might reveal common ground.'

Jamie made a thin laugh down his nose.

Marika Morcanu walked a few steps, then leaned on a low wall. Her hands were in her coat pockets now. 'We want the business shut down and no loose ends.'

'You mean without any loss of profits?'

'No,' the woman moved her hands together, closing her coat. 'Profit is negligible, the risk nonsensical.'

'Risk?' Jamie looked at her.

'My brother and I, our businesses are legitimate, profitable. We're nothing to do with the unit.'

'Shag City.'

'The unit,' Marika Morcanu went on, 'is my father's. We've tried to persuade him to let it go for years. Even got him to shift the leases to six month options, hoping the rents would go up and force his hand, but...'

'But?'

'But the economic downturn: the decline in exports caused by the new bureaucracy. Property companies are just happy to have a tenant. Everything else was sold to uncles and cousins at mate's rates. Maybe he wanted one last thing so he could say *look, I'm still a player*.'

'And was he?'

'No. He was an old man raging against the dying of the light.'

'So why don't you?'

'Because of the Pole: Bakula and the people behind him. Poppa was supposed to be selling it to them. Doing a few months handover while they finalised their foreign business clearance.'

'So why didn't the deal just run its course?'

'Bakula began leaning. Making threats. Shutting him out. In the old days, my father would have spit in his eye. Poppa was a big man. Nothing would make him back down. He said nothing in Britain was frightening when you'd faced the Securitate back home.'

'Securitate?'

'Romanian secret police. They were everywhere in the Ceausescu years.'

'And?'

'He never said, but I'm guessing – the Pole is in his thirties. My father is a pensioner. When we saw the change, that's when my brother and I did some digging. Got an idea who he was dealing with.'

'And you shit yourselves.' Jamie had his hands on hips now, breathing slowly.

'My brother and I, this was never our world. That's what he'd protected us from; why he'd made sure we went to good schools, studied at good universities.'

'Poor little rich girl.'

Marika Morcanu's voice stayed measured. 'I know I've been lucky and I know my father made that luck. So yes, I am rich. Yes, I am privileged. But I know where I came from. He'd never allow us to forget.'

'And that was you trying to make a connection,' Jamie spat into the gutter. 'Tell the prat: "I know I've been lucky, but we're all the same." See if he bites.'

'It's not what I am saying. I'm saying my brother and I have been trying to close it down for years. Risk versus reward? Non-starter.' Maria Morcanu held a practised calm. 'All we ask is a chance to get out from under, work with you in a way that can't be traced back to our families.'

'What the bloody hell paid for your expensive education?' Jamie stared down the road. 'The big house with Peak District views? What was the seed corn? The manure, the shit that fed your growth?'

'But we were children. Years ago. He went to work, he came back. It was only after university we saw it. Saw it and didn't want it,' the frustration was slipping into her voice now.

'Then why is it still here?'

'A fair question,' Marika Morcanu reclaimed her calm. 'Yes, we should've tried harder. Time passes. You live a different life. Things drift and... he is still our father and deserves some respect.'

'So do the girls.'

'Agreed, Sergeant Seagrief. And that's what I'm saying. We want to help.'

'Want to save your skin from the Polish mafia.'

'Yes, sergeant, we do. But one outcome only helps the other. We can access records, show links, help you control the explosion. We can argue about our motives, but maybe if we focus on the outcomes?'

'Focus on the outcomes. Christ, it's not a business seminar. Maybe we could exchange mindmaps.'

'What do you want?' Marika Morcanu's voice tensed. 'Your endgame?'

'Nail the bastard responsible.'

'Bakula, or my father.'

'Both.'

'Well God's done half your job already.' Marika Morcanu kicked herself upright from the low wall and straightened her coat. Then, reaching into an inside pocket, she held out a photograph.

Jamie took it: an old man with his heavy moustache, but its weight seemed too much for the face as it dragged his mouth down and pulled on his eyes. Less a face, more a house with slipped foundations, still recognisable, but all structure failed, flesh fallen like shifted bricks.

'The stroke was July. There's been no improvement.'

'Any kid with Photoshop—' Jamie began, but Marika cut across.

'Sergeant Seagrief, when you have had time to recover from the stress of your exercise,' the dam of her suppressed anger was breached now. 'You can give me a call.' And she placed a business card on the wall where she'd been leaning.

Jamie watched the swirl of her coat as her heels beat a retreat towards the Land Rover. He squared his shoulders and, hands on hips, locked his eyes on Marika Morcanu through the windscreen then, slowly rotating, kept his stare unbroken as the Land Rover drove past and on until it turned out of sight.

When Shona arrived, Jamie was updating his duty record. A business card was on the desk. Shona's hand slid across.

'Morcanu's rich-bitch daughter. Mihai, his old pal, gave it me,' Jamie didn't look up.

'You should call,' Shona pushed the card back.

'Yeah, we could do brunch.'

'It's a lead. We can't afford to… seriously, Jamie…' Shona stood. 'Do you want a tea? I'm buying.' She knew confrontation was a road to nowhere.

When Shona returned from the canteen with two cups, the card had gone and so had Jamie.

'Great,' Shona said to herself. 'Two teas, that'll keep the old lady plumbing flushed out.'

But then Jamie came through the door. 'Sorry, been for a slash. Made some room for the freebie tea.'

'Effortless,' Shona shook her head. 'Remind me again why you don't wear your Eton Old Boys tie to work?'

Once Shona had finished her tea she picked up a laptop. Just off the corridor was a small, windowless office where she sometimes went when she wanted some privacy. Eventually, Jamie stuck his head round the door.

'Wondered where you'd gone,' he said. 'I'm off. Sorry to interrupt your Christmas shopping. Not Black Friday fortnight is it?'

Shona answered him with a single middle finger.

Back home, Shona's evening spread into morning again as she continued her trawl through the endless hours of body-cam images. Around midnight she checked the table of data she'd pieced together: body-cam numbers, corresponding video and audio clips, and timings were almost filled in. Only the *Possible Voice* column was relatively unpopulated.

Shuffling to the bedroom, Shona buried herself under the duvet. Everything was black.

Jamie had been out on the edgelands until late. If he'd slept well, he'd have had nearly five hours sleep, but he hadn't slept well. He'd felt his phone vibrate as he was pulling on his rucksack ready for home but, before he'd gotten his gloves off and coat unzipped, it had stopped. Calling back, it was unavailable. But there was a message.

30

'Pull up over there.' Shona opened the passenger side door.

Jamie watched her walk into the coffee shop. After a couple of minutes she emerged holding two take-away cups.

'Open the door nobhead,' Shona's voice was muffled by glass. 'You can see my hands are full.'

'Lottery numbers come up? Tea yesterday, coffee today.'

'Something to drink while you tell me what's on your mind.'

Jamie took both coffees as Shona got back in the car.

'So?' Shona blew, then sipped.

Jamie didn't speak. Shona let the silence grow.

'I met this woman last night.'

Shona stayed quiet.

'Flash cow. Bloody electric Range Rover and clothes to match.'

After twenty seconds of Jamie describing torque and gearbox ratios, Shona cut in.

'So anyway, this rich bitch?'

'Sorry, yes,' Jamie re-focused. 'Marika Morcanu. She gave me her card, not Mihai.'

'And…'

'Some shit about shared goals.'

Shona sipped again. 'So, was she offering a bribe?'

'No, some rehearsed bollocks about her father already being in prison. Apparently God's locked him up.'

'So, how…' Shona began, but Jamie reached into a pocket and passed her a print-out.

'Looks authentic.'

'So, you can tell Photoshop just by looking?'

'No, but I know a severe stroke when I see it,' she looked at the wreck of Neculai Morcanu, propped on pillows to prevent him toppling sideways, a sore crusted track etched into his chin where the dribble leaked from the corner of his lip. 'Fuck sake, Jamie, he looks like a waxwork someone's left by a radiator.' And Shona threw the paper into his lap. 'No one's faking that.'

'Yeah, well…' Jamie folded the print-out back into his coat pocket and opened the car door. 'I'm going for a walk.' He was out and striding to nowhere in particular.

When he got back, he lifted his coffee out of the cupholder. It was cold.

'At least we're not stuck in the school run traffic,' Shona tried to coax him into conversation as she drove.

Jamie was monosyllabic minimal, but Shona was persistent, making him respond to addresses and information.

The main Vulpes office was in the city centre, and the estate agents were the same, or in the Eccleshall Road vicinity. But they began with the Morcanu list: taxi offices, a car mechanic, a wholesale cash-and-carry and six corner shops. Quick scan of the outsides, an occasional foray inside, but any talk kept casual.

Splitting their list, Shona and Jamie systematically quizzed the out of town estate agents.

Finally, back in the car, they began pooling what they'd gleaned.

Shona leaned back, closed her eyes, then straightened. 'These last few estate agents? All city centre,' she began. 'Doesn't really need both of us.'

Jamie gave a slight nod.

'This Marika rich-bitch,' she continued, as Jamie pressed the start button. 'Maybe if I dived into the Central Library with my laptop, then you WhatsApp me when you're done?'

Jamie began to move away. 'You get yourself in the library. Sit by a radiator. Don't worry about me out in the weather.'

Shona hadn't been settled long when the phone vibrated in her pocket. 'Never bloody finished already.' But as she took out the phone it wasn't Jamie. It was a text: Katya.

Sorry slow reply charger lead fall out.

And there were fourteen numbers.

31

After an hour, Jamie texted.

Done, dusted. Meet M&S?

Shona was already in the cafe and logged onto the Wi-Fi when Jamie walked in.

'See… Always thinking,' she pointed towards the coffee and biscuits waiting on the table. 'How'd you get on?'

'Bugger all.'

'And Vulpes?'

'What you'd expect. High-end, corporate bland. More disconnected than obstructive. Lad I spoke to said low price rentals get subbed out.'

'To Solar Properties?

'Nah. Blank stare. Like everywhere else. What about you?' Jamie cupped cold hands round the coffee.

'Had a quick check through the local Morcanu stuff. Nothing else coming up dodgy, but I'm getting a picture of your posh totty.'

'So Lady Rich-Bitch looks what?'

'Rich,' Shona inhaled. 'Seriously rich… and legit.'

'Or the smarmy Romanian tart is just good at concealment.' Jamie slurped at the froth on his coffee.

'Maybe, but she's all over the internet. Her and her husband.'

Shona turned her laptop towards him.

'Major business interests with her brother, Dominik,' Shona clicked another Instagram image. 'Registered as owners and directors of Trajan Enterprises.'

'Trajan?' Jamie swiped his phone screen. 'See what Google says.'

'Roman Emperor: Trajan's column,' Shona continued. 'Saw it in Rome. Story of his conquest of Romania carved into it. Violence, torture.'

'So, nod to the heritage,' Jamie put his phone back in his pocket. 'What do—'

'What do they do?' Shona cut in. 'Numerous, varied. There's an investment wing, consultancies, big in IT systems. And Marika runs a pet project, managing high end retail refurbishments. Got a flat and prestige offices in Butler's Wharf.'

Jamie's face registered non-recognition.

'South Bank,' Shona explained. 'Near Tower Bridge. And then there's her husband.'

Jamie's mouth twisted like it was tasting something rancid.

'Shipping broker, huge. Offices worldwide. Buys and sells space on the biggest ships in the world. His income looks like a mobile phone number.'

Shona watched Jamie flick from tab to tab: Marika Morcanu standing in front of Trajan Enterprise offices, rolling fabrics across her Butler's Wharf floor, clients looking on; luxury cars, Marika in sparkling evening dresses, surrounded by black-tied men at a flock of industry award dinners.

Shona let the rage fade in his eyes and eventually said: 'These say she is who she says. Despise her as much as you want, I've found nothing that isn't legit.' She closed her laptop. 'The money from Shag City… Why would she risk it? It's peanuts in her world.'

'Because that's what they do. These leeching bastards,' Jamie's voice was low. 'It's not about balance sheets, it's about arrogance; about taking it because they can; because they never imagine they'll be caught.'

'So everyone with money should be distrusted and despised?'

Jamie tapped his knuckle against a window.

'Anyway, Christmas,' Shona moved on. 'What's your off-duties looking like?'

Jamie stopped tapping. 'I'm on late Christmas Eve, then back in the morning, twelve hours from eight o'clock.'

'So you're not—'

'Yeah, well. We have Christmas on Boxing Day. Jacko, our Mandy's bloke, they've been together since they were fourteen, always pulls a double shift Christmas Day. Couple of hours with the kids while they open presents in the morning, then works through till early hours of Boxing Day. He's maintenance. Hardly any work going on, so usually no breakdowns and no bosses coming in to check. Pays for Christmas, the old triple time.'

'So, you're Uncle Jamie?' Shona grinned. 'How many?'

'Two boys and a girl... anyway,' Jamie changed tack. 'Clegg. She doesn't need the overtime. Off on holiday. Have you downloaded the blanks?'

'Nearly all filled in, just the space saying why we need access.'

'Money laundering, proceeds of crime. Cleggy loves a bit of white-collar. And whatever's on the warrant? Maybe one thing leads to another and once the toothpaste is out the tube...' he looked self-satisfied. 'Anyway, bit of momentum now. Got that flash tart Meccano out the woodwork.'

'Meccano? Morcanu you pillock. She isn't a construction set.'

'She's a piece of work. Phoning me at one in the morning. Trying to catch me half asleep so she can—'

'Phoning you at—'

Jamie already had his phone out and was scrolling through the options. 'Here, read,' and he threw it across.

'So, which date did you choose?'

'Haven't,' Jamie stared ahead. 'Fuck her. Let her wait. Anyway, Christmas and stuff. Need to give it some thought... and, Clegg...'

As Jamie spoke, Shona was seeing calendar pages blowing away in her head.

'Remember what I said? Always gets clear before Christmas and the shit season really takes hold. Usually slips off early. Got to keep an eye on that tomorrow. Catch her when she's in a rush, so she signs without digging.' He leaned back in his seat. 'Even then, where do we start?'

Shona took a breath. 'This might come in useful.' She held out the text from Katya – three pairs of numbers and a string of eight digits. 'Already googled the sort code, so we know where to look for the account number.'

Around four, Clegg crossed to her office; a constable from the front desk was following like a Sherpa, carrying bags from various leisure-wear shops. The constable left and the vague frosted-grey silhouette of Clegg moved across her glass wall.

'Trying stuff on,' Shona said, watching from her desk.

The shadow play went on for a few minutes, then a woollen pom-pommed hat was visible above the frosted line.

'Holiday head on,' Jamie said and they crossed the room and knocked on Clegg's door.

'Spyder, top make,' Shona picked up a ski-jacket upon stepping in. 'Didn't know you were a skier.'

'I'm not, so it's a necessity. Can't rely on exercise to keep you warm when you're sitting on a terrace with a brandy and hot chocolate.'

'And being still, boss,' Shona joined in. 'Means a fashion statement's more essential than when you're just a fast-moving dot on a mountain.' The two women shared a smile.

'Be glad when I'm on that plane. If ever a shit day was designed to make you want a holiday. Thought I'd never get out for my retail therapy.'

Shona and Jamie stayed quiet. They knew Clegg would go on.

'Regional HQ, plastic chairs. Early start and fuck off before twelve, so they don't have to put on food.' Clegg looked over the frosted glass in the direction of Moonlight. 'Look at the prat. He was there. Came back all inspired. He'll be at it soon, giving his minions a bit of motivational speaking.'

Shona and Jamie peered through the glass.

'They can sound tough,' Clegg continued. 'Safe in the knowledge that people like him will balls-up any operation that's more sophisticated than kicking doors, or throwing the occasional sacrificial lamb to pet journalists to delude the masses. Fucking Moonlight.' Clegg shook her head and the pom-pom swung from side to side.

'Holiday well earned, boss,' Shona picked up one of Clegg's brochures and began turning pages.

'Before you go, ma'am,' Jamie passed over a warrant. 'Need access to a suspect's bank accounts.'

Clegg read the name on the warrant. 'Solar Properties and recipients of said company's moneys or goods. But Vulpes,' she was talking as she signed, 'is a no go. If it does crop up, you do nothing till I'm back. Don't test me on this,' and she pointed her pen at Jamie. 'None of your maverick *sorry I misunderstood* pissing into the wind.'

'You've seen the names and addresses, boss. Strong wind, to blow piss on us from Marble Arch.'

'Just make sure I don't come back to an office full of yellow snow. If I do, I'll have your balls for Christmas baubles – think on.'

Clegg picked up the phone and Jamie and Shona left. A couple of minutes later the desk constable appeared and renewed his Sherpa duties, trailing Clegg towards the door.

Across the room, Moonlight was holding forth now. Shona didn't catch what he was saying, but the Peepos began a synchronised bout of clapping and chanting.

'Fuck this,' Jamie unplugged his laptop and made for the door.

Shona found Jamie on a chair in the corridor, apparently filing emails. His body language was clear – any attempt at conversation would be one-sided, so she took out her phone. Walking in casual loops, her voice descending into chatty, raw Glasgow. After ten minutes, the briefing room door opened and the herd jostled out. Jamie shut the laptop and dropped it into a supermarket carrier and followed the stragglers towards the canteen. Shona tried to keep up, still on the phone.

'Got to go now, hen. Something's come up.' A couple more walking sentences and the requisite three 'Bye nows,' and a 'Love to Tam and Kirsty,' and she put the phone in her jacket pocket. 'My cousin Marie,' Shona explained as she caught up. 'Keeping tabs on the Glasgow gossip.'

In the canteen, Shona felt Jamie's hand on her elbow, but she didn't need reminding not to creep too close; not after the last queue argument. Luckily, lots of the canteen tables were occupied, so they could sit adjacent to the Peepo group without it looking like they were trying to get within earshot.

'Chance to kick the PR politicos in the bollocks.' A voice was reiterating Moonlight's speech. 'We're chasing thick bastards, when the real prize is Operation Smartarse, run by their police and customs puppets.'

'Yeah. Strengthens Miss K's hand if we could embarrass some of the wobbly bastards.'

Shona watched Jamie stare into his cup, he was making sure nothing in his body language gave a clue that he was listening.

At home Jamie finished a microwaved meal and took out his laptop. He heard ringing, then a voice, but no image, just the spinning circle of doom in the middle of the screen. Then it cleared.

'Hi, Jamie, we weren't expecting you,' Claudette was beaming.

'She's not here. School Christmas party. Miriam Turay is bringing her home. You remember Miriam?'

Jamie smiled. Miriam Turay, lead nurse and his nemesis – "Don't come here with your battle ground heroics Mr Seagrief. We run a calm and quality establishment."

'Yeah, I remember Miriam. Good friend to Cara and me. Five star nurse in a two star tent.'

Claudette smiled back.

After general chat and a promise to be online to watch the grand Christmas morning present opening, Jamie was back alone. He needed distraction and began to assemble his edgeland gear, then a wave of rain swept across the window, distorting his view of the world. Going back to his laptop, he clicked on BBC weather. A series of thin clouds drifted across a graphic of Sheffield.

'Jesus, Carol, get a grip,' he cursed the absent weather girl. 'Don't need a forecast. Just look out the fucking window.'

Jamie disassembled his outdoor kit, then sat at his desk. He reached for a rough jotter. On sheets of printer paper, he re-drafted his notes, then took his hard-covered chronicle with its high-quality paper and opened it so that it lay comfortably parallel to the edge of his desk. Next, he laid out his drawing and writing equipment and took a pencil and ruler and marked a faint box, divided into regular lines drawn with a lightness that was almost invisible. After a while he was ready for permanence. Thin black lines formed into shape and shade from the end of his needlepoint pen, cross-hatching restrained, as he resisted the domination of shadows. The storm beyond his window seemed to be settling in. The BBC were still showing light clouds, but his efforts on the ordered page had soothed him. He was ready for his bed and the green lava lamp.

In her flat, Shona had finally finished. The depression of dark winter nights and hours of collating nameless body-cam videos to ID numbers were taking their toll. Dave would have the sign out list. The thought brought some comfort as she dragged herself towards her bed.

The clouds of the previous night still besieged the city and, between his front door and the car, a skirmish of rain had caught Jamie in the open. Although the underground car park meant his entry into the police station was sheltered, as he entered the briefing room his hair was still flattened against his skull. The central heating was cranked up and there was a radiator by the desk. He hung his coat on the back of his chair and it began to steam.

Shona was already in. 'Didn't the grey clouds give you a clue, detective?' she smiled. There was an umbrella near her, drying on the pipes.

As Jamie sat down, Shona showed him a print-out of her body-cam info.

'Yeah, this is good. You must've really—'

'Nipping up to Dave's. Get a copy of that sign-out list. That and Katya's numbers. Could be a double Christmas present.' Shona pushed back in her seat.

'Except it's not just Clegg on the slopes over the holiday.' Jamie met her eye. 'His brother's got a ski business.'

'Bastard,' Shona hissed through her teeth and kicked a chair into the desk. A couple of Peepos turned.

'It's only Aviemore,' Jamie leaned forwards, his voice quietening. 'Probably just be driving up for a few days.'

32

The sort code traced back to a bank just off the Peace Gardens and, half an hour later, they were shown into the manager's office.

'Sorry to wake you,' Jamie said as the woman struggled to lift her eyes from the desk.

Shona read her lapel badge: Janine Bowker, Manager. The young lad who'd shown them in stifled a laugh.

'Don't,' she pointed and the lad left.

Jamie took out the warrant.

'I'll take your word for it. My head's banging. Do you want a coffee or something? Anything that doesn't involve me trying to focus on a page of accounts.' She pressed an intercom and, a minute or so later, the young lad came in with a tray. The woman glowered at him until he backed out the door and closed it behind him.

'So, what can I do for you, Sergeant Seagrief and...' she squinted to read their IDs. 'McCulloch?'

'Long way from Villa Park aren't you?' Shona reacted to the woman's accent. 'Or are you a Bluenose?'

'Walsall, not Birmingham.'

Jamie grinned. 'Where they serve pigeon peas in the pubs.'

'Grey peas and bacon bits, now you're talking. Original Black

Country balti. Don't think I could face it this morning though. Some prat persuaded me to try a Traffic Light last night. Not my finest hour.'

'Traffic Light?' Jamie looked bemused.

'Yeah, you know. Like a cocktail. Layer of crème de menthe, layer of limoncello, layer of raspberry liqueur: green, amber, red. I don't usually drink, but it's Christmas and I didn't want to look snobbish.'

'What, with coming from Walsall?' Jamie was amused by the mismatch between job, clothes and what came out the woman's mouth.

'I only had the one. God knows how people do it every night.' She reached for her coffee. 'Anyway, fuck it, won't happen again for a long while. Show us what you've got.' She began flicking through the papers, then said: 'Obviously, I can just pull this one up. Our sort code and account number, but it'll take a bit longer to trace any activity linked to…' she squinted at her computer. 'Solar Properties… anyway, leave it with me, I'll work on the presumption you're chasing bastards.'

'Can you…?' Shona unfolded photocopies of the Companies House pages. 'The directors' names were about as legitimate as its Marble Arch postal address.'

'Yeah, that's what we've got,' the bank manager turned her computer screen for them to see. 'But bank I.D. checks? Easy to set up an account in a false name.'

Jamie stood and offered his hand. 'Thanks, appreciated. If there's any chance you could print off a few months' transactions.'

Shona did the same.

'No problem,' the woman stood. 'Do a search on the credits and debits, list any banks and account holders. Anything to distract me from my headache for a bit.'

As they walked away, Jamie looked at his watch. 'Clegg'll be in the air now.'

Shona's phone buzzed. There was a text. 'Seems everyone's on the move.' And she showed Jamie the text.

Bastard home for Christmas. Lock up fuck off.

'Need to meet her.'

Jamie nodded. 'Tell her to get a taxi into town. We'll pick her up. Use the Christmas pissheads in the city centre as cover.'

Across the meeting space, the Peepos were waiting for their official end of shift. The room was raucous and distracted by Hobbes falling on his arse while trying to head a balloon that was hanging from the Christmas decorations. Shutting out the festive chaos, Jamie and Shona moved their chairs closer together.

'Cash is king,' Jamie sucked his teeth. 'But you can only spend so much in notes. Pin down those transfers and…'

'Bakula must have accounts somewhere.' Shona was tracing down a bank statement. 'Katya mentioned a Black Forest House. Wonder if Katowice knows about that?'

Jamie was leaning on his car as the taxi pulled up along the street. Katya was wearing leather trousers and a hip-length parka in a leopard-skin print. Shona stepped from the shadows of the tram stop shelter. Her coat was a similar cut and style, but with a bulkier fur trim and, despite the weather, she was wearing a sparkly mini-dress and over the knee boots.

'Could do a double act dressed like that, you two,' Jamie said as the two women got into the back of the car.

'Yeah,' Shona glared. 'Katya said she could get me a job working with a better class of person than now.'

'And bit more respect,' Katya added.

Jamie sensed an evening of female solidarity looming before him.

Concrete steps led up from a tarmacked area behind Shona's flat, but the high-security door led into a hallway that was wider than

Jamie expected. Everything was wider. More rooms, bigger rooms.

'Wouldn't think you were over a shop,' he said with no sense of snide.

'High-end wine merchant underneath. They used to live here. Him, his wife and a couple of kids. No garden, but the park's just over the road. When the business took off they moved nearer to The Peaks.'

'Nice till it snows, or it's pissing down in a gale,' Jamie carried on taking in the flat.

Shona indicated they should sit. Jamie slanted an armchair towards the sofa where Katya sat.

'Drink?' Shona was at the kitchen doorway. She disappeared and came back with three teas. Two were Earl Grey with lemon. Shona settled next to Katya and offered mince pies. 'Only supermarket,' she apologised.

'So, Bakula?' Jamie got no further.

Shona angled her shoulder to isolate him. 'This one has Monika Jarosz and Konrad Parol. Too much money, but we can look.' And she opened a magazine.

Jamie leafed through the Christmas Radio Times as the women chatted over glossy fashion pages. He knew better now than to interrupt Shona when she was using "soft skills".

But then, 'You don't know me,' an edge in Katya's voice pierced his personal bubble. 'How I was. I was here before. Here with bastard husband, but the girls...' and the tales flooded out. People sealed in lorries, behind walls of boxes, hoping the customs couldn't be bothered to climb up to look, or phone for the sniffer dog. People paying over their last euro just before the ferry sailed then, as they landed in the UK, immigration police ripping open their containers or power-hosing them from their hiding place on a lorry's chassis. For most, a couple of minutes of freedom, then handcuffed for re-export... but then there were the chosen few. Those deemed young and beautiful... being told the van was their way out. Being panicked away from the detention centre flock…

When Katya's words finally ebbed, they left a trail of young lives smuggled in one container until they arrived in another: this one inside a factory unit, kitted out with a bed, mock curtains and a cheap bordello decoration job.

'Tea?' Shona's eyes told Jamie he would be making it.

Jamie was reaching for mince pies as he heard Shona at the kitchen door. Stepping in, she sucked air to the bottom of her lungs and her eyes began to moisten.

'Give me a minute,' and she breathed out slowly. 'Christ almighty… monetised like battery chickens. If it were my family…'

Jamie slid the mince pies back. The kettle boiled and he made the tea and carried the cups through on a tray.

Shona breathed again, and dabbed her face with a kitchen roll, then opened the door.

'How's that phone charger going? No problems hiding it around the house?' she faked nonchalance and placed biscuits on the low table and sat again.

Katya blew on her tea.

'Safer not in your room?'

'No problem,' Katya shrugged. 'I can watch while they kick shit out of wrong person?'

Shona put her arms around Katya and gave her a hug. Out of the corner of her eye, she saw Jamie smile.

'We had a film. Taken at the docks,' Shona's voice was soft. 'People herded towards a different van.'

Katya nodded.

'Little lights kept bouncing off that group, but not the others,' Jamie's voice was quiet.

'Yes, girls say clip-on things. Shiny plastic, like put on children to walk school on dark mornings. Lorry driver at last service station. He look and tie on some – mostly young ones.'

'So, when they land in England in the dark, it's easy to find the beautiful girls,' Jamie's tone remained quiet.

'Yes, mainly girls. Nearly all…' Katya reached for her tea and Shona and Jamie mirrored her actions as the lull in words held.

'While you're here, Jamie,' slowly, Shona stood. 'My cooker hood. One of the lights has packed up.' She headed to the kitchen, and he followed. 'Enough for one night,' Shona dropped her voice as the kitchen door almost closed.

'Yes, just the bulb,' Jamie's voice was back on loud. 'See if I can pick you one up.'

Back in the lounge the conversation switched to Christmas and general chit-chat. In the hall the two women adjusted coats, scarves and hair.

'Ready?' Jamie was holding the front door latch.

'Lucky for both of us you not hang mistletoe over doorway,' Katya's voice was deadpan as she passed Jamie. Shona had to suck in her cheeks to stop herself from sniggering.

Back in the shadows near the taxi rank, Katya stepped onto the pavement. Shona handed her a couple of twenty pound notes. 'Pay for the cab,' she said.

'Not that much,' Katya looked at the money.

'Police expense account.'

Katya smiled. 'Cash always help, specially now Buzzard bastard say he want rent cash early.'

Shona gave Katya's hands a last squeeze before releasing. 'And Bakula? Is he back after Boxing Day… St Stephen's?'

'No, say back open New Year Day night. Waste of time. Business be crap. Punters all hungover, but Bakula say Christmas, New Year, long time listening to wives. Men need change.'

'Be good to meet again. If you…?' Shona said and stepped back into the shadows as Katya beckoned to a cab.

'Early collection?' Jamie asked as Shona approached his car.

'Probably doesn't want all that cash hanging around, especially with the weekend and all the bank holidays coming up.'

'Plans for tomorrow?' Jamie started the car.

'Drive to Glasgow. Couple of days family time. And you?

'Overtime,' said Jamie. 'Then my sister's.'

33

It was twenty-five past six as the bedside iPad blustered through his last vestige of sleep. His alarm was set for half-past anyway, but she was already on his screen, gap-teeth grinning and holding a shiny, wrapped present.

'Daddy… three, two, one.'

Claudette's voice was in the background, admonishing. The sound of ripping paper masked her words.

Smiles and thank yous and how-did-you-knows filled the next half an hour. Clothes tried on, or held against bodies, toys examined and occasionally demonstrated. At one point she disappeared out of shot, then reappeared in a sequined dress that rippled green in the bright morning.

'Auntie Mandy sent it,' Baggage held the hem and pirouetted.

Eventually, Jamie stood and, checking the webcam was picking him up, began his unwrapping. Baggage was clapping and shouting 'Yay, Daddy,' as Jamie smiled at two presents. The first was a box, gift-wrapped, care of Amazon – new trainers, but the second had stamps and address labels stuck onto brown wrapping paper. Inside an inner layer of Christmas paper was a book and, cosseted in bubble-wrap, two picture frames. In one frame was a recent photo of Baggage, in the other she was a baby cradled by two smiling parents.

'Nanny said you'd like these and the book...'

Jamie tilted his head so the tears were hidden from the camera. 'I do, sweetheart. I really do,' and he fought against the crack in his voice. 'And the book...'

'I know you've got most of his, but...' Claudette's voice came from beyond the visual range.

As its wrapping fell away, Jamie saw David Attenborough – *Life in Cold Blood*.

'Thanks. Yes, thanks. Exactly what I wanted.'

Conversations felt comfortable for a while. Video call communication had been the norm for so long. In time, as his shift approached, there was one last flurry of blown kisses and, as the screen blackened, Jamie felt the emptiness of his room.

In the car, he leaned back and the tears came again. 'Oh Cara, why isn't either of us with that little girl at Christmas.'

He finished work just after midnight. It had been quiet. Christmas day, even the villains were turkeyed out. Jamie settled with milky coffee and a plate of mince pies. He texted love and season's greetings to Mandy. Her phone went silent from eleven till seven, so there was no danger of waking her.

About ten minutes after the demise of the last mince pie, he pulled on his thick coat and dropped his phone in a pocket. Walking to the busy road, he scrolled down missed messages and tapped *Reply*. The number was obtainable now.

Second option – he began to type. *Unless I tell you different*. And he carried on walking.

'There you go, rich bitch. Merry Christmas.'

Dinner at two, Mandy had said. Jamie knew that meant at least half-past three. For once the drive to Manchester would be borderline traffic-less.

The sky was rain-heavy, but the Peak District landscape was

still a sight to behold. A gap appeared in the clouds and a shaft of sunlight tracked across the hillside like a theatrical spotlight, transforming the shaded olives and muted browns into a drifting patch of emeralds and golds. Jamie pulled into a lay-by as the narrow sunbeam rolled along the edge of the Ladybower Reservoir and performed its magic on the grey depths, lifting them into azures and jades and tipping their ripples with twinkling jewels.

He leaned on a limestone wall and, peeling the foil off a clod of pork pie and piccalilli, watched the track of light as it transmuted base vegetation into brief fabulous moments. The wind made his eyes water at the corners and, eventually, it closed the rift of light and the beauty of the moors darkened into unbroken rugged again. Jamie licked the last sourness of piccalilli from his fingertips and checked his phone: a couple of emoji-ridden WhatsApps from his niece, but nothing else.

Mandy opened the door in the promised paper hat and gave him a hug. Jacko shook his hand and said: 'Alright mate.'

Central heating and an all day turkey-laden oven wrapped itself around him in a meaty, oniony blanket and, as he sat on the sofa tipping a bin bag full of Christmas wrapped presents across the carpet, a niece and two nephews swarmed over him in a horde of hugs and thank yous, while a spaniel tried to get in on the act.

At quarter to four, retro prawn cocktails arrived on the table and everyone made their way to a chair and paper hat. Jamie refused to put his on, so Mandy snatched away his starter until he accepted the inevitable.

An hour later, gravy stained plates and industrial quantities of sausage-meat stuffing returned to the kitchen.

'I saw this recipe for Christmas pudding ice cream and thought that'll be lighter,' Mandy distributed large pudding bowls, then scooped clumps of brandy butter onto the adults' desserts.

Cheese arrived and the children departed towards toys, video games and a Disney cartoon, while the adults remained at the table. Jacko had a small glass of port. Jamie and Mandy were content with the coffee pot.

Eventually, everyone slouched towards the television. No one really watched and soon Jacko and Jamie were head back and snoring. When Jamie woke, the dishwasher was humming and Mandy was sat with a magazine. 'Bit of peace while the kids are occupied.'

Jacko yawned into the kitchen and stretched. A cup of tea and general chat and Mandy was up, organising cards, penny-a-time gambling on card games that the children won, while the grown-ups faked indignation at losing their money.

At about ten, his niece and nephews gathered at the door to give Jamie a last hug. Mandy did the same and Jacko replayed his *alright mate* handshake.

Reaching the edge of the Pennines, he parked in a lay-by to check his phone. Nothing but a photo-message of a bottle of scotch from Shona with the caption *Christmas pudding – Glasgow style*.

'Must still be full of the stuff, sending me that,' Jamie put the phone in his pocket. Behind him the lights of Manchester rippled across the horizon. Ahead, Sheffield was imprisoned beneath heavy cloud.

In the post-Christmas lull, neither woman felt the occasion needed sparkles. Katya stepped from her taxi in jeans and a parka. Shona's coat was long and quilted. Again Jamie watched, parked in the shadows.

'How's your Christmas been?' Jamie asked, as Katya and Shona got in the car.

Katya shrugged. 'Walk four banks today getting rent cash for bastard Buzzard.'

Jamie left the chat to Shona for the rest of the drive.

At Shona's flat there was cake, but the soft-skill bonding was shorter.

'At the docks,' Shona let Katya register what she was saying. 'They had a film in our office. But the pictures and sound? All bouncing around. If…' Shona waited a moment. 'Katya, last time, did you tell us everything?'

'Katya,' Jamie spoke and Shona froze. 'I understand you aren't sure if you can trust us. But, let's be honest,' and his voice dropped. 'It's already—'

'Shit or bust,' Katya nodded again. 'The uniform one – ski-mask.'

Shona breathed and looked at Jamie. His head was nodding, almost imperceptibly encouraging, and Katya was meeting his gaze.

'Uniform one. He mostly get out van before final drop-off. One girl…'

'One girl?' Shona spoke into the pause.

'Kaliningrad girl say it, but think some others just stay quiet. She say he fuck her against van. But she say she start it. She flirt, tease. She girl with plan. Russian, from Kaliningrad. You know it? Little bit of Russia on Baltic. Big navy base. She different from rest of us. She whore back home. All those sailors… boom town Kaliningrad.'

'But she had a plan?' Shona leaned in.

'Yes, move London. High end, West End, good clothes.'

'And she encouraged him?'

'Her plan. Obey. Seem happy. And when look other way…'

'She went?'

'Yes. Only here week.'

'You don't think she was…'

'No. Only in unit few days. Fitting in. Being no trouble. Then gone. Think she have contacts already. Just need get in country.'

'And a lift to London?' Shona asked. 'Easy from Sheffield.

Straight down the motorway.'

'Easy anywhere for her. Men would stop.'

'But other girls, you think…?'

Katya nodded. 'Maybe. Probably. Not talk about van. Bad memories: Some faces look…'

'These girls. These possibles?' Shona began.

'No, no. Good girls then. Just off ferry. Not like Kaliningrad girl. She already whore.'

'And this Kaliningrad girl, did she describe him?' Shona probed a little.

'Kept ski-mask on. Was swearing… couldn't get belt off. Hook got stuck to…' Katya drew her hand from her hip, indicating diagonally across her chest. 'Kept whispering as he fucked her. She say he smell nice. Clean. Slim, nice muscles. Not many we get clean, smell nice.' Katya half-smiled.

After a few seconds, Shona spoke again. 'Last time, when you were saying about the shiny disks being tied on the beautiful ones, Jamie said girls and you said girls *mainly*. So…?'

'Bakula say room for few pretty boys. Charge extra. Say gays rich. Can pay more.'

'And at the unit?' Jamie's tone was soft now.

'Our unit? Only Jakub,' Katya was blinking now, and a film of water was forming.

'Jakub?' Shona stretched out a hand.

'Jakub my friend. He young. Fifteen, but passport say nineteen. Parents die. Car crash. He was in…' Katya seemed to be searching for a word.

'A home; an orphanage,' Shona helped.

'Yes, but Jakub hate it, so think better in UK. Parents leave him money, but controlled by boss of home. Jakub get account numbers and stuff. Did transfers. Clever boy. Should be school, not…' a tear sat on her eyelashes.

'But if—' Jamie began.

'There's fruit cake,' Shona cut in. 'If Jamie could find his way around my kitchen?'

As he went through the door, Shona slid her hand towards a magazine, but stopped herself. 'Katya,' she began. 'I hope you can trust us now. If you can't, me taking out the Reserved catalogue won't change anything.'

Katya looked down.

'If I got some photographs. There might be a face...'

'Punters?' Katya asked.

'Maybe, but ...' Shona looked at Jamie as he came back carrying a tray.

'Want photo of Buzzard? Can take own.'

They both stiffened.

'Wait at house when he come collect cash. You see bastard Buzzard.'

Shona placed an arm on Katya. 'Oh, sweetheart, I think you've just given us a late Christmas present. Bugger the tea.' And she went to a cupboard and came back with a bottle of single malt.

'Shame you not give me present. Arrest him tonight,' Katya tipped back her whisky. 'Save me month rent, tomorrow.'

'Tomorrow?' Jamie shot forward in his seat.

'Most times he come first day of month. Come between eleven and twelve. After we wake up and before anyone leave for afternoon shift. But this week? Banks shit. Christmas, New Year.'

Shona poured herself and Katya another whisky and Jamie went to the kitchen and made himself tea. The talk became chat as everyone recognised the natural end of business and the potential of tomorrow.

34

Wednesday, in the nether time when Christmas staggers into New Year. Jamie and Shona had mapped out their morning and were on the move. Jamie received a text.

2nd option confirmed. Please advise if any problems.

And there was a location.

But he was driving when it came, a muted beep, deep in a pocket.

They were parked by ten; an hour early. Shona had a flask of coffee.

'Made some progress,' she handed Jamie a plastic mug. 'Tying names to body-cam IDs.'

'But the sign out list? That prat covering for Dave, hasn't he got it?'

'Yeah, but,' Shona took out her phone and tapped the camera icon. 'He's a bloke. I've got tits. Seemed happy to comply with my request to check a couple of the more distant boxes on the farthest shelf while I stood by his desk.'

A dark blue Nissan pulled up.

'Relax,' Shona sipped her coffee. 'Not before eleven.'

And then the driver stepped out.

'You bastard,' Jamie slid from the car covering his face with a scarf and low-pulled woollen hat. The man was in similar, with only a hooked nose exposed to the cold air, but the bulk of his winter coat couldn't hide the loose, predatory rhythm of his movement.

Jamie shambled towards the corner. Every few houses, an arch-topped tunnel led behind the terraces. Jamie picked one with a good line of sight. The Buzzard hammered on Katya's door.

One of the girls let him in and Shona swapped to the driver's seat. Ten minutes later he re-emerged holding a bright orange carrier bag, his face already wrapped against the weather.

Pulling out before the Nissan moved wasn't much of a gamble. Just short of the city centre, Shona eased into a bus stop until the Nissan passed, then maintained a next car but one tail until it entered a multi-storey car park. Jamie leapt out.

'Park and—'

'Just go,' Shona cut him short and he was running, again pulling at his woolly hat and scarf, racing to the back of the car park and the exits.

The storms and general grip of winter meant Sheffield was a city of woolly hats and scarfs, but Jamie didn't need to track. The sort code told him his destination: Pinstone Street.

Watching the Buzzard enter, Jamie pretended to be on the phone, then gave it thirty seconds before he opened the bank's plate glass door. The Buzzard was already in the queue, his back to the entrance. Jamie hunched over a small ledge, seemingly writing. He could see the cashiers' counters mirrored in the window. The bright orange carrier stood out on the reflection and Jamie glanced over his shoulder briefly, to note the time and cashier as the Buzzard reached the counter.

The reflection was fractured by the movement of people in the street, then there was a flash of orange as the carrier was squashed into a pocket. Jamie stayed huddled until the Buzzard passed into the street where Shona waited in her all-consuming parka hood. Trying to rush inconspicuously, Jamie signalled that they split either side of the street full of post-Christmas bargain hunters.

Just after the Town Hall, Jamie looked across and Shona shook her head. Their target lost, Jamie jogged on, while Shona traced back towards The Peace Gardens.

After a few minutes Jamie was on his phone. 'Back to his car,' and he was running, reaching the car park stairs, racing up, checking each level, until he reached Shona and the space where the Nissan had been.

Leaning out from the multi-storey, Jamie watched people emerging from doors and realised what had happened. They'd run along Pinstone Street, unaware that some buildings had rear exits that cut through. There was a beep as Shona unlocked their car, but he turned for the stairs and the top floor.

Standing in the open, Jamie felt the wind strengthen, its direction had shifted, colder now as the late afternoon gloom marshalled itself against the last remnants of an earlier brightness. He took out his phone and drew breath. Then he registered the notification. 'Fuck off...' After a microsecond of reading, his thumbs were tapping across the letters.

Reaching their car, he tapped on the window. Shona got out.

'Back to the bank. They'll have CCTV.'

The bank staff were tidying beyond plate glass. Jamie knocked with his knuckle. A woman in corporate colours pointed at her wrist and he held up his police ID. Coming near enough to read their details, she called the security guard.

Opening the door a fraction, the woman listened and said: 'I'll phone up, but I'm sure she's gone. Managers' monthly meeting at head office. Be the morning now.'

'Got your text,' Janine Bowker flicked the hair from her face as Jamie and Shona sat down. 'Got in early so I could make a start. That cashier and time, Solar Properties.' She slid a set of highlighted print-outs across the desk. 'Big cash deposit.'

'Great, and could get us a look at the CCTV?' Jamie asked.

'Yeah, should be easy enough when the technician's back on duty, but he rotates around all the local branches. And this week? Christmas and crap. Be pushing off myself in a bit. Time owing and the New Year pilgrimage back to the family shrine in Walsall.'

Jamie went to speak, but Shona nudged his leg.

'But your text yesterday,' Janine Bowker went on. 'I've had a trawl. Balance between cash and card payments follows what you said. There's some maintenance bills, but they're pretty low. Not what you'd expect. Most landlords crank it up, so they can set it against tax. And,' she pointed to a series of orange highlighter lines. 'Foreign sort code.'

'Poland, Katowice?' Jamie leaned forwards.

'No. But there is a Polish account as well,' her finger briefing flicked across a patch of fluorescent yellow. 'But this one's Germany.'

Jamie and Shona waited.

'Deutsche Kredit Landesbank. Branch address is Munich. Solid choice and they make it easy to set up accounts for non-German residents.'

'So whose account is it?' Shona was scanning the paper.

'That's a bit more of a problem since—'

'Since we told Europe to fuck off,' Jamie finished the sentence.

'Yeah, pretty much. Need a load more paperwork to get anywhere near identifying account holders abroad now. But sort codes?' She drew a highlighter line across the print-out. 'That's Katowice, like you said. And...' Janine Bowker flicked her fingertip along a series of lines. 'Munich deposits are a close match to the UK cash business. And what goes to Poland tallies with the traceable payments.'

'Traceable?' Jamie looked.

'Card payments, e-transfers, occasional cheques.'

'So...' Jamie waited.

'After the pilgrimage, I'll have another dig.'

Clicking on her intercom, the bank manager called for another round of teas and coffees, but Shona, sensing Jamie's frustration, stood and smiled diplomatically.

'Thanks, but got to get back to the station,' she said. 'Inspector wants an update and she's due in a meeting.' And they made their way towards the exit.

'Bit sloppy, not keeping the tax down?' Jamie made a half-hearted reference to Janine Bowker's early remark as he zipped up his coat.

'Not really,' Shona said. 'Marble Arch. Fake address and IDs. Just shut it down. Open up another fake company. Not like any government's ever been big on tax evasion.'

Back in the police station, Shona parked and went to the boot. The new leather shoulder bag was slim, like an up-market laptop bag. Back at their desk, she fiddled with the clasp.

'Christmas present? Moda Polska?' Jamie held eye contact.

Shona pointed at an embossed trademark – RLL and the word Polo. 'Cousin Marie works in John Lewis. Gets first dibs at post-Christmas sale prices.' She pulled out a document wallet. 'Morcanu, we've talked about,' she began taking out clipped piles. 'But Vulpes and the Fox family,' her hand rested on a series of clipped sheets. 'To state the bleedin' obvious – they're very rich and very diverse. Companies House again. Numerous property concerns, several quarries and a couple of golf clubs in Berkshire. And then there's the ancestral pile... that's not far. Just into Derbyshire. Surprised it's not National Trust.'

Jamie's fingers twitched, but he didn't break the silence.

'And yes, everything looks legit,' Shona unclipped one sheaf of papers. 'But I'll keep digging.'

Suddenly, Jamie stood and waved. Dunky was crossing the office. The Peepos parted and formed a corridor of backs.

'Grab yourself a seat, mate. Shona was just getting us a coffee,' Jamie smiled as Dunky reached the desk.

Shona glowered, but didn't want to draw any more attention. When she came back, she had three coffee mugs and a saucer of sugar on a tray.

'Dunky's hit the bullseye again down the records office,' Jamie said. 'Overcome all obstacles.'

'Yeah, that girl Moonlight was chatting up got a bit above her station, just because she'd moved up a desk,' Dunky looked pleased with himself.

'Up a desk?' Shona looked at them both.

'Yeah, auntie had her usual pre-Christmas cold. Couple of days home alone with Amazon, sorting the presents. Anyway, the girl started on about restricted this, special permission that... until she scanned my pass and it came up *access all areas*. Really was about to—'

'Seems to confirm the theory that Solar is subcontracting from Vulpes,' Jamie cut across. 'If you show...'

'And here, dates and addresses,' Dunky held his phone screen. 'Photoed the documents. If I just...'

'Could be a signature?' Shona squinted over Jamie's shoulder as the email pinged and he opened the attachment. 'Thanks Dunky. You know you shouldn't,' Shona tapped the screen. 'Seriously, Dunky. We're not sure who we're dealing with.'

'Mafia, anything,' Jamie put in.

Shona flashed him a look.

'Always think, Hitler's train timetable,' Jamie continued.

'What?' Dunky looked bemused.

'He means, don't take unnecessary risks,' Shona jumped in.

'Hitler's timetable. It's a bit of mantra.' Jamie leaned back in his chair. 'If you were in charge of the train timetable for Hitler's death camps, would you go with your conscience and feel like a hero when they shot you, leaving some really efficient bastard in charge who'd get the trains running full speed? Or would you keep your head down so you could save some, but feel guilty because you could've saved more, if you'd taken a risk?' Jamie smiled. 'It's called a moral dilemma.'

'Cos, thing is,' Shona continued. 'You have to keep yourself safe, so you can save others.'

'Dead heroes...' Dunky was nodding now.

'Guilt or death,' Jamie was grinning as he said it. 'It's our motto. We're thinking of having badges made.'

Dunky mirrored Jamie's grin. 'Nah, mate,' and he tapped his temple with his finger. 'Be smart and save them all... then rip up the rails.' The two men laughed.

Shona grabbed at the tray. 'I'll clear your mess.' And the mugs and sugar nearly slid off.

Just outside the main office was an alcove with a sink and kettle. Shona slammed the tray onto a work surface, then, checking no one was around, kicked a cupboard.

As she re-entered the office Dunky was crossing the central briefing space. 'Speak soon, sister.' He gave her a wave. He had his sunglasses on now.

Shona placed two hands on the desk. She leaned towards Jamie and hissed: 'You twat.' Jamie looked amused. 'You selfish twat.'

'I didn't tell him to do anything.'

'No, you didn't. You just quietly lit the fuse on the silly sod's hero complex. Fuck sake,' and she straightened. 'I need a bit of time not looking at your smug face.'

The wooden dividing wall of the kitchen alcove shook. Jamie looked up and saw a shadow against a frosted window. There were words spoken, but they were muffled by the glass.

'What was happening in the corridor?' Jamie asked when, a few seconds later, Shona slumped opposite him at the desk.

'Bit of a heated discussion,' she opened her shoulder bag and began leafing through her diary.

Jamie noticed the acrylic nail on her index finger was missing. The office door opened. It was Hobbes. His shirt collar was twisted and his face flushed. He stared at Shona and the anger almost clawed its way across the air towards her. She didn't look up.

'So?' Jamie whispered across the desk.

'Tell you later. Don't want that shithouse thinking he's worth talking about,' Shona pretended to smile.

Jamie looked again. Hobbes was still staring at Shona. Across his eyelid and brow there was a red scratch.

'So?' Jamie began, as the last Peepo group pulled on coats and went back on duty. Shona kept focused on her laptop, until he touched her arm.

'Hobbes expressed an opinion I thought needed correcting,' her eyes stayed on the screen. 'That cuppa Dunky had when you were talking to him…'

'Yeah, coffee. Usually does.'

'Well, Hobbes broke his cup,' Shona made eye contact. 'Held in between his finger and thumb and said *whoops*.'

Jamie's face was momentarily puzzled.

'Dropped it on purpose. And when I asked him why, he said "because he hadn't got any bleach".'

His face showed the reality was sinking in but, as his mouth opened, she spoke again.

'Said he didn't want to risk it touching his mouth if it hadn't been bleached.'

Jamie spun on his heels. 'I'll fucking kill the little turd.'

Shona grabbed his shoulder. 'Leave it. It's not like you don't abuse Dunky in your own way.'

Jamie shrugged her hand away and began walking away. 'Fuck off,' he hissed then, turning back, he grabbed a file of burglary follow-ups off the desk and headed for the door.

Paper trails. Frustration, anger, adrenalin: Shona was too twitchy to focus. 'Bit of flexi time. Make it up tonight,' and she stood. Her kit was in the car boot. Moving to Sheffield, her one indulgence was enrolling at an up-market gym.

Wireless headphones on, she ran in sync with the music video on the big screen. To her left was a glass expanse, opaque from outside, but from inside she had a clear view of the floodlit car park. 5K done and Shona was draped over the treadmill rail, when she saw the crown and trident logo on the car that pulled in.

A girl in a fur coat and short dress got out, walked towards the reception and peered in, then walked back. Shona watched her point a set of keys and the car's roof slid open. The girl got in and lit a cigarette.

Shona took her notebook and phone out of her handbag, dropped them into the treadmill's water bottle holder and began a gentle jog. After a while, a man she recognised left the building. Grabbing her notebook and phone, she ran for the stairs. Pushing her phone into a gap between the reception doors, she hit video. The girl leaned over and opened the passenger door. The man cupped the girl's jaw in his hand and they kissed. Then she leaned back and the engine hummed.

'Batting way above your average,' Shona kept filming until the car pulled into the traffic, then made her way back towards the stairs. There was a black man with a mop and bucket.

At home, she picked up her iPad and tapped *share*.

The video was shaky, but Jamie still whistled as he saw the car. 'Maserati. Not one to leave parked outside the kebab shop on Page Hall Road.' He was squinting at the shared video. 'Jesus,

GranCabrio. You could buy a couple of houses on Page Hall for less.'

Time and movement had blunted their earlier mutual irritation.

'And?' Shona spoke from the screen. 'The girl.'

'Oh, yeah. How's that bastard afford her?'

'It gets better. The registration. Bet you can't guess who Miss Fur-Coat-and-No-Knickers is?' and a series of images appeared.

Jamie looked. 'Jesus. He'd just be a bit of rough in her universe, him and his Mercedes.'

35

It was option two day and Jamie's mood wasn't helped by the realisation that delaying his initial reply had backfired. When he'd mumbled "There you go rich bitch," he hadn't considered his message was going to a work phone that was in a locked office drawer, because Marika Morcanu didn't mix business with her family Christmas.

As he waited, he checked the postcode, even though he knew the destination well enough. While he was setting the satnav on his phone, a message beeped.

Watch to the end. Won't spoil the surprise. Could be a game-changer. Call me and I'll put flesh on the bones.

'Fuck off, Dunky, you muppet,' he registered a link to follow, but just closed the app. 'Game-changer. You couldn't change your pants. Like I've got time to watch YouTube.'

When he looked up, Shona was crossing the car park. He gave the horn a blast.

'Like I'd put on a sprint to get to you,' she said, opening the car door without giving eye contact. During the drive, Jamie broke the silence by giving his version of Shona's role at the meet. Nothing in her manner suggested she was listening.

You have reached your destination.

'Stay in the car,' Jamie yanked on the handbrake and was out walking.

Shona waited a few seconds, then got out and leant on the bonnet. Jamie looked back, but said nothing. Marika Morcanu was alongside her Land Rover, wearing wellingtons and a Barbour. Her hair was tied back under a wide brimmed leather hat. She remained near the wing mirror and, as Seagrief reached her, he lifted his foot onto the Land Rover's front bumper and tightened his shoelaces. When he straightened, he'd left a muddy sole-print.

'So,' he began. 'Always glad to serve the landed gentry.'

Marika held a professional smile, but Jamie was aware of her eye-contact drifting over his shoulder.

'Thank you for coming.' Her eyes came back. 'As I said before, I believe we have common ground. But we need to establish a degree of… mutual trust.'

Jamie looked into the Land Rover, there were two child seats in the back; one contained an empty McDonald's milkshake cup.

'Sergeant Seagrief?' Marika broke the lengthening silence.

'Sorry,' Jamie smiled back. 'I was waiting till we'd got past the management-speak platitudes.'

'Maybe if we stretch our legs? My father used to bring Dominik and me up here when we were young,' Marika, starting to walk, moved beyond Jamie's obvious provocation. 'You and your colleague will be fine up here on the cinder path. Wellies are only needed lower down where the ground gets boggy.'

'Leaves are virtually all gone now,' Jamie ignored Shona, as she trailed behind. 'Last stragglers are generally clear by Christmas.'

Marika nodded, as if lulled by his new-found civility.

'Oaks are strange,' he continued. 'Some lose their leaves early, others cling on to the last.' Walking on, he looked about. 'Ash is good if you've got log burners. And hedera, okay up here but you don't want much in the garden.' Jamie continued for about a hundred yards, just trailing out random woodland chat.

As they emerged from under a tracery of branches, Marika Morcanu stopped. Seagrief felt her eyes harden.

'So? Any particular reason why you've been dropping in wrong names for various plants and trees?'

'Gives me a clue,' and he looked along the path. 'As to whether this cosy daddy-daughter walk in the woods scenario is just bullshit.'

'Yeah, well – my father knew plant names are based on Latin, just like Romanian. So, the ash tree you pointed at was a beech. That's fagus not fraxinus and hedera is ivy – that one, hedera helix hibernica, Irish ivy, you can tell because the leaves are bigger – and the big mushroomy thing back there was a bracket fungus. I'll tell you what, let's start by making one deal. I'll cut out the management-speak platitudes if you cut out the working-class hero bollocks.'

He could feel Shona smiling behind him.

'But maybe one last bit of management-speak,' Marika Morcanu adjusted her hat brim. 'Listing your issues, as I see it. You don't think we're genuine about not losing money. I'll give you accounts, leases. Whatever you want related to the unit. You think my father deserves punishing. I say God got there first. The man who used to be my father is gone. The man who ran the business is gone. But you don't believe the photograph. Maybe if you've lost the last one,' she pulled another photo out of her pocket. 'Get it tested. Then stop giving me your Photoshop bullshit.'

Jamie sank into his shoulders.

'Accounts, leases,' Marika continued. 'Profits, turnover: Companies House, HMRC. Christ, check the numbers. The unit money wouldn't pay for our postage stamps.'

'Yeah, I'm sure you've laid a neat trail of convenient information for me to find. Made sure all the figures fit what suits you,' Jamie glared, trying to save face.

'Look us up,' Marika's stare was unwavering. 'We might be rich, but we're not rich enough to fake Google.'

Jamie turned and started back to the car. As he passed Shona, he spat. 'You coming?' But instead she walked forwards.

'Nice to meet you Ms Morcanu. Hopefully, we can work something out.'

'Yeah, well we might get somewhere if your friend decides finding a solution is a higher priority than waving his metaphorical dick about.'

'Aye, well. Let's call it work in progress,' Shona smiled, lifted an arm and the two women shook hands.

Walking back to the car, Shona watched the silent burst of hostile words from behind the windscreen, then waited until Jamie had performed a frustrated U-turn before opening the passenger door.

Jamie stood next to Shona in the canteen queue, but made no eye contact. He bought a packet of sandwiches, blueberry muffin and a large coffee. 'Things to do,' he said and turned for the stairs.

Shona took her tea and biscuits to the windowless office. Taking out a cheap phone, she checked messages. It was there. Just an acknowledgement, but the speed of reply was encouraging. 'Maybe something more concrete in a day or two.' But she knew this was the best she could have hoped for, when she'd scribbled her name and number on the post-it and stuck it to the palm of her hand.

Beyond the briefing room's windows, the afternoon was heavy. Cones of low light oozed from reading lamps across filing cabinets, where occasional Peepo ghosts moved through the gloom. Jamie reached for his muffin, as Moonlight's shadow crossed to a desk and clicked a switch. A soft funnel of yellow seeped across his hands as they drifted in and out of the ellipse light.

As Jamie shook the last crumbs into his mouth, Clegg entered. She looked at Jamie. 'Had a lovely holiday. Thank you for asking. I trust all my instructions have been followed to the letter and I won't fall into a yellow snowdrift of your making.'

Moonlight's shadow sniggered.

After a few minutes Clegg peered above the frosted glass and beckoned. 'Update?' she pointed at a chair and Jamie concentrated on the bank angle. 'So, bit of progress. But no incursions on the Vulpes front, as per.'

'No, boss,' Jamie leaned back, trying to appear casual. 'Name's come up in the trawl through accounts, but just legit transactions like you'd expect.'

'And no—'

'No boss. No digging off-piste.'

'Off-piste?'

'Thought some skiing vocab might ease your transition back into the world of work.'

'Taking the piste, more like,' Clegg stood and looked out across the room. 'What's this big operation those twats are on?'

Jamie nodded towards Moonlight. 'Heard some Peepo prats blabbing about a network smuggling in clever bastards...'

'Can't want it found then, can they? Our lords and masters,' Clegg eyes followed the same line as Jamie's. 'Not if they've given it to Moonlight and his mob.'

'But since the election. It's so...' Jamie began. 'Do you never think—'

'No,' Clegg cut across him. 'Not if there's an alternative. It is what it is. And on another day, it'll be something else. I go to meetings. Meetings you don't go to because you're a menial sergeant,' Clegg grinned at Jamie. 'And in the corners people talk... Police tasks?' Clegg looked like there was something rancid in her mouth. 'Slipping towards those bald-headed bastards.

And redundancies and promotions? Some of the smart-arses have compiled a database. You're a detective. Have a guess what political views are sitting on top of those two piles.'

'And you think that's okay?'

'I think it's like watching a roundabout at the fair. Stand outside, wave at whoever's signing your pay-cheque this month and wait for things to come round again.'

Jamie's mouth began to open.

'And the only thing that goes on my social media is a photo of my dog, or a particularly spectacular pudding.'

'Bloody social media. I prefer a pen.'

'I know,' Clegg's voice dropped. 'Be surprised the stuff that gets put in police personnel files since the last election. Yours? Just a photo of your niece's first Holy Communion. Word to the wise. Keep it that way.'

Jamie stood, but Clegg reached the door before him and leaned on it. 'Remember...' her eyes flicked towards Moonlight. 'If anybody, copper or not, is playing fast and loose with the immigration laws, it's us that catches them, not him.'

'But—'

'But bugger all, Jamie. There's pointy-headed politicians and their shit-rag newspapers gagging to paint Moonlight, or one of his clones, as a cross between Winston Churchill and Sherlock Holmes.' Clegg stood away from the door.

After pulling out of the police station's underground car park, Shona parked in a side street where she could get a signal. She read the text again.

Can be available this evening. Sorry about short notice. Got work in my London office and need to be back for New Year's Eve. But be grateful if we can get ball rolling.

Below it, there was a postcode and a door number.

36

There was a single door squeezed between a chemist's shop and a taxi office that led to a flight of narrow stairs. As Shona began to climb, a door at the top opened.

'Tiled floor,' Marika Morcanu smiled. 'Bit of an early warning system,' and, as Shona reached her, she extended her hand.

'Sergeant McCulloch,' Shona mirrored the other woman.

Marika indicated a metal-legged sofa and crossed to a stainless steel sink and lifted a mug.

'Tea please,' Shona sat.

'Glad you were available at such short notice. My home and businesses are all London based now, so Sheffield... I flit back and forth.' Marika clicked the kettle on. 'And I need to make a start. Really, the gangster aspect. I have children.'

For a second, Shona saw beyond the professional polish.

'My uncle,' Marika pushed back into breezy conversational. 'It's his taxi business. Away for a few days. Taking my aunt on a mini-break. New Year in Edinburgh.'

'Aye well,' Shona said. 'Takes all sorts. I'll be jumping in the car and racing home for New Year myself.'

Marika looked puzzled for a second, off-balance. 'Oh, yes. Your accent – Glasgow?'

Shona nodded.

'Rival cities.' Crossing to the sofa, Marika placed two mugs on a low table, holding her hand still for a second. 'Bit rushed this morning. The nail varnish. I know. Too red,' she smiled.

Shona recognised the *making-a-connection* opening gambit. *Should've used a fashion magazine* flashed across her mind.

'Thank you for coming.' Marika moved on. 'I know your colleague thinks I'm…what? Just slick and sales? But you, you're…'

'Pragmatic.'

'So you'll be willing to—' Marika was cut short.

'Base my judgments on what you actually do. We've sent the photograph for analysis. I don't expect it to be fake,' Shona paused and smiled. 'But if it is, obviously, that's a game changer.'

'It isn't, so at least that'll be one hurdle out of the way.'

'Small one,' Shona nodded. 'But if you've…'

There was a folder already on the low table. Marika reached out. 'Leases. You can match them with what's at the council and land registry.'

Shona nodded.

'I've included sites where you can check out my companies, and my husband's. Easy enough to cross-reference, so you know it's not me just pushing you towards information that backs up my version.'

'And the unit's accounts?'

Marika shrugged. 'Pretty sure figures since Poppa fell ill are false. On paper income's in line with when Poppa was running it… well, slightly up, maybe ten per cent but… truth? My cousins say more girls, more punters coming in. Much more.'

'Your cousins?'

'Yes, they still have the taxi contract. Said it must be taking plenty because they're doing so many more trips.'

'But it won't be showing because taxis take cash,' Shona stared into her tea.

'No, it will. They're licensed. Everything's booked and matched to their fare metres.'

'So you could quantify?'

'My uncle's booking logs are all computerised. But that could put my cousins in danger, if it looked like they'd gone to the police with evidence.'

'If it came to that,' Shona met Marika's eyes. 'You could just tell us verbally and later, when we were doing the official evidence stuff, we could just put in a court order saying our surveillance had noted the taxi traffic, so computers were seized.'

'But your partner?'

Shona's eyes flashed at the word.

'Colleague, Sergeant Seagrief,' Marika corrected.

'Yeah, Jamie he—'

'Has trust issues, as the Americans might say.'

'Oh aye… but don't feel special. It's not just you.' Shona flicked at the pages in the folder. 'Look, this stuff is okay. Good. But you'll need an angle with Jamie. If, next time we speak, you could give me something significant about how you're going to get the girls out of this. Give them a chance of a new life?' Shona's eyes came up from the papers. 'Because,' and Shona leaned forwards. 'That's the one thing that's bothering me – the girls. You mentioned them before. But tonight nothing. So, what are they now? Collateral damage?'

'No,' Marika's voice was quiet. 'I've been thinking, but no, not collateral damage. We can do something. You're right to pull me up.'

'Pragmatic, remember,' Shona stood and held eye-contact with Marika. 'So, leap of faith time. Someone's got to take a chance to move this on. Leave it with me. I'll work on Jamie. But if I bring him, I'll need to hear how this is about the girls and not just nailing the Pole and keeping your family out of the blast zone.'

Marika nodded.

'And let's be honest, if it's just your family? Jamie won't buy it. The girls. Work on the girls angle and I'll chip away at the rest.'

'Thank you,' Marika Morcanu extended her hand.

'But remember,' Shona made eye-contact, smiled and held the handshake. 'Fuck those girls about, and if you think Jamie's an angry bastard, I'll make him look like a vegan social worker. But, thanks for this.' Raising the folder, she walked through the door.

'Where've you been?' Jamie was at a filing cabinet.

'Had a drive near the girls' houses. Spate of break-ins up there, so two birds…' Shona began rooting in a drawer.

'Dave's back,' Jamie's words brought her head up. 'His brother had a three day gap between bookings.'

Shona grabbed a notebook.

'How was it?' Shona leaned around Dave's door.

'Good powder.'

'What, snow? Or a pile of coke.'

'Why would I want coke when I've got all this excitement?' Dave was shuffling the contents of a jumbled in-tray.

After the ritual coffee, Shona said: 'That raid. London Gateway?'

'Day that politician was here for his PR photo-op?'

'The body-cams—'

'Don't.' Dave reached for a list.

Shona peered at the gaps in the signature column. 'And?'

'That little Peepo twat came down and asked for a load. I told him to piss off. Told him every number needed a signature.'

Shona waited.

'Then that lanky, big-nosed prat came up. Said it'd look bad if all his blokes were out of the office while the politician was there, so I told him to send them in groups.'

'And they all signed.'

'The first ones did, but then I had to go on a course, *Collating Evidence in a Digital Age*, and they sent bloody Pollard up from the front desk to cover,' Dave pointed to a signature and column of dittos. 'Little twat must've come back and Pollard must've…'

Shona knew that hoping Dave had some secret belt-and-braces system was clutching at straws.

'First thing I saw this morning,' Dave's finger moved to *Returned By*. Shona looked at a single signature and every other box was a ditto.

When Shona got back to Jamie, the photocopy in her hand was shaking.

'Five. Still bloody five we can't pin down. And guess who…' she slammed the paper onto the desk. 'I'm away for a coffee. Need a break from this shit.'

Jamie didn't follow her to the canteen.

Eventually, when Shona returned she was carrying a print-out.

'What are you—'

'Downloaded from my phone. Front desk's photocopier's got Bluetooth,' she sat back at the desk. 'Miss Fur-Coat-and-No-Knickers and her Maserati. Pampered cow probably thinks shagging Moonlight is edgy. A bit of rough to parade in front of her West London slaggette mates.'

'Good to see you maintaining a professional detachment.'

'Her clothes,' Shona jabbed her finger into the printed image. 'First glance, typical High Street Slut-U-Like stuff, but the cut, the accessories. To paraphrase Dolly Parton, costs a lot of money to look that cheap.'

'And she's on your agenda why?'

'Light relief. Change from body-cams and balaclavas,' she puffed out her cheeks and opened her laptop. 'Back on it now… and tonight… and the night after.'

Jamie came round and leaned.

'Getting there,' her screen was split, video and a table. 'If I track body-cam numbers around the Beautifuls, sort out signed-out names from blanks.'

Jamie nodded.

'These two numbers are close for a bit, but then drop away. He stays close until they're nearly half-way across the field. And the body cam he signed out...' she nodded across the briefing space to where the lanky second-in-command was writing on a whiteboard. 'That's him, sweeping across the field, like a sheep dog, making sure none of the sparklies get detached... and then this body-cam. Whoever was wearing this number? He's with them till they're virtually in the van.'

'How long does each individual film go on for?' Jamie touched the time signal in the corner of the screen.

'Varied,' Shona sat back. 'Under an hour and most are de-kitting, ready for the return journey, but there's eight on migrant mini-buses, filming all the way to the detention centre... could've been so much more,' Shona's voice was tight. 'If Dave hadn't been...'

'Step in the right direction,' Jamie's voice was measured. 'We can shake a few trees, see what falls out. Anyway,' he looked at the clock.

Later, after Shona had left, Jamie began filing odds and ends. As his in-tray diminished, Clegg crossed to her office. He gave it two minutes.

'Thing is boss,' Jamie stood in Clegg's doorway and began his edited version. 'Dave's pissed off because he thinks it reflects on him, even though it was that dozy Pollard that allowed the multiple signings.' Jamie showed her the list. 'I know there's—'

'Nothing concrete, but...' Clegg didn't need hints. 'Chance to talk about professional standards. *Protocol there for a reason* conversations.'

Jamie nodded. He knew she'd seize on the chance to throw some shit and, as he walked away, she was already on the phone. In his mind he could hear her. *Bloody Peepos. Bunch of jumped-up security guards pretending to be a professional police force...*

Shona showered at the gym, came home and changed into her pyjamas. When she'd finished the slow-cooker meal that had bubbled all day, she slouched on the sofa, tapped her phone and selected recent contacts.

37

'I'll keep switching between cheap, pay-as-you-go phones,' Shona was conversational as numbers were ascribed to fictitious names. 'So if you... Got a couple already?' She listened as the voice at the other end of the call explained. 'Glastonbury... Pick-pockets and flimsy doors... Yeah, I can see why a campervan would be... Exactly, own toilet and shower. So, if you... Remember, key to getting Jamie on board is what you plan for the girls. I'm off duty from lunchtime tomorrow, so before I'm back. That's forty-eight hours max.'

Shona was washing the early morning drinks mugs when she felt the buzz. The kitchen alcove was empty, so she took out the burner.

Was already sketching some ideas. Please find attached time scale and draft proposals for possible employment/accommodation opportunities for the ladies...

Shona pressed download and read. She made two coffees and began to type. She already knew her next step.

Good start, she began typing. *Suggest face to face with our friend. More impact from the horse's mouth than me just telling him. Need a meet. Same location? Detectives visiting taxi operators, movements of villains, missing persons, easy to explain away.*

Shona's face was calm and her voice business-like brusque as she sat opposite Jamie for her shortened shift. It was a front. He had to know. Get it over with. From the alcove, she'd diverted to a toilet cubicle to rehearse words. She needed to get Jamie somewhere they couldn't be overheard when the inevitable verbal explosion came. 'Press the detonator and fuck off,' she'd told herself driving into work. 'Zip up to Glasgow and stay a couple of days till the shit settles.'

If she pushed it, she could be back in time for an early evening drink that would inevitably become an early morning drink, as the first hours of the New Year slid towards the traditional four-in-the-morning taxi queue. Across the room, the Peepo bulk had dispersed. Shona leaned across the desk and whispered: 'Car, now.' Then she stood and headed for the basement.

Shona was already in the driving seat when Jamie got in the passenger side.

'What?'

'Not here.'

The deep, overnight frost lay undiminished. Gritters and the traffic kept the main roads ice-free, but, turning into a side street, the car slid.

'For fuck's sake,' Jamie swayed in his seat.

Shona tightened her grip on the wheel as tarmac became cobbles and they trundled onto the gentrified peninsula of Kelham Island. Passing swathes of trendy, new-build flats, then a cluster of restored Victorian monoliths and the towering crucible of a Bessemer furnace. Cobbles reverted to tarmac in a claustrophobic passage and, beyond a gate, trendy became pock-marked. Shona parked towards the far end where the River Don almost encircled them and limited any approach to the single road they had used. Stepping from the car without speaking, Shona walked further along the isolated splinter of land. She focused on the brightly painted cast iron arches of Balls Road Bridge and clenched her teeth.

'Fuck's sake.' It seemed to be Jamie's phrase of the morning. 'Couldn't you find anywhere colder?'

Shona eased herself even further out on a limb, hoping the surge of water over Kelham Weir might drown out the initial impact of Jamie's reaction. It didn't.

As he ranted she paced, first in circles, then retreating across the brick-strewn land. Jamie's noise followed her as she clung to the handrail, pushing close to the weir. Hanging over the torrent, she tried to blot out everything but the sound of tumbling water, fixing her eyes on the turmoil of white churning over the weir.

Eventually, she became aware that Jamie's ranting had ebbed into chuntering obscenities and she near whispered: 'When I talked about it to Jephcott—'

'Jephcott. Fucking Jephcott…' The name acted like a detonator.

Again, Shona tuned out the words, but backed away from the raging eyes, pointing finger and the eruptions of spit that burst from every hard-edged consonant.

It was as his tirade pressed her into the weir wall that the third explosion came. It wasn't planned. It was just there. Shona inhaled and the dam of her anger burst.

'See you, you fucking…' she pushed off the wall, long striding, shoulders rocking towards Jamie. His mouth was open, but she heard no sound. This time it was her eyes, her legs apart, drawing power from the ground, her finger pointing and her mouth back in a Glasgow playground. The bastard needed telling and fuck the calculations. Jamie stood and took it, silenced and shrunken but, lost in her fury, Shona was beyond empathy as her hand hit him in the chest. 'Read this, you fucking wanker. Read it and try and get your head around somebody else's life except your own.'

These were the first words Jamie had understood for a while and he looked down at Shona's hand. The fist pushed into his chest held a sheet of paper. Her fingers opened and he took it, flattened out the creases and began to read.

'It's what she's agreed. Access to her father's bank account,' Shona talked while he read. 'She's already given me details of leases and her own company's balance sheets. But I've told her we need to hear what she's going to do for the girls. I've told her we'd get the other stuff eventually, and the only place where she can add value is by giving the girls a way out. I've told her that'll be the only thing that might stop you nailing her and father's arses to the nearest wall.'

'And she'll agree?' Jamie's voice was strangely conversational now.

'That's what we'll find out when we meet her. I've told her I need to see something concrete and long-term for the girls. If we see what she comes up with. If it sounds genuine, thought out, checkable; or whether she thinks she can play the smart-arse and just give us bullshit and flannel.'

They walked back to the car through cleared air: words taken on merit, now the storm of the morning had blown itself out. Pulling off the island, Jamie was looking out the side window as she steered past the brewery.

'Sorry, if I said anything… back there. But…' she flicked on the windscreen wipers.

'Nah,' Jamie looked back. 'Understood more when you were speaking Polish. Must be why the BBC use subtitles when they film in Glasgow. All I got was a couple of *See yous* and a *Boil ya heed*… Is that some kind of vegetable?'

'Oh, aye,' Shona grinned. 'Your head. Yeah, it's a vegetable.'

Fifteen minutes later she'd dropped Jamie back at the station and was heading north. Pulling onto the motorway, she breathed to the bottom of her lungs and exhaled. Jamie: it'd finished better than she could've hoped. If she pushed it, she could still be in Buchanan Street with her cousin as the evening kicked off.

38

A couple of wheelie bins were out beyond the neat dwarf wall that separated the new build houses from the pavement and road. A man was squeezed between them, knee-huddled and hidden from the stabbing east wind. Those who took a sly glance saw a slit of eyes between a low-pulled hoodie and a nose-high scarf. He'd been there before. He'd been there a while, in his cheap white trainers and sagging, jogging bottoms; anonymous in the grey uniform of the underclass. No one looked close enough to register that his frame was denser, more athletic, than the usual sparse druggie. As the dark solidified, he shifted forwards, still huddled, but now in a position where he could observe. The nearest parking space in the cramped street was fifty yards away. It would make things easier; give a bit of time. A car turned the corner, a Ford. It slowed and then reverse-parked and its throbbing exhaust died. The driver got out and pointed his key. Lights blinked and the wing mirrors folded in.

As the man watched, his hand slid into a supermarket bag-for-life and closed around the tool of his trade. The man knew to remain still until the last possible moment. He'd got to this point the night before, but someone had come out of a nearby house and stood smoking, so he'd just remained between the bins.

As the distance closed, the man scanned along the street. Still clear. Just the driver; walking now. The man's grip tightened, but his hand remained inside the supermarket bag as the driver walked, upright and long-striding; closer and taller. Then there was muffled music and the driver pulled a phone from his pocket.

'Dunky Lal. Enforcement,' and his head was nodding. 'Okay, Mum, okay. No, I didn't forget, just getting home. With you in an hour, tops. Plenty of time for you to put a bit of chilli heat into your party food. Relax. New Year's Eve, long night. Be ten o'clock before Auntie Suki and her lot turn up.' He stopped and listened. 'You're where?... Okay, mom. Thanks, but you didn't need... Got enough shirts to last the week... Yeah, yeah, course I'm staying at yours. Promised Dad the first beer by eight.' Then the phone was gone and he was walking again; feeling for door keys now, reaching a mark.

The man's hand was out of the supermarket bag. A final glance along the empty street and he stood, timing his movement to intercept as keys and front door met. Observation told him that there was a double lock. That would give him the pause he needed. The mortise lock had turned and the Yale key was just below eye-line as the grey figure arrived parallel.

The strike sliced deep into the soft crevice beside the larynx and was then pulled outwards, severing the carotid artery. Dunky Lal fell, eyes lolling, unconsciousness the moment his blood surged towards the door instead of his brain. As he toppled like a tree, Dunky registered a peripheral figure, a split second of pain and thirty years of accumulated thoughts and memories seeping onto the pavement with the warm blood that was pumping between his fingers.

The grey man kept walking. A flick of the thumb and the blade retracted into the handle and he slipped it into his pocket. Experience had taught him that a good quality roofer's knife was money well spent. In his other hand was the bag-for-life.

His route was planned for speed and anonymity. A turn into an area between flats, communal yards, doorways, passages, garages. Plenty of out of sight corners, multiple ways in and out and, as his scouting had told him, no CCTV. In a passage within a passage, a place of echoes that would warn of approaching feet, he stopped, opened his bag-for-life and lifted out its contents; two black bin liners, bags within bags. One was empty, he shook it, then rolled it so it sat open on the floor. His hoodie went in first. There was no visible blood. As he'd calculated, Dunky's fall sent the spray in the opposite direction from where he struck the blow. Easing out of jogging bottoms, trainers and socks, he dropped them into the open bin bag. Lastly, he removed the latex gloves and they fell onto the mass of grey. Standing in his t-shirt and underpants he tied the bag's top and picked up a second bag. It contained clothes and a small rucksack. Stepping a couple of metres away, he shook out its contents and placed the full bin bag inside the empty and tied again. Then he re-dressed in jeans, bottle-green sweat-top, dark brogues and a compact kagool, before stuffing everything into the rucksack and slinging it on his back. Lastly, he pulled a woollen hat low across his eye-brows and ears. As he re-emerged into the street, his metamorphosis was complete. Stepping onto the tram, he was just another figure going home from work.

A few stops along the line, he got off and made his way to a block of commercial properties where he'd scouted out the location of an almost full skip. Dropping the bin bag into a gap, he pulled a couple of plasterboard remnants over the top and weighed them down with a few bricks.

It wasn't far to the station. Train south and away. His night was over and, apart from Dunky Lal, he'd left nothing behind that would cause any excitement.

Cars drove past, but Dunky lay beyond the beam of their headlamps, slumped against his own front door. Earlier that evening his mother had let herself in with her key. She'd hung his shirts in the wardrobe and was hoovering again; keeping her son independent and clean. She looked at her watch. Where was he? In the hallway, she unplugged the hoover and took out her phone. A few seconds later she heard *The Ride of the Valkyries* muffled from beyond the front door. As she clicked the latch on the Yale lock, the door and Dunky fell inwards. His blood and a few green chillies that had burst from a bag in his pocket spilled across the yellow carpet. That was when the screaming started. A young boy walking the short distance from his house to the corner shop stopped at the door and looked in at the blood-drenched woman. In the light that oozed from the hallway across the pavement, he could see his own shoes, clotted red around their soles and he realised his feet were small islands in a vast lake of gore. He was still staring as a neighbour with a phone appeared.

Police cars arrived first. Women were trying to get the dumb-struck boy to tell them his name and address. Forensically, it was carnage; so many feet tramping Dunky's blood up and down the pavement.

Then the ambulance arrived and, eventually, the paramedics lifted Dunky's head from his mother's lap and eased her to her feet. 'I told him Malik is best.' She kept repeating as they led her to the ambulance. 'If you want fresh chillies go to Malik's. I was always telling him.'

Official calls went back to the station; unofficial ones rippled out across the city. Jamie answered his phone. He listened, and nodded. 'Yeah. Okay.' And that was it. The death of Dunky Lal. Soon everyone would know.

39

Shona was on the M74 sweeping towards Tollcross when the message came through. She exited at the intersection, circled the roundabout and was back on the opposite carriageway. Her only stop was when the petrol gauge touched red a hundred miles from Sheffield. After nine hours driving, she repaired the remnants of streaked mascara before getting out of her car.

'Okay, kid,' Dave stepped away from Jamie as she reached the desk and cradled an arm around her shoulders. 'Didn't expect you so soon.' His eyes flicked up towards Clegg in her office, pacing around, holding her phone. 'She beat you in by a quarter of an hour. Still, that four miles from Whirlow is a bugger of a journey.'

'Had a word with the SOCO on site,' Jamie's voice sounded strangely detached. Shona saw his eyes and smiled weakly.

Cozza shuffled towards them, hunched in fleece, moaning about taxis, muttering how he could've driven, how he'd had a couple of hours sleep after the pub and the patrol cars were chasing killers, not breathalysing.

All the police and their civilian staff had trailed in. Those who'd heard early evening were soberly dressed, later arrivals were dressed in various levels of New Year party clothes, but the alcohol in their bloodstreams had been crushed by sorrow. The Peepo side of the room was unpopulated, except for two overnight admins.

The uniformed officers who were first on scene arrived. One, who wasn't long out of training, stared at the floor.

'It's Kieran isn't it?' Shona put a hand on his shoulder.

The older one, Robbo, wore the mask of thirty years in the job. 'His mum was processed quickly,' he began. 'I know that scrawny SOCO can be an awkward prat but, fair play, he was there fast and had a bit of kindness in his voice.' The man looked down at a maroon blood line caked around the sole of his boot. 'We were processed at the scene. Me and him,' he nodded, but the young officer remained immobile.

'Family liaison?' Shona focused on business.

'Yeah. Tracey,' Robbo confirmed 'Real empathetic, but misses nothing.'

'And statements?' Shona had a notebook.

'Tracey says not yet. Says the old lady's in shock. Just talking trivia: chillies and hoovers. Says we'll get nothing useful tonight. Wait for the psych.'

Clegg's office door opened and the room quietened. There were ritual *Thank you for rushing ins*, and the obligatory *One of our own* speech.

Shona watched the eyes look nowhere. Clegg turned for her office and the sound resumed. A girl came in carrying a laptop. Jamie lifted a hand.

'His diary was electronic, so I've emailed… and printed… last three months,' the girl placed a wad of paper on the desk. 'Thought it might be easier if you had both.'

Shona smiled encouragement as Jamie flicked the edge of the print-outs.

'And this,' the girl took out a large exercise book. 'He used to scribble in this all the time. Like a day book, I think.'

Jamie opened a page.

'Don't know what's in it,' the girl shrugged. 'We used to take the piss, but he said if he told us he'd have to kill us.'

Jamie didn't look up, but Shona reached across and touched her hand. The girl blinked, then strode across the room, trying to reach the door before the tears overwhelmed her make-up.

Beyond her frosted glass, Clegg was pacing again; tight circles, phone inevitably to her mouth. In the briefing room, Shona found activity revolving around her. There was no collective decision, but she was the centre that held: listening, communicating, maintaining procedure and logic. Jamie needed no instruction. His task was closed: diary pages, cross-reference contacts. A couple of times Shona saw him looking in the day book and noticed a slight smile. At midnight the boom of fireworks reverberated against the windows and, for about ten minutes, the sky shimmered with coloured fire. No one noticed.

Shona mapped out duty rosters and coordinated the constant radio chatter and phone calls. In the briefing room, people made her lists their point of reference: no ranks, no egos, just pulling together. Jamie raised his eyes for a few seconds, but then turned back to the print-outs. Shona left him to it. She knew he'd be trawling key times and contacts: the whens and wheres of Dunky's last days.

Cozza made tea and ferried food back from the canteen. 'An army marches on its stomach,' he said, placing a toasted sandwich and a banana next to Shona. 'Good job someone's playing the general.'

Clegg emerged from her office and stood until her stillness brought attention. She was already in her coat. 'Listen, I think I've secured more help on this. Dunky deserves the best.'

Shona scanned the loose circle of staff, just in time to see Jamie's back pass through the briefing room door.

'But for tonight,' Clegg was saying. 'Tie up any loose ends, then go home. The real work begins in the morning when we start knocking doors. Good work everyone.' And she whisked a long woollen scarf around her shoulders and began walking. At the door she stopped. 'Just tidy up and go. Get some rest. Tomorrow will be here soon enough.'

Shona's desk acted as a deposit point. Information was laid out and Dave Collins was attaching notes and labels when: 'Bloody hell, Jamie,' he said as Seagrief crossed the room. 'That needs sealing up and signing for.' Dave held out a hand and Jamie passed him the day book.

It was after two in the morning when Shona pulled on her coat. 'And you Jamie. We'll do more good tomorrow if we're fresh.'

Jamie nodded and carried on reading pages.

Shona was back in the station just before seven o'clock. A couple of Peepos drifted about filing. They didn't speak. Dave Collins looked in and picked up the previous night's folders.

'Need to be in my office,' he said. 'So I can stay on top of the evidence bags.'

Shona smiled.

Cozza phoned and explained how he wasn't supposed to conduct post-mortems on people he knew, but he would be in the room, making sure that the on-duty pathologist didn't miss anything.

Then it began. All those from last night arrived. Other stations sent people. Just after eight, Clegg crossed to her office, beckoning Shona over.

'About half-nine, I want to call everyone together,' and she hung up her coat. 'So where are we?'

'Be easier if you came over to my desk, ma'am.'

As they walked from the office, Clegg called to one of the Peepos. 'Oi, you bring that over,' and she pointed to a flipchart. The man bristled and his mouth opened, but Clegg hardened her eyes and he did as he was told.

Transposing notes onto large flip chart sheets and blu-tacking them along a wall, Clegg and Shona gave shape to the day.

As Shona re-checked task allocations, Clegg called everyone together and reprised her motivational speech from the previous night, ending with: 'Stock yourselves up with sandwiches. Long shift ahead and I don't want any of you flagging.' As the room emptied, Clegg asked Shona: 'Where's laughing boy?'

'Had a text last night. Says he's drawn up a list of things to follow up, so he's made an early start.'

'Playing the Lone Ranger again,' Clegg pursed her lips. 'Thought you were getting him out of that.'

Shona bounced from location to location – scene of crime, family liaison, the on-ground door-to-door organiser – while, every couple of hours, updating Clegg and, as the last sliver of midwinter daylight faded, she stood outside Dunky's house, staring into the arc lights and tents. Huddled locals shuffled by. Someone knelt and added a bouquet to the river of flowers that flowed around the crime scene perimeter. Talking, listening, moving between from colleagues, Shona ensured she had a clear picture of progress before matters were left to the overnight team and the uniformed officers who had been tasked with mopping up potential witnesses.

When Shona returned to the office, Clegg's door was open and she was standing in an irritatingly familiar pose – holding a phone. Shona went to her desk and began updating her notebook. After a few minutes, she became aware of a door shutting. As she turned, Clegg was striding towards the corridor.

'Ma'am,' Shona began.

'Save it for the morning please, Shona. I'm already fifteen minutes late.' Her coat was buttoned and her scarf around her shoulders.

'Jesus,' Shona spoke under her breath. 'We're all fifteen minutes late for something.'

Over an hour passed as she checked notes and mapped out morning shift deployments.

That was when the message flashed.

Shona gathered her bag, pulled on a coat and began moving, trying not to appear hurried as she made her way out. Inside her car, she checked the text again and pressed the phone icon.

40

'For fuck's sake,' she blurted, a few seconds into the call. 'He's where?'

Jephcott launched into a factual description, but his voice betrayed anxiety.

Eventually, she said: 'Okay. Leave it with me.' And, as the call ended, a postcode pinged onto the screen.

Shona drove. She didn't need the address, she recognised wannabe, refurbished Victorian decor anyway. The police seasonal drink-driving campaign meant the car park was quiet, but punters, seizing on the last alcoholic hurrah of the New Year holiday, had seeped out of the crowded pub onto the street.

Pushing her way through the clustered drinkers blocking an inner corridor, she opened a pair of etched glass doors. Her eyes scanned the cavernous room. Seated revellers crammed around tables and spilled from alcoves and around the bar was a deep crush of hardcore drinkers. The far end of the room was a mirror-image of where she was standing, except the etched glass doors opened directly onto the pavement. And then she saw them, close by the exit: Peepos. About four of them, mouths open, draining lager and laughing. She edged away until the crowd cut across their line of sight, then she carried on her search, praying Jamie would be this end and she could smuggle him out without being spotted. Shona could feel her own breathing shorten as she moved between tables. Then she saw him – alone in an alcove, his space defined by a wall of backs. Shona sensed his segregation wasn't random.

Jamie's eyes seemed focused below the table at his hands and, as she got closer, his mouth was forming words. A man and woman turned and glared at him, then chairs shuffled and the wall of backs closed even tighter.

'Sorry, sorry…' Shona kept smiling as she squeezed through and sat herself alongside Jamie in his quarantined space. 'There you are,' Shona's smile was broad and seemed to knock Jamie out of focus for a second. 'Nearly missed you in the crowd,' Shona was giving no gap for his words until she was settled and had a chance to exercise some control. A woman in the wall turned. 'Thought I'd lost him,' Shona mouthed. The woman's eyes rolled. 'Making new friends,' Shona's voice dropped.

Looking into his hands, she saw Jamie was holding his wallet, staring at the photograph she'd seen before, the copper-skinned toddler with the bright eyes, held in black, elegant fingers. Jamie looked at her, stuffed the wallet into a pocket and reached for his pint.

After a deep swallow of beer, he wiped his mouth. 'Are you stalking me?' His volume became exaggerated. 'Someone call the police. This woman is hunting me down.' He made to stand, but Shona pulled him back into the seat. 'Check her bag.' He kept striving for an audience. 'It's full of mistletoe.'

Backs shuffled. No one turned. Shona reached under the table and dug her fingers into Jamie's thigh and whispered through still smiling teeth: 'Keep this up and next time it won't be your leg.'

Jamie's eyes focused.

'Now,' Shona continued. 'We need to be about getting out of here.'

Jamie squared his shoulders. 'What, and leave all my new

friends before they've finished staring up their own arses? You should've been in earlier. We had a lovely Christmas discussion about how so many people in this country think they're God's gift to the world, because they live in a decent house with cupboards full of food.'

'How long you been in here?' Shona tried to shift the conversation.

Jamie pointed at his watch.

'Christ. How many pints?'

He held up a single finger. Shona was about to speak when he chipped in. 'But I had three double vodkas first. And there was another in the beer.'

'And how did our friend?' Shona didn't use Jephcott's name in public. 'How'd he… know?'

'Because he phoned with some bollocks and I told him "fuck off, I'm in the pub" and sent him a selfie of me and the vodkas.' Jamie grinned.

'At least you put in more time than Clegg,' Shona's voice was quieter now. 'Fuck knows what she's doing to drive this investigation forward. Jesus Christ, there's got to be more to being Senior Investigating Officer than spending hours on the phone.'

'Loves a phone, our Cleggy. Needs surgery to cut it off her ear,' Jamie looked at Shona. 'What's it say in the manual? "The SIO will work long and arduous hours in the initial stages of an investigation". Long and arduous, my arse. Fucking hell – you're more use than her. At least you're rallying the troops.'

'Thanks for the compliment,' Shona felt a tinge of amusement.

'Bet you a month's pay she's passing it on,' Jamie continued. 'Telling The-Powers-That-Be how our team is too emotionally involved. Sound professional, then fuck off home and open the Shiraz. Speaking of…'

Catching Shona by surprise, he was out beyond the chairs and tables and heading for the bar. Shona made a grab for his arm but missed and knocked his coat into a gap between the seat and a radiator. Lifting it out she saw, rolled up in a pocket, the printouts from the exercise book that the girl had called Dunky's day book. As her eyes flicked up, Jamie's back lurched into the crowd around the bar. She swallowed, waiting for the explosion but, by luck, he seemed to have hit a line of teens on the borderline of legal drinking, who shied away rather than assert their rights.

Despite reaching the bar, it was a while before Jamie was served and, checking there was no escalation of conflict, or Peepo sight-line, Shona scanned Dunky's accounts of dustbins and parking disputes. But then she saw paragraphs underlined in red biro. These had titles like Surveillance *19 Dec 1715hrs*. Some entries were detailed conversations; some labelled *Unit Girl*, and then some inane details; a couple referred to the security guard on the overnight delivery depot at the end of the industrial estate. Often the action was marked *As per JS discussion:* or *Police info request*. Glancing up, Jamie was still within the bar crowd. Another red scored page told the tale of a barbed exchange with Moonlight at the records office – it was headed *Enhanced access deployment*. Absorbed in Dunky's film-noir journaling, Shona was surprised as Jamie plonked back onto the seat.

'Tribute to your heritage,' he placed two whiskies on the table, then saw the book. 'Enjoy your gloat.' And his face turned away.

Shona pushed the papers into her bag then reached out and put a hand on his wrist. Jamie made to pull away, but didn't. He let her hand rest, then, after a few seconds he began to rock, just a fraction, but rhythmically in his seat.

'It's not—' she began, but Jamie turned his gaze away. Shona lifted the whisky. 'Single malt. Choice of the connoisseur,' and she tilted the glass so a microlitre touched a taste bud. 'You've—'

'Yeah,' Jamie downed his whisky in a single gulp. 'The chronicles of Dunky Lal. Reads like Philip Marlowe meets Adrian Mole.'

'Shall we just,' Shona sensed the hurt in Jamie's words and

stroked the back of his hand, but he pulled it clear and took another swig of beer and bumped the glass down on the table. Then his arm arced towards the distant clump of Peepo heads.

'Bastards,' he slurred and Shona grabbed his arm, pulling him close. 'What you looking at you tosser?' Jamie's face was peering over Shona's shoulder as she held on, desperate to make him less visible. 'Never seen a pissed bloke before? Am I offending your quasi-middle class sensibilities?' Jamie glared. 'Quasi – look it up. Not a word you'd have come across in your quasi-education.'

Shona pulled his arms down, clamping him in the seat like a naughty child, all the time smiling and mouthing apologies to the man with the quasi-education. The man turned away, but Jamie slowed his words as he addressed the wall of backs.

'Enjoy your drinks. Enjoy your cosy, central-heated lives.' And then, seemingly at random, he turned back to Shona. 'Remember that fire in London? The tower block where they kept the poor people wrapped in cut-price cladding. Metaphor for Britain. Metaphor for our glorious government and their rich mates who were offended by the brickwork. Bastards.' The last word was spat out and Shona could see the backs of the people stiffen, but in her hands she felt the tension drain from Jamie's body and his voice fell to a whisper as he spoke again.

'I pulled them out, Shona... toddlers. A baby. A wave had swamped them. They'd been for dead hours. These bastards...' his arm swept out again. 'These bastards...' again he was addressing the wall of backs. 'This government and the bastards who voted for them... they think people stuff their kids in death-trap rubber dinghies because they want a damp bedsit and food stamps...'

Then, lost in his own speech, he made to stand. Shona changed tactic and, picking his coat off the seat, she edged him around the table.

'You lot... you fucking lot think you're middle-class because you're dad bought his council house. Think you're landed gentry cos you had a picnic in the Peak District once... they're laughing at you, you thick saps. They're pulling your strings, you brain-dead Little England morons.'

'C'mon now. C'mon,' Shona's smile was in overdrive as she squeezed Jamie towards the door. 'C'mon, before somebody punches your lights out... I'll take you to Glasgow next time you decide to get pissed. Talk like that in Glasgow and they'll pay for your beer and give you a microphone.'

Shona used the general crush to cover her exit. Apologising every step and smoothing Jamie's arm, while clinging on tight, she edged him towards the street.

Outside, Shona struggled to steer him towards the narrow driveway opposite as he swayed in the cold air. Gripping his hand and clamping an arm around his shoulders, she manoeuvred him towards a car that waited by an unlit warehouse. Jephcott opened a door and Shona shoved Jamie into the passenger seat and locked him vertical with the seatbelt.

'Real crush in there,' she spoke through the open car door. 'Few bald-headed bastards, but they were at the far end, so...' Shona took a carrier bag from her jacket and opened onto it Jamie's lap. 'Just in case,' she said, but as she closed the door, Jamie's head lifted and he grabbed her hand. 'Wind him up and watch him go, that's what you said. Wind him up and watch him go.'

Shona stepped back onto the pavement and stared until Jephcott's brake lights turned out of sight.

'Oh, Jamie boy,' she whispered to herself, as she stood in the shadows. 'More to you than meets the eye. Maybe your skin isn't as thick as you wish it was.'

Shona had received the message that Jamie was tucked up in bed just before she'd got home. Visualising Jephcott guiding a semi-conscious Jamie into his flat then depositing him in bed in his underpants made her smile. She'd sniggered out loud when

Jephcott mentioned the recovery position.

Jamie woke early, but the world was blurred, so he went back to sleep. He woke again a few hours later but, by now, the anaesthetic effect of the alcohol had faded and he stared at the red insides of his eyelids. He hauled his head off the pillow and tried to focus on his bedside clock. Eventually, the fuzzy digits said 10:43. Jamie groaned and sank back. It was nearly eleven thirty before he steeled himself enough to fight the pain and depression for a few seconds. Swinging his feet onto the floor made him heave. He stood and wobbled; a pre-vomit constriction clamped itself around the back of his tongue as he tottered towards the toilet. Hovering above the white bowl, he waited, but nothing came. After a couple of minutes he knelt and positioned his head, then pushed a finger into his throat. He heaved. Another prod – a projectile surge. Two more surges, then two more dry heaves and he was empty.

'Always drink responsibly,' he muttered and slumped down the wall, face cold against the tiles, trying not to think about what might have splashed around at that height since the last time he'd bleached.

The weight of Dunky's death pressed on the police station, colouring every voice and movement. Someone had put a Tupperware box by the door and cut a hole in the lid; a felt pen label read *Dunky*, and Shona could see the silhouette of coins and notes inside. Moonlight came in and out, ignoring the box. Shona's shift ended at half past three. On the way home she went shopping. Fruit juice, bottled water, vegetables. When she opened her front door the smell of meat and onions was warming the flat. The slow cooker she'd filled before she'd left was doing its work. She made dumplings and sat them on top of the gravy, then put potatoes in a saucepan, with broccoli sitting above them in a steamer.

Jamie had showered in the afternoon. That helped. 'Keep drinking water,' he told himself, then cleaned his teeth. The electric brush throbbed inside his skull, but he kept brushing, scouring out the memory of vomit. He made a cup of tea. The print-outs were on his kitchen table. After a second cup, he began to read and finally looked for his laptop and phone. His eyes swam, but doing nothing wasn't an option. He found an unopened packet of extra-strong mints and crunched his way through three before slowing to a suck. Mints, two teas and a gallon of water was the sum total of his day's nutrition when the doorbell rang, just after seven.

41

Shona was standing on his step, holding a bulging carrier in one hand and an insulated picnic bag in the other. Jamie stepped back. The kitchen was off the hallway and she plonked the bags on a work surface.

'Warmed some plates,' she smiled and opened a bottled water. 'Thought you might be ready for something by now. I'm guessing you didn't have *The Full English* this morning,' she reached into the picnic bag. 'Won't be many minutes. It's still warm.' She began clearing the kitchen table. 'Got any tablemats?'

Jamie went to a drawer.

'What's this?' Shona reached past him and pulled out a tablecloth. 'Who knew you were this civilised?' She gave it a shake and draped the red and white gingham across the table by the far wall of the kitchen. 'Bloody hell Jamie, you'll be telling me you've got a gypsy violinist locked in a cupboard next.'

Shona talked about the day at work. How little she'd done on her own. How she'd just cleared the decks a bit. 'Ready for us to make a start… if you sit down, there'd be a bit more room to plate up.'

Jamie sat and Shona went to the oven.

'This'll *stow ya oot* as they say in Glasgow.' And she placed his meal in front of him.

Jamie smiled. After the first couple of mouthfuls his appetite made a come-back.

Shona talked. Jamie nodded a lot. She didn't mention Dunky. She didn't mention anything of consequence. Chit-chat. Glasgow, its sights and culture. Her flat in Birmingham and its views of the canal.

'My brother's still in Glasgow. Gone up-market now,' Shona sipped her water. 'Walks his cockapoo in Kelvingrove Park. Used to be a mongrel in Drumchapel. I told him, "Cockapoo? Just another social climbing mongrel".'

'Like the rest of us,' Jamie chased the last trace of gravy with a potato and sat back.

'There you go,' Shona smiled. 'A man restored,' and she poured more fruit juice, then reached into the carrier.

'Dessert?' she placed a doughnut in the centre of the table.

Jamie's hand shot out. Shona, grabbed it and held. Still holding his hand, she reached for a knife.

'Don't want you having a sugar rush. Half each,' she said, jam oozing onto the plate as she began to cut.

Licking the last of the sugar from her fingers, Shona said: 'Italian, medium roast okay?' and stood. Again she went to the carrier and took out ground coffee bags. As she reached for a couple of cups she glanced at a cluster of framed photographs on the wall. 'This your sister's family?'

'Yeah, that's our Mandy and her brood. Her and Jacko have been together forever.'

'Just a sister, then?'

'And our mam, but...'

'But?'

'Mandy sees her sometimes.'

'Surprising how we need the bitterness,' Shona slid a coffee across the table. 'Can't stand the sweetness just hanging around.'

'Could've managed a whole doughnut though,' Jamie smiled.

Shona made another jug of coffee and they moved into the lounge. Jamie sat in an armchair, Shona on the sofa and they talked – not about work; about holidays, films, about why Jamie had such a small television.

'Don't watch much,' he said. 'I like books.'

'Nature?' Shona said.

'Yeah, I prefer to be out, watching the life. There's bits of green hidden all over the place that hardly anyone sees, except the occasional dog walker. The things that happen at night. People have no idea.'

Jamie went to a shelf and his hand rested on a spiral bound notebook with a high quality, linen cover.

'It's like a hobby. Our Mandy just takes the piss,' his hand left the book and he came and sat on the sofa. 'So, that's it. My idea of fun. Walking around in the dark, watching nature; the flow. Life, death, seasons. What goes around comes around.' And he smiled. Then they both moved together and kissed. It was a kiss of recognition, of comfort. As the kiss ended and they parted a little, their eyes held a second of soft embarrassment, and then they kissed again and settled into each other's warmth.

The time was slow, relaxed, almost easy and, in time, they moved to Jamie's bedroom. At about half past four, Jamie felt Shona move in his semi-sleep. She kissed him and slid out of bed. His eyelids twitched, then settled and his breathing slowed. When his alarm woke him, he found a note on the bed.

I'm not sorry… S xx

The office door opened like any other morning. Shona crossed the briefing space like any other morning, but as she reached the desk she leaned across.

'I meant what I wrote,' she whispered. 'But maybe not quite ready for people noticing us arriving at the same time, from the same direction, yet.'

Jamie's eyes angled towards the desk, leaving Shona staring at the top of his head. His hand reached for a post-it. He began to write, then slid the paper towards her.

I'm not sorry either.

Shona folded the note carefully and tucked it into her purse.

The day was spent on the street. Shona was everywhere. Uniforms, plain clothes, support staff came to her; ranks and roles subsumed into the hive mind. Jamie fell into his solitary norm, slouched against a wall scribbling on an OS map. Shona left him to it. Over the afternoon he trudged the lines he'd marked, finally settling in a network of passages. He showed Shona and she sent in a search team, but they both knew it was a gesture.

Shona went back to the station to collate the day. Clegg was already gone. When she eventually got home, she phoned Jamie.

'Falling asleep standing up,' she said. 'And I'd only got a microwaveable meal for one in the fridge.' She mentioned Clegg and Jamie had a mini-rant, but then conversation slipped back into generalities. 'So, see you in the morning,' Shona eased towards conclusion. 'Should I be picturing you in your jim-jams?'

'Not unless you want to risk being too excited to sleep.'

'Oh aye,' she snorted. 'Excitement, terror, dream, nightmare. Some words are just too easy to confuse.'

42

Moonlight entered and switched on the wall-mounted computer screen. The room quietened, except for Jamie's voice. Shona tapped his arm, then they both lifted papers, faking disinterest but, as Moonlight launched his PowerPoint monologue, Shona angled her laptop's webcam across the room.

'The net is closing,' Moonlight pointed at a map. 'And we are the centre of the spider's web.'

Jamie suppressed a snort.

Moonlight's eyes flicked up. 'Entry points,' he continued, his hand indicating ports. 'Major cities, motorways and rail links – and Sheffield...'

Shona peered over her file.

'Where we stand,' Moonlight's arm swept over his men. 'Is the potential battleground where we take on the nest of vipers who are subverting the will of the people. Civil servants, politicians, policemen... whoever.' He held still. 'They think they're clever. They think they're safe. But they are not. We have them in our sights.' His voice and shoulders rose. 'And we will hunt them down. Them and their smuggled vermin.'

Shona watched Jamie turn his back on the fists and chants and pretend to be filing, while his lips formed a stream of silent obscenities.

Across the room, Clegg slid into her office. Ten minutes later she emerged, long-striding towards the corridor. Then Shona's phone rang.

Reaching the station's front desk, Clegg had already shook the hand of Dunky's father and had both hands clamped around the mother's. 'I promise all our team are totally focused on finding your son's killer. Every single person in this station thought of him as one of our own.'

The old lady was nodding.

'Whatever we can do for you,' Clegg's hand was beckoning now. 'Detective McCulloch will take care of you all.'

'Shona,' Dunky's mother looked across. 'My son told us how they worked together.'

Clegg smiled and, holding each of the Lal family's gaze for a moment, shook each hand again and moved away. 'Keep me briefed, Shona. And if I'm still in my meeting, make sure you call me out. This family don't leave without me speaking to them again.'

'Ma'am,' Shona moved forwards. 'He was very much one of the team,' Shona was talking as the family made their way towards the briefing room. Mercifully, on arrival, it was devoid of Peepos.

'And this is—' Shona began as they approached the desk.

'Sergeant Seagrief... Jamie,' the old lady was pacing ahead and, as he stood, she clamped him just above both elbows. 'Your name. He was always telling us. Said you were more than colleagues. Always kept him in the loop. A real pal.'

'Showed us your photo on his phone,' the father was nodding.

Jamie smiled, shook hands, made remarks about a valued friend, used words like *irreplaceable*. And all the time Shona looked at his eyes, unblinking, like glass holding back water.

Dave's arrival cut short Jamie's agony. Again the round of handshakes and expressions of sorrow and then Dave lifted a briefcase onto the desk.

'Personal belongings from his desk. Sorry, but there's a few items: phone, diary, that sort of thing, we've had to keep for the investigation.'

'Quite right,' Dunky's mother agreed, nodding. 'Nail the bastard.' The words sounded wrong in her mouth.

Jamie was sitting now, head bowed, hand masking his eyes as the family listened to various staff and their stock condolence phrases and assurances of no unturned stones.

'So,' the mother drew herself up. 'We understand about coroners and forensics and why the funeral must be delayed. Anything to catch our son's killer. Anything.' Her eyes focused on Shona. 'But... Prayers must be said. Thoughts shared. So there will be a memorial service at the temple.' A younger man stepped forward with a large envelope. 'So please,' Dunky's mother pulled out a wad of posters. 'Put these around the station. We have taken some to the Housing Department. Dunky thought of you as friends, as do we. His loss has hit us all.' And she put a hand on Jamie's shoulder.

A few more ritual words and Shona was walking with the family towards the corridor. As they reached the front desk, Clegg appeared and eased into well-rehearsed remarks.

The office resumed its bustle, but Jamie remained at his desk. Shona kept a constant check from wherever she was in the room. It was like watching a suspect left alone in the interview room, unaware that the outside world was watching on the security camera. Fetching a tray of coffees, Dave's handiwork revealed itself in a trail of blu-tacked posters: around the canteen, on doors, dotted along corridors and stairwells.

A couple of hours later, Jamie stood, pulled on his coat and made to leave. He gave a slight nod to Shona, but no words. Later, she had learned that he'd stopped by the lift and began reading. She knew the words on the poster.

In memory of our son. You are all invited to the Temple.

There was a map insert, marked with an X.

While we await the release of his body, we will say prayers and remember. Friends and colleagues, Dunky loved being with you and the acceptance and respect you held for him. As a family, this brings us comfort and so you are invited…

And the date and time was in red.

As the briefing room door closed behind Jamie, she'd continued scanning witness reports for a few seconds before the noise erupted. Sprinting, she saw one of the civilian staff clinging onto a Peepo, while two uniformed police were trying to unpeel Jamie's hand from the man's throat. Crumpled between the wall and floor, another Peepo was groaning, blood seeping between his fingers as he held his face.

'My office now…' Clegg was just behind Shona.

Jamie turned, but carried on twisting his fist into the man's throat.

'Now…' Clegg raised her voice and Jamie slackened his grip and let his restrainers pull him away a little. When a gap opened up, Jamie lifted his hands to indicate he was calm and the officers released their grip. Letting his shoulders ease he took a step away, then turned and lunged at the Peepo again. The man lurched back, his face terrified for a second. Jamie stopped short, before he could be grabbed again. He grinned at the man, then brushed himself down, making a show of straightening his clothes.

As he passed, Shona shook her head.

'What have you done now?'

'Broken that bastard's nose for a start,' and nodded at the crumpled Peepo. 'Heard it pop.'

43

Clegg's office walls did little to hide the contents of the encounter. Her voice echoed around the briefing room but, above the line where the frosted glass became clear, everyone could see the non-impact on Jamie, as he stared, unflinching, at her. Shona knew the look; knew, inside his head *yeah, yeah, now fuck off*, would be repeating on a loop.

Eventually, Clegg opened her office door. Jamie walked slowly, looking around, daring a challenge. Peepos glowered, but kept their distance. Clegg followed him out for a couple of steps.

'Forty-eight hours. Remember, I've said it at least three times. I'll email to confirm. And now this lot,' Clegg's arm indicated the room, 'are all witnesses, so don't try your "I didn't understand what you were saying" shit.'

Jamie didn't look back. Shona watched until the door closed behind him. It didn't slam. Clegg looked at Shona and called her over.

Inside the office, Clegg pulled out a chair for Shona, then sat on her own side of the desk. 'He's forced my hand,' she began. 'You know that don't you? Case so close to home? Shouldn't be us dealing with it. Against my better judgement, I've been fighting our corner, but now...'

Shona opened her mouth to speak, but Clegg carried on.

'He's cut the legs from under me. You can see that. I won't be able to fend them off after this, the National Crime Agency. They'll send in a specialist murder team and that'll be that for our Dunky's case.'

Shona said 'Yes ma'am,' and she stood. As she reached the door, Clegg lifted a finger.

'Forty-eight hours, I've told him. I don't want him near this station. It should be a suspension, but I'll log it as compassionate leave. Say he was under emotional strain.' And she lowered her voice, as if trying to draw Shona in. 'Truth be told, those two bald-headed goons got what they deserved, but don't tell Jamie I said that. You see,' and she leaned towards Shona. 'You have to play the long game. Explaining that to Jamie?' And Clegg smiled.

Between shepherding the diverse elements of the Dunky team and giving Jamie space, it was shift end before Shona phoned. But the number rang out. Across the evening, she tried again, several times. Finally, around midnight she had a text. *Been for a run. Having a walk. See you tomorrow. Meet you outside.*

Shona was in early, so were the rest of the police and civilian staff. Most wore black. A mass of Peepos sneered around the briefing room. No one spoke to them. By the time she'd got her first tea of morning, Shona knew the story. Gerry off the reception desk and a couple of young constables had seen it all.

'Should've broke the other bastard's nose as well,' Shona made sure her voice carried across the room. She looked at the Peepos, but no one met her eye.

At about nine o'clock, Clegg moved into the briefing space. She stood, feet apart, and glowered. The Peepos took the hint and skulked away. Police and civilian staff entered in dribs and drabs and waited in a quiet whisper.

'Colleagues,' Clegg began. 'It is a sad day for us all, and I appreciate how you've sorted rosters so we can release as many people as possible to attend the memorial service. I know the family will appreciate a big presence at the temple. I'm happy to hold the fort with a skeleton staff for a couple of hours. Shona,' and she spoke across the crowd. 'Please make sure Dunky's family know why I'm not there.'

As the room began to clear into car-sharing groups, Dave and Cozza beckoned across. Reaching reception, the slow beat of rain moved up tempo against the floor-to-ceiling windows.

'Left my brolly upstairs,' Shona turned and ran for the lift.

Crossing to her desk, Shona saw Clegg's office door was open and her back turned.

'Yeah, piece of piss,' Clegg was on the phone.

Shona moved quietly and listened. After a minute, she eased her way out. In the lift she leaned back and kept repeating, 'Two faced cow,' until the doors began to open and she saw Dave tapping at his wrist.

In the car, Cozza and Dave made conversation.

'Fuck's sake,' Shona said when she saw the terraced streets clogged with cars and realised how far they'd have to walk.

Jamie was leaning on a low wall that surrounded the temple.

'Forty-eight hours doesn't ban me from funerals,' he began, but then Shona grabbed his arm.

'I hate anything like this.' She pulled in tight. 'Good job, I've got you two for support.' And she reached out for Dave's hand and gave it a squeeze. After a couple of steps, she loosed Dave, but clung onto Jamie until they were through the main doors.

'Where are you parked?' Shona leaned close.

'Nowhere. Fancied some fresh air.'

'You'll get more than air by the look of those clouds.'

Jamie shrugged.

'We can squeeze one more in Dave's car. Drop you home when this is over.'

The tribe from the police station added their shoes to the line of footwear inside the temple foyer. Shona loosed Jamie's arm, took a silk scarf from her bag and draped it over her head. An elderly man in a turban passed along the line of visitors with a selection of bandanas for the men to tie around their heads.

'Always fancied trying the heavy-metal look,' Cozza whispered when the man had moved on. Shona shook her head at Cozza's socks, a grimy toenail poking out of one.

Beyond a door, a large square expanse became ornate and out of kilter with the dirt and damp of the building's exterior. Bright net and silk swept upwards like a rich tent above a raised platform with its own canopy of elaborate gold cloth.

As they stopped, Dunky's mother looked towards Shona and motioned to a girl of around ten years old, who walked over and held out a hand.

'Nani said you should sit with us.'

The three men squashed together and Dunky's father stood and walked along the cross-legged rows on the men's side of the swirling carpet. Reaching Jamie, he stopped. Jamie shook the offered hand, but had no words.

His eyes locked on his fingers as they lay in his lap, he became aware of the smell of incense and the quiet lament of a harmonium. It felt both strange and familiar, like meeting a distant cousin.

An old man in an orange turban walked towards the raised platform, bowed to a book, opened it with a silver-tipped pointer and began to read in a high-flown chant. Time passed. Jamie's hands and eyes hardly drifted apart.

Eventually, the people rose. The family moved together and mourners trailed past in a line of sad words. Shona shuffled in behind Jamie. Stock *sorry-for-your-loss* phrases eased most people through their tongue-tied duty.

'Jamie,' his eyes stayed low. 'Sergeant Seagrief,' the mother smiled and enclosed his hands in hers. 'Dunky's favourite colleague.'

Shona watched Jamie's eyes lift to meet the old woman's. She saw the weak smile and lip of water that balanced on his eyelashes until he had shaken hands with the remaining family and could pretend to sneeze and hide his face behind a large tissue.

Mourners clustered in the narrow car park, no one wanting to be the first to drive through the knots of people. Shona searched the faces. She saw Dave and Cozza and expected to see Jamie standing with them. She'd mentioned a lift but, instead, she saw his back moving away up the hill, heading away from where he lived.

Catching Dave's eye and pointing, they hurried towards the car, but hordes of mourners were snaking their vehicles slowly into the road and jamming the narrow streets in all directions. After a minute Shona got out and looked again, but Jamie was nowhere. The street rose steeply and the tangle of branches from its numerous trees concealed the pavements long before Jamie reached the brow of the rise. Shona's hand slammed down on the car roof. A huddle of Asian women spun around, shocked.

Eventually, traffic began to stutter away. 'Where the fuck...' Shona began as they pulled up at the first set of traffic lights.

'It's Jamie,' Cozza shrugged. 'What does that prayer say? Grant me the serenity to accept the things I cannot change.'

'Away and shite,' Shona hit the back of his headrest, jolting him forwards.

'Sheffield's still here.' Clegg was standing in the doorway of her office, as the returning mourners trailed in. 'Preserved by myself and my small, but expert team.'

Back at her desk, Shona began checking messages. Nothing

from Jamie. Out in the corridor she found a quiet corner and dialled.

The caller is currently...

The same thing happened twenty minutes later and again after forty. This time, as Shona returned, Clegg was talking to a man in a blue suit. She motioned for Shona to come into her office.

'Shona,' she began. 'This is DS Jackie Milhurst.'

The man offered his hand. Shona shook it and sat down.

'Known Jackie for years,' Clegg was conversational. 'Just out of training when he was with me.'

'Yeah, mean streets of Norwich,' the man grinned.

'I was a sergeant then. God, we were terrified of the tractor thieves and badger-baiters back then.'

'Different with all the county lines and drugs shit now,' Shona joined in.

'Yeah,' Clegg was smiling. 'Could've done with some drugs to keep us awake in Norwich back then. Shona,' Clegg shuffled in her seat. 'Jackie has been sent because of our current situation. Bit of an advance-guard.'

Shona waited.

'You know I've been fighting our corner, what with the Dunky case meaning so much to us all. But protocols say murder should be investigated by officers with no connection to events...'

Shona stayed silent.

'I'm not blaming Jamie. Smacking those bald-headed bastards probably just sped up the inevitable. But Jackie...'

'I'm scouting out the logistics, offices, accommodation, so my boss and the team can hit the floor running,' Milhurst's voice was well-practised. 'Murders linked to organised crime. It's our bread and butter.'

'Specialists,' Clegg tilted her head. 'Be for the best in the long run. For Dunky. But, the murdered prozzie? No conflict of interest there, personal emotion-wise. So that's still ours.'

Shona gave a cursory 'Ma'am' and shifted in her seat.

'If you can get staff in at twelve. Don't give them any details. I'll do that.'

Shona stood and, as she moved to the door, Clegg spoke again.

'You know I've put my neck on the line to try to keep it with us. You know that. But that temper of Jamie's.'

44

Shona saw Clegg leaning on her office door frame and hated her.

'Make sure they get everything,' Shona stood over a desk where two female constables were sorting files. 'Don't give her pal any excuse for letting Dunky's family down.'

When she looked round, Clegg had sidled over and was nodding towards Moonlight. 'Took a few days, but looks like he's had his bollocking re: body-cam signature non-compliance.'

Shona's 'Ma'am,' was minimal.

'He'll be into blame shifting mode now,' Clegg turned away from the desk.

Across the room, Moonlight was standing in the doorway of his office, holding a piece of paper. After a few seconds, he began tapping the door with his knuckle. The room quietened. Then he beckoned. One Peepo shuffled forwards, his gait unmistakable as Moonlight's door slammed behind him.

Shona and the rest of the police contingent were head-down working when Hobbes returned to the herd. Moments later, Moonlight strode across the floor and, as the doors to the corridor swung together, a murmur rippled across the room.

Hobbes, now no one of consequence was in earshot, squared off his shoulders and launched into his version of his ritual reprimand.

'Your orders,' Hobbes began. 'I was only following your orders. That's what I said. If the protocol was so bloody strict, why did you tell me to break it? I mean, if there's any problems, stitch-up wise, there's plenty of my mates will back me up. They know why I signed those crappy body-cams out.' Hobbes was sealed in a bubble of self-importance, as the other Peepos suppressed grins. 'I told them,' Hobbes lifted his voice to cling to the moment. 'I won't be anyone's fall guy. No, I'm nobody's scapegoat, I said. Your orders. Your cock-up, I told them… Not my arse.' Hobbes felt the attention sweep back. 'I told them. "Your cock up, my arse? I'm not having that".' His jaw jutted and his hands were on his hips. 'No, I told them. I'm not having it. Your cock-up. My…'

The Peepos and everyone in the briefing room exploded in laughter.

'What?' Hobbes looked confused for a second. 'Oh fuck off…' he glowered as the penny finally dropped and he stomped towards the door.

Jamie looked up at galvanised gates and jagged metal fencing. His coat was bulky and, Dunky-style, he pulled up his collar and took out a hat. In a drive that ran parallel to Shag City, he mooched around a plumbers' merchant, like he was checking materials for a job. Then he found it: a narrow walkway between units. Off-cuts and pallets littered the metre-wide gap and, edging behind a stack of plastic guttering, he could see Shag City's entrance and parking bays. Nearly an hour passed and a smattering of crumpled men shuffled through the door.

'Must be pension day down the Post Office,' Jamie grinned to himself. Then a red transit pulled up: a battered VW with Polish number plates. Jamie recognised the description of the thick-set man that shambled out. He had the look of muscle.

Bakula opened the van's back doors. Jamie could see industrial-sized containers of, maybe, cleaning chemicals or fuel, or both. There were ropes, hoses hanging from hooks and, on the floor, a large tarpaulin that could be concealing something, or just stiff and rumpled up into a random shape. He remembered what Katya had said about sausages and carcases. Bakula climbed into the van and moved some toolboxes. Now Jamie could see a chainsaw and a disc-cutter.

'Shit, trees and kerbstones. God help human flesh.' He could taste the potential for atrocity in his mouth.

Bakula grabbed some spanners, locked the van and went in. Jamie knew it was stupid, but he reckoned if he kept tight to the buildings he would be beyond the range of the security camera until he was so far up the street he would be blurred, or of no interest.

Emerging from the pallet-strewn gulley, he walked towards the large through-the-night delivery firm until he was at the end of the unit line that housed Shag City. Head down, close to the walls, he dodged under the sweep of the CCTV as he approached. Then, edging towards the back of the van, he crouched and sniffed. Even through closed doors the smell was unmistakable.

Moving away, tucked below the overhanging rooflines he reached the galvanised gates, took out his phone and made for the bus stop.

I'm okay. Sorry. Couldn't take anymore smiles x

'Maybe one day I'll rate a capital letter kiss.' She glanced up and Clegg was beckoning. The office was in flux. Shona squeezed through Milhurst and his NCA oppos as they boxed up files.

'Better if they're based in the main headquarters building,' Clegg explained. 'Only cause friction mingling with the team here.'

'Ma'am,' Shona sensed that Clegg recognised the resentment in her voice and lifted her tone. 'Only natural. Can see it's for the best.'

Clegg relaxed a little.

'Family appreciated the presence this morning,' Shona moved things on. 'All those hairy-arsed coppers with bandanas around their heads. Looked like extras from Pirates of the Caribbean.'

There were a couple more minutes of inconsequential information and Shona chattily repairing her earlier resentment. Then Clegg's phone rang.

Shona walked into the corridor, ducked into the small windowless room and took out her mobile. She tapped *Jamie*, and it rang out. But then he spoke.

'Sorry, didn't hear it at first. This bus is noisy and the road's full of potholes.'

'I've seen Clegg.'

'Wha…?' Jamie's voice fought against the background noise. 'Sorry. Got on one stop before the bloody high school. It's me and about ten thousand self-obsessed teenagers.'

Shona smirked at the thought. 'Okay. Look, I'll come round later. I'm on shift till five, but I'll go home first.'

Shona left the insulated bag with various hot food dishes inside in the passenger footwell of her car and walked to Jamie's door and knocked. There was no answer and no lights on. Sitting back in the car, she restarted the engine.

'Sod global warming,' she pulled her collar up. 'I'll give him ten minutes.'

Halfway to her deadline, a familiar outline of baggy sweat-top, flapping shorts and rolled-down football socks appeared at the corner. As he passed under streetlamp, light fell on his face and Shona saw him smile as he noticed her huddled in the car.

The insulated bag sat on Jamie's kitchen table as Shona stood by the oven.

'Get yourself a shower, then you can put back some of the calories you've just burned off.' As Jamie walked towards the bathroom she said: 'Might not just be the food that gets reheated.'

Jamie turned to reply, but stammered and, seeing him blush, Shona grinned.

'And maybe you'll find a way to lose the calories again.'

As she searched for cutlery, Shona saw pictures of Mandy's family on the unit above the drawers. Then, jammed between books, she noticed a photograph frame. Sliding it out, she recognised the image as a bigger version of the one in Jamie's wallet. Now the fine features of the copper-skinned girl were in focus, as were the elegant black fingers on the hands that cradled the child's waist.

As she pushed the frame back into place, its glass wobbled, pulling the copper-skinned girl with it. Behind was another photograph: an image she hadn't seen before.

After a couple of minutes, she heard the bathroom door open and managed to get the photo frame back in its place.

'Shower was scorching,' Jamie arrived in the kitchen wearing his dressing gown. 'Think I might start a support your local lobster group.'

'Shame,' Shona kissed his nose. 'The pink skin really compliments the ginger in your hair.'

The meal was chit-chat at first. What was in the sauce? Why was the pudding shop bought? But they both knew it was just tip-toeing around the elephant in the room.

'It wasn't your fault,' Shona looked at Jamie and his eyes dropped to the table. 'It was always going to happen. All you did was give her a bar of soap to wash her hands in public.' Shona let her words hang for a few seconds. 'Her door was open when I went back for my brolly. She was on the phone.'

Jamie's eyes lifted for a second.

'Don't know who was on the other end. Could've been that Milhurst. More likely his boss.'

'But I made it happen.'

'No. You were just the excuse. Just her doing her usual – both ends against the middle. Trying to look good to the troops and all the time letting her bosses know she was following the regulations down to the last comma. You might've brought it forward by a day or so. Don't even think you did that.'

Jamie waited.

'Ready to go, as per. That's what I heard her say.' Shona reached across the table and held his hand. 'This afternoon she went on about this Milhurst being here to get everything organised for their team, but it was all bullshit. I heard her confirming which offices at Regional Headquarters had been allocated. Christ, Jamie she was saying they'd booked hotel rooms instead of using police accommodation to make sure those NCA twats weren't socialising. She hadn't done all that in the time since you chinned those two Neanderthals.'

Shona recognised the fall in Jamie's shoulders and she smiled. 'Anyway, Punchy, you never told me what happened.'

It took Jamie a few seconds then: 'That poster.'

Shona's hands were on top of his and she squeezed.

' "Typical of his lot," the bald-headed bastard said. "Waiting for the January sale so they can get a discount on the funeral".'

'So you hit him?'

Jamie nodded.

'Good lad,' Shona leaned across and touched his cheek. 'See, Jamie, if you were a middle-class twat you'd just have started blubbing, then felt self-righteous for getting in touch with your inner ponce.' And they both smiled a little and Shona watched him blink, to make sure his eyes showed no trace of his inner ponce.

Red and cheesy pasta brought its comfort and Shona's voice softened and slowed. 'Suppose I've always sided with the outsider. Maybe it was being shuffled about when my mother was ill. Living with my auntie and her Polish relatives.'

'That's the curse,' Jamie's eyes lifted for a second. 'Do nothing, others suffer, but it doesn't touch you. Do something and when it goes wrong… Liliana Normova. Logic. You. Jephcott. All say it wasn't down to me, but that's not how it feels. Like you and the girl at New Street Station. How could you know?'

'Girl at New Street. Yeah,' Shona stared into her wine glass. 'That one was forgivable.'

Jamie began clearing plates and took them into the kitchen, so he couldn't hear the silence.

After a few minutes she drained the dregs and walked through. Jamie was washing up in rubber gloves.

'So,' Shona said. 'Sheffield?'

'Ticks all the logistics boxes: motorway links, trains. Back home – Manchester? Too many cupboards, too many skeletons. In Sheffield, I'm just a copper. And it's near enough to nip over to see our Mandy and the kids.'

'So, how'd ya…?'

'Contacted pretty much as soon as I was back in England. Only been at our Mandy's for a couple of days. Someone phoned. Didn't tell me his name then but, long story short, it was Jephcott. Best guess, one of the guys I'd worked with on the boats in the Med mentioned my name in certain circles. Anyway a month later I had a job interview and an apparently long-standing flag-shagger social media presence.'

'Flag-shagger.'

'Yeah, y'know. Those prats who abuse anyone who doesn't have a bulldog wrapped in a union jack as their profile picture. Anyway, Jephcott, he organised all that crap and more.'

Shona looked quizzical.

'Surely you remember our illustrious leaders' bull-shitting manifesto promises? No ex-serviceman to be left jobless. Actually, can't argue with that one. Pity it was such a brief gesture. Anyway, window of opportunity and Jephcott did his stuff – and suddenly my army records said I was a detective sergeant in the military police instead of a medic. Got me on this conversion course; military police to normal police. Even kept my military rank. So, Jephcott? Might be a posh prat with a broomstick up his arse, but he's good at his job. Conversion course was six months intensive. By the time I finished I'd learned enough to fake it till I could make it.'

Jamie finished the washing-up and hung his rubber gloves over the tap, then dropped coffee bags into two mugs. As they eased towards the sofa, he asked: 'So, Sheffield. What's your story?'

'Beyond the Jephcott deployment aspect? Fresh start. Back at it.'

'At what?'

'Detective.'

'So you…'

'Acted out of character.'

Jamie looked bemused.

'Brief flirtation,' Shona cut the silence short. 'With promotion… Listened to a bloke who told me, "transfer to traffic, you'll make inspector faster".' Shona grimaced at the coffee's first bitterness. 'Didn't tell me the price of power was a frontal lobotomy.'

'And the bloke?' Jamie's voice dropped and hardened.

Shona leaned back into the sofa. 'Like I say, brief flirtation. Chief Inspector. Record breaker, rank ascent-wise.'

Jamie's eyelids closed a millisecond too long. 'So, how did it go?'

Shona shrugged. 'Started in Birmingham. Ended in tears.'

'Fucking hell,' Jamie's mouth hardly opened. 'How can I compete with the glamour of a man who commands the traffic flow on Spaghetti Junction?'

Shona pushed him in the chest. Then bent forwards and kissed him.

After about twenty minutes kissing on the sofa, Shona excused herself and went to the toilet. 'Flashback to the teenage years,' she was saying as she came through the door.

Jamie was looking through his latest edgeland journal. Shona sat next to him.

'What's this?' she asked as she looked down.

'Television substitute,' Jamie flicked the pages. 'Remember?'

And this time she was invited to see more than the spiral binding.

'These are beautiful,' Shona extended a hand, but then felt she shouldn't touch the pages. Her eyes scanned across the fine ink-line drawings and meticulous hand-written text. For a minute she was absorbed by the journal's elegance; gradient and plant density calculations, species names in scientific Latin. 'Cozza called you encyclopaedic once, when you were out of earshot,' Shona rested her head on his shoulder and smiled to herself as the last page turned and the journal closed.

Jamie held her hands and stood.

The sheets were clean. Shona could smell fabric conditioner. Jamie was in the bathroom when she flicked the switch on the battered lava lamp and, as he entered, familiar green amoeba were tracing their trails across the room's surfaces.

'Always fancied a night in a 1970's disco,' Shona sat up and smiled, her body awash with random green.

Jamie mumbled something about feeling seasick and reached for the plug. In an instant, the random green was replaced by the flat beige of a low wattage bedside lamp, and he was slipping out of his dressing gown and into bed.

Shona held the sheet to her nose. 'Lenor... always an aphrodisiac.'

Jamie's eyes were shut. His pattern of breathing told her he was in a deep sleep.

She snuggled herself into his shoulder, then whispered: 'That photograph. She was beautiful.' Shona sensed a slight shift in the rise and fall of Jamie's chest. 'And the little girl, those green eyes against that copper skin, gorgeous.'

Jamie's eyes didn't open and his breathing held its rhythm. Shona stared at the ceiling and imagined green amoeba and soon her breathing synchronised with his.

45

Jamie didn't hear Shona's alarm, but then the Yale lock dropped. He went to the window and watched her car's rear lights shrink into the dark.

Around six he woke again and, this time, he got up and pulled on his kit. A twenty minute loop around the park in the cold and dark. He ran it twice. Lactic acid, the gift that keeps giving on Sheffield's sloping streets. Still, he could feel the improvement. Back home, showered and fed, he assembled his equipment and checked his phone. The reply he wanted was there.

Up to my elbows in a deceased pensioner. Collect from Lauren. Bring back before weekend – Personal property, not department shit so be careful. Included tripod. Need a steady hand for long-shots. Enjoy C

Jamie edged back into the spot he'd found the previous day in the pallet-strewn gully. Cozza was right about needing a tripod with the zoom lens. A handheld trial shot of a streetlight looked like a fluorescent banana.

The coming and going of the industrial estate's day began long before the January sunrise, but not in Shag City. Jamie was half way down his flask before a woman, hunched under layers of winter clothing, opened a metal side-door. After fifteen minutes, she came out, minus her layers, wearing an overall. Jamie squinted behind the tripod and the Nikon lens captured pin-sharp images of the woman's face and mop. Over the next hour, the woman made repeated appearances, shaking dusters and emptying buckets down a drain. Then the door stayed shut. Around eleven o'clock she came out again, but now dressed in barmaid-chic. Leaning against the building, she lit a cigarette.

'Bloody hell,' Jamie lined up the camera. 'Film-noir – Yorkshire style.' Twelve million megapixels zoomed in on crow's feet ridged with make-up and a lip-stick ringed cigarette filter.

The woman breathed out a final cloud of smoke, trod on the cigarette butt, and turned. She fiddled with a bunch of keys and the big roller shutter rattled up. Jamie was back at the camera. Inside, the light was fluorescent and tucked against a wall was an exercise bike and a bench with weights.

'Fucking man spa,' he grinned to himself. 'Boys toys for Bakula, more like.'

Near the door there was an office and a reception area. He could see containers in neat rows and stairs leading to a mezzanine floor and the impression of more cuboids. Then the woman went inside and must have flicked a switch because fluorescent lights were replaced by strings of dim multi-coloured bulbs zig-zagging between the containers.

Around noon a smattering of blondes straggled in and sat in the reception area, seemingly chattering, while the earlier woman sat behind a counter, her face hidden by a computer screen. About the same time as the day before, the first customers arrived; a sparse succession of the elderly, unemployed and occasional shift-workers trailed across the lunchtime.

'Jesus,' Jamie whispered to himself. 'Stick a couple of girls on the Meals on Wheels van and they could really rake in the grey pound.'

Around three-thirty, the red VW van arrived. Bakula stepped out and opened the van's back doors. The courtesy light came on and its contents stood out in the falling dusk. Jamie eased the zoom to maximum. The whole incident seemed to play out in slow motion. Bakula loaded on a couple of large containers of liquid and a tarpaulin and then he was slamming doors, checking handles and climbing into the driver's seat, reversing onto the drive and away.

Jamie packed up his equipment, shuffled back down the gulley and retrieved his car. A mile or so later, he pulled over and sent a text.

Enjoy your night. I'm back in the morning and he added a winking emoji. Shona had a visitor and Jamie was glad. He'd enjoyed the comfort of her in the bed next to him, but since Cara and Sierra Leone his default setting had been to live inside his head. Happiness, comfort: these were feelings that could only be endured for brief intervals. Like a diver who fails to decompress, a rapid transition risked disaster.

'Enjoy your night, hen?' Jame spoke in faux-Glasgow across the desk as the morning shift began.

'Aye, had a nice meal and a natter up by the Winter Gardens, then back to mine,' Shona had told him about her cousin stopping-off on her journey to a job interview in London. 'Wasted a few quid on transport though. Three taxis and no drink. Marie said she wanted a clear head for this afternoon and was on the early train to give herself time to settle.'

Chat and routine merged and attention fell on a manila envelope of Clegg tasks that were supposed to fill the Dunky gulf. Jamie snorted and pushed them across the desk, then took out his phone and plugged in a lead that trailed from the computer.

'Didn't waste my suspension.' A folder of images appeared on the monitor.

'So, overall?' Shona shuffled her chair until she had a clear view of Jamie's pre-van images.

'Overall?' Jamie was scrolling. 'Like fairyland meets zombie-apocalypse, with the cadaver of Marlene Dietrich on the front desk.'

Swiping the screen, the Bakula van images appeared. Jamie's fingers zoomed in and Shona leaned close. A handle lying between boxes held the possibility of a chainsaw and the containers, their labels enlarged and legible, matched what Jamie had smelt the previous day: *Sodium Hypochlorite* – industrial bleach.

'That's it,' Jamie placed two hands on the desk. 'I need to see inside that place. Get a sense of the locus.'

Shona didn't speak, but her face was saying *fucking locus*.

Jamie flinched and flustered. 'Need to speak to Katya. See if she can get a key or something.'

'Yeah, well now Bakula's back, a few words brushing past her in a shop is about the best we can manage without putting her in danger.'

'There's that phone.'

'Oh yeah,' Shona was stony. 'Like she can chat away on that in English, confident that no one else in the house is going to hear.'

Jamie disappeared to the canteen and Shona trawled back through the images. An email pinged onto her phone; a list of low-level burglaries.

'Clegg,' Shona pushed a print-out towards Jamie as he returned with two mugs. 'Just wants us tied up so we don't irritate her pet out-of-town Crime Squad boys.' Shona pulled on her coat

'Don't worry.' Jamie stretched back. 'I've seen this before. She hasn't got the stamina to keep it up. More interested in going out to meetings. If we split up. You keep focused on Shag City stuff. Me? Bit of breakfast, then make a minimalist gesture.'

Shona gathered files and her laptop and decamped to the

windowless cube. A morning of cross-referencing lay ahead. The dull grind of detective work: financial records, times, locations, boring shit.

'Got myself a sandwich,' Jamie poked his head round the door. 'So, I'll drive up and make a start.'

Shona visualised the pile of food wrappers on his back seat.

'Knock a few doors. Get a couple of replies to write in the log, then shove a load of these through letterboxes and pretend no one answered.' He held up a wad of *sorry-to-have-missed-you* postcards.

Around noon, a message appeared on Shona's phone. Five minutes later, she was in the car park opening Jamie's door, but he was sat in the passenger-side.

'She's got it sorted. Says anytime before two,' he held up his phone. 'You drive, I'll call as we go. I'll be like a fart in a colander till I find out.'

In the city centre they huddled through the winter-wrapped shoppers. Suddenly, Jamie ducked into a shop. Shona swore. A minute later he was out with a pasty.

'Training tonight. Be rammed in half-an-hour.'

Jamie gradually slid more pastry out of the greasy paper as he ate his way down, finally scrunching the empty bag into a waste-bin outside the bank. Inside, they showed their ID cards to the lad on the reception desk. He pressed a buzzer and they were led through.

'Greggs?' the Walsall bank manager looked up as Jamie stepped into her office. 'Know that cheeky pastry flake anywhere.'

Jamie wiped his hand across his mouth.

'Anyway, rather than keep you in suspense with tales of the Walsall pilgrimage.'

The bank manager turned her laptop towards Jamie and Shona. A video clip showed the rent-collector in the queue: a narrow strip of flesh exposed between his hat and his scarf. But then he reached the counter.

'You bastard. You fucking lanky, hook-nosed bastard.' As the man pulled down his scarf to speak, Jamie was staring at a face he'd seen countless times before.

'Could've just emailed it, but...' and the bank manager handed over a small memory card.

Jamie was almost at the door, as Shona struggled to get out her *thank yous* and *we really appreciates*.

'I know,' Janine Bowker exhaled. 'We had a Jack Russell like that once.'

And repeating her *thank yous*, Shona strode to catch up.

46

'He won't be there. You saw the notice. Anyone of his rank is at that Harrogate conference.'

Shona knew driving was her best chance of keeping Jamie out of conflict. From the corner of her eye she could see frustration and anger rippling off him, like air shimmering over a bonfire. After twenty minutes on the road, the January sun gave up the ghost and Jamie was reduced to a silhouette against the light from shop windows. Shona kept driving. Then, somehow, she sensed the change in Jamie's shadow and knew its anger was shifting from The Buzzard to self-loathing. Ten more minutes on the ring road and she turned right towards the reservoir behind the university car park.

'It's not...'

Jamie glared.

'It wasn't obvious. Wasn't even close. Balaclavas, stab vests, riot-duty overalls. Could've been any one of them. You can't blame yourself for not being omniscient. Even in your own little world, you're not God.'

Jamie's eyes were lower now. Even in the dark, Shona could tell.

'Guilt, blame. That's what I told Jephcott drives us all on,' Shona said. 'We all have it. If we didn't, we'd do no good. We'd all be self-satisfied little shits with no regard for anyone else's life.'

'And because you were slow finding your way around New Street Station you'll carry the guilt to your grave?'

'You can be a bastard sometimes, Jamie.'

'Yeah well, the girls all love a bastard. Wasn't there some comedian did a routine about that?'

Shona sagged and went quiet. Then, across the dark, Jamie squeezed her hand in a wordless apology.

'New Street Station. If only,' Shona whispered to herself.

Jamie lifted Shona's hand and pressed it to his lips.

'Those little number plates,' Shona's head shook a little. 'And the car. Same make and colour. Same nationality. What were the chances?' She looked at Jamie. 'Armed Response.'

'You were Armed Response?'

'No, but my boyfriend, Mr High-Flying Traffic, was co-ordinating the road closures for the hard stop. I was following. You know how it works, Armed Response forces them to stop, then a processing team jumps in and makes the arrest.' Shona seemed lost, looking at her hands, but then: 'So we were trailing a Czech gypsy gang. Big players. Mainly illegal tobacco, but some arms. Usually they dealt in old revolvers for street gangs who just want a bit of crash and flash, but this one was different.'

Jamie waited.

'Intel said they had a couple of machine pistols. Street sprayers. Hundreds of rounds a minute. Anyway, Hard Stop was classic. One car in front, one box in from the side, then the third screaming in behind. There was all the usual shouting – "Armed police, hands on head," blah, blah… Prosecution tried to say it was inadequate planning. Should have had a Czech speaker doing the shouting.'

'Like we're littered with Czech speakers,' Jamie's voice was low.

'Well, maybe, but the shots came before all the words were out. Three shots, rapid. Story was, his hand moved – that he was reaching under the seat.'

'Makes me sick the way barristers tell it,' Jamie squeezed her hand again. 'Supercilious bastards, unpicking details like everyone's got hours to reason it all out. Maybe if they knew what looking down a gun barrel felt like.'

'Except it wasn't all by the book,' Shona's eyes rippled with tears. 'And it was a cock-up. Wrong car. Like I said, same make and colour. Probably just saw CZE and the little flag on the number plate, not the actual number. They were builders.'

'But his hand moved.'

'Reaching across his body. Probably just undoing the seat belt so he could get out.'

'Would've known it was police, though.'

'Yeah, but maybe not understood the *hands on your head* bit.'

'But you said he was reaching forwards... maybe under the seat.'

'Or maybe just folded in half by the first shot. First shot was body. Next shots were virtually immediate.'

'Thought standard protocol was subsequent shots were only if the danger was ongoing.'

'It is. That's the way we told it in court.'

As Jamie looked, Shona's eyes focused nowhere.

'We all said there was a gap. Between shots one and two.'

'But?'

'But there wasn't. Shot one. Split second. Two and three – bam-bam. First shot folded him in half. Second and third went through the top of his head. Medical evidence said he might've survived if there'd just been one shot.'

'But it all happens so quickly. Easy when it's not your split second decision.'

'True, but he had previous. Armed Response had turned him down a couple of times: too gung-ho. Type of prat who spends his days off playing *Call of Duty*. He was always going to fire those extra shots. But I went along with it... the co-ordinated response.

Amazing how many police cars arrived simultaneously. How many officers were out of cars with a clear view of the whole situation.'

'But sometimes…'

'Sometimes,' tears were running down Shona's face now. 'You should do what's right… because in the end it only gets worse.'

'The court case went tits up?'

'No. Some days I wish it had,' Shona's hands were shaking now. 'Not just some days… the court case was long over. We were all well out of any frame. No blame attached. God, no blame. No come-back…' and Shona's words fell away into sobs.

'Seems so significant, here,' Jamie passed over a pack of tissues. 'The death of a stranger or two. In Africa…'

Shona's eyes cut across Jamie, but then she mopped her cheeks, set her face and started the engine. 'Think I'll have an hour or two at the gym. See you at work.'

'The gym?' Jamie unclipped his seatbelt. 'Thought we were… so… morning then. Suppose I might as well go for a run myself then. Sure you…'

'I'm tired.' Shona pushed the gear stick into first. She let him kiss her on the cheek as he got out of the car, but she'd pulled away before he'd reached his front door.

The dark seemed a comfort as Jamie ran, episodes from Shona's story washing in and out on the tide of thoughts.

'So, you've still got a sliver of space for me in your life, now you've finally trapped another unsuspecting woman?' And Cara's voice was there with its familiar, teasing tone.

'Sorry, I'm…' he stammered. 'I was…'

'Will you tell her you talk to your dead wife? That'll go well.'

'No. I'm not mental. I know it's not you. I know it's just my imagination, saying what I think you'd say.'

'Or hope?'

'Yeah, well, that's the danger. I make excuses and use your voice so I can kid myself it's not just selfishness.'

'I am the voice of your hopes? Then why do I spend so much time bollocking you?'

'Maybe I just miss it. Or maybe it's easier to face uncomfortable truths if I hear them in your voice.'

'Maybe you should listen to another mouth. One that's still breathing.'

'Like who?'

'Like, who do you trust? Claudette? You always called her the voice of reason; especially if she was disagreeing with me.' Cara's smile formed in Jamie's mind. 'Who else?'

'Mandy.'

'Yes, Mandy,' Cara echoed. 'So there, two voices not in your head. Have you told Mandy yet?'

'Not something for the phone and... early days.'

'You're seeing her tonight?'

'No, just running.'

'Running? And this woman's...'

'Said she was going to the gym. Needed a rest.'

'Can't imagine a woman wanting a rest from you, Jamie.'

'Maybe when she told me about the Hard Stop.'

'Hard Stop?'

'Come on Cara. You're with me. You know what I know.'

'Sometimes I see and hear what you don't, though... seems so significant here.' Cara was tutting. '*Death of strangers...*'

'I just meant Africa is different. You adjust to the norm. Two dead strangers? Be a quiet morning for us some days.'

'And you said that to her?'

Jamie could feel her incredulity. 'Not...' he stopped running and leaned back hauling in air. As oxygen flooded back, the insensitivity of his words washed in and he went to speak, but Cara had said her piece and slipped back into the depths behind his eyes.

47

'But that's just him,' Shona reached the top of the concrete stairs that led to her flat. 'Not like I didn't know it before I climbed into his bed.'

The security lighting cast random stripes into the shadows. There was a rippling sound. Shona froze for a moment, but then recognised it as the familiar flapping in the wind of next door's weft of washing lines.

Where the stairs opened onto a small walkway by Shona's door, there was a timber shelter for her bins. A flash of orange supermarket bag was trapped in its door. Actually, it was two bags, heavier than they looked.

Once inside her flat, she tipped the bag's contents across the floor: two identical signs: *Dacian – Taxis to Trust*.

There was a note taped to the bag, but she knew who they were from.

Spare set from my uncle. Might help. His cabs are everywhere.

The signs were flexible, but didn't seem to know if they were supposed to be metal or plastic. Sticking one to her fridge, she unlocked her phone.

Shona picked up a folder and stood as Jamie reached the desk.

'Sorry, didn't mean…' he began.

'Okay. Water. Bridge. New day.' She gave a slight nod and began walking. Jamie waited for a couple of minutes and followed to the car park.

'Lunchtime.' Shona opened her boot and Jamie looked in. 'I texted her overnight. We'll take her in for her afternoon shift. She says they block book taxis last thing at night. Multiple girls finishing similar times. Slacker earlier on, so they start in dribs and drabs and make their own way in.'

Shona touched his hand as they walked back to the lift. 'You were right about Clegg not keeping it up. She's at Regional HQ today, but there's no updates on yesterday's job list.'

'Like I said, she's always the same. Too many horses and only one arse. Just one thing on her mind today. How to get to the front of the buffet queue.'

'So, I'll see if that bank manager can stick some more flesh on our potential skeleton,' Shona began to text. 'If we could see her before lunch—'

'Put these in your text,' Jamie reached inside his jacket. 'She might have a chance to dig something out before we get there.' And he handed her a folded sheet of paper. 'From Dave. Not sure if he hacked the central computer, or just sidled up to a filing cabinet in personnel.'

'Would it help if I just got you a key cut, then you could just let yourselves in?' the bank manager shoved a plate of biscuits across the desk. 'But anyway, that stuff you sent. Lucky my regional manager cancelled, so I had a spare hour. That sort code and account number? Colleague managed to access the paying-in details on his wage records.'

'The Buzzard,' Jamie was scanning the transactions record.

'Hayden,' Shona leaned in. 'His name's Hayden.'

'Yeah, but it's a business account. Solar Properties and...' Janine Bowker turned her screen. 'Pays in on a similar day each month. Always uses the company's paying-in book. Always cash. Anyone can deposit, but he's not on the account so he can't make withdrawals or transfers. My guess is he just keeps an agreed wad of notes. Actually, more than a guess. That sort code and account number in the name of Hayden. Not one of our branches, but it's local and I know the manager. His brains are in his balls when he's talking to me. I've only got to mention rigorous fiscal discipline.' Her eyes flared over the rim of her tea cup.

Shona half-suppressed a laugh.

'So yes. The name is Hayden and,' she reached for another print-out. 'No payments or receipts linking him with the account that he's paying into here. Mr Solar Properties? That's somebody else. This bloke, Hayden,' she leaned towards Jamie. 'His account just shows the usual stuff: council tax, gas and electric. But not many cashpoints, or shopping paid by card. So, if he has a wad of cash each month... but this Solar account? Keeps a bit of a balance, but mainly it channels money elsewhere. There's a UK deposit account with links here. Then there's those other accounts. Poland and Bavaria. Again, pretty much a single monthly payment to each. But, if I can get time? Trawl through in a bit more detail...'

Jamie propped his chin on a hand. 'Play that security video again.'

'If you've still got the receipt for the charm lessons, I should ask for a refund,' the bank manager clicked her mouse.

'There. That carrier bag. Like you said,' Jamie was pointing as The Buzzard walked away from the counter. 'Hundreds of quid in notes, looks like fuck all in a carrier.'

Katya dodged out of the café as Jamie's innocuous grey car pulled up, with Dacian Taxi signs stuck to its doors. Shona was lying in the back. Katya squeezed in, squinting down. A couple of corners turned, the road was quiet and Shona sat up next to her.

'Sorry about that. Thought if someone saw you getting into a cab that already had someone in it...' Shona went through the small talk. Comments on clothes, how good Katya was looking and so on. Then she said: 'We know who he is... The Buzzard. He's Peepo.'

'But not the top man,' Jamie turned towards the university car park. 'He's just the bag carrier. Someone else is skimming off the real money.'

'Bakula?' Katya sounded unconvinced.

'Yeah, but not just him,' Shona said. 'Most likely Mr Solar Properties is a Brit who works with Bak—'

'Only saw Buzzard,' Katya cut in. 'Only when he collect rent.'

'And there's no one else you...'

'Only one that Kaliningrad girl say smell nice. She say he boss man. Shouting orders on way to van.' Katya stopped for a second. 'Kaliningrad girl saw Buzzard collect rent, day or two before she go. Buzzard flirt with her, but when he gone she say "Not waste shag on him".'

'And none of the other girls... with this boss man?'

'Not say, but one night, Kaliningrad girl, she joke about shagging against van. Loud bitch. Laughing, say about struggle with belt. Copy what he say. Pretend she drown in his nice smell. "Sweet as," she say, and two girls...' Katya moved her head and eyes.

'Flinched?' Shona supplied the word

'When say, smell good. Sweet as...'

Jamie's eyes narrowed.

Katya shrugged. 'Girls say was man shouting orders, when they run. Dark. They scared. Not sure. But say, later, van stop. Hear someone get in.'

The conversation paused. Shona took out a flask from her bag. As Katya sipped her coffee, Shona passed a cup to Jamie and reached for a magazine. After a few minutes there was a lull in the dissection of the glossy images and Jamie coughed.

'Might help if I could—'

Shona's head turned, then froze in position.

'If I could get a proper look,' Jamie's voice was quiet and measured. 'Inside, I'm sure something would...'

Katya's eyes stayed steady. 'One way in and out. Metal on windows.'

'So, I'd have to pretend to be a...'

'Then make your excuses and leave. As the old tabloid journalists used to say,' Shona sounded calm.

'Your face...' Katya spoke slowly. 'You round unit and shops a lot. If someone see you... you have that look... police way of looking at people.'

'Wear a disguise,' Shona offered. 'And hope the girl you get doesn't mention that you paid, but didn't do anything.'

'Maybe wear no disguise...' Katya was holding back a grin. 'And hope girl goes into shock and lose memory.'

Shona began to chuckle and took the coffee cup off Jamie and drank its dregs.

The drive to the unit was more magazines and soft skills and Shona was lying down again well before they reached the galvanised gates.

As she got out, Katya turned. 'Unless you wear disguise and book me.'

When Jamie pulled onto the main road, Shona gazed out of the side window and said: 'Need helluva disguise. And Katya? If someone has seen...'

Jamie turned on the radio. Some prat was apparently disappointed by a shortbread biscuit and raspberry coulis.

At the station, Milhurst and two grey suits went into Clegg's office. One of the canteen staff appeared carrying a tray of coffees. There was raucous laughter as they opened the door for her.

'Bastards,' Jamie ground his teeth and reached for the list of post-burglary follow-up visits and a pile of *sorry-to-have-missed-you* postcards.

Clegg's head appeared above the frosted glass.

'Here she is, our flexible friend,' Jamie grabbed his coat and was across the briefing room before Clegg opened her office door.

'Shona, if you and Jamie can bring Jackie and his gang up to speed on the state of play with the Lal case.'

'Sorry ma'am,' Shona entered the office, nodding to the suits. 'Jamie's cracking on with the Gleadless estate burglary list.'

'Jamie, cracking on. Not words that usually inhabit the same sentence. Still,' Clegg turned to Milhurst. 'I know there's nothing that Shona hasn't got a handle on. She was de facto coordinator on the ground.'

Jamie spent twenty minutes pushing postcards through doors to establish a presence, then he was driving again, heading for the environs of Shag City. Ghosts of hooded youths shouted in the twilight at the precinct's heart. Jamie wandered about, as if he might absorb knowledge by osmosis. There was a café. Jamie peered in, then entered.

Ordering a mug of builder's tea, Jamie carried it and a milkless china cup to a table. Mihai looked up.

'See,' Jamie moved the cup towards the old Romanian. 'I remembered, Earl Grey.'

It was shift end when Jamie got back to the station and Shona was in her coat. She'd sorted a pile of documents and she was going to drop them off with an admin clerk to be scanned for Milhurst.

'Enjoy your fresh air?' Shona kept her eyes on the papers.

'Yeah, then practised my legendary soft skills over a cup of tea.'

'Legendary? More like mythical,' Shona's focus remained on the scan fodder.

'And you…?'

'Forty minutes of being patronised and a couple of hours doing this mindless crap.' Her eyes lifted for a second. 'Nothing I'm not used to.'

Jamie turned away, then stopped and shuffled back. 'If I'd gone in there with them. With Clegg spouting bullshit. You know what would've happened.'

Shona exhaled.

'Talked to the old guy, Mihai,' Jamie stared at the floor.

'And it was worthwhile?'

He shrugged.

'I was serious,' Jamie said as they walked to their cars. 'About getting a look in that unit.'

Shona lifted a key and her car beeped. 'Took something out of the freezer this morning. Going to the gym now, but if you want to come round later?'

She opened her door. Jamie smiled and dropped his eyes. He looked up as her engine revved, then watched her drive away before turning towards his car. Getting in, he began scrolling through his messages. A van pulled up and a man in a hi-vis jacket got out, carrying a plastic case and a clip-board. Jamie read the side of the van, got out and followed the man into the station.

48

'Another step away, Fatboy?'

Cara was in his mind even before his car pulled onto the main road that ran past Shona's flat. Behind him, wrapped in a thin dressing gown, Shona smiled from her window.

'Don't think I didn't notice you switch my pretty green light off the other night. Seems you prefer beige these days.'

By the time Jamie reached home his mind was sparking, a thousand miles from sleep, and he could only think of one cure.

Before slamming the door behind him, he pulled on a head torch. Turning a corner he kicked into a sprint, but his change of pace was leaden. Offering up the sacrament of his pain, he forced his legs towards a canal bridge. This wasn't Liliana's bridge, that was a few miles away, but it would do. Jamie jogged down then sat on a wall, letting the January wind slice through his sweat-soaked shirt and claw at his bare legs. He looked up and waited for Cara to speak again. He could feel her but no words came. Even in life, she'd known when to leave him to face his demons alone.

The pre-dawn moon was hazed with frost. Stillness and the ice of the night cooled his body. He tried compiling a mental list of nearby shrubbery to distract himself, until the pain reached an intensity that might pay back some of the debt he owed for his brief hours of feeling human warmth in Shona's bed. The moon fragmented into white slivers as the wind rippled the black water. Jamie looked down and imagined a disjointed torso drifting just below the surface. The cold passed into numbness and Jamie felt his eyes close. For a few seconds he enjoyed the dark, but deep down he knew he didn't deserve the slow drift into unconsciousness that hypothermia could deliver. He stood, shook himself and began to jog, easing up to the bridge and the world of streetlights.

Back in his flat, he stepped into the shower, gritted his teeth and turned up the flow, so the intensity of the numberless pin-pricks multiplied until the heat of the water brought him back to a warm-blooded state.

Dried and in bed, he knocked the beige bedside lamp off. The message light on his phone was winking. He flicked the screen, then texted back: *Good. Stops us treading water and wasting days – X*

Three hours later, Jamie crossed the briefing space on aching thighs. As he sat, Shona leaned forwards.

'You stay there, I'll get us both a coffee. Men's legs have usually stopped wobbling by mid-morning after a night with me.' As she walked down to the canteen, her phone vibrated. She recognised the number.

Hope package useful. Drafted out some details. Face to face? Both of you? Same place? Possible dates/times?

'More time-filling crap,' Shona pointed at an email from Clegg on her laptop. 'But her heart's not in it.'

'Couple of hours max,' Jamie leaned over to read. 'More—'

'More my sort of thing,' Shona tilted her head.

'Means I could have a word at that firm with the Shag City contract, like I said last night. Pick you up after?'

'Always happy to help the police,' the manager pointed at the desk. There was a checklist on a clipboard, a handheld scanner, lanyards, an array of hi-vis and a plastic attaché case. 'You can have all the kit whenever, but if I can have a headshot? For your ID card, not an assassination.' The man grinned. 'If you email one over. Just let me know when you're ready and I'll have everything sorted. Company mobile and we've got overalls in stock, all sizes.'

'Perfect.' Jamie held out his hand. 'Real big help. Some people wouldn't…'

'Twenty-five years as a fireman, so…' and the meeting eroded into nostalgia.

Shona's day was filled with the grind of evidence: bank transfers, dates; the vital boring slog of paperwork and account checking and a minimalist sweep through Clegg's time-wasting crap. At the end of the afternoon traffic was building up. It was a short drive home, so she dropped her car off and walked the few minutes to the tram stop.

The last light of the day retreated towards the Pennines and the fluorescent-lit bubble that was Meadowhall shopping mall glowed against the gloom. She'd told Jamie to meet her in his car so they could get Clegg's crap over with and, at some point, she'd mention the real business of the evening.

Shop after shop, manager after manager, she was given the same old message: 'Out of town. Stealing to order. Could be anywhere by now.' Most shrugged. It was an old story. Organised gangs. Building Meadowhall next to the motorway wasn't just convenient for shoppers. Eventually, they'd made their gesture.

'Go left,' Shona left it to the last minute as they were pulling off the car park. 'We've got an appointment.'

Light washed across the pavement from the chemist's window. Next door, the taxi control room was dark, except for a girl in a headset haloed against a low-watt light bulb. Shona watched Jamie get out of the car. He hadn't spoken since she'd told him who they were meeting. There was a doorway with steps inside. At the top were three doors. Jamie stopped, but Shona reached past him and knocked.

Stepping into the office, there were folders spaced equidistantly across a low table. Marika Morcanu was standing, wearing jeans and a simple knitted crew-neck.

'Coffee, tea?' she indicated they could sit on the small sofa and, as she flowed through the opening pleasantries, the kettle kicked in.

Jamie leaned and whispered: 'Dressed down. Tried to make us feel at home.'

Shona remained quiet; the cut of Morcanu's jeans spoke to her, even though any logos were hidden under the ribbed waist of her jumper – *Paul Smith* in a muted lemon cashmere.

Marika Morcanu placed mugs on the low table, then sat opposite Jamie and Shona and reached for one of the equidistant folders. 'I expect you've already done some checks on these? Leases, accounts, balance sheets, as per email.'

'Enough for now,' Shona held Marika's gaze. 'So maybe move onto proposals that might convince us that you aren't going to treat your father's human assets as disposable?'

Marika passed over two folders. 'Identical copies… if you'd like to look over them.'

Jamie pored over the pages. Shona contented herself with checking it matched what she had already been told. If this didn't do it for Jamie, she couldn't think of a plan B.

Marika Morcanu waited. Shona imagined her in numerous business meetings, looking confident while the other side checked the details.

After a couple of minutes, Marika said: 'So, we'd be looking at doing a skills audit and matching it to vacancies and projections.'

'But given that you can't speak to the girls till Bakula and whoever else is out of the picture?' Shona's tone was steady.

'Yes, but once we're there it can be pretty quick and…' Marika turned a page. 'If the audit goes the way I expect, jobs won't be a problem.'

'Easy to say, but there'll be employment costs,' Shona held eye contact.

'There always are, but the family businesses are expanding. Staff coming and going? Happens all the time. I thought, if we agree to pay their accommodation for what, three months after? Give us time to assess them. Some of them might need to be patient, agree to best fit rather than perfect fit, but…'

'But then what's to stop you giving them the sack soon as the case is shut?' Jamie kept looking at the spoon as he stirred his tea.

'Nothing. But, like I say, we're hiring. Vacancies cost us money… some of these girls? Sounds like they're something of a community. Makes them more reliable than a twenty something with a boyfriend in another town. But…' Marika Morcanu looked across the table. 'Let's be honest. I'd be naive to think you wouldn't keep a file of evidence ready to launch if you thought we weren't keeping our word.'

Jamie kept flicking through the papers, but then he stopped and Shona saw him look directly at Marika Morcanu for the first time.

'Yes, that would always be on the cards, but,' his eyes hardened, 'I'd probably just take the simple option. Email a man in Katowice.' Then he stood and took a step.

Marika Morcanu looked down and began tidying pens into a line.

'So,' Shona spoke into the tension. 'To summarise. We have accounts outlining the insignificance of the money generated by the unit, and the leases and your exit strategy from them.' Shona held up her folder, then moved towards Jamie. 'And the plan of how you will integrate the girls into legitimate family businesses.'

Jamie half turned about to speak again, but Shona eased the folder against his shoulder and guided him back towards the door.

Jamie reached the street, flicked a key and the car beeped open. The engine was running before Shona had crossed the pavement. She was still struggling to pull her door shut as the car lurched into the traffic.

'Thought we could…' it was five minutes into the drive when Shona spoke.

'Stuff to do,' Jamie's focus didn't waiver from the road.

'Look, it was just—'

'Three doors. Lucky you knocked on the right one,' Jamie gripped the steering wheel tighter.

Shona sank into her scarf.

Fifteen minutes of traffic and Jamie pulled up at the front of her flat. 'Save me turning round in that car park at the back.' He didn't turn off the engine.

'Like you're Mr Transparent,' Shona reached for the door.

Inside, Shona sat. Then stood. Too many thoughts to sort out sitting. She changed quickly and minutes later she was wearing her quilted winter coat and had her gym bag slung over her shoulder. At the bottom of the steps she looked at her car, but she needed air. The gym wasn't far. Fifteen, twenty minutes' walk.

Selecting a high tempo playlist, Shona pounded her frustration into the treadmill. Twenty-six minutes later she was leaning over the rail, gasping, and 5k was flashing on the display.

Peering into the floor-to-ceiling mirror, she could see the doorway.

'Oh shit. All I need. Talking to that prat,' she pulled her headphones down and lowered her head into the crook of her arm.

Behind her, Moonlight was in his kit, talking to the attendant.

She'd spoken to the man before – Somali – he'd shown her family photos on his phone. Moonlight was smiling; obsequious, his default mode. Shona held her head just off her chest. Moonlight's lips stopped moving and he patted the man on the shoulder. Shona exhaled as Moonlight half-turned towards the door. Then she watched as his index finger traced across the man's collar bone and came to rest under his chin. He lifted the man's face a fraction, then moved to the door. The Somalian's shoulders fell and he reached for a broom. His brushing was fast and pressed hard into the floor.

Shona looked back towards the gym reception as she walked into the dark. With the atmosphere with Jamie and what she'd just seen at the gym, she was glad she'd walked. She needed the headspace. Lengthening her stride, she pulled down her scarf so she could taste the cold air. Near the ring road her phone pinged. There was a postcode. She texted back her apology and opened a taxi app. Not Dacian. It was three minutes away.

49

Jamie was driving when his phone buzzed. A few minutes later he was parked and shambling across the street towards a large Audi.

'Shona hasn't replied yet,' Jephcott said as he opened the passenger door. 'Thought she might be with you.'

'We're not joined at the hip.' Jamie slumped in.

After a minute, Jephcott broke the silence. 'You've told her—'

'I've told her nothing. I know her game. Empathise. Manufacture some shared experience bullshit. She thinks that New Street and the other crap means I'll have to… I'll have to do fuck all.'

'Other crap? She told you about the Hard Stop, the court case?'

Jamie was tapping his teeth.

'What the gung-ho bastard did a year later…' and Jephcott recounted the tragic epilogue that Shona cut short from her version.

Both men sat in darkness until, after some minutes, a taxi's headlights slid into their silent space.

'Sorry I'm late. Was away from my car.' Shona shuffled into the back seat.

'Not a problem,' Jephcott began, then lapsed into coughing for a moment. 'Jamie hasn't been here long.'

As Jephcott rambled through a few pleasantries, Shona

registered the false ease in his voice.

Eventually, he turned to business. 'Jamie, I know you've got more than enough on your plate, but I've received a draft schedule. If you're...'

'Might as well,' Jamie rolled his shoulders.

Jephcott held a list.

'Already got that. Remember?' Jamie's eyes flicked up to the mirror on the sun visor and made eye-contact.

'Yes,' Shona looked back and the dead detachment that had been in his eyes last time they spoke was gone. 'Said you'd got it on your computer.'

'Okay. Entry point,' Jephcott took out another sheet of paper. 'And the incoming transport.'

Jamie asked a couple of questions, then said: 'Immingham: Piece of piss.' He began reading the details.

'Eight men, four women, mainly engineers,' Jephcott said what was on the list. 'One civil, the others a mixture of mechanical and electrical. It's a well-rehearsed run,' he said for Shona's benefit. 'Motorway west, melting away in twos and threes via taxis at various service stations.'

'Like I say, piece of piss,' Jamie said. 'Checks minimum. Not like Dover and the south coast. Migrants dream of London, not Grimsby and easy access to Hull. Especially when they're already in Sweden.'

'Jamie,' Jephcott shuffled the papers back into order. 'If you draft the drop-off timings and map out alternate routes in case of problems. Then, on the night, it's just a matter of monitoring communications, in case...'

'In case of what?' Shona asked.

'Peepo or immigration service activity; traffic, or if any of the cars have a problem.'

'You can do it.' Jamie turned and looked at Shona.

'But—'

'I'll teach you the comms stuff. Piece of piss. Phrase of the night.' Then Jamie looked towards Jephcott. 'If that's it?'

Jephcott started the car.

'I suppose you'll be needing a lift?' Jamie was already unbuckling his seat belt and his door was open. Shona scrambled around the car floor trying to find her bag, then rushed to follow, watching his back as it moved into the darkness.

The drive back to Shona's was almost wordless, but not a hostile quiet.

'See you in the morning,' Jamie parked close to the steps that led up to Shona's flat.

'Aye, bright and early,' Shona smiled for the first time that evening and opened the car door.

Jamie watched until he saw the light come on inside her flat before starting the engine. Reaching the main road, he glanced up briefly. He thought she'd been at the window looking down.

When Clegg reached her office door, she stopped and crooked a finger in Jamie's direction.

'Shit,' Shona's eyes and voice stayed low on the desk. 'Looks like she's had a good course.'

The pair stood and began walking.

'Don't sit down, you're not stopping,' Clegg's eyes narrowed on Jamie. 'Re, the yellow snow warning.'

'I didn't, boss. I didn't dig into the Vulpes thing.'

'No? Well take this as a timely reminder. I've had a couple of days from hell at that Holiday Inn conference. Subject – Immigrant: capture and repatriation thereof. And fucking Moonlight was there. Him and all the other bald-headed bastard commanders in Yorkshire. Twats on equal footing with police. Some of the shitbags even got to the biscuits first.'

Jamie's mouth opened, but Clegg went on ranting., 'Like I said, give them nothing. No excuses. No treading on powerful toes who might see them as a route to political clout.' Clegg pointed a finger at Jamie, 'So, no cock-ups. And if there are any coppers free-lancing in some covert resistance, make sure we nail them first. Moonlight and his mates don't get a sniff.' Clegg's hand hit the desk, flat-palmed and echoing.

'Some other prat's been inspired by his course,' sitting back at their desk, Shona nodded across the briefing space.

Jamie followed her eyes. 'Yeah. Be tragic if he'd bigged himself up with his bosses and then fell on his arse.'

Shona's head dipped and turned a little. Jamie leaned in.

'I mean, what if me and my mini-bus went one way and him and his minions another. Look a prat in front of his masters…'

'And bonus,' Shona was nodding slightly. 'It'd cheer Clegg up. Pity she'd never know it was down to you. You could do with the brownie points.'

Across the briefing space, the screen behind Moonlight lit up and the milling herd shuffled to face it. In minutes the room was raucous with chants and Clegg was glowering over the frosted glass line at Jamie, but then she grabbed her coat and was gone.

Jamie and Shona watched the propaganda rant for a couple of minutes to give Clegg time to clear the building, then Jamie mimed drinking tea. As they stood, Moonlight stopped and looked over.

'Ah, good. I was about to ask you to give us the room. Operational reasons, I'm sure you understand.'

'Yeah, no problem,' Jamie smiled and lifted a cardboard folder off the table. 'Operational reasons. That's usually what the airlines say when they don't want to tell you your take-off's delayed because one of the wings has come loose.'

The room remained silent as Jamie and Shona made their way out. At the door, Jamie turned, smiled and waved the folder.

Sitting at a canteen table, tight in a corner, their conversation was fragments of routine information, spaced between significant silences.

'The death of strangers,' Jamie's words came from nowhere. 'Just because Africa normalises… doesn't mean it's ever trivial, especially when…'

Shona looked and a shadow of a smile came and went.

'Jephcott, he told me how that gung-ho bastard did it again. Shot into a car. How the bullet went right through the man's shoulder, then through the seat… and the baby… strapped directly behind. Not surprised you—'

Shona's eyes told him that was enough. Jamie reached out a hand and, with the angle of his body shutting off the room, held on gently until a slick of noisy Peepos pushed through the doors and flowed towards the counters, filling trays with bulky breakfasts before they seeped towards Jamie and Shona.

Draining the last of his drink, Jamie was about to stand when Shona kicked him under the table. He looked and followed her eyes.

'He's given me all the transport and hire firms to traipse around and give these out,' the Peepo rippled a pile of business cards between his fingers.

'Taking action at last?' Jamie leaned across. Shona kicked him again, but he didn't flinch. 'Transport. Good work. Probably need to look at transport if people, or things are being moved around. Ever thought of becoming a detective?'

The Peepo with the business cards raised a middle finger. Jamie grinned, then moved behind Shona to ease her chair out. As Shona began to walk towards the door, Jamie turned and took a couple of strides back to the table.

'Oh,' he grinned and held the folder up. 'Wouldn't want to leave this lying about where nosey prats might be tempted. Operational reasons.' He held his grin for a second, before moving away.

In the corridor Shona turned. 'That folder? Why's it so…?'

Jamie flicked it open. It was empty.

Across the briefing room, Moonlight was clipping papers into a ringbinder. Jamie opened his laptop and began googling and printing.

'I'm out for a bit,' he called across from the printer. 'And one of the security guys at Meadowhall messaged saying he'd identified some of the shoplifting gang on a CCTV recording.' And he began walking back to Shona. 'Keep Clegg thinking we're putting some time in,' his voice lowered as he reached the desk.

'And I think Dave's in, so when I get back I could check...' Shona began collecting documents.

Jamie opened the folder he'd been carrying in the canteen and turned it towards Shona. Now it was full of print-outs: various paragraphs, a map of Hull docks and a ferry timetable with a single highlighted line. He laid the folder flat, staggered the papers a little and then dragged a light pencil mark across their edges. He closed the folder and placed it carefully an inch from the lower left-hand corner of the desk. Shona looked across to show she understood.

In the lift Jamie said: 'Look better if we both leave in the same car. If we both log out as being at Meadowhall.' As Shona opened the driver's side door, Jamie took a bag out of the boot. 'If you can drop me just off the ring road. Easy enough to walk back.'

A few minutes later he was pointing at a turning that disappeared under a brick railway bridge. Shona parked and he opened the bag.

'Reserved didn't do my size, so I went to Screwfix,' he pulled on a bulky work jacket, then added the obligatory scarf and hat and scrunched the bag into a pocket.

Shona watched him shamble away, then made a U-turn and aimed for the retail delights of Meadowhall.

Two hours later Shona was back in the police station. Hobbes and a couple of other Peepos were loafing in the far corner of the briefing room. She glanced at the folder, still neatly equidistant from the desk's edge, then tucked her laptop under her arm and headed for the corridor.

Poking her head around Dave Collins' door she smiled. 'If I fill the kettle, can I settle here for a bit? Can't stand listening to those Peepo wankers.'

50

A hundred yards from where Shona had dropped him, Jamie turned left. The street had dilapidated Victorian remnants down one side and a brutalist sixties tenement on the other. After a couple of minutes he reached a pot-holed cul-de-sac. At its far end was a van hire depot. There was a CCTV camera over the large roller-shutter entrance, but Jamie's face was an eye's only slit between his scarf and hat.

Inside, a man was blasting a van with a pressure washer. Jamie looked at his sodden clothes and the icy haze thrown off by the water jets and shivered. In the corner was a glass-sealed reception area, with an electric heater glowing on the wall behind the desk. He walked over and pushed open the door.

'Bloody freezin' out there. Pity that poor sod with the hose,' Jamie put on a scouse accent. 'I'm full of cold already. Keep sneezing and getting the shakes. And the snot running out me nose. I dread pulling this scarf down.'

The girl moved back and took out a form.

'So, if I want a minibus?' Jamie shuffled from foot to foot. 'Need it overnight.' And he unrolled a paper with a date on.

'That's a Wednesday,' the girl scanned her monitor. 'Be cheaper than a weekend.' She wrote down a figure. 'And there's an excess mileage charge if you go over a hundred and fifty miles.'

'Nah, just to Hull and back,' Jamie watched the pun sail over the girl's head.

'You can leave a deposit, but you'll need to bring in—'

'Driving licence and National Insurance Number.' Jamie finished her sentence for her. 'Going to a couple of others to check for prices, but your quote? That's fixed.'

'Unless we have a rush.'

'Thanks. Might be back. Can I?' Jamie picked up the paper with the price on. There were three more vehicle hire companies within a mile's walk.

Shona felt her phone vibrate. It was a text.

'Jamie's on his way back. Should be about fifteen. Shall I?' she moved towards the kettle. 'Time for a quick one before our little ray of sunshine sparkles his way back into our lives.'

'Yeah, go on. Always enjoy a coffee and double entendre,' Dave licked the end of his felt-tipped pen.

When Jamie arrived there was a cup with a saucer on top to keep its contents warm. Shona guessed he'd come via the car park and the Screwfix clothes were bagged up and in her boot.

'Alright for some,' Jamie lifted the saucer off his cup. 'How have you pair been spending your time?'

'Coffee and innuendos,' Dave passed him a biscuit.

'Innuendos?' Jamie plonked himself in a chair. 'I thought they were some kind of Italian suppository.'

'When you two boys have finished…' Shona moved towards the door.

The briefing room was quiet as they entered. A couple of older Peepos hardly looked up from their document sorting. Reaching their desk, Shona dropped her carrier bag well away from the still neatly placed folder. Checking that the Peepos had their heads in filing cabinets, Jamie held the folder still on the desk, then opened its flap. The corners of the papers were neatly together and the pencil line hidden. Jamie closed the flap, then looked at Shona and winked.

Shona turned to Jamie as they entered her flat. 'C'mon, I've got something for you.' On a small side table was a key. 'Save you knocking.'

'Thanks,' Jamie picked it up and, when they reached the kitchen, he slid it onto his key ring.

'You okay with beans? Forgot to take something out of the freezer this morning.'

Jamie took his tea through to the lounge and switched on the television. The cerise jacket of Moonlight's favourite politician radiated from behind the newsreader. 'Bitch,' Jamie muttered under his breath and clicked the television off again. He stood and walked back into the kitchen as Shona was tilting a saucepan.

'Baked beans and wholemeal toast,' Jamie said, looking over her shoulder. 'That'll do nothing for global warming.'

As they ate, Jamie recounted his van hire routine.

'But when you don't pick it up?' Shona stared across the table.

'Nah, went into four places. Won't all have phoned it in. Just looks like I picked the van up from someone else.'

After they'd eaten and cleaned away, Shona shuffled off and came back a few minutes later in a dressing gown and pyjamas. 'Keep feeling my eyes closing. At least if I nod off, I've just got to climb into bed.'

Shona resettled on the sofa and leaned onto Jamie's shoulder. The chat was slow and low-level. Jamie could feel his own eyelids flickering. Twice he'd felt himself nod forwards.

'Make a drink,' he stretched. 'We can take it with us.'

Jamie cleaned his teeth and, when Shona came in holding two mugs of warm milk, he was lying in bed wearing a t-shirt and a pair of boxers she'd washed for him. Shona took off her dressing gown and they both hunched their knees up as they drank. In a couple of minutes the mugs were empty and Shona reached across, switched off the bedside lamp and settled her head on Jamie's chest. He could feel the brushed cotton of her pyjamas against his arm and legs. There was a gap in the curtains and streetlight fell on Shona's face, soft orange above the duvet. Jamie felt her breathing slow. After a minute or so, she shuffled from his chest onto her side, pulling him close so that the curve of her back fell into the front of his body. She pulled his arms around her and, bending her knees, their legs kept contact from hip to calf.

'Spoons,' she mumbled without opening her eyes. In a few seconds Jamie's breathing synchronised with hers.

The early morning routine was becoming just that. Whoever was on home turf left last, so they could lock up their own house and arrive without giving a clue that they'd both set off from the same place. This morning Jamie was in first. When, about twenty minutes later, Shona appeared, Jamie already had folders spread across the desk.

'Anything new from Clegg?' She looked down on the paper-strewn expanse as she hung her coat on the back of the chair.

'No,' Jamie kept his focus on the documents. 'And there won't be, not today. Spoke to Gerry on the front desk. She's at the monthly budget meeting, so she'll be going straight to regional HQ, then she's taking that Milhurst on a tour of the rest of the city's stations and introducing him to that councillor prat who's just been elected Police and Crime Commissioner.'

'And that'll include food, courtesy of everyone's council tax.' Shona lifted a paper that Jamie had been scribbling on. 'Be best if we take this away from prying eyes.'

They looked across the space at the gradual arrival of dark shirts and shiny scalps. Jamie nodded and they both reached for paper clips, post-its and stuff they needed to give shape to their mass of paper.

'Make a bit of progress this morning, before I get off,' Shona said.

Moving to the windowless office, they pored over documents, tracing cash from country to country and account to account, trying to estimate the possible totals that the camouflaged cash might reach each month.

'What the Buzzard takes is small change,' Shona was looking across a spreadsheet. 'The rest? You've got the traceable, non-cash transactions. Payments to Vulpes are industry standard for rentals like Katya's place and it matches the girls' direct debits. Then there's the payments going to Katowice. That's around ten percent above the takings when old man Morcanu was in charge.'

'So Bakula's father-in-law is seeing profits within the expected ballpark,' Jamie followed a row of underlined figures.

'That leaves the bulk of the takings, the extra rent the girls pay and the money shelled out by all those punters who are filling up the taxis, all in non-traceable cash,' Shona scanned up and down the print-outs and scribbled figures in the margins. 'The money that ends up in that Bavarian Account is close to what Katowice sees. And,' her finger went to her pencilled totals. 'There's a similar amount in the end of month balance, before it's transferred to whatever account that number belongs to. Means whoever controls this account is getting a good percentage of the cash non-traceables.'

'So, like we thought,' Jamie took in the numbers. 'Bakula and whoever is paying The Buzzard.'

Shona nodded. 'Need a face to tie to that Solar account to nail the bastard... but those foreign accounts... even if we know, we've got no jurisdiction.'

'There's always back channels,' Jamie straightened the edges of the papers.

Another hour's work and the major patterns and offences were roughed out on a grid.

'Needs typing up and presenting to Clegg,' Shona sat back.

'Needs emailing,' Jamie said. 'Make it look like we're sharing.'

'Yeah, email. Something dated, with a footprint, but maybe not today's date,' Shona understood the logic. 'And maybe think about the subject line.'

'Right.' Jamie's voice brightened. 'Get this stuff out of sight, then time for an early lunch.'

In the canteen, they began browsing the chiller shelves. Shona picked a salmon sandwich and a banana. Jamie stretched for a flapjack, then moved along and began joking with the woman on the hot counter while she assembled him a sausage and egg sandwich. As Jamie stacked cups onto a tray, the double doors banged open and a mass of shaven-heads lurched towards the food.

'And two teas,' Jamie held up his bankcard, ready to tap.

'Fucking hell,' Hobbes turned to the mass. 'Can't we even eat without listening to your flat Manc vowels?'

'Flat Manc vowels. Open your ears, you Essex moron,' Jamie turned. 'You're in Yorkshire, world leader in flat vowels.'

Shona felt the world go into slow motion as Jamie moved towards Hobbes, smiling and shaking his head.

'Y'know, I've only ever seen Essex people on reality telly,' Jamie said. 'Thought you all had fake tans and cosmetic surgery.'

'No darling,' Hobbes seized the chance of attention. 'Some of us rely on natural perfection.'

'Jesus, looks more like the plastic surgeons assembled you from the bits the other bimbos had sliced off.'

The Peepo clump looked at Hobbes.

'Tell 'em lads,' Hobbes tried to inject some bravado into his shoulders. 'I'm a sort-after man, Yorkshire nubilia-wise.'

'Yeah,' one of the Peepos whispered to his mates. 'Yeah, remember when he went night-clubbing in Hull and they had to close the Humber Bridge to stop the local women throwing themselves off like lemmings.'

And there was a snort of derision.

After a few seconds of bluster, Hobbes stepped towards Jamie, pointing his finger. 'Yeah, well, we're onto something. Maybe even onto you …'

The Buzzard leaned through the mass of dark shirts. 'Moonlight sealed the meeting room. You know why.'

'Yeah, but this network… Manc bastard's so…' Hobbes voice was shrill. 'He's so *look what I'm doing…*'

'Sealed room, you twat,' the Buzzard's hand slammed onto Hobbes' shoulder and dragged him back until the dark herd closed around him.

It was still only half past twelve when they piled the litter from their lunches onto a tray.

'So, this afternoon. Remember I told Clegg it was my nephew's birthday.'

'Yeah, said she couldn't believe you had family. Says she imagined you dropped outside A&E in a cardboard box.'

'Whatever, but I'm going to get my head down for a bit. Long night ahead.'

51

Jamie knew he wouldn't sleep, so he drove down towards Bridgehouses Roundabout and the river. The Upper Don Trail was a gentle nothing of a walk, but he needed to feel the intrusion of nature amongst the industrial decay. It gave him hope, as if the city were composting itself slowly back to a state where more species than just humanity could have a sense of belonging.

'Domestic bliss, Fatboy,' Cara was just there. 'Moving beyond the old wham-bam thank you mam, then Jamie? Beyond the making the-effort stage. Never thought I'd see the day. Beans on toast now. Getting a bit complacent? Must be—'

'What in the name of holy shite would you know about it?'

'Holy shite, Jamie. That's what I said when I saw you two lying together like a pair of old spoons in a drawer. Her in her comfortable jim-jams. Brushed cotton, Jamie. We never had a brushed cotton sort of a relationship, did we?'

But as his mouth opened to answer, he could feel her gone.

Near the bridge and weir at Furnival Road, there were three people with cameras and various measuring equipment; all wore woolly hats and kagools. 'Winter plumage of the species, Universitas, biologicus, twaticus.' Jamie shuffled riverside.

A girl turned. Her smile was open.

Jamie felt a pang of guilt. 'Spraints this far into the city.' He bent to look at what she was collecting. 'Wouldn't have found them five years ago.'

'No,' the word spraints injected a moment of surprise into the girl's voice. 'And, unless this government restores the old anti-pollution legislation, we won't be seeing them here much longer.'

'Otter shit and other signs of decontamination,' Jamie knelt down and looked at a spraint. 'Could be sequel to *Ring of Bright Water*.'

'Taken decades to get them this far,' the girl stood. 'But that means nothing to the politicians.'

'Maybe you should campaign for universal otter suffrage. If the otters could vote they could set up a pressure group.'

'Otters more common at home,' a youth spoke with an accent. 'Estonia. Politicians say keep water clean, like old laws in UK.'

Jamie mooched around and chatted easily, falling in and out of the scientific language that formed their common ground.

After about ten minutes he said his goodbyes and headed towards his car. Two hundred yards on, there was a heron. He stopped and watched it hunch its wings against the low sun to form a shadowed hunting zone. Jamie and the heron remained motionless for a while until the bird's neck snapped forwards, then back and up, gripping a small fish, still wriggling.

'Brushed cotton.' Cara's voice darted in and out and Jamie writhed for a second, looking for words to form an answer, but she had hit her target and vanished. Jamie moved on along the bank, his movements fast and jerking, grinding his teeth. Reaching the car, he slumped into his seat. Despite the outside wind, the car's glass had trapped the winter sunlight. He leaned back and let the soft warmth wash over him. It felt good, but he couldn't surrender to it, not today. He began to drive. A couple of miles into the forty mile journey, he pulled up on a steep street. He took out his phone and messaged Shona, so she could find somewhere private. A few minutes later she rang back. The conversation was functional; contingencies, schedules, etc.

'Speak soon,' Jamie finished.

'Aye, break a leg. I'll be home soon and set up. Oh, and good news.'

Jamie waited.

'When I went back, the baldies were all either out on the streets, or still in the canteen. The projector screen was off, but I took a chance with Moonlight's laptop.'

'And?'

'And he hadn't shut it down. When I flicked the mouse-pad... there was a map of Hull.'

Jamie picked up the carrier bag and rucksack from the back seat of his car. The front door opened as soon as he pulled onto her drive. Family birthday, overnight visit; normal family stuff, if anyone asked.

Mandy had a meal ready for him. There were sandwiches for his rucksack and she filled his flask.

'Surveillance,' he'd told her. 'Meeting a Manc detective. Using his car, so can I leave mine on the drive?'

He caught a bus that dropped him near the van hire depot. It was closed, but a minibus was parked a street away. A handshake, a set of ignition keys and he watched his contact walk towards an old Volvo.

Then he was on his way; east for Immingham Docks, via the M62, then south on the M18.

Jamie was in good time as he exited where the M180 gave way to the main A180. There was a petrol station just off the island. He filled up then aimed for the nearby truck stop. The map called it a diner, but Jamie knew it had *Café* painted on its roof. He'd used the shadowy corners of its large lorry park before. It was a good twelve miles to the docks, but this was the nearest west-bound stopping point where a lorry would look inconspicuous.

Parking up, he shuffled into his bulky jacket and repeated his high scarf, low-pulled hat routine as he stepped out of the cab. Even with the trees breaking its flow, the wind had a spiteful cold. Jamie grinned and imagined the Peepos taking the full blast as it swept down the Humber, with nothing but frozen plains and the North Sea between Hull docks and the Urals. He pictured their pinched faces and their sparsely-worded, shivering conversations, then grinned and opened the door to be met by the muggy heat rippling off the ever-burning griddles and stoves.

Returning to the minibus, he drank his take-away coffee and waited until the app on his phone confirmed the arrival of the ferry. He'd still have a wait until the lorry unloaded and trundled its way to him. He checked the time. Wouldn't be long before the Peepos got excited at the Rotterdam ferry pulling into Hull, but that wouldn't last: not in the bitter wind. He knew what was in the folder, the clues. He imagined them laying out their vehicle inspection lanes and targeting the particular lorry. He'd chosen carefully; the bright green enviro-sympathetic outside camouflaging the stinking, filthy contents inside. He checked the time again and took the burner out of his coat.

'Everything's on time. Probably be just another boring night. Thought I might divert over the Humber Bridge. Nice sea view and get onto the M62 that way instead.' He heard Shona inhale. 'Could give Moonlight and his boys a wave as I go past. I hope they choose old Hobbesy to climb into the container. Be nice when they open the doors and get a whiff of what de-regulation smells like.'

'Just don't be more of a prat than your daily average,' then she confirmed times, service stations and taxi rendezvous' points.

'Cheers you up though. Moonlight holding his nose and

Hobbes or one of the other twats having to crawl over all those stinking rubbish bales, heaving and getting scratched to bits by all the wire bindings… anyway, be dropping the minibus off before their office opens. I'll post the keys in the late return box and get the train back.'

Shona mumbled some *keep me posted* phrases and the call ended. Jamie opened the driver's side window and looked towards the road.

It was about twenty minutes later when the headlights flashed. Jamie did the same and waited for the lorry to back itself into shadows by the trees. The driver got out, made no sign of recognition and walked towards the café. Jamie eased the minibus close and got out. Next came a well-practised routine. Finding the anti-tamper seals on the container doors, he cut them from the handles and stacked them in the designated place. On his return, the driver would use a special tool that re-fixed them so precisely that nothing could be noticed, unless an inspector was motivated enough to turn up with forensic equipment. As the doors opened, Jamie could see a faint glow. Shapes and shadows began to move.

'Wait,' Jamie held up a hand. He stepped back and took a final look around the lorry park. 'Okay. Quickly and quietly please.'

Hunched under rucksacks and well-wrapped against the cold, Jamie led a dozen figures to the minibus. The warmth of the heater met them and their faces lightened. As they arranged bags and coats, Jamie climbed into the driver's seat.

'Forgive me if I don't tell you my name,' he turned, illuminated by the minibus' dull courtesy light. 'But I need to check yours.'

Faces smiled back as Jamie read out his list and, holding a small LED torch, began handing back papers.

'Emergency contact numbers, should something happen between being dropped off and reaching whoever's waiting at your accommodation. Never had anyone need to use them yet, so let's make sure we don't break any patterns.'

Jamie piled his coat, hat and scarf on the seat alongside him and started the engine. Then he turned and spoke again.

'We're mainly on motorways, autobahns. I'm dropping you off in twos and threes, yes?'

Heads nodded along the bus.

'We stop at service stations and there'll be taxis. Make sure you have all your belongings organised on a seat close-by, because I need you on your way quickly and we'll be pulling up in the dark corners, away from the main buildings.'

The heads nodded again.

'So, Klaudia and Jan, you're first: Sheffield. Taxi from Doncaster North Services,' Jamie made sure they were giving him eye-contact. 'Listen, you have the longest taxi ride. About forty kilometres, okay?'

Klaudia and Jan nodded. 'Forty kilometres in the taxi. We have the longest journey.' Jan's English was accented, but clear and fluent. Jamie raised a thumb.

Fifteen minutes along the M180 and colour was returning to faces and chatter was growing and relaxing. At Doncaster North, Jamie headed for a far corner in the car park. He knew which counterfeit taxi sign would be on the car and its registration. He pulled up and hopped out. The driver's window slid down and, after a couple of words, he beckoned to the minibus. The back doors opened and Jan and Klaudia stepped down and slung rucksacks over shoulders. Quiet good wishes followed them and the remaining ten waved as the taxi moved away.

'Give it a minute,' Jamie said. 'Let a few other vehicles go first. Then, Konrad, Henryk and Rafal, you're leaving us for Leeds, so that's Ferrybridge Services next stop. Then, ladies, it's a short hop to Hartshead Moor, so Zofia and Olenka, that's you for Bradford.'

52

Beyond Bradford the minibus began the climb into the Pennines and it started to snow. Just dots at first, but then fattening and multiplying. There was no moon and cloud sat on the mountain tops. Jamie slowed.

'Thank fuck, we're not on the Snake Pass,' the burner phone began to vibrate on the seat beside him. He reached down and hit speaker.

'How's your progress? Taxi says he'll be late.' Shona sounded metallic.

'Him and me both. Been driving through snow for a bit. Not settling yet, but visibility's crap.'

'Okay, keep me posted. I think it's a car issue with him. Says he's in a red Mondeo now. Same plates though,' Shona paused. 'Snow? We've got nothing.'

'Yeah, well, I'm up a bit higher than you. Cracking heater on these Fords, though. We're all driving along in our underpants.'

'Please, I'm cursed with a vivid imagination and weak stomach.'

Jamie smiled and the call ended.

As he descended towards Birch Services, the snow turned to rain. Pulling in, Jamie headed for the corner of the car park where the taxi rendezvous was supposed to happen. After ten minutes he pulled on his coat, hat and scarf and stepped out. Mindful of the CCTV, he didn't go far. The red Mondeo wouldn't arrive any quicker just because he was looking for it. After a couple of minutes he was back in the minibus and its bubble of warm air.

'Slight delay,' Jamie turned to the remaining quintet in the back. 'Nothing to worry about.' Attempting a smile, he reached for the phone. 'Been here over fifteen minutes,' he said as Shona answered.

'Okay. He told me everything was sorted. Let me try and raise him again. Any message?'

'Yeah, tell him I'm where I'm supposed to be.'

'Other than the bleeding obvious. The bloke's doing his best. Cars go wrong. Snow falls. Not everything bends to your will, Jamie.'

'Okay, okay. Let me know when you've got something definite.'

He turned and smiled again. The smiles that came back were polite, but unconvinced.

After ten minutes, Jamie saw the headlights ease towards the agreed position in the car park. He could tell it was a Mondeo, but not the colour. As it closed he read the number plate and breathed.

'Okay, Norbert, Isabela, Marek, this is you. Bags and coats.'

While the girl and two young men got sorted, Jamie walked over to the red Mondeo. The driver was already out and opening the boot.

'Sorry, mate. My Zafira was knackered. Came out to find a pool of clutch fluid on the drive.'

'Didn't you feel it going spongy?'

'Wife's been driving it the last couple of days.'

'Nuff said,' Jamie nodded and walked back to the minibus. The two young men shook his hand and the girl hugged him. 'Okay. Just me and you two left. The dynamic duo. And you're Jacek and Kristian, yes?'

'Yes, driver,' a voice came from the back of the minibus. 'You have delivered the right packages to the right cities. Just us now.'

'Okay, gents, bit different for you,' and he handed them an address. 'I'm going right into the city. Liverpool's the end of the line. I'll drop you at the main station, Lime Street. There's taxis coming and going twenty-four hours a day. You just hop in a taxi and tell him this address. This'll be more than enough,' and Jamie handed the men a twenty pound note each. 'Get straight in a taxi. Don't hang about. I'll be there myself after a few minutes, so I don't want to see you, okay.'

'Okay,' both the men nodded. 'Not good if we all on station CCTV together.'

'Exactly,' Jamie said. 'Keep hats, hoods and scarves on. I'm doing the same when I come back.'

As they passed the sign that read *End of Motorway 1 mile*, Jamie spoke.

'Nearly there. Remember what I said?'

The two men nodded.

'I'm pulling up at the 24 hour petrol station in a bit, so pretend to be asleep.'

The men nodded again. Leaving the motorway, Jamie carried straight on along Edge Lane.

Fuelled up, he headed for the city centre. Even on a dark winter morning in the rain, the great stone and glass arch of Lime Street Station was impressive. 'Buildings as loud as a Scouser's gob.' Jamie tapped the window. Turning into Lord Nelson Street, he pulled into a loading bay. 'Okay, lads. This is you. Liverpool. You've fallen on your feet. That's a taxi rank there.'

Jacek and Kristian grabbed their bags and began to walk, then turned and waved as they headed for a black cab. If they were smiling, Jamie couldn't tell. They'd buried their faces in scarves and hoods as per instructed.

The van hire terminal was on a street a bit back from Princes Dock, but it would be hours before its office opened. Posting the keys in the late returns box, Jamie walked towards the river and Pier Head. He stayed on the shoreline, letting the breeze off the water drive away the tiredness of the night. Reaching Albert Dock, he turned his back and let the wind push him towards the shops and up the hill, back to the station's great glass arch.

Scanning the departures board, he found what he was looking for. 'Manchester. Got twenty minutes.' And he looked for a coffee shop.

When Shona came into the office just after nine, Jamie was already at the desk.

'Early train,' he leaned in close as Shona sat. 'Got into Manchester about half six. Taxi to our Mandy's. She'd done me a flask and sandwiches. Been in about half an hour.'

The overnight Peepo staff shuffled about yawning and waiting to go home. Eventually, a skeleton day shift arrived, but not Moonlight. Jamie got up and strolled around making random remarks to the sparse Peepo deployment as they drank coffee and eased themselves into a little light filing.

The morning was blessedly mundane. Clegg was in and out. 'If you could…' she called over a couple of random tasks as she passed. Jamie and Shona waved, signalling *yes boss*, and went back to what they were doing.

'Could do with some air,' Shona looked across the morning's cluster of cups. 'Might go over…' she forced her eyes wide, trying to scan the mountain of bank records yet again. Leaning back and breathing to the base of her lungs was a temporary help.

'Walk around. Talk to those prats,' Jamie nodded towards the scattering of Peepos. 'Two birds with one stone. Wake you up and they register you were here early.'

Lunch was in the canteen.

'The oven's on auto-time,' Shona poked at a yoghourt. 'Should be a goulash and jacket potatoes, if you're interested?'

'Brushed cotton on a plate,' Jamie gave a slight smile.

The afternoon followed the morning.

Shona had used her app to turn the heating on early and warm air carried the smell of long-cooked herbs and paprika. Potatoes, sour-dough bread and thick red gravy eased the tension from Jamie's shoulders and he began to recount the previous evening. Shona wanted descriptions, background, impressions of the people and how they looked as they first entered the minibus and their body language as they walked towards their transport. Jamie was most animated speculating on Moonlight and his crew and the delights of a North Sea wind in January.

There was a cheesecake and coffee, wine for Shona and easy listening music, almost subliminally low, to fill the conversational gaps where angst might have re-established itself.

When they moved to the sofa, the inevitable tiredness flooded in. Shona stood. 'I hate it when you've been asleep and then you have to get ready for bed.'

Faces washed, teeth brushed and within ten minutes they were both asleep, spooned together. It was half-past eight.

Jamie was awake by five. He slipped into the shower and made himself tea and toast. Shona was still asleep. He leaned across and kissed her. Her eyes opened briefly.

'Have another couple of hours. I'll make something up if anyone notices you're in late.'

Shona managed another hour or so and stretched to cancel the alarm on her phone. The message light was blinking.

Shifts changed. Put on different hours.

Shona took out her phone and tapped *Recents: Jamie*.

The early start meant that Jamie was looking over the rim of his second tea as the briefing room door opened for a couple of seconds and Shona's head appeared. After brief eye contact, the door closed again. Jamie looked down at his desk and pretended to be engrossed in papers until he deemed his movement would seem disconnected with leaving the room.

Shona was waiting in the small, windowless office. 'Change of plan.' She held her phone for him to read.

Lunchtime start. Can have taxi 11:30. Usual place?

53

Jamie pulled up a couple of streets away. Shona was sitting in the back, talking and checking the time. Eventually, she tapped Jamie on the shoulder and ducked down as Jamie started the engine. Katya was waiting in her calf-length quilted parka. As she slid into the car, the coat fell open and Jamie's focus was taken for a split second by the band of flesh between her mini-skirt and thigh boots. Katya met his eye and pulled the coat closed.

Shona wittered something along the lines of: 'Looks warm,' and 'mine's too short for these bitter days,' then, as they moved beyond the traffic lights, she sat up. When the chatter moved into substance, Shona asked: 'So, the sooner the better?'

'Maybe,' Katya looked out the window. 'Bakula talk about busy times, lulls and crap. Say work when tell us. Say owe him for Christmas holiday. Point at us, "Got new catalogue." Bastard flick pages.'

'Catalogue?' Shona moved closer in her seat.

'Bakula's catalogue girls, not clothes. "Phone boss in Poland," he say. "Click and collect. Bodies in. Bodies out. Keep things fresh," he say. Bastard.' And Katya's head bent.

Click and collect. Jamie and Shona stared at nothing.

Eventually, Jamie coughed, then: 'Bit of good news. Found a

way to have a look around that means you don't have to be locked up with me for an hour.'

Katya almost smiled.

'Jamie... They seek him here, they seek him there...' Clegg stood in her office doorway and crooked a finger.

Through the open door Shona could see Milhurst and one of his oppos slouched in chairs. Walking towards the office, Shona dug her fingers into Jamie's arm.

'Thought you might want an update,' Clegg was behind her desk.

'So,' Milhurst straightened. 'Forensics and witness statements confirm that no known DNA trace has been found, and the wound was delivered with one movement using a sharp blade, causing massive blood loss. The drop in blood pressure would have resulted in unconsciousness within...' he clicked his fingers. 'Witness statements reveal nothing, except a vague reference to a man in a hoodie in recent days, but he doesn't show on any CCTV in the area or any transport hubs.'

'So, basically nothing to report that wasn't in Cozza's post-mortem and the reports I gave you?' Shona was slow and precise. Jamie stared at her for a second.

'But the confirmation gives us a good starting point,' Clegg attempted to hold a line.

'Same starting point we were at days ago,' Shona's face and voice were still expressionless. 'Unless I've cut in before you'd finished.' She began to rise in her chair.

'If there are further developments...' Milhurst retreated into stock phrases, but Shona was standing now, with a hand on the door.

'Ma'am,' and she was into the briefing space, Jamie struggling to get out of his chair and catch up.

'What was...' he began as they sat back at their desks.

'Thought I'd better get in first,' Shona ground her teeth. 'You'd have only lost your temper.'

About ten minutes later, Milhurst and his oppo headed for the door. Neither man's head made the slightest turn in the direction where Shona was seated.

After the shift, Jamie drove home and parked his car. Shona picked him up from the other side of the park and headed out towards Page Hall estate. Shona locked the car doors as Jamie nipped out to the convenience store. A couple of minutes later, he was back and Shona started the engine.

Jamie sniffed as Shona's flat door opened.

'You're getting too used to casserole,' Shona hung up her coat. 'When you've worked out what you're saying, I'll dial for a pizza.'

Shona made coffees and when she brought them to the table, Jamie was tatting with the phone he'd just bought.

'Am I being paranoid,' Shona's hands circled her coffee mug. 'Or would it be better away from here when you make the call?'

'Million to one,' Jamie shrugged. 'Be in the canal by this time tomorrow. But, if it makes you feel…'

As they drove to a random location a couple of miles away, they rehearsed a routine of *so you'll say… and if they say…* scenarios so that, when they parked, Jamie had a series of alternatives depending on the reaction when the phone was answered.

'Well,' Jamie looked at the digits on the phone. 'Good a time as any. This'll be the mid-evening lull.'

And he hit speaker. The dialling tone dragged out.

'Shite, it's going to voice—' Shona was cut short as a voice answered.

'Sorry to call so late. Took a chance,' Jamie slid into his faux-scouse accent. 'Had a colleague phone in sick. But we're up against a deadline. Statutory annual checks. I've got a full day tomorrow, but I said I'd do a couple hours overtime in the evening.

Bonus really, me and the wife have just booked a holiday, so bit of extra spending money for—'

'Hang on. Breathe,' the voice matched the woman Jamie had seen mopping out and opening up. 'What are you going on about?'

'Oh, sorry. I'm always doing that,' and Jamie told her the company name. 'You can phone to verify in the morning. Fire safety check. Mandatory for business premises. Extinguishers, emergency exit signs…'

'Thank fuck for that. I thought you were going to ask me to ghost-write your autobiography.'

'Wha…?' Jamie feigned confusion. 'Oh yeah… so, like I say. Tomorrow evening. I'm having to pick it up off my mate's round. He's—'

'Sick, yeah. And you need to work overtime to pay for your piña coladas.'

'Yeah, ready when you are,' the ex-fireman had said when Jamie called early next morning. 'I'll be here till six.'

Jamie got there at three. Everything was as promised, including his own photo ID.

'You can keep that as a souvenir,' the man had said. 'But I need all the other stuff back. Especially that hand-held scanner. Can't pick them up off the shelf.'

When Shona opened the door, a little after five, Jamie was on the sofa using sellotape to shorten his overall legs.

'Give 'em here,' She hung them over the ironing board. 'Get yourself a snack now. All goes well, we'll pick up a take-away on the way back.'

After tea and toast, Jamie slid into the overalls and Shona pinned the legs to length and fixed them in place with iron-on fabric tape. Then he pulled on his hi-vis gilet with the company logo and reached for his ID lanyard.

'Shit,' Shona squinted at the badge. 'Give it here.'

Jamie passed her the badge and, scrunching up the fabric tape she'd used on his overalls, she began dabbing it with the iron. Jamie went to speak, but she got there first.

'Better if you don't look too life-like.' The adhesive from the tape had made the photograph look old and worn. 'You next.' Shona took the pair of supermarket glasses with a black, plastic frame that he'd worn for his photo ID. Next she took out hair gel. 'There you go, flatter and darker.'

Being almost eight o'clock, most of the units were locked and the few windows and doors where lights showed were very much in wind-down mode. Only Shag City and the big through-the-night transport operation at the far end of the access road showed signs of any real business.

Jamie stood under the roller shutter wearing overalls and carrying his plastic attache case. The strings of LED bulbs hanging between the containers hardly had the energy to cast light as far as the floor, and in the gloom the office stood out as the only point of real brightness. Beyond the office there was just the occasional pastel rectangle of light where a container door had been left open.

'Took some finding,' Jamie's hi-vis gilet announced his arrival.

As he approached the office, the mop and bucket queen of Yorkshire Noire peered over an old desktop computer.

'Safety check. I phoned,' Jamie held out the ID card on his lanyard. 'Seen better days.'

'What, you or the card?'

Behind the woman, around a coffee table on low seats, sat a cluster of girls, wrapped in oversized quilted coats, vying to get near an electric fan heater. Katya was the only non-blonde. On her shoulder was a young boy, his head bent, pale skin and eyes nowhere. Katya lifted the boy's head gently and stood. As she reached Jamie she held out a hand.

'Got price list in room. No kissing on mouth.'

'No, no. Just here to…' Jamie held out his lanyard again as if it might provide some protection.

Yorkshire Noire woman started to chuckle. 'Leave the poor lad alone, Katya. He's only here to check entrances and pipework.'

'Entrances and pipework. We must be in same business.' As Katya turned away, Jamie flustered in his case and took out a small torch.

'Meters this way?' And he began following a run of pipes along the wall until he'd passed the first row of containers.

At right-angles, corridors of shadows stretched in gloomy lines, despite the incongruous strings of decorative bulbs zig-zagging between container roofs. As the dimness stretched back, a blue glow washed across the darkness, but Jamie couldn't see its source.

Following the wall, Jamie's torch picked out windows – all obscured – wired glass and grills. Scanning around, he took in the lit-up green signs that indicated fire exits. He pushed the bar on one and there was a distant whooping of an alarm. He closed the door again and the siren stopped.

'That's a pass,' he shouted in the direction of the reception area. On the floor was a chain and padlock. He walked on, pretending to mark off the list on his clipboard. Standing alongside the wall, a steel stairway stretched to the mezzanine deck. Jamie looked up. More containers and zig-zagging lights. Ahead, half-way down a row, a girl was leaning over the scaffold-tube handrail around the metal steps that led to her container door. She was wearing cami knickers and a sheer net wrap.

'What fuck you do, opening doors,' the bulky silhouette of Bakula was striding between the containers.

'Annual check,' Jamie slowly released a paper from his clipboard, and re-clipped it behind the top sheet. 'Twenty minutes, half an hour max and I'm gone. Nothing to worry about for at least a year. Just routine, photograph the metres and pipes to prove no one's nicking the gas. Surprising how many people do that. Specially if they're running a cannabis farm.' Jamie smiled and stood, legs apart.

'I said, what fuck you open door?'

Jamie repeated the paper re-clipping routine, then looked up. 'Legal requirement. Fire exits, extinguishers, gas supply. Maybe I should recommend a random visit.' He kicked the padlock and chain.

Bakula glared at him.

'Like I say, everything's okay so far. Fairly new building, so hopefully...' he looked Bakula in the eye. 'But if I have to phone the supplier, they're obliged by law to cut off all gas till a thorough assessment has been done. Don't think January would be the ideal time to have your heating cut off. Think some of those girls might catch a chill.' He nodded towards the leaning girl and her gaping lingerie.

'Hurry fuck up. And keep away from customers.' Bakula turned and stomped away.

Under the steel steps Jamie saw a couple of metal cuboids, five-foot high on wheels. *EezyCleen Laundries* was stencilled on the side. He opened one. It was full of sheets, so he gave them a poke. 'Jesus,' he dropped the lid. 'Smells like a fishmonger's watch strap.'

Switching off his torch, he traced his way along the pipework. The further he ventured from the reception area, the more the blue glow filled the rear of the unit. Dotted outside random containers was a selection of cheap exercise bikes, cross-trainers and other second-hand remnants of New Year fitness resolutions. 'Bloody hell,' Jamie reflected on the cut-price cover story. 'Man Spa, courtesy of eBay.'

Skirting past closed doors and sounds of activity, he reached a side branch where a sliver of light indicated a door ajar. Jamie listened, then gave it a push. Tip-toeing onto the entrance steps, he looked in. Pink netting drapes hung in swags, dimming the already low lighting, with curtains framing a painted-on window. Jamie took in the crude attempt to make a metal container seem exotic. Two paces in, he sat on the bed and smoothed his hand across a sheet; still warm. A brief thought of submarines and hot-bed systems flitted across his mind. He leaned back and there was a low clang as the thin netting did nothing to protect his head from the metal wall. In the corner was a wooden dressing screen, concealing a jug, plastic bowl and large roll of blue paper, like car mechanics use to wipe the grease off their hands. He almost laughed, then backed out and headed deeper towards the blue glow.

Beyond the last metal cuboid, his view widened. There was a desk with a computer and projector. A large screen almost covered the back wall. Jamie looked around and tapped the computer's mouse and the blue glow became white light, then red overlain by a monochrome image: a stereotypical smiling blonde, head and shoulders, huge across the screen.

'Hey, what fuck?'

Jamie looked back. Bakula was standing at the head of the corridor between the containers.

'Sorry,' Jamie waved and called back. 'Kicked the desk and the mouse moved. Accident. Be finished soon.'

Bakula turned and clomped away. Jamie remained still. When he turned another image was automatically rotating up in the sequence; another blonde stereotype, smiling, monochrome with red flooding into where the white should be. Jamie took out his camera and began taking photos, clicking and WhatsApping them back to Shona. The blonde face faded and a spreadsheet appeared. Then photos. White now and smaller, like a sheet of postage stamps. As Jamie watched the word *znak* appeared on a face, then another – question marks blinking on and off at random on each girl.

Then red again and Jamie froze. He felt his tongue tighten and his stomach clamp.

Liliana Normova, smiling down, her head as tall as two men; life and light still in her eyes, even as she floated on a red tide. As if on auto-pilot, he raised the phone, tapped and WhatsApped and then it was another excel sheet. He steadied himself, trying to ensure he captured the text, pin sharp. He tapped once more and then it was the first face again. Jamie moved to the darkness at the edge of the space and photographed through the cycle of faces and spreadsheets as it rotated through again. There was a jumble of leads alongside the computer. Jamie looked over his shoulder. His line of sight back to the roller shutters was clear. The reception desk and anyone there was beyond a corner. He looked at the leads. Standard USB-Cs. He pushed one into his burner phone. New device appeared on the screen and he right-clicked, selected copy and minimised. The slide show resumed. He looked back. Still clear. Watching the corridor for activity, the seconds of file copying stretched themselves on the rack of his anxiety. But then *Download Complete* and he breathed.

Grabbing his phone, he took out a torch and scanned the walls, again as if tracing pipes, then leaned against the scaffold bannister around the steps to the container with the open door. Inside, a woman's voice crackled from a speaker above the bed.

'Five minutes. Ladies, please ensure all gentlemen vacate the suites and are back in reception on or before time. Overstays will be charged to the next twenty minutes, at the discretion of the management.'

Looking back from his place in the wall's shadow, he saw Bakula pacing the grid of corridors at the far end.

Jamie pretended to return to his paperwork. Over the next few minutes, six doors opened. He strained to see if he might spot a face that could prove useful to him – someone he might be able to lean on – but all he saw were hunched men shuffling in sad scarfs and high-collared coats.

As the last punter disappeared beyond the roller shutters, Jamie collected his equipment and walked towards the reception.

'Done for another year,' he nodded at Yorkshire-noire woman on the computer. 'All okay. I won't be cutting off your heating.' She looked, but didn't speak.

The girls were sat back in reception, like taxis waiting on a rank. Jamie walked towards the exit and fresh air.

'Got everything downloaded,' Shona reached into her kitchen cupboard, then carried on scrolling down her phone screen. The kettle boiled and she dropped teabags into mugs. 'Be able to see better on a laptop screen. Anyway, tonight. We said take-away.'

She looked at Jamie, sank in his seat, shoulders heavy and elbows bent across the table. Shona tapped his shoulder.

'Sorry, not really that hungry.'

'Adrenalin. You're allowed.' She moved alongside and put an arm around his shoulders. Shona had seen Liliana's photo and knew words had no function. She stood and made the tea and placed biscuits on a tray, then took them to the low table by the sofa. 'Come on,' she called through and tapped a cushion as Jamie appeared in the doorway.

When he sat, Shona put her head on his shoulder and drew her arms around him. She could feel his tension ease, like an old-fashioned clockwork spring, slowly unwinding.

'I'll be in work early,' Shona just knew he would be going home to sleep. 'Hopefully, I'll have organised an easy day for us.'

'Thanks,' Jamie stood. 'I might be a few minutes late in the morning. Got some calls. Family stuff.'

'Mandy?' Shona wished she hadn't spoken and quickly moved on. 'Your coat's on the back of the door.'

Jamie said thanks as he looked down the steps to his car. Their kiss was a brief touch of the lips, followed by a hug that was held for a little longer than just goodbye.

54

Jamie was showered, dressed and early. He forced down toast and made tea in a pot for the first time in months, which he kept topping up with hot water. At seven o'clock he reached for his iPad. It was something he needed after last night. A moment or two in the lost life he should be living.

'Wasn't expecting you Jamie,' it took a couple of seconds for Claudette to settle into focus. 'We're a bit behind this morning. Christmas holiday knocks us out of rhythm and getting back to school takes a few days.'

'Thought I'd take a chance.'

'Okay, can't let you miss her. Emmy, get yourself down here child, Daddy's on the iPad.' Claudette looked back at the screen. 'If we're late I'll explain things to this new, young teacher she's got. I like explaining things to her, in her youth,' Claudette chuckled and Jamie knew such an encounter would only go one way.

'Daddy,' Emmy was ready for school, except for the unrestrained mass of her hair.

'Missed you honey,' Jamie began. 'But I had to see my girl, wish her happy New Year and tell her I love her.'

'It's past New Year,' Emmy's head tilted and both hands went to her hips.

'Well maybe I'll just have to leave it at I love you.'

Emmy's mouth opened and she popped out her tongue. 'Got to get my bag ready.' And she darted out of shot.

'And sort your hair, or I'm coming up with the brush and you don't want that,' Claudette slipped back in front of the screen. 'She's fine. Getting cleverer every day. Like watching Cara grow up again.' She smiled.

Jamie's head bowed a little. 'Thanks. I don't tell you enough how much I appreciate what you do. Not near enough.'

'And there was me feeling taken for granted. Go on with you. I have a young teacher to educate. Tell her the truth about youth and knowledge. Remind her that when an old person dies a library burns.'

'Okay,' Jamie's face leaned in. 'Got a long shift ahead. I'll call again soon.'

And as the iPad image closed, Jamie smiled to himself. A library burns. He'd loved to hear Claudette say it when Cara was getting above herself.

He breathed in, then stood, ready for the day.

'You look brighter,' Shona had already mapped out the day and written up the paperwork to dismiss the last of Clegg's fictitious tasks. 'Come on, canteen. I've been here since six. We need to make up for that missed take-away.'

'At least your appetite's back.' Shona tidied the scatter of plates on the table. 'Called Jephcott for a debrief. But the photos? Those score sheet things. If we go in the corridor room? Got them on my laptop now. Had a quick scan first thing, when there was hardly anyone around, but—'

'Need to drill down.' Jamie finished her sentence.

Parked at the back of the university again, Shona sent a confirmation message. A minute or so passed and the expected car pulled alongside. Shona and Jamie got out and crossed to Jephcott's Audi.

'So, these are the potential victims,' Shona said from the back seat. 'Suggests we've found two out of three.' She leaned forwards and passed her phone.

Jephcott absorbed each image. 'And the text pages?'

'Each girl's monthly takings. Sorted in order.'

'There's more than three,' Jamie cut into the exchange. 'The bastard's been in charge since July.'

'Maybe not,' Shona leaned and touched Jamie's shoulder. 'Might not have started right off. Forensics from the canal. End of November, early December... and Tree Girl? Cozza says two months before, from the insect analysis. So, there's no guarantee he went to one a month right off the bat. See what Katya knows for definite.'

'Ask her by all means, but what are your priorities here?' Jephcott's voice was measured.

'Follow the money, more forensics,' Shona took her phone back. 'Quiz Katya again. And Marika Morcanu, see—'

'Fuck her and her family. There's a clock ticking for one of those girls, and that bitch is playing you for a prat. Self-preservation bollocks. Need some air.'

Jamie opened the car door and moved away. There was a large boulder set in a circle of gravel. Shona and Jephcott watched him stomp over and sit down.

'Bloody Rodin's Thinker in a woolly hat,' Shona tried to sound calm.

Jephcott held his gaze on Jamie and his motionless pose. 'Maybe ease back. Give him a day or two.'

Shona flicked open her phone screen. The face of Liliana Normova stared back.

Beyond the windscreen, Jamie stood up and walked about, taking deep breaths, then he returned to the boulder. This time his feet were up and his face buried between his knees. Shona gave the occasional glance, but used the time to talk next steps through with Jephcott.

'What did Jamie say about this?' Jephcott had listened to the outline.

Shona shrugged, then looked out towards the boulder. Jamie was on his feet and striding back.

'End of the month,' he was talking as soon as he'd pulled the car door open. 'That's the priority. The bank docs and where they lead. Girl three, or however many there are. Gone already. This operation needs to speed up. Any information? Evaluate and decide. Like triage. Check. Act, or move on. Don't waste time on those beyond saving.' His tone was flat now. No aggression. Nothing for show.

Shona looked at his face and sensed the hand of his past: of Africa, of life in a world where tossing a coin between life and death was everyday business. As she continued to stare, he flicked his phone and held up the spreadsheet image.

'Every few seconds,' he turned the screen towards her. 'They'll be seeing that... who's winning? Who's standing on the trapdoor?'

'Bloody market forces,' Shona nodded. She'd seen the frequency and price data; the way, towards the end of the month, the girls in the relegation zone tried to up their strike rate by dropping their prices. 'Pile 'em high, sell 'em cheap,' her voice was a whisper and the genesis of a tear blurred her vision. 'Black Friday and the January sales.'

Shona drove after they left Jeffcott. Jamie's assessment of priorities encouraged her to think the storm had passed, but maybe not to push a conversation.

Approaching the city along Hanover Way, Shona kept sweeping east. Her gaze flicked to the side as she drove. Jamie stared, out and away, fixed on passing streets, but she needed to speak, needed eye contact somewhere open and preferably green: somewhere less constricted by hard-faced buildings.

Shona pulled up in a neat estate that overlooked the parkland that surrounded the Cholera Monument. 'Jephcott said you should ease back. Last few days you've been through—'

'The Buzzard's just a bag man, an errand boy.'

Shona was surprised by the randomness of Jamie's mind and its constant rotation of evidence. 'So who else is in the frame?' She consciously softened her voice.

'I know who I'd like it to be,' Jamie made brief eye-contact.

'Logical. Next up the food chain.'

'Nah. Hasn't got the bottle. He's all mouth and daddy's money. Love it to be, but nothing nails it down. Christ, I wish there was,' Jamie's hand flexed and he hit the dashboard. 'Love it to be. I'd love it.'

'But what? I think we sh—'

'We should focus on the evidence. Not make it fit what we want. Keep focus. We owe it to those girls.'

'And if we can't nail the paper trail between Bakula and Mr Solar Properties?'

'Or Fox.'

Like that's not making evidence fit conclusions went through her head, but she said: 'A meeting with Katya, take an hour or so; bit of time planning questions beforehand. Could give us nothing, but…' she shrugged. 'We need to keep meeting, keep her feeling valued… so, yeah. You're right. Don't get deflected. Keep on the docs. But Katya… I'll text her. There might be some detail.' Shona reached across and touched his hand. 'And Marika…' she softened her voice. 'We need—'

'Fuck sake,' his hand pulled away and he was out the car, storming towards the Cholera Monument.

Shona slammed back against the headrest and swore, then

looked out. He was already a small figure heading for Clay Woods.

'Away and shite,' she started the car, her voice resigned, not angry.'Walk to the city centre won't kill him.'

Shona decided against the claustrophobia of the station for her afternoon of grinding document interrogation, so she retraced her way back to the university. Checking her police ID, the librarian led her to a row of largely unoccupied study carrels. Shona plugged in her laptop, arranged her folder of banking papers and, turning to the highlighted sheets, she began cutting and pasting financial transactions, hoping for an unbroken link to an account with a name. Around five she began packing away. Her eyes were tired. She looked across at a young student in designer glasses and wondered if she should visit an optician. A final tidy and she stood and banged the edges of her folders into a neat block. 'Bollocks,' she felt the words in her mouth. 'It needs to move on.'

The news was on the car radio so, after she'd finished texting, Shona switched to Radio 2, hoping for a stream of sing-a-long music to fill the space where she might have to think. She wanted a few minutes respite but, inevitably, thoughts of Jamie intruded. 'The minibus run, the fire safety man act, not long apart. Lot of adrenaline. Maybe he's just hit overspill?' she tried to rationalise as she drove.

Inside her flat, food was waiting courtesy of the auto-timer on her oven. Too much for one. Shona opened her recent contacts and tapped. An evening of bank data stretched ahead, but the voice at the other end of the phone would decide if it was on a full stomach or solitary pot noodles.

Shona laid the kitchen table and the rich smell of chorizo-spiked chilli seeped around the flat. Jamie arrived and hung up his coat. He was quiet and Shona knew better than to say anything that held the potential for ignition, so she gave a casual update of the non-events of her afternoon and Jamie responded with occasional extended sentences about nothing remarkable.

'Still,' Shona told herself. 'Step in the right direction. You were right.' She continued, trying to maintain a positive connection. 'End of the month deadline. Everything else? Mop it up later.' *Deadline*. Shona swallowed as she registered her own words.

The evening came and went in a predictable progression from food, to washing-up bowl, to bed. Later, when Shona's head was just above Jamie's heart and his arms around her, she said: 'I texted Katya. Hopefully, she's on the day shift.'

Jamie nodded.

'And,' Shona took a deep breath. 'Marika Morcanu.'

'Oh yeah, what's she got to say?' She felt the muscles in his arms and chest tighten as he stared into the darkness.

'That photograph of her father after the stroke.'

'So he's reaping the whirlwind. What goes around comes around.'

'Maybe. But you know it's not really Photoshop don't you.'

'Unless I can put my finger in the holes made by the nails. That's what my Nan used to say.'

Shona lay still and counted the rise and fall of his breathing. When it reached twelve, she said: 'If she'll let you do that, will you listen?'

In the quiet, Shona could see him staring at a patch of ceiling where the dreary streetlight fell on the plaster relief. Eventually, she felt the grind of his teeth lessen and his breathing soften and slow.

The morning shift's first couple of hours were memos, phone calls and various forms. Jamie and Shona just accepted the mundane clearing of decks as the price to pay for some autonomy in the day.

Around ten, Shona arrived at the desk with two lidded coffees. 'Nipped to the canteen,' she sat down and watched Jamie take a couple of sips. 'Anyway, this afternoon?'

Jamie shrugged.

'We'll have dropped Katya off by half twelve. You're right, keep the bank stuff front and centre, but I can make up those hours at home. But maybe not have all our eggs in one basket?'

Jamie gave the slightest of nods.

'Okay, so that's one decision, and I've made another,' and she stood. 'Too much coffee, I need a trip to the little girls' room. Get this stuff sorted while I'm away. Don't need nosey neighbours for what we're doing next.'

'Two birds with one stone,' Shona sat in a toilet cubicle and took her burner phone out of her bag. When she came back, she and Jamie grabbed pens and paper, made their way to the beige cube and began mapping out the who, what and wheres of their interrogation of Katya.

'Anything said by Bakula? Any threats or intimidation?' she began her list.

'If we talk about me going round as the gas man. What I saw. Make it more conversational. Give her space to go with what's on her mind.'

Shona jotted down Jamie's thoughts.

When they'd finished, they took two coloured pens and underlined whether it was Jamie or Shona asking a particular question. Then they rehearsed for a while, watching the clock.

55

The taxi signs, the lying in the back seat. The pick-up of Katya was as per. As Jamie drove to an unpopulated green space, Shona kept things light with her usual feminine-bonding chat.

'Nice touch, the teasing,' Jamie parked and turned to face Katya. Shona looked quizzical. 'Said she'd get me a price list when I was at the reception desk. Good bit of misdirection. Attack, always the best defence.'

'Like you with Bakula,' Katya smirked back.

'Like him with everyone.' Shona shook her head.

'Weird place,' Jamie went on. 'Fairy lights, painted on windows, chiffon drapes. But it's basically a big shed full of metal boxes.'

'Like inside punters' heads. Nothing real.' Katya shuffled in her seat.

'Must make you…'

Katya shrugged. 'Work in box. I try keep it there.'

'But when three girls have disappeared? Girls you knew?' Shona slipped in one of the questions.

'Only Liliana. Not others.'

'So Bakula, he's—'

'Has other unit,' Katya cut in. 'Doncaster, near motorway.'

'Doncaster?' Shona repeated.

'Him, yes. But others. Leeds, more than one. Bradford. Others in charge.'

'You've been there?'

'No. He talk about them. Once girl from Leeds, Slovak, bring her for two weeks when three girls sick.'

'Did she say…'

'No chance. Not stay. Came and went on train. Arrive for evening rush. Get first train back in morning. Shit for her.'

'That blue light,' Jamie changed tack.

Katya was looking at her hands. 'Better than faces and number sheet.'

As Shona looked she saw Katya's eyes fix and moisten. 'But you, Kasia,' Shona used her real name. 'You're strong. Your numbers. Every month, never outside the top quarter. Nothing for you to worry about.'

'Nothing for Katya. No worries for her. But Kasia? She know things change. Kasia see her friends. Watch them break. Every day more cracks…'

The conversation petered out. Jamie drove. A glossy magazine opened. Shona wittered. And they were there at the galvanised gates. Kasia got out and walked down the drive in her Ugg boots. She was carrying Katya's stilettos in a creased Moda Polska bag.

Shona drove and made occasional conversational forays. Jamie was responsive at first, but, as close-packed terraces became council estates, Jamie's word-count diminished. Shona sensed his mind shifting to the business of the afternoon. Semi-detached gave way to hedged and wide-drived detached and then to dotted, edge-of-the moors islands of solid stone set in a sea of winter-brown bracken. Then they were out towards The Peaks: Hathersage, Bamford, that general direction.

'Christ, not a country pub with a blazing fire?' Jamie was looking out at a road sign. 'If I'd known I'd have worn cords and a Fair Isle jumper.'

Shona sucked her teeth and carried on driving. The land rose and flattened; gorse became golf club, became hillocked sheep country.

'Driving towards Hope,' Shona tried a weak smile as they passed the road sign that said Hope Road and led to the village of the same name. Jamie held his silent, side window stare.

About ten minutes later, on the other side of the village he said: 'Beyond Hope now.' But his face remained fixed on his side of the road.

Soon, there was a gravelled lay-by. Jamie recognised the eco-friendly Land Rover and shifted in his seat. The driver's side door opened and Marika Morcanu stepped down and fastened her quilted coat to shield herself from the wind that funnelled between the peaks. This time it was Jamie that recognised the brand.

'Canada Goose,' he said. 'Get five of my Berghaus for what that cost.'

The gravel grated under their feet.

'I could drive us,' Marika got straight to the point. 'But…'

'We'll follow,' Jamie cut in before Shona could reply, turning back towards their car.

The smug Land Rover snaked away, slowing to allow Shona's hatchback to latch on. The scenery continued to be bleakly beautiful; thin grass pierced by bones of white limestone giving way to colour-starved heather and fingers of snow reaching down from the tops. Fifteen minutes later, on the edge of a village, the Land Rover turned between tall, gritstone gateposts. A hundred yards of drive passed through lawns and led to a frontage whose construction was a modern take on imposing Edwardian.

Marika Morcanu parked, walked towards the entrance and waited. Shona got out and moved towards her, but Jamie stood facing into the bitter wind. At the decorative porch there was an intercom. Two plate-glass doors swung inwards automatically. Shona followed and, as she signed in, heard Jamie's feet dodge through the doors before they shut.

The duty manager stepped beyond the reception desk.

'I've ordered drinks,' Marika turned to Shona. 'He's being showered. Takes a while: hoists, wheelchairs.'

'Most of our residents are just seeking a safe and comfortable home from home,' the duty-manager nodded towards a group playing chess as he led the way from the reception desk to a pair of well-upholstered sofas. 'The more specialised facilities are concentrated at the rear of the building in an annexe,' and he smiled and moved back to his station.

A tray arrived with cups and biscuits. 'That he should end up here,' Marika reached for the cafetiere. 'It was opened by the Duke of Kent. He would have liked that. Big fan of the aristocracy.'

'I'd have thought Romania… given the peasant life,' Shona arranged the cups, trying to ignore Jamie grinding his teeth.

'Came a thousand years ago. Still on top. That's what he admired. Big reader of history. Battle of Hastings was a favourite soapbox.'

Shona waited.

'Duke William and his bandit mates,' Marika continued. 'That's what he called them. Came here. Took a chance and won.'

'So he admires killers?' Jamie focused on a window.

'More what came after. The longevity,' Marika's voice was measured. 'Every family is just a generation from a Swiss ski chalet or the shit-heap. One of his sayings. Could've been our family motto. Set the family up for generations, that was what he wanted. Said money alone wasn't enough. Said it was about attitude, values, being responsible. Legacy, but that wasn't a word he used.'

'So he started a business exploiting whores,' Jamie's eyes turned towards her.

'No,' Marika met his eye. 'He started a corner shop. Open all hours, and the whores came in. He had a couple of store rooms he wasn't using. It was safer than the street... warmer.'

'Christ, are you sure he wasn't Mother Theresa?'

'Oh, he charged. Rented space by the hour, but like I say, warmer... and more comfortable. The girls could earn more.'

'So an equal opportunities pimp. It's political correctness gone mad.'

Shona's eyes bored towards Jamie.

'If you like. But not really a pimp. No compulsion. He charged rent. Work or not. Leave or stay. It was up to them. Always has been. Always... right up to the time that bastard Bakula showed up.' Marika's voice hardened.

'So like hairdressers renting a chair?' Shona tried to diffuse the tension.

'Yes. Good analogy,' Marika's tone softened again. 'He would let them book ahead and take a deposit. But a pimp. No. Pimps control, threaten.'

'Yeah,' Jamie stared at her. 'That's what they do. Never known a working girl go any length of time on the street without a pimp. So...'

'Oh there were pimps in the early days. Didn't like what my father was doing. There were threats.'

Jamie snorted. 'And he was a shopkeeper?'

'He was a big man, strong. Grew up on a farm where the closest thing to a machine was a donkey. Hard times. Fight or go under. All those families – clans. Vendetta. Same word in Romanian. Do you think some mouthy woman-beater would bother a man like my father? Urs, Mihai would call him – like Latin, Ursa – the bear.' Marika paused and now it was her gaze that went to the window. 'Age is cruel. Maybe if it was just a slow decline in the power of his arm. But then the TIAs and worse.'

'TIAs?' Shona repeated

'Transient ischaemic attacks,' Jamie said. 'Mini-strokes. Sometimes the episodes seem to pass, other times it just masks personality changing damage. Matches what Mihai said.'

Shona and Marika looked.

'Medic, remember? They didn't just teach us about bullet holes and trench foot.'

'Then at home, he shouted at my mother. He would never do that. And with me and my brother, one time, discussing business, something and nothing chit-chat, and he hit the desk... Later, Mamma told us how he would cry, frustrated, not knowing where the anger came from.'

A nurse approached and smiled and they stood and followed down to a glazed walkway, then the annexe. Here the corridors were flat plaster, functional but light. The nurse reached the third door.

'Use the beeper if you need anything,' and she stood aside.

The room was light and warm. Its far wall was mainly glass: landscaped gardens against a backdrop of distant hills. Jamie recognised winter-bare fingers of mountain ash and the stark white bark of Himalayan birch.

Inside, flowers and plug-in air fresheners masked the leakage of decrepit old age and, like a waxwork left too close to a fire, the ruins of Neculai Morcanu lay propped on a pillow in clean pyjamas. Shona saw Jamie's shoulders sag as his eyes fell on the old man.

'The photograph,' Marika moved to the bed and kissed her father's forehead. 'Unless you're going to say something crass about 3D printers.'

Jamie shuffled back and his gaze fixed on the floor.

'Sorry,' Marika Morcanu softened her voice. 'What you said about the TIAs... that was helpful.'

Between the bed and large window was a sofa and two armchairs; heavy plaids and cabriole legs. Marika walked over and put a folder on a low table. Shona joined her on a sofa and, slowly, Jamie moved to an armchair.

Shona checked developments about job creation and housing for the girls. Jamie sat back as the women talked. Shona sensed his change of mood, but kept him in her peripheral vision, ready to fill any conversational gaps where he might bludgeon in.

'After the 2008 crash, commercial property prices dipped. Luckily we weren't overcommitted. Since then,' Marika pointed at a block of text, 'most of our non-residential properties are on six month, renewable leases.'

'So you want us to let you keep Shag City open for another six months,' the return of Jamie's cynicism took Marika by surprise.

'No,' a hint of red eased across her throat. 'This is old ground. One unit, six months' rent,' and she looked directly at him. 'Actually less than three before it falls due for renewal.' She held her gaze on him. 'First time we met, Sergeant Seagrief, I told you the money was irrelevant. Told you we'd wanted out for years before this Polish business. It was just out of respect for his feelings.' And she looked towards her father's motionless shell.

Shona followed her eyes, but then Marika was up, pulling a handkerchief from her sleeve and dabbing the trail of spittle that was drooling from the corner of the old man's mouth. When she sat back down, she took a deep breath and spoke now towards Shona.

'You've got the paperwork. Everything in mine and my brother's name is legitimate. Always has been. Moving out, being legit, it was all he talked about. "Make sure you and Dominik never have to walk in farmyard shit." That's what he would say. Delusions of dynasty? Maybe.'

'But you and your brother? Easy money, sense of entitlement,' Jamie relapsed into type.

'Go for it,' Marika hardened again. 'Investigate. Make a prat of yourself.' And she stood and moved back to the seat by the bed.

'There's nothing and you know it. So what's this? How you get your entertainment?'

'Bringing down entitled bastards? Yeah, I suppose you could call it a hobby. Bastards living on inherited money and other people's sweat. You, Fox, you're all the same.'

'Fox?' Marika sneered.

'Vulpes – Fox, his lordship and his slutty daughter. Skimming cash off the girls' rents.'

'Fox?' Marika shook her head. 'Fox wouldn't touch anything like that.'

'Mr Nice Guy is he?'

'No, he's a bastard and his daughter is a slut, but risk and reward? Too much risk for not enough money.'

'Not enough money? At least five hundred a girl every month, and that's just on the rents.'

Marika's shoulders began to shake and then she laughed quietly. 'You really have no idea how the other half live, do you? Five hundred a girl, a month. A tenth of a point on his currency investments, an hour or two getting a lawyer to check a contract, a couple of bets at the casino. Five hundred pounds a month, a girl – he's probably lost more money at the dry cleaners because he hadn't checked his pockets.'

Shona had moved away and was now leaning on the window ledge, looking out at flecks of snow floating into the winter-sparse garden

'If someone's skimming that money off the girls,' Marika continued. 'It'll be a middle-man, or one of his staff pulling a scam. He has sharp accountants – a spike like that would leap off the balance sheets.'

'But him, men like Fox, they're your father's heroes,' Jamie spoke with a slow cold.

'Men like him? No, not men. I told you – longevity. That's his hero. Dynasties who keep the ski chalet and avoid the shit-heap, generation after generation.' Marika paused and almost smiled. 'Knowing that after he was dead, his yet unborn family would trace back the line of their riches and find him sitting there – the founding father, the first one out of the farmyard, even if he still had some shit on his boots.'

The old man in the bed shifted and took a breath.

'Yes, papa. Abraham, Duke William, Neculai Morcanu. We used to laugh.' Marika Morcanu turned and her voice recalibrated. 'And now you want your justice? You want to put what's left of him in a prison. In prison? Don't you think God's put him there already? Be honest with yourself, Sergeant. What is it you're after? Justice or vengeance?' Marika's jaw hardened and lifted. 'Is that all you've got, Sergeant Seagrief? Vengeance?'

Shona turned from the window, but didn't move.

'And what would your vengeance consist of? Harder bed? Rougher toilet paper. Look at him, he wouldn't notice the difference.'

Jamie looked to Shona but her face didn't flicker.

'And the girls? Where do they go? Trying to tie in my brother and me? Good luck with that, because you'll find nothing. Nothing in our name. No connection. That was what our father was working for – for us to never have shit on our boots. Right from the start, we were insulated, locked in a sterile bubble. So carry on with this vengeance that you call justice, and what happens? We're forced to jump ship and your vengeance turns into what? If the girls are lucky, the Polish mafia maintain their interest. If they're not? My cousins hear rumours of Albanians looking for a toehold.'

Shona remained motionless, like a camera recording the scene.

'So have your vengeance and tell yourself it's justice, but it's the girls that'll pick up your bill for the chip on your shoulder. Look at him.' Marika sank into a chair and faced her father. 'Look at him. Christ, do you really think the CPS will prosecute? Thousands of pounds from the public purse to pay for his care, when they can leave the family to pick up the tab?'

Shona straightened, but came no nearer as she watched Jamie move to a chair facing Marika. She saw his swagger but knew it for what it was: a sham that hoped to cover up his capitulation. Easing down the room, she settled on a seat a couple of feet behind his shoulder.

After a few seconds Jamie cleared his throat, then: 'The girls... their future safety...'

'Like I've—' Marika caught herself. 'Like we've said. Finishing a skills audit should be quick. Across the family, there are jobs, potential ways up and out... so much gone,' she reached across and held her father's hand. 'There was never a room where you didn't know he was in it. Look at him now. I hope his soul is gone. I hope it doesn't feel what this body has become. He did so much... knew so much.'

'In Africa there's a saying. When an old person dies a library burns,' Jamie spoke, as if talking to himself and Shona felt the air change.

'My father's books are burning fast,' Marika looked at her hands. 'Just waiting for the fire to destroy the roof and walls.'

56

'So, back to following the money,' Shona had been driving for about ten minutes before she broke the silence. 'Nailing down who's behind Solar Properties.'

She dropped Jamie and made her way home. They'd kissed a *see-you-in-a-bit* married couple's kiss and he'd got out of the car. So many loads had shifted over the course of the afternoon, Shona recognised the need to give them time to settle.

Inside his flat, Jamie opened the fridge; there was a pierce-the-film cottage pie. He checked the use-by date and went to sort out his running kit. Fifteen minutes later he was pounding the pavements, watching his shadow shift as he moved from streetlight to streetlight.

'Careful Fatboy, I ain't giving you the kiss of life.' A kid on a bike zoomed past. Jamie gave him the finger. Five minutes later and he was under the trees in Endcliffe Park. He clicked on his head-torch and the shadows of overhanging trees yawed in rhythm with his running.

'She's given you a route to an endgame. You know that don't you?' And there was Cara, closer than the darkness that skulked beyond the torch's brief bubble of light.

Jamie upped his pace a little.

'Can't blame her for living up to her father's dreams. Not everyone that does well needs to be despised.'

'Substantial majority.' He sucked through his nose and spat into the bushes.

Cara's voice laughed in his head. 'But you know it makes sense, don't you, deep down? Like us in that bush hospital, eeking out medicines. You know you can't save everyone. No shame in just doing your best… and laws, Jamie. Since when did you become so fixed on what a law said? Certainly not immigration law.'

Jamie ran on, sucking air, hearing Cara in the lurching shadows, but he had no answer, so pushed deeper into pain, hoping oxygen debt would blot out thought. Beyond the park the gradient rose and he was sick.

'Glad I didn't pierce the film,' he wiped his mouth on his sleeve. 'Been a waste of pie.'

Shona had another evening traipsing through bank documents: Sheffield, the fake Marble Arch operation, Poland and Bavaria – the same rotation of payment codes in and out, the same old dead-ends. She fell asleep around midnight, and launched back into it after her first coffee of the morning at work.

Jamie was out at court, but finally appeared around lunchtime.

'How'd it go?' Shona looked up as he hung his coat on the chair back.

'Same old, same old. Bring everyone in, witnesses, me, couple of social workers, then plead guilty five minutes before getting called in.'

Shona gave a slight tilt of the head. She'd seen the routine a hundred times before. Jamie offered to fetch some sandwiches and they drank coffee and ate at their desk.

'Clegg's told me to look into that spate of posh car thefts in Whirlow. Reckons they get driven straight onto a transporter, then into containers. Twenty-four hours later Belgium, then India, Far East. Big business.'

'Enjoy,' Shona waved a hand.

'Yeah, might fall lucky with a distraught housewife whose only way of dulling the pain of losing her Porsche is getting tanked up on lunchtime prosecco and throwing herself into random sex.'

'Dream on. More likely to throw herself under a random bus if you knock on her door.'

Jamie pulled his coat on. 'See you at the end of the shift?'

'Aye, I'll wait.'

At about quarter past six, Shona's phone buzzed.

In the car park.

Jamie was hunched in his driver's seat reading an RSPB magazine with a small LED torch when Shona tapped his windscreen.

'Got a mountain of work, but there's food if you want.'

Parking by the steps at the rear of Shona's flat, Jamie looked at his phone. There was a missed call. Ten minutes later he was sat at Shona's kitchen table with his hands wrapped around a coffee, marvelling at her ability to set an oven to come on at a preordained time. Parboiled potatoes had roasted as they sat alongside some Scottish variation of goulash. Jamie leaned down and peered through the glass panel in the oven door.

'Another one to Stow me oot.'

Shona poured a kettle onto frozen peas. 'It's no good unless I get a run at it,' Shona picked up her mug and pulled her laptop from her bag. 'It'll be here somewhere, but it'll be a slog.'

More coffee and Jamie washed up, while Shona spread papers across a table and a couple of other horizontal surfaces. When Jamie had stacked everything on the drainer, he pulled on his coat. Shona followed him out to the hall. At the door she leaned against his chest and they kissed.

'You know it's...' she tucked her chin into the quilt of his collar.

Jamie kissed her forehead. As he opened the door he turned. 'Sunday.'

Shona waited.

'Had a text off our Mandy. Says I've got to go for lunch.'

Shona had a text as well, but hers was from Janine Bowker; one for the morning, so she went back to hours of bank statements and blurred vision. There was a possible. She took a photo of a page of rainbow highlighter lines and attached them to a WhatsApp. Then she filed everything into a ringbinder and went to bed.

'Leave the packet. We've got guests.'

The bank manager clamped a multiple-ringed hand on the young bank clerk's wrist. He'd arranged a few biscuits on a plate, but was moving away with the rest, still in their wrapper. His smile was nervous as he placed them back on the tray next to the teapot and crockery and turned to leave.

'Yeah, I know I'm a cow,' Janine Bowker waited for the door to close. 'But some days, well most days, you wouldn't believe how boring this job can get. Jesus, one day we had Garibaldis and I had to phone me nan to get her to crochet some bunting... so, I've had a look. Someone was having a late night. But if you've got your originals?'

Shona stood by the bank manager as she scrolled around her computer screen. Jamie sat quietly with the biscuits.

For a few minutes she pored over Shona's ringbinder, going back and forth to her computer screen. Then she said: 'Yeah, Dublin. You're right, originated in Ireland.'

'Good job for you they've got that London agency, then,' Shona leaned towards the desk.

'Not really,' Janine shrugged. 'Records are on their Dublin server and the Irish can be particularly awkward since our government screwed them over that crappy customs deal.'

Jamie looked at Shona.

'But all is not lost,' Janine Bowker was irritatingly cheerful. 'I was trailing through our Solar account again…' she opened a drawer and took out a concertina of printed paper. 'There's cashpoint withdrawals. Not many, but…'

'I saw those,' Shona squinted at where Janine Bowker was pointing. 'But we already know it's the Buzzard using this account.'

'Nah,' Janine shook her head. 'Business account. Different tiers of access. He's pay-in only.'

'So, Mr Solar Properties? You've had the bastard's name all along.' Jamie's voice made Shona flinch.

'Mr Fake I.D.' Janine shuffled more papers across the desk. 'The names, utility bills. I've checked it out. Doesn't match.'

'But…' Shona began.

'It's a bastard,' Janine reached for a biscuit. 'Getting new accounts. Nicking each other's customers. Big business. Piece of piss to mock up a couple of bills and stuff. Driving licence? Photos are crap. Don't really want to catch 'em out. New customers equals bunce time. Manager's targets. Bonus for the counter staff. Might even have been done online from some random public computer.'

Shona and Jamie sank into their chairs.

'But this card. It has full rights. So withdrawals, transfers,' Janine Bowker went on. 'And Mr Pay-in-only Buzzard bloke doesn't.'

'So someone might recognise him? Mr Solar Properties?' Shona rose a little.

'We've got loads of staff. Hundreds of customers every day. Like I say, dead easy online. Imagine a scanned driving licence. Utility letters? Bit of tippex, put your name above the address, take a photo. Job done.'

'So, gets us nowhere,' Jamie's head bowed and Shona recognised the loop of obscenities as his lips moved silently.

'He's a fucking ray of sunshine isn't he?' Janine looked at Shona. 'Anyway, there's more than one way to skin a cat,' and she turned the concertina of papers around to face Shona.

'There's occasional cashpoint withdrawals, but few and far between, so no pattern for you to stake out.'

Jamie was still locked in his silent obscenities loop.

'But, if I ask nicely, our boffins can snatch the recording when the specific card is used,' Janine Bowker turned back to her screen. 'And most cashpoints have built-in CCTV. Just means a bit of a waiting game.'

'How long?' Shona's face lightened and Jamie broke out of his loop and looked up.

'So this account goes back about six months and the longest gap is… three weeks.'

'Three fucking weeks,' Jamie's fingers locked and strained against each other.

'Yeah, but the last time he used it was before Christmas. So three weeks max? We're not far off.'

'And the boffins?' asked Shona.

'If I push, and I will – couple of hours.'

Shona's head went back in her chair and she sucked down air. Jamie straightened his fingers, sliding them along his thighs and the meeting slipped into banter and chit-chat.

An hour later, when Shona was back at her desk, an email came in. The subject line read *Walsall – Paris of the Black Country*. There were several attachments. Copies of ID documents used to set up accounts. Janine Bowker had been right. Shona looked at the scanned driving licence.

'Christ, with the exception of Beyoncé and the Pope, it could be almost anyone on the planet.'

57

The road was quiet. Sunday, dull grey and still, but the sky was lightening. It was January, so it could pass for a good day. Shona had flowers. She'd been surprised to see a carrier full of comics, a small Lego model and something pink and sparkly on the back seat of Jamie's car. As they got out, he reached for the bag. A child's face popped up in the window. He seemed to turn and call. Jamie was still locking the car when Jacko opened the door. Three children crowded behind him.

'Jamie…' Jacko held out a hand.

Jamie strode up the path and they shook, then the children swarmed forwards. The girl and the youngest boy hugged Jamie around the legs, the elder boy peered in the carrier bag.

'Star Wars?' he asked.

'Go with the stuff from Christmas,' Jamie lifted the box.

'Be through in sec,' Mandy's voice came from the kitchen as they stepped into the hall. 'Just got my hand up a chicken's bum.'

Jacko smiled at Shona and led her and Jamie through to the lounge. The little girl whispered something behind her hand. The adults sat and the children scrambled onto a shag-pile rug. Jamie began his introductions.

Mandy was by the door, wiping her hands on a tea towel.

'Shona, really happy you could come. I could say our Jamie's told me all about you, but we both know that wouldn't be true.'

Shona stood and went to extend a hand, but Mandy threw the tea towel to Jacko, stepped forwards and gave her a hug. Both women smiled as they stepped back. 'Actually, he has said a couple of things, and the WhatsApp photo doesn't do you justice. Nowhere near.'

There was general chit-chat. Teas and coffees. Shona helped take the wrapping off the pink, sparkly tiara and magic wand set.

Mandy stood. 'The dog's been in that back porch long enough and I don't want her under my feet in the kitchen.' She looked at Jacko.

'Okay kids, get your coats,' Jacko reached for a frisbee from behind the sofa. 'You got a coat mate, or do you need to borrow my old kagool again?'

Shona took a step towards the door.

'No,' Mandy smiled. 'Stay in the warm. It'll give me a chance to talk to someone who looks like they're listening.'

A tangle of dog and children piled into the back of Jacko's van. Jamie got in the front.

'Peace at last,' Mandy shook some potatoes into a roasting tin. 'Hope chicken's okay?'

'Yes, great. Love a proper roast.'

'Good,' Mandy picked up a brown cuboid in a tin foil dish. 'Nut Roast. Jacko can take it work for his dinner. Had it in reserve. Be just like our Jamie to drop a surprise vegetarian on me.'

Mandy opened the oven door, lifted out the chicken and pushed a probe into a pocket of deep flesh. 'Near enough. Probably only a danger if you're a pensioner or breast feeding,' she teased, and then poured boiling water into a couple of cups. 'So? You and our Jamie.'

'What's he said?

Nothing. But you're a woman and you're here.'

'And that's…?'

'Unheard of,' Mandy looked over the rim of her cup. 'Never even a vague, nameless hint of anyone before.'

Shona took a sip of tea and remained still. Then, after a few seconds: 'But you're the only one that really knows him.'

'Really knows? I doubt he really knows himself.'

'But he tells you things. You talk.'

'Old ground mostly. Bits drip out over time. And Claudette.'

'Claudette?'

'Emmy's grandma,' Mandy fiddled with her teaspoon. 'We Skype sometimes. He doesn't know.'

Both women sat back a little

'But now he's got you…' Mandy lifted her eyes and smiled. 'Bringing you here. He must trust…'

'Trust? Maybe in some ways… but to talk to? Doubt I'll ever reach that favoured status.'

Mandy reached for her tea again. Shona followed suit.

'So, you know?' Mandy spoke again.

'Seen a couple of photos. Odd words. Sierra Leone. His wife died. He has a daughter. Her grandmother looks after her. Odd words here and there.'

'And he told you how she…'

'He said Africa.'

Mandy nodded. 'Not Ebola? Not how?'

'Well, I know that's why he went. Military paramedic, with the marines.'

'But not Cara?'

Shona waited.

Mandy pulled her chair forwards and shuffled closer. 'He wants you to know. He wouldn't have brought you here if… but, you know Jamie… look.' Mandy went to a drawer, then came and sat next to Shona on the sofa. 'This is Emmy.' She opened an album, then flicked the pages. 'And this is when she was born.'

'And that's his wife, in the green dress,' Shona recognised the photo. 'That one's in his flat. She's…'

'Yeah… Cara was… you and her. Not frightened of batting above his average with either of you. Must be his effortless charm.'

'Effortless something.' And both women laughed.

'And here. They were at work.' Mandy held a photograph of Jamie in scrubs, with a plastic face visor perched on his head. Cara was in a white coat with a stethoscope around her neck.

'She was—'

'A doctor. Yes. Specialised in tropical medicine. Trained in London then went back home to Sierra Leone. Didn't he tell you?'

'Christ. Her looks *and* a doctor? Nothing to challenge a girl's self-confidence there then.'

Mandy flicked through more photos: more of Emmy, Claudette, their house in Freetown and then the tented medical station.

'Official line was an outbreak of Yellow Fever, easy to pass off the symptoms apparently…' and Mandy laid out the tale: the jealously, the argument, the taking the Yellow Fever job, Claudette's description of the goat stealer, the mass graves, bodies slaked in lime and Cara with the flies on her eyelids. At the end both women were holding hands, without remembering when it happened, their tears falling into the silence. After some minutes – neither of them knew how many – they shuffled apart and straightened themselves.

'Here,' Mandy stood and went to the drawer again. 'Use this…' and she passed Shona a wad of tissues. 'Best get ourselves sorted before those daft buggers get back.'

After dinner Mandy and Shona washed up.

'Should we?' Jamie nodded towards the kitchen.

'Nah,' Jacko was at one with the sofa. 'They enjoy it. Gives 'em chance to talk and play the martyr. Be the highlight of their afternoon.'

When Mandy and Shona emerged from the kitchen with a tray of teas and a giant Toblerone, the children grabbed chocolate then sneaked off to video games and Cartoon Network. Jacko had the football on with the volume down. Jamie was spark out, his mouth open and the dog sprawled across his lap.

'Thought I'd enjoy a bit of footy while he's zonked out,' Jacko looked towards the unconscious Jamie. 'He always moans if he has to watch it.'

Jamie and Shona got in the car. Everybody hugged everybody and, as they pulled away, Shona looked back in the mirror. The smiling and waving kept going till they turned at the end of the street.

'She's nice, your Mandy. Well, all of them. Nice family.'

Shona followed the headlamps as they picked their way between the bends and drystone walls, as Glossop gave way to the Peak District. Jamie gave a slight nod, then clicked on the beam and peered over the steering wheel.

'You look knackered,' Shona searched in her bag for her keys. Jamie had parked right at the bottom of the steps to her flat. 'Got my central heating on a phone app. Switched everything on an hour ago. Be cosier than your place.'

Jamie looked towards the steps.

'There's a bag of your washing in the kitchen. Just needs the shirt ironing.'

There was a comfortable warmth as they closed the flat door behind them. It'd been a long day with a big dinner. Shona was already asleep when Jamie got back from cleaning his teeth. The bedside lamp on Shona's side of the bed was dimmed low. Jamie set his phone alarm and, as he plugged in the charger, noticed he'd left a Google page open. The company logo and chairman stared out from the screen – *Vulpes – a name you can trust*. Jamie scrolled through Google, reading articles and looking at photographs until the phone slid from his sleeping hand.

Jamie's shirt was still warm from the iron as he stood in the dark at the top of the concrete steps. He zipped his coat and sucked in the icy mist that hung in a bright patch below the security light. It made him feel alive again. A small window became a square of light. Shona was in the shower. She'd make her own way later, in her own car.

'Fuck sake,' Shona seethed at the email.

'Welcome to Cleggworld,' Jamie was already scribbling next to names and addresses on the print-out. 'A planet where serial killers rank lower than nicked cars… if the car belongs to a rotary club mate.' Jamie finished writing. 'It' a non-job. Leave it with me. Couple of hours PR. We're-pulling-out-all-the-stops bollocks.' Jamie zipped his coat up.

Shona went back to the grind. Paper to computer doc, to CCTV and body-cam footage. Around ten she had a text. No name, but she knew the number. Jamie was back before lunchtime. He sat and began typing.

'Crime log already?' Shona tapped his laptop. 'Mr Efficient.'

'Mr Fuck-it-off-and-forget-it.' Jamie looked up. 'I'll tell Clegg it's the Belgium container gang. She can have a photo-op in the local rag with her rotary club mate looking sad, just before he buys an upgrade with the insurance money.'

Jamie went back to his typing and ten minutes later he and Shona shuffled off to the canteen and a distant corner table.

'Been listing it,' Shona began. 'Where we are? What's nailed down? What's circumstantial? The Buzzard – CCTV and bank account evidence is rock solid. Body-cam number identifies him herding girls towards the Glamour Wagon.'

'And shows him working with at least one more Peepo, but we

can't match him to a name.'

Shona nodded agreement. 'But is that Mr Big from the banking docs, or just more hired help?' She tapped her spoon against her cup. 'There's voices, but…'

'Never stand up in court. Voice recognition is crap, even when it's crystal clear. And we've got?'

'Body-cam audio bouncing up and down on someone running.'

Jamie was quiet for a few seconds, then his jaw tightened. 'But we could nick the old man. Got the paperwork to prove living off immoral earnings.'

'So that'll do for you will it? Nail the easiest target, then tell yourself job done. What's next? Phone the Lithuanian police and say tell the grieving parents that the British police can't be arsed to find out who killed their daughter. Tell them we're too busy bullshitting shop managers and car owners about our chances of ever catching anyone. Send a photo of that crippled old man, tell them justice is done because we're locking him up some place where the pillows are lumpier.'

Jamie made to speak, but Shona continued.

'And if you think that's job done, maybe you'd like to have the same conversation with Dunky's mother?'

Jamie's eyes flashed, but Shona didn't flinch.

'Ultimately,' she dipped a Kit-Kat in her coffee. 'The only way we'll nail the bastard behind this is if the prat stands in front of a cashpoint.'

Jamie drained his cup and shoved it away.

A couple of minutes passed and Shona stacked their crockery on the tray and walked to the washing-up hatch. Jamie stayed seated until she'd almost reached the canteen door, then he stood and slouched off behind her.

The silence held all the way back to their desk and beyond. Eventually Jamie mumbled, head down.

'Keep seeing that screen, the faces carouseling, smiling. And that excel sheet. The bottom-of-the-table girls, desperately trying to shag themselves out of the relegation zone.'

Shona looked across, but his head was still down. Glancing to check they were in no one's eye-line, she reached across and cupped a hand over his as it lay on the desk.

58

A text arrived:

Been looking at the photos you took on my camera. Meet up after work?

The signature of choice was a winking emoji sticking its tongue out.

Jamie showed Shona his phone, then sent a line of emoji thumbs. The immediate reply was Cozza's venue of choice.

The pub was terracotta painted brickwork with lintels and doors picked out in black.

'What's he see—' Shona began.

Jamie pointed at the CAMRA badge on the door, then along the road at the Shalesmoor tram stop. 'Lives just off Woodbourn Road, so real ale and door-to-door service.'

'Unlimited mustard,' Cozza tilted his head towards the pork pie that was quartered on a plate in front of him, as Shona and Jamie reached his table. There was a jar and a knife and each of the meaty segments were hidden below a yellow render. He took a bite and sucked the mustard into his mouth. Lips quivering, he reached for his pint. 'See, if the mustard's really hot, I have to take a swig of beer for health and safety reasons.'

Shona sat and Jamie crossed to the bar. He returned with a pint, a red wine and a lime and soda.

The conversation paddled in the shallows of small-talk for while, then Cozza said: 'Good chance of DNA.'

'But in the—' Jamie began.

'Yeah, industrial bleach,' Cozza licked some mustard off the side of a pie slice then lunged for his beer. After he'd swallowed he went on. 'Neutralises everything it touches, I know, but think about it. Chainsaw. Disc cutter. Giving them a spray and a wipe, probably won't do the job. There'd be spatters of blood and all sorts getting thrown everywhere, and power tools? Full of gaps and crevices. If you could get hold of one, I reckon you'd have a good chance.' Cozza sat back and took yet another swill of beer and waited for thoughts to settle.

'So,' Shona spoke for the first time since the small-talk faltered. 'We can tie the Buzzard to fraud and people trafficking and, if we get the German bank account details, that should link Bakula to Solar Properties.'

'But DNA on Bakula's cutting gear,' Jamie's fingers clawed at his knees. 'Ties him into the actual act of murder.'

'But that'll take round-the-clock surveillance to get his van,' said Shona. 'And he might not still have the tools in the back. Extra staff, overtime costs. No way Clegg'll approve the expense.'

After a few more observations, words drifted into small-talk; global warming, the migration patterns of swifts. Shona felt her eyelids close. It only seemed like a second, but when she blinked Jamie was on his feet and heading towards a Gents sign.

Cozza eased forwards. 'And you two?' he tilted his head and winked.

'What?'

'You and Jamie.'

'Me and – yeah, right. That'd be the day *after* I'd booked my flight to Switzerland for an assisted suicide.' The blush that climbed up her neck like red ivy told a different story.

'Now, you know me,' he touched Shona's hand. 'The dead tell me their life stories, so working out two people with a pulse is a piece of piss.'

And he straightened in his seat as Jamie re-emerged from the toilet and returned via the bar, carrying a tray. Again lime and soda, a red wine and two pints of some faux-rural ale.

'Bonus pint for the possible DNA lead,' he slid the glasses towards Cozza.

Cozza's mouth opened, but he caught the look in Shona's eyes. 'Jamie,' he said. 'I hear you've been taking great strides towards passing your routine fitness test. Regular exercise, shedding a few pounds.'

'Yeah, Cozza, like a Mancunian antelope. It all comes back when you're a natural athlete. Did I ever tell you how I came third in the North Manchester Schools' cross-country?'

And Shona's breathing eased back to normal as the moment passed.

'More posh car shit,' Jamie was reading an email from Clegg. 'Garages, container firms, traffic CCTV. I can double up. See about Bakula's van at the same time.'

Jamie reached for his coat. Shona stayed at the desk with her follow-the-money paper trail. Across the day, she stared at spreadsheets and lists, a highlighter pen in her hand, occasionally daydreaming about Moonlight with Miss Fur-Coat-and-No-Knickers and the Somali cleaner at the gym. The money patterns, the man himself – the thoughts kept circling like crows over roadkill.

A couple of hours after shift end, Jamie was at her door. He used his key. Shona called for him to come through to the kitchen.

'Final push,' he said. 'Got the test date. Been home for a shower and put my kit in the washer. Tried shuttle runs up Southgrove Road.'

Shona grinned and turned to the oven.

When the meal was finished, Jamie slumped onto the sofa. 'Christ, I'm knackered. That hill really catches up with you. And shuttles, not jogging.'

Shona handed him a tea and carried on towards the bedroom, carrying her cup. 'Mindless programmes and hot milk helps me sleep.'

Jamie sat in the bedroom, propped on a pillow. As he waited for Shona to finish her night-time cleansing rituals, he began aimlessly flicking through WhatsApp. Scrolling back, he saw *Dunky* and his last unopened message. A vague memory. Guilt. Whatever. For a few seconds he just stared at the screen, remembering his cocksure dismissal of any possibility that Dunky could ever find anything of value. But then he clicked open and read:

Gamechanger.

He shook his head and clicked on the link. YouTube. A video with an opening title banner: *Wraggs to Riches*. After a few seconds the words dissolved, but as the camera began its slow zoom, Shona's electric toothbrush stopped whirring. He pressed pause and stood, ready to take his turn in the bathroom.

'And make sure you use the brush head with the green ring on,' Shona was at the doorway in her dressing gown.

When he came back, the bedroom was illuminated by a single bedside lamp. As he slid under the duvet, he adjusted a pillow. Shona switched off the lamp and put her head on his chest, her face lit by the glow from his phone.

Jamie unpaused YouTube and, on the screen, two distant men in armchairs sat below images of innumerable shops and delivery vehicles, all with identical logos. A dramatic commentary faded as the camera panned in tight.

'I like this one,' Shona's head raised for a second. 'Wraggs to Riches.'

'What?'

'Wraggs to Riches, the show. Tom Wragg. It's his name. The interviewer.'

'So what's he…?'

'He interviews successful entrepreneurs. How they started with nothing and got rich. Hence the title.'

Jamie pulled himself up a little and focused. The interviewer was listening to a young businessman. His look was vaguely Mediterranean, but not his voice.

'Something about him.' Jamie touched Shona's cheek.

'Spent too much time with E-fits, that's your problem.' Shona's voice was a low mumble as her eyes flickered between micro-sleeps and her head settled again.

Jamie sensed she'd slipped beyond listening.

'My parents were professional, affluent,' the man was saying. 'But I didn't fit in. Especially after the furrow my brother had ploughed.'

Shona's breathing confirmed her unconsciousness, as the businessman began to explain how, when he told his parents he hated school, they told him he'd forfeit his share of the family inheritance.

'Not interested in academics, see,' the man went on. 'I was at a good school, for a while. Parents paid high fees. Had my future mapped out. Big brother had paved the way – champion four hundred metre runner, he captained the debating team. Debating team… what sort of school has a debating team? Anyway, I didn't fit in. Kicked out eventually, and got a job loading for a Turkish grocer. He had six shops. I saved up and the moment I turned seventeen, I paid for driving lessons. All my own money. A man with numerous shops needs to shift a lot of stuff around. I knew that a driving licence was a passport to a pay rise. And trundling around in a van? Better than stacking shelves.'

'Full of shit,' Jamie was trying to set the sleep timer, without waking Shona. 'All I had from my parents was thirty-thousand pound start-up capital and a loan guarantee for a hundred k.'

'Parents gave me nothing,' the man on the television was saying. 'Be a professional; law, finance, dentist, my father told me. Be like your brother. Go to university. No university, no money. So I left home. Sofa surfed for a year. I had plans for the money I earned.'

'And now?' the interviewer offered the opening.

'I was twenty-three when I turned up at home in a new Mercedes. That was six years ago.'

'Had a few business lunches since then,' Jamie felt his eyes closing and propped himself a little higher.

'Flavour of the month when they saw the car,' the man continued. 'Took them on a tour of the shops and warehouse. Even sweeter because my shining brother was starting to rust. Dropped out of university in his final year... a couple of weeks after my parents signed over a flash house and the contents of an investment account to him.'

'And?'

'And that was the time we really took off. So I took them to the house I'd just paid for with my own money. Launched the *Jyoshna* brand in six regional hubs. Same model. One or two shops to test the demographic, then buy more, reach half a dozen and open a wholesale warehouse. Model's a real winner. Got clusters in every major conurbation from Bristol to North Yorkshire.'

'And your brother?'

'Parents are in touch. He and I don't see eye to eye. Had all the advantages, so he felt grafting was beneath him. Like he always was. I'm told he's a real gym bunny now. But just for show. Vanity muscles. No poke,' and he hit a fist into his palm. 'While he was thinking up get-rich-quick schemes, I was doing proper weights: lifting boxes and loading vans, all the hours that God sends. Him?

Entitled. All talk, style-over substance flannel. People would give him money. For a while. Parents did for years… until he stiffed them. My mum still can't see it.'

'So he?'

'Fell on his arse… repeatedly. Drifted into one of those political cliques a few—'

'But you?' the interviewer cut in.

'Strength to strength. You don't get anything worthwhile off the ground without a bit of grunt and grind. Starting up, you're the one gettin up before dawn, loading, driving. You're the one still behind the counter at eleven o'clock at night – the one with the mop and bucket.'

'And that's how you got Jyoshna out of the starting blocks?'

'Out of the blocks and kept it growing… but now I have people to load and drive and stand behind counters.'

'All the menial stuff.'

'Nothing menial about it. It's where the money's made. That's why I'm known for paying good wages. Want to keep my shops a cut above, so I need people who are there for the long haul.'

'Doesn't that cut into your profits?'

'Not as much as having a constant turnover of low-grade staff that keep generating repeat training fees and recruitment costs.'

'So good people and then you can be—'

'Eternally vigilant. Always dropping in. Always checking. What's flying out, what's dragging its feet? You can't leave that to others. I know my staff and they know me. I go around trying to catch them doing good things and then I tell them. And when I occasionally find—'

'Yes,' the interviewer continued. 'I think I can skip a few questions. I was about to ask what advice you'd give to a young entrepreneur, but I think you just gave it. So, Jyoshna. Interesting name and your company logo, a rising moon. Is that…?'

'Islamic? No. We're Hindu. At least my father is. My mother's from Cardiff. The name, it's from the Hindi. A nickname we gave our grandmother, well the English translation. The other one, the Cardiff one, was Nanny Gwen. Hasn't got the same ring.'

'So if I put the name into Google Translate I'd get?'

'Hindi is a different alphabet. There's a couple of versions.'

'But you'll tell us tonight?'

'Marketing is about keeping your brand in the customer's mind. If I tell you now, thousands of people all over the country will be going *oh yeah* and forget it as soon as they've heard it.'

'So?'

'If I leave it a puzzle, some of them will be looking it up, finding the translation. Keeping my brand in their minds.'

Suddenly the screen cut to a different shot. Adverts. A close up of some energy drink. Jamie rested his eyes, waiting for the skip option to appear. Hovering between wakefulness and sleep, his mind descended into random generation: emotions rather than thoughts, fluctuating between guilt and anger. For a few seconds he had dim awareness of music, then nothing else until the morning alarm.

There were still at least two hours of January darkness ahead when Shona opened her eyes. Jamie was awake, but unmoving except, she thought, he was grinding his teeth. She stood and made her way to the bathroom. Fifteen minutes later, when the shower had worked its magic, she wrapped herself in a towelling robe and made her way to the kitchen. She could smell toast and when she sat down there was a tea waiting. 'Thanks,' she lifted her mug.

'It'll be that Fox. Baron or duke or whatever the nobhead is,' Jamie's words appeared at random. 'It's in their blood, thinking they're too clever for the plebs.'

'But looking at—' Shona rubbed her hair with a towel.

'It's the distancing. That'll be the bastard,' Jamie's eyes narrowed on his inner thoughts. 'Making sure some minion who's daft enough to let his name go on the papers takes the fall.'

'Been checking loads of business and finance sites. Honestly Jamie,' Shona moved to the toaster. 'This cash in carrier bags malarkey. He wouldn't even know he'd got it.'

'That's what I'm saying,' Jamie's movements were suddenly jagged. 'It's what they do. Just because they can. Fucking obvious.'

'Except if you—'

'Fucking obvious,' and Jamie's feet were moving towards the bedroom.

For a few seconds Shona was transfixed. The last few days he'd been calmer, but now *Bad Jamie*, out of nothing. By the time she collected her thoughts he was dressed and in the hallway, pulling on shoes and grabbing his coat. The flat door shut heavily. Shona moved to the window. She heard the tyres as Jamie's car lurched onto the main road.

'Looks like another Bring-a-Prat-to-Work day.' She watched his rear lights dwindle towards the park.

59

More Clegg crap. If you cover will dig about Reynard Offices

'Bloody Reynard,' Shona couldn't help but smirk at Jamie's crap code name for Fox. 'Spirit of Bletchley Park.' She screwed up the post-it stuck on the desk.

Clegg was true to form. Two hours of gesture jobs dressed up to look like a day's work. Shona flicked between her own laptop and the office PC. Jamie finally appeared with the last of the daylight. He pulled out a chair and hunched into his coat.

'Christ,' Shona hissed across the desk. 'Never seen anyone scowl from their feet up.'

Jamie mumbled about how he'd found nothing at the Vulpes offices in Sheffield and Rotherham. 'Just Doncaster left, but bollocks to it today. Sat nav said forty minutes this morning. Just turned three? Bloody hour and a half.'

Shona resisted the temptation to mention the predictability of evening traffic.

'Waste of time anyway,' Jamie started picking paperclips out of a box. 'Bastard has it down to a fine art.'

'Fox and his slag of a daughter,' Shona forced a smile. 'Be great you can find a link but, as of now, monies to Vulpes? I'm only finding electronic. Business like that? Cash just slows the admin down. But Solar? Transfers to Bavaria? Dublin account via that London agency? Total them up. It's well in the cash payments ball park.' Shona looked across. Jamie was making a chain with the paperclips. 'Got a meet with Katya in the morning.' She felt her voice tighten. 'If you can fit it into your busy schedule.'

A bank of rain swept across the city. Jamie swore as he knelt in a puddle, attaching the taxi signs to his car door.

Katya was waiting in the usual place, her parka zipped to her chin. A sudden squall snatched the fur-trimmed collar from her face as she crossed towards them and, getting into the car's front seat, the wet tip of her bobbed hair stuck to her mouth. She blew it free, then called to a teenage boy who was huddled in a shop doorway. The boy's collar was high around his face. Jamie flicked the central locking.

'I trust him,' Katya's eyes didn't flinch.

Jamie pressed the door release. The boy looked shocked when he went to sit and saw Shona lying on the back seat.

A few streets away, Jamie pulled up and Shona and Katya changed places and the boy leaned his head onto her shoulder. His eyes were grey and hollow, so was his face. He took a breath, closed his eyes and shuffled deep into Katya's collar.

Driving along Manchester Road, Jamie turned onto a narrow track in a cluster of woods. Bones of trees bowed above them as the rain slid into sleet and gusted dark against the sky.

'Blackbrook,' Shona's teeth locked tight at the memory of a net dangling high in winter-bare branches.

'Concentrate the mind.' Jamie's smile was lifeless. 'End of the month, maybe nothing for Miss Top Quarter, but for those in the relegation zone?'

Shona stared as Jamie glowered out of the windscreen. Turning to Katya, her eyes softened. Katya crooked a finger below the boy's chin. The boy's eyes opened briefly, then slipped back into sleep. Shona smiled, but Jamie began drumming multiple fingers against the steering wheel.

'Nearly hour,' Katya said. 'Need be at work then.'

Jamie's drumming quietened, the movement of his hands being the only clue that he wasn't a victim of locked-in syndrome.

'He likes faux-fur,' Shona smiled at the sleeping boy, pulling Katya's attention in her direction. 'Before, you said…'

'Maybe nothing,' Katya's voice was quiet. 'Not want make people frightened to…'

Shona reached back and held her fingers. The boy's eyes opened for a second.

Katya's head tilted towards him. 'He happy when he sleep,' then she looked back to Shona. 'Mention Kaliningrad girl few times. Say about "Shit, thought he in charge. Waste of shag." Watched faces. Two girls. In their eyes. And Jakub.' Again she tilted her head and tips of fur rippled as he breathed. 'Something…' and a tear weighed on her eyelashes.

Jamie had stopped drumming now.

'On my floor,' Katya seemed focused inside her own head. 'He sleep on blankets. When he dream… sometimes he shout so loud he wake himself up.'

'When…' Shona began.

'Has room, but always on my floor,' and she curled her body to indicate. 'At end of bed, across my feet. Like puppy I have when girl.'

Shona looked and her eyes shut a little longer than a blink.

'Not be late,' Katya ran a hand across his hair. 'Sleep good for him. Take time. Not swing car around when drive.'

The drive towards Shag City was almost silent. Shona tried to lift the weight of Jamie's resentment with occasional remarks about a coat, or pair of boots some woman on the pavement was wearing. Jakub snored a little and, every now and again, Katya stroked his hair and whispered: 'Spij kochanie, spij.'

Just within the galvanised gates they turned off the main drive and parked. Jakub blinked and yawned as he stepped onto the pavement.

'*Spij kochanie, spij* – Sleep sweetie, sleep,' Shona repeated as she watched Katya link her arm through the boy's and pull him close, then begin to walk. After Katya and Jakub were out of sight, Jamie touched the window switch.

'Leave it,' Shona's face was turned away. 'Need some air.'

'It's bloody freezing.'

'Not as cold as some bastards.' Shona pushed her door open.

'How will you—'

'Bus, taxi. Plenty of choices to travel with fucking human beings.' And she stepped onto the footpath.

Jamie began a three-point turn. By the time his car was facing the right way, Shona had turned into a narrow walkway that linked through to a cul-de-sac on the neighbouring estate.

When Jamie was back in the police station car park, he phoned. It went to voicemail. He texted. Nothing. Texted again. This time there was a reply.

Fuck off

Back home, Jamie rang again.

The caller is unavailable.

He threw his phone on the bed and pulled a crumpled running kit out of the tumble dryer.

Later, when Sheffield's gradients had extracted his penance, he showered on legs of stone. The mirror in his bathroom was misted and, as he dragged his hand across it, he looked at himself. Around midnight he texted again.

Sorry I was an arse

The text was unanswered when his alarm woke him at six in the morning, so he sent it again.

By eight o'clock Shona hadn't made an appearance. Another text. Another no reply. About half past, Clegg crossed to her office. She was still hanging her coat up as Jamie knocked.

'Trouble in paradise?' Clegg turned.

'Just wondered… got a missed call, but I think her battery must be flat or something.'

Clegg sat. 'Wasn't flat when she called me.'

'So…'

'She said tell you to look in the top left drawer. There's a red folder. You can have a turn at the paperwork.'

'And she's?'

'Clarifying info with Milhurst's team this morning, the dentist this afternoon.'

'Did she say…'

'No, nothing, but…' Clegg stood and reached for her coat. 'Working with you. Bound to need the occasional day of respite care.'

Jamie took out the red folder – print-outs, Day-Glo lines and post-its – and surrendered to its tedium. His behaviour of the previous day demanded atonement and he accepted the justice of his sentence.

An hour into the morning and, by osmosis, he absorbed the truth in Shona's follow-the-money approach. After an hour, his appreciation of her relentless focus was complete. By twelve, he'd broken the back of the set tasks and he headed for the car park. Clipping his phone into the holder suctioned against his windscreen, he tapped directions on the sat nav. At least the journey time was short outside the evening rush.

The light was just beginning to dip as Jamie pulled back into the police station car park. He spoke to the uniform on reception. As expected, no sightings of Clegg. No signs of Shona either.

Stepping into the beige cube room, fluorescent lights sensed his presence and flickered on. Outside, an occasional muffled conversation dopplered up and down the corridor. Jamie's hand went to his phone. Messages: Shona's string. He began tapping.

Tell Katya Sorry. I will say it to her face next time we meet. My fault. Sorry again. Red Folder – Thanks for that. Doncaster this pm – Estate agents and rentals. Maybe should've bought shotgun or got dinner suit. Cheeky prat in office said try the bastard's grouse moor or roulette table. Said Fox in area for a few days shooting. Sorry again. J xx

60

Back at his flat, Jamie dipped a sandwich in a cuppa soup then stuffed a Mars bar in his pocket and reached for his Gore-Tex coat and rucksack. It wasn't eight o'clock yet and he had time to fill. Shona's bed and slow cooker had distracted him from his edgeland chronicling too much lately. Somehow it made him twitchy, diminished; not being out amongst it, the life, absorbing the range and detail.

He parked just off Sheffield Parkway in a litter-strewn street on the borders of abandoned industry and a rough-wooded scrubland. Jamie remembered an attempted murder – a missing machete and a finger-tip search across discarded buildings; concrete footprints eroded by roots, weeds and other outriders of urban decay.

At the end of the cul-de-sac, a security light reacted and flooded the zone where tarmac disintegrated into hard-core and mud. Jamie heard a snuffling and pulled a head-torch out of his pocket. Pointing it towards the sound, its beam reflected from the hedgehog's eyes and the tips of its prickles.

A few steps further and the security light clicked off. He waited for his eyes to adjust to the darkness before crossing the rough ground ahead. As always, he settled downwind of his observation site. It was cold, almost cloudless now. Jamie huddled and watched. Soundless voles rippled the grass and there was an occasional scurry of a ubiquitous rat, but no apex predators; no owls, foxes or representatives of the weasel family. Still, his major purpose was achieved. He'd filled in time. Around ten he packed up and moved on.

Back home, Jamie washed, checked his messages and selected Shona again. Then he turned to the mirror, did his top button, pushed his tie up and reached for his only smart jacket. Where he was going, the wild life didn't really start moving until the early hours.

Shona's eyes had cleared when she'd read the text. No problem focusing by then. The visit to the gym had helped, but she'd had to abandon the treadmill. With the state of her balance then, running on its rolling belt had the distinct potential for a comedy moment. She'd got through the step class, trying to ignore the young girls behind her that kept giggling. Sauna, shower, taxi home and a sleep. Shona checked her watch and did the count back. A unit an hour. She read the text again. *Lucky I didn't try and keep up with Katya*, went through her mind. The sequins made the dress easy to find in the wardrobe.

The walkway from the car park was a corridor of potted greenery and security men in crisp white shirts and narrow ties. The casino frontage was illuminated by blue floodlights and the imitation flames of four large orange beams that rippled through chiffon as it spiralled on an updraft of air.

'Membership?' the security man gave an expected greeting. Jamie showed his police I.D.

Inside, well-dressed men and a selection of women in backless and low-cut gowns formed settlements around the various gaming tables. Jamie surveyed the room. Fox was easy to spot; a cluster of tuxedos radiated around him. At the bar Jamie ordered his customary lime and soda then moved into earshot, leaning on a chest-high table, with his back to the group, imitating mindless phone scrolling, while listening to a stream of anecdotes about game-keepers, shotguns and missed birds. Eventually, as the ice melted in his drink, the groups ebbed into the room and Fox took up residence at the roulette wheel. Jamie shuffled into the knot of hangers-on as Fox and a friend placed a bet each.

'All contributions gratefully accepted,' Fox grinned as the chips were raked in.

'Might as well have stayed in the bar and handed you a fifty every few minutes,' the friend shook his head.

'*Nils desperandum*,' Fox put a hand on the man's shoulder. 'Think how sweet it will be if you win and I have to watch my money disappear into your wallet.'

'Suppose it takes the edge off the fun,' Jamie leaned alongside Fox's arm. 'Knowing any money you're losing is just in transit to your own till.'

'Asked my accountant about it,' Fox smiled, without missing a beat. 'Apparently, I pay gambling tax on any winnings, but if I log it as a security check then any losses are tax deductible.'

'Always one step ahead,' Jamie's jaw tightened. 'All these stupid people's money tonight, then in the morning, some wannabee landed gentry paying you the price of a car to blast a few defenceless grouse.'

'Yes, my accountant tells me HMRC would rather I won than lost on my own tables.' The practised smile didn't waiver. 'But grouse season finished before Christmas. Tail end for pheasant at present. Hope I can cope with the loss.'

'You know something—' Jamie began, but a hand landed on his shoulder and pulled him away. It stayed there until he reached the door.

'Christ,' Shona twisted her fist into his jacket and pushed him out. 'What were you expecting? Fox standing with a martini in his hand telling all his mates about the peanuts money he was making from a knocking shop and illegal rents? Jesus, you're a fucking wanker sometimes.'

Jamie slouched towards the car, like a child whose mum has just been told he's been suspended from school. Shona continued the lecture as she drove. It was comforting. Better than silence. She dropped him off outside his front door. Standing on his top step, he turned and looked back.

'Go on. Fuck off.' Shona mouthed through the car window, waving the back of her hand.

Half an hour later, Jamie's phone blinked. The screen read Shona.

Did you tell him you were police?

No, Jamie messaged back. *Didn't get chance. Doorman saw my I.D. but Fox won't mingle with the minions. What about you?*

Did what you should've done. Put on a sparkly dress and slid myself between a gaggle of regulars. Shona pressed send and rolled over in bed.

About five minutes later the light pulsed again. Shona looked at the screen.

Sorry X

She stared, unsure what surprised her most – the latest apology, or the X.

'Capital letter, bloody hell,' she smiled to herself.

X yourself.

61

By nine there was no sign of Clegg. Shona strolled down to reception and the duty sergeant stared into the diary page on his computer.

'Combined Yorkshire Police Conference,' the duty sergeant said. 'Two days, Harrogate.'

'So she'll have left Betty's Tea Room as her emergency contact number.'

The duty sergeant smirked.

When Shona returned, Jamie had the red folder in front of him; more follow-the-money osmosis.

'Come on, canteen,' she tilted her head towards the door. 'Need a drink before I start fiddling with my laptop.'

Jamie smirked at the innuendo.

'I texted over your apologies,' Shona and Jamie were leaning over two cups of tea, tucked on a corner table. She saw the moment of disconnect cross his eyes. 'To Katya. You say it yourself. Face to face, when we see her. Don't make me have to remind you.' She dunked a biscuit and stared nowhere. 'Lucky it was so late, or I'd never have dipped under the breathalyser limit.'

Jamie looked confused.

'Finish your tea and we'll get a bit of fresh air,' and she pushed a biscuit towards him.

It was cold, but bright and the light made the most of the yellow sandstone walls in the Botanical Gardens. Jamie and Shona strolled towards the great glass pavilion. '*Galanthus nivalis*,' he nodded towards a cluster of snowdrops pushing above the grass. 'Be hyacinths next. February. That's when you notice the light coming back. Bit of new life,' and he nodded towards where the low winter sun flooded across a mass of bare trees. 'Even when everything looks dead, it's there if you know how to look. Most people would say that tangle of twigs was brown, or maybe grey but, if you really look, so much is soft pinks, lavenders and golds.'

'Christ,' Shona turned her face. 'You're a little ray of sunshine this morning.'

'Anyway,' Jamie changed tack. 'Breathalyser. What's all that about?'

'Need somewhere quiet.'

Between the main domes of the pavilion, apexes of glass formed functional plant houses. Visitors were sparse everywhere but the café.

'Cactus and succulent. If we can find somewhere to sit,' Jamie looked around for a bench.

There was something comforting about the warm, dry air and a view of hunched figures outside being harried by wind-driven leaves. Shona plugged a set of earphones into her phone, handing Jamie an earpiece, then pushing the other one into her own ear and they sat, knee to knee, with the lead dangling between them.

'Met Katya at lunchtime,' Shona began. 'Brought her back to mine. She had to get the bus to the unit though.'

'And you…?'

'She brought vodka. "Helps work. Couple of big ones before a shift of little ones," she said. Bright girl. Not easy to be funny in a second language. Some people can't manage it in their first.' Shona held her gaze on Jamie. 'Told her I'd just have a sip because of the car.' Shona touched the phone and she and Katya were talking, their tinny voices coming through the earpieces. Jamie heard Shona say about needing to drive.

'Bollocks,' It was Katya's voice. *'Not drink alone. I get there easy. Walk across park, catch bus.'*

'But you might be—'

'No. Look.'

Shona tapped Jamie's arm. 'She had this blonde wig. Said it was business equipment.' There was a clunk – a bottle on a table.

'This best vodka. Polish, not Russian piss.'

'That's Katya,' Shona stated the obvious.

'Always vodka with bison grass. Long grass standing in bottle.'

There were sounds of pouring. A tinny jumble of noise echoed in the earpiece. 'And that's me choking and her laughing.'

'Bison grass give it flavour. Specially if bison piss on grass.'

There was more laughing

'Not worry about bison piss. This vodka disinfect toilet.'

'Did she know?' Jamie said over the sound of more pouring and general clattering.

'About the phone being on record?' Shona shrugged. 'Saw me put it in the middle of the table.' As Shona talked, Jamie tried to follow the words in his earpiece.

'Sorry about—' it was Shona's voice on the recording.

'No, he right. He was pig. Tick Tock twat, but he right. No time.'

Jamie took a breath.

'I get girls. Say everyone my room. Cheer up. Had other bottle of bison piss vodka.' Katya began unfolding events. *'Need get mood right. Not rush. Chit-chat, jokes. Let vodka kick in. Most girls have story of docks and van. I say about Kaliningrad slag say, "Waste of shag. Thought he was boss. Still he smell nice. Smell sweet…" And I watch faces. Couple of girls…'*

'So you think?' Shona's voice.

'In eyes, something. And...' there was a shuffling. *Jakub, he wake up. Rest is back to chit-chat. Not talk when Jakub listen. Not after what happen in van.'*

'What did happen to him?'

'No detail, but sweet-smelling man, seem not just like girls.'

'He told you?'

'Hear bits. He talk in sleep. Broken bits he say. Sometimes awake, few words, then he shut up. Bite lips. Curl up. Cry.'

'But no—' Shona was cut short.

'Not ask. Can't ask. He just cry.'

'If we could just get a bit more,' Jamie stood and winced as his earphone pulled out. 'There'd be something in the detail.' Jamie was pacing. 'If she – we, could just lean on that Jakub a bit, I'm sure...'

'No chance,' Shona was wrapping up the earphone flex. 'Already hinted. Nearly jumped down my throat. She's very protective of the lad.'

Jamie went to speak, but then didn't. They moved through to a café and had a general chat over tea.

When it turned half-past twelve, Shona tapped her watch. 'Might as well have a bit of lunch. Better than the canteen. Could lift our spirits for the afternoon ahead.'

The afternoon ahead was filled with paper, computer screens and mindmaps. The investigative equivalent of glacial flow. By six the office had emptied, except for the usual overnight Peepos snuffling from filing cabinet to computer screen, living in hope of the occasional phone call to break the monotony.

'You got much left?' Shona looped her scarf and fastened a zip.

'Few sets of notes need transferring to the database. Shouldn't be long.'

'Okay,' Shona pushed her chair under the desk. Forty minutes later Jamie's car parked behind her flat.

'I think we need to step away a bit,' the bedside lamp flickered as Shona sat up. 'What prat said a good meal and make-up sex made you sleepy?' And she was on her feet, reaching for her dressing gown.

Jamie followed, via the toilet. In the kitchen there was coffee and a selection of papers and pens.

'Need to sort what's speculation from what's solid?' Shona smoothed out a sheet of paper and pencilled in a grid. 'Buzzard,' she wrote his name. 'Take yours in the other room.' Shona sketched another grid. 'Best if we start with our own thoughts, uninterrupted.'

Around twenty minutes later, Jamie called through. 'How you getting on?'

'Pretty well finished. Couple of minutes,' Shona was leaning across the kitchen table. 'I'm numbering mine. One: cast iron. Two: highly likely. Three: possible. You do the same.'

Jamie came through and laid out his paper.

'Number twos,' Shona placed her list next to Jamie's. 'That's where to focus. Ones, job done. Threes? We're in real trouble if they're our best shot.'

Shona scanned the papers. They both had Bakula and The Buzzard as number ones for fraud/money. Jamie had Old Man Morcanu there as well.

'No paper trail,' Shona tapped. 'Not like the other two.'

Jamie had Marika and Dominik Morcanu listed as twos. Shona only listed them as threes, but she had Moonlight in two.

'Wishful thinking.' Jamie tapped the name. 'Nothing solid. Make my day if you're right, though. But the Buzzard's cast iron for the financial stuff. More evidence needed on people smuggling and living off immoral earnings.'

Shona nodded. 'And the killings?'

'No,' Jamie was barely audible. 'He's a silly bastard out of his depth, not a psychopath.'

Shona pushed her papers towards him. Wherever Shona had written *Moonlight*, she'd added highlighter pen to link several notes. 'These,' she said. 'If we could just make one or two of these concrete, they'd all fall, like dominoes. Remember, Hobbes said there's often a van waiting, that none of them recognise, and Moonlight doesn't travel back with everyone else.'

When they eventually crawled back into bed they'd slugged out priorities, balancing out likely guilt against the solidity of evidence already amassed.

Shona was laid back on the pillow again. 'You think Moonlight's unlikely. I think Marika's an asset, not a suspect.'

'You sleepy yet?' Jamie rolled onto an elbow.

'Yeah,' Shona closed her eyes. 'Surprising how satisfying paperwork can be... knock the light off.'

Jamie knew he should be tired, but his mind was still running as Shona fell into the rhythm of sleep. He stared at the ceiling then reached for his phone. It blinked awake and he plugged in a set of earphones, opened YouTube and turned the phone to landscape. A circle rotated in the centre of the screen, then two men in distant armchairs appeared. Jamie gripped a biro. He was used to taking notes in the dark.

62

'Christ, you look rough.'

'Crap sleep.'

'I've made tea, and there's bacon.'

Jamie crumpled into a kitchen chair. Shona bustled around singing along with the radio. Jamie flicked at his phone. Shona didn't seem to notice that there were no words coming from him. When she came out of the shower, his car was gone. There was a post-it on the kettle: *See u at work*.

It was the usual and, a little later, when Jamie looked up from his desk and saw her, he grabbed his coat from the back of his chair. 'Car park, before Clegg gets in.'

Shona watched her wing mirror as Jamie reversed out of the parking space.

'Bakula's van. Thought about it again.' Jamie pulled into the traffic. 'If it's empty. No tools, no DNA, we're fucked. Even if we did nail him? He's not working on his own. Might as well ring a warning bell for Mr Solar Properties, or whoever.'

Jamie turned and they were in a narrow street of Victorian buildings and the red brick walls that enclosed their yards. He parked and rummaged in a pocket.

'But this…Dunky's last gift. Might be nothing, but could give us a look inside his head.'

Jamie was scrolling across his phone now. Shona looked down and had a vague sense memory of what was on the screen.

'I said about his face,' Jamie tilted the phone towards Shona. 'But then you fell asleep.'

Shona listened as the young business man recounted his rise and the schadenfreude decline of his brother, peering at the screen until Jamie pressed pause.

'He's similar, I grant you. More business lunches, less exercise and eye-brow wax.' She stared at the face again. 'Even the voice.'

Gym bunny, political clique, entitled style-over-substance merchant. The contents of the programme assembled themselves like a computer graphic of a jigsaw.

'When he says about his brother blagging a house off their parents, and him turning up in a Mercedes.' Jamie touched the phone screen. 'And taking them to the house he'd bought outright. Then the adverts came on and I nodded off.' Jamie pressed play again. 'That's why I watched it all again. Watched what came next. The real rubbing his nose in it bit'

'But it wasn't just your Mercedes? Each birthday…'

Shona listened as the interviewer teed up the answers.

'Yeah, a few months later it was Dad's birthday so I turned up in a new Mercedes, and this time I left it with him. Become a bit of tradition ever since. Every birthday, he gets a new Mercedes.'

'So there's no hard feelings?' The interviewer probed.

'No. Sometimes, I think it was his way of toughening me up. Giving me drive. The old lion and the young lion.'

'Like he really believes that.' Shona shook her head.

'My brother…? All show. While he was working on his six-pack, I was loading them by the hundred into vans. Might look better than me with his shirt off, but real strength, in here.' He jabbed a finger against his skull. *'And here.'* His hand slapped against his heart.

'We grew up with a voice on each shoulder. Parents. One to care. One to drive. Mummy's little stars. The second coming. And Dad applying the stress test. Pushing us on to see who'd make the hard yards.' Again the man slapped his own chest.

The interviewer eased into closing remarks and Shona looked up from the phone.

'Reckon Philip Larkin had it right.' Jamie made eye contact. 'What did he say about parents fucking you up?'

'Aye, maybe, but more of a convenient excuse than serious poetry.' Shona closed her eyes and ran her fingers through her hair. When she opened them, Jamie was tilting the phone towards her. He'd opened Google Translate.

'Jyoshna,' he said. 'The name of that bloke's company.'

'God, yes.' Shona read the screen. 'Not concrete, but near enough... shit. Like you say, helluva look inside his head. Let me...' and she held the phone.

'So, Milhurst's mob,' Jamie asked as they drove back to the station 'Where are they with Dunky's murder?'

Shona shrugged. 'Few similar hits, London area. Nothing anybody else couldn't have found out from our notes and access to police computers.'

Simultaneously, both their phones beeped. Identical emails from Clegg, each set up to force acknowledgement of receipt. The gist was *Get back to the station, I need some paperwork sorting ASAP.*

'Fucking Clegg.' Shona didn't look up from the desk full of papers. 'As if the Assistant Chief Constable is going to ask for all this lot at the monthly meeting. How many of them around the table? Lucky to get a couple of minutes each. Lazy bitch,' Shona slumped onto the desk, then sent an email.

Across the briefing room a steady flow of Peepos coagulated in chattering knots. By three o'clock, the spaces between groups had filled and heads faced towards the screen. Shona stopped moving papers and stared towards Moonlight as he droned on. Just some nondescript pep talk on routine admin. Jamie shook his head as her lips formed silent obscenities. As Moonlight finished, Shona tapped Jamie's hand.

'Drink. Sandwich,' and she was crossing the briefing room. As Jamie caught up, she turned and began speaking again. 'So, I don't usually bother with YouTube, but there's this one show, Wraggs to Riches. Tom Wragg. Interviews, successful business people, that sort of thing.' Her voice was cranked up, deliberately loud. 'Had this guy on. Self-made millionaire. All those shops. Every year buys his a dad a—'

Jamie grabbed her arm to move her away. Moonlight looked up, but she was nearly at the door.

'What the fu—' Jamie was still holding her as they stepped into the corridor.

'Yeah, well…' Shona straightened her shoulders and began walking towards the canteen.

Dave Collins was already seated near the window. Shona slid the tray onto the table.

'Bit of creative tension,' Dave looked at Shona's face as she and Jamie shuffled onto their chairs.

'Paperwork,' Jamie stuttered. 'It can get you that—'

'You watch much YouTube?' Shona cut in.

Dave shrugged.

'You heard of Wraggs to Riches?' She put her phone on the table, turned it towards him and hit paly. 'Ring any bells?'

Dave stared then said: 'Yeah,' as a face came into focus. 'Bit porkier, but yeah see what you mean.'

Jamie glowered.

'Apparently he owns that chain of supermarkets.' Shona flicked her phone. 'You know the ones, Jyoshna.' And again she turned the screen. Google Translate was already loaded.

Jyoshna: A girl's name (Indian) from the Hindi/Sanskrit word meaning moonlight.

On their way back to the paperwork there was a knot of people waiting for the lift.

'Might be quicker up the stairs,' Jamie said.

Shona's eyes remained focused on the numbers, tracking the lift's progress to their floor. The lift capacity said ten. Twelve squeezed in.

'Good job we're all way below national average weight,' Jamie tried to steer any conversation.

'That show I was telling you about. Wraggs to Riches. Did you give it a look?' Shona was on autopilot. 'My cousin told me about it. I can send you the link, but if you go to YouTube and search Wraggs to Riches.' Again, Shona's voice volume was a couple of notches louder than the social norm.

Jamie felt sick.

'She said this bloke was a dead spit for one our illustrious leaders. She'd picked me up from work one night and ogled him.' Shona had a salesman's smile. 'So I watched it. She was right. Wasn't just the looks though. Real family saga. Like a corner shop Cain and Abel. Worth a watch. Like I say, Wraggs to Riches, on YouTube.' And, as the lift doors opened, she said the name of the show again.

'Was there a point to all that?' Jamie scowled as they reached a bit of personal space in the corridor.

Shona carried on walking. 'Maybe,' her tight-lipped smile widened, 'But it'll only take one. If one watches it, you can guarantee it'll be all round the station, twenty-four, forty-eight hours max. Then watch him. Not a man to cope with humiliation. And anger? Short step from angry to careless.'

The office desk was still a clutter of folders and a spreadsheet simmered on Shona's laptop. Jamie began ordering papers, then tagging to indicate status. He didn't speak. If they could get through the afternoon and out of the station without Shona lobbing another verbal grenade, maybe he could get some sense out of her when they got home.

'You just made that up,' Jamie drained the spaghetti, then handed it to Shona. 'About humiliating Moonlight to make him careless.'

'Doesn't mean it's not true though.' She stirred the pasta into a casserole dish.

'But you going off at random,' Jamie sat at the table.

'Pot, kettle,' Shona began plating up. 'Goose, gander, sauce.' And she pushed his food towards him.

It was a quiet meal, then Shona's phone beeped. 'Katya,' she said. 'Got something for us.'

Jamie was twitchy as he waited for Shona to finish reading, then she passed him the phone.

'Lunchtime, usual routine,' she began talking whilst he was reading. 'Pick her up. Be your chance to say sorry in person.'

It was their customary separate arrival, fifteen minutes apart. Shona pushed the briefing room door open. Jamie was on his feet, making eye-contact, then looking towards the front desk. Moonlight was sat, bent low, sorting items in his desk.

'Early start,' Shona smiled as she passed him. At the back of the room, Jamie winced. 'Be a while before your boys are in,' she continued. 'They'll still be shovelling down bacon and black pudding.'

Moonlight looked, then went back to the contents of his desk.

'Jesus,' Jamie leaned across the desk. 'Are you taking the piss? Bad enough gobbing off in the lift.'

Shona smirked. 'Nah, lots of people hearing? Just buries where it started and spreads quicker.'

Across the room Moonlight seemed to be checking the wireless link between his phone and computer projector. A series of random images flashed up and rotated. He put his phone in his pocket, checked his belt and the leather strap that looped off it and through his epaulette.

Shona watched him preen, standing, eyes steady. Jamie swallowed and Moonlight strode towards the door.

'Let him feel it,' Shona's voice was calm. 'Bet I'm not the first. You watch.'

About twenty minutes later the first raucous Peepos of the morning entered. Over the following quarter of an hour the numbers and noise increased. Then Moonlight returned.

It was there. Shona and Jamie watched it. The angle of eyes, the hidden sneers. It had no form but they could see it, and the way it touched Moonlight. Then he flicked his phone so that the wall screen woke. The Peepos stood. Moonlight's jaw elevated as he spoke and scanned the room.

'He knows,' Shona whispered, her head just above the desk. 'The way they're looking. All those bastards sniggering at him inside their heads.'

Eventually, Moonlight dismissed his men and they dispersed to the tasks of the day. Jamie watched them; the angle of the eyes, the glances over shoulders, the pockets of suppressed laughter. Almost invisible, but as real as concrete.

'Christ, Shona,' Jamie kept his teeth clamped. 'You know what you've done. He's like a ticking time-bomb, and you've set him to random.'

'Better nail the bastard before he goes bang then.' Shona looked at her watch.

63

A mile or so into their drive, Jamie pulled up under a bridge, went to the car's boot and took out the magnetic taxi signs. Shona turned on the radio, then climbed out and sat in the back. It was The Eighties Show: George Michael, Elton John. Jamie got back in as she joined in with *Don't You Want Me Baby*.

'Look,' he talked over an instrumental break. 'I will say sorry to her face. Let me get that out of the way before anything else comes up. If she's got that kid with her again,' Jamie went on. 'Might be an idea to use that car park where we met Jephcott, in the park by the reservoir.'

Even at eleven in the morning the sun hung low, fogging the dirty windscreen. 'By the alley,' Jamie flicked the washer-wipe switch. 'Her and the lad.'

Katya opened the front passenger door and Jakub looked down at Shona curled on the back seat as he sat.

'So what've you…' Jamie looked at Katya, but her eyes flicked towards Jakub.

'Hey, misio,' she smiled at Jakub, mimed playing guitar, then flicked her phone and pressed a couple of buttons on the car radio. 'Bluetooth music. Keep Jakub relaxed.' And she paired her phone to the car speakers.

When they pulled up for the customary seat swap a couple of streets away, the car had a soundtrack of Polish pop. Again, as Katya took her place in the back seat, Jakub snuggled into her collar, but this time there was an occasional humming along with the music.

'So,' Jamie had got the message. 'Nothing in front of...'

Another sugary Europop tune washed around the car.

'Hey misio,' Katya put her hand under Jakub's chin. 'Come on little teddy bear, sing. You know this one.'

Jakub smiled and when the chorus began, Shona joined in. Jamie turned and raised his eyebrows.

'Nineties hour. Staple diet when I was with the family. Golden age of Polish pop.' Shona danced in her seat. 'Unexpected consequence of Solidarity and the fall of communism.' And she picked up the lyrics as the chorus came round again.

Katya was singing all the words and tapping the rhythm gently on Jakub's shoulder. The park appeared and they turned and followed a track until Jamie pulled up close by a clump of trees.

'Idź spać, misio,' Katya folded her coat and laid his head on it, then tapped her phone, cutting the music as they got out of the car.

Jamie went to the boot and pulled out his ski jacket and draped it over Katya's shoulders. 'Before we start, so nothing gets in the way. I want to say sorry. I can make up reasons – time, worried about getting things wrong. But whatever, there's no excuse. You're putting yourself in the firing line. I know that. So... sorry. Everything you've done. It's appreciated.' And he held out a hand.

Katya shook it and gave a slight nod and a sliver of a smile.

'I use phone like you,' Katya looked at Shona, then down at her screen, tapping as they walked the few metres to a cluster of trees. 'And 'nother bottle of bison piss vodka.'

Shona's phone beeped. There was an email with an audio file.

'Not want scare them. At least two, maybe more I think – and Jakub, but keep him clear of this. He break too easy.' Katya touched Shona's hand. 'This is audio I send you.' and she tapped her own phone and there were voices. 'First bit just chat,' Katya raised the volume. 'But Bison vodka soon do its work.' And she handed the phone back.

'English?' Jamie seemed surprised as they leaned in close.

'What we speak,' Katya stated the obvious. 'Only me and Polska in room. Others? Three Baltic, two Slovak, one Bulgarski.' And she held the phone up.

'Waste of shag, but smell nice, Kalingrad slag say.' It was Katya's voice on the phone. *'Good day if we smell soap, eh girls.'* And her laughter was raucous.

'Smell nice, Mr Sweet As.' It was another voice. *'Then bang my head against side of van and rip my skirt.'*

'Bulgarski,' Katya spoke over the phone.

'And angry when couldn't get cock out of trousers.' Another voice. *'When shoulder strap stick on belt. He hold my hair. Twist my face down. Make me undo clip.'*

'Asenka,' Katya again. 'Latvian. Not here long.'

'He hold my hair all time, till he come. Sweet As…'

'Yes, Mr Sweet As…' It was the Bulgarian girl again. *'Sweet as… he say it as he come.'*

'Couple of others. Could see it in faces when they say "Sweet As, when he come." Same story in bit from Nina – one of Slovaks. Not expect it.' Shona was holding the phone flat in her hand. 'Face not show anything before.'

Then Jamie looked back to the car. Shona and Katya followed his eyes and then they heard it. A dull, slow thumping. They looked at the side window and heard the scream trapped behind glass.

For a moment all three stared. The sun, the dappled shade through the leafless trees. They froze for a few seconds as if unable to take in what they were seeing. Katya was the first move, then Jamie was past her.

Jakub's head was swinging like a pale hammer, crashing against the window and door pillar. Before each new strike he paused, held his head back from his shoulders and inhaled before launching himself forwards. His forehead was split and, from where the flesh was pulled apart, a stream of blood was flooding into the recesses of his eyes. Jamie pulled the door open. Unfettered by the glass, Jakub's screams echoed from a point deep in his body. Katya had her arms on his shoulders, then she was in the car, pulling him close, clamping him against her, his blood and tears pooling on her neck, shoulders, seeping down her back. The screaming collapsed into spit and snot, like a toddler distraught and unable to find the words for his despair. *Sweet As*, he kept repeating in amongst the dribble-choked words.

'I heard *Fuck*, what's the rest?' Jamie looked to Shona for a clue.

'*Dupa* is arse. The rest?' she was pacing. 'Too fast for my crap Polish.'

Katya was rocking now, slowly with Jakub. Rocking and soothing and shushing. It was then, as it went quiet, that they all seemed to hear it at once. *'More vodka. Can smell the bastard in my nose.'* It was the Bulgarian girl and her words transfixed the trio as she spoke from the car radio. *'Mr Sweet As. Hear him grunting. Feel his fucking ski mask on skin. Come on, Katya.'* She was slurring now. *'More bison piss vodka.'*

All three were motionless, bewildered then, with nothing said, they all knew and Katya was scrabbling into her pocket, desperately floundering for her own phone while hugging Jakub close and trying to shut down the vodka voices that had been silent outside, but coarse and clear via Bluetooth and the car's audio speakers.

'Fucking Bluetooth,' Jamie stared at the trees. 'How far is it?

Five, six metres. Shit.' Now, both women were comforting Jakub, tightening and rocking each time his wailing threatened to burst out.

'Fucking Bluetooth.' Jamie was pacing back and forth. 'Fucking Radio. Should've turned it off: walked out of range. Shit. Fucking six metres and that bison piss, sweet as bollocks…'

'Take us house.' Katya held a blood-soaked tissue to Jakub's head. As the minutes passed, his breathing slowed. 'He not work like this. I clean him up. Got steri-strips in home. Close wound. I take photo. Tell boss he bang head on cupboard.'

Jamie drove as close to the house as he dared, parking in a high-fenced alleyway that ran behind a row of shops.

'I phone 'nother taxi when he settle.' Katya had Jakub hugged close as they began walking away from the car.

'We'll wait,' Jamie turned off the engine. 'Least we can do.'

After forty minutes Katya turned back into the alleyway and got back into the car. Nothing was said for a while, then Shona spoke.

'How will the boss react to you being late?'

Katya shrugged.

'And Jakub. Is he…'

Katya held up her phone; Jakub, bleary-eyed with half a dozen steri-strips clawing the gash in forehead together. 'Asleep. Give him double dose of Night Nurse and a drop of the vodka.'

'Vodka…could that?' Shona's tone was quiet.

'Not much… and better than him being awake. Nina watch him'

'Good luck with the boss,' Shona said as they parked outside the galvanised gates.

'Thank you,' Jamie added as Katya stood. 'Look after yourself.' Once she was out of sight, he did a U-turn. 'It was me,' he said. 'I was driving. I'm the one who should've made sure the radio was off.'

'But it was her that switched the radio on and…'

'Yeah, well,' Jamie didn't look at Shona. 'I'm the one with the car keys and Bluetooth radio – I'm a bloke. It's my job to remember that stuff.'

Shona's burner beeped. It was Katya.

Message back when you have this. Need to delete before go into work.

And there was an attachment – the sound file. Shona downloaded it and played a couple of snippets, emailed it to herself, then pressed *Reply* and typed.

Thanks for magazine

64

The morning was a slog, consisting of avoiding Clegg's crap. Around lunchtime, Shona stood and picked up her car keys.

'Can I leave you to it for an hour or so?'

'Thanks a mill—' Jamie began.

'Dunky's mum.' Shona's words cut short any objection. 'Messaged to say she'd be in town. Could we meet for a coffee?' She turned her laptop. 'Reckon this'll be next on Clegg's agenda.'

There was a pro forma summarising progress for ongoing cases on the screen.

'How'd it go?' Jamie was tidying away sandwich wrappers when Shona got back to the desk.

'As you'd expect. She was lovely and kept thanking us all for our efforts. I gave her some old guff about Milhurst and a team of national specialists brought in,' Shona dropped her head. 'Is there a window open?' She'd left her coat on and pulled it tight.

By the time the shift ended, she wanted to close her eyes and an ache had crept across her shoulders.

'Are you…' Jamie watched her gather her stuff, ready for home.

'Yeah,' she disappeared beneath a scarf. 'Thank God for phone app central heating.'

'Okay,' he dropped his voice. 'Be about half an hour behind you.'

When she got back to her flat the shivering had increased. Jamie made her a tea, but she couldn't get warm and couldn't face the food that the oven's auto-timer had simmered to perfection.

'Had your flu jab?' Jamie held the back of his hand against her forehead, then began sorting through a bag with a chemist's logo on it. 'Bought this on the way back.' He boiled the kettle and stirred a Lemsip into a glass. 'And this,' he handed her an ibuprofen.

While Shona shivered over the steaming glass, Jamie sorted out a couple of duvets and made himself a bed on the floor.

'Give you space to sweat,' and he kissed a finger and touched her cheek.

Overnight, Shona continued to shiver. Jamie did a couple more back-of-the-hand temperature checks. Around four he heard a phone beep, but Shona was asleep.

When Jamie woke, Shona was deep in sleep. He showered, dressed and had a tea and four digestive biscuits. He found a thermometer in the bathroom cabinet. One of those thin plastic strips that display digits if you get a good contact. Shona stirred as he held it against her forehead.

'Not bad. Keep wrapped up and hydrated. Might be one of those here-today-gone-tomorrow bugs.' Again he kissed a finger and tapped her cheek. 'Drink. Don't forget.' He'd already placed a jug of water and glass on the bedside table. 'And only get out of bed for the toilet, or if you feel you can manage some food. I've left a couple of energy drinks in the fridge and there's a cheese sandwich wrapped as well.'

Jamie went into the hall and pulled on his coat, then came back and stood just inside the bedroom door.

'I'll call when I can. Check you're still heading in the right direction. Should crack on well this morning. Had a good night's sleep for a change.' Wish I'd known how comfy your floor was before I wasted all that time in your bed.'

Shona pretended to throw a pillow, then slumped back. Walking to his car, Jamie read a message on his phone.

In from ten to eleven this am. Be there. Message back soon as you receive this.

Driving, he kept muttering 'Bollocks. 'Another day of Clegg-generated pointlessness loomed.

Jamie was late, but the Buzzard was still setting up the obligatory morning briefing PowerPoint as his tribe trailed in from the canteen. A couple of minutes later, Moonlight entered and the Peepos turned to face him, but Jamie could feel it – the ripple of words from the corners of mouths, like teenagers when it's the crap teacher's day to take assembly.

Moonlight squared his shoulders and his hands slapped onto the desk. The Peepos straightened and fell silent. But it was there. Moonlight's posture, the clip and clarity of his voice was self-conscious, under pressure.

'Like the boy with his finger in the dyke,' Jamie muttered to himself.

As Moonlight finished, Jamie watched the Peepos. There were a couple of sarcastic fist-pumps as they moved to the tasks of the day.

Clegg arrived, swathed in tweed. Jamie took in the smartness of her dress. Another buffet day. She didn't take her coat off as she bustled around in her office. After a couple of minutes he saw her sit and his email pinged. The sender was obvious, so were its contents. He was still taking his boss's gift and its hours of tedium and irrelevance when she loomed over his shoulder.

'Where's your oppo?'

Jamie gave a slight shrug. 'Phoned in sick. I didn't take the call.'

Clegg leaned over and tapped his laptop.

'So this is down to you, then. Crucial. No excuses. In on time. Got the monthly divisional meeting first thing tomorrow.' Clegg straightened. 'Pro forma first. To me by three at the latest, so I can check. Mandatory that it's circulated by shift-end.' She told him what he already knew. 'Then a one-page bullet-point summary I take with me.' She tapped the monitor again and waited until Jamie gave her eye-contact. 'Crucial. No excuses.' And she pulled up her collar, then buttoned it into place before turning for the door.

'Thanks for another shit day,' Jamie stared at the pro forma. Crime case statistics, main evidence, progress assessments, time estimations. Its columns scrolled on beyond the screen edge.

Trawling through computer directories and filing cabinet drawers, Jamie began to populate the pro forma until his arse felt like it had been injected with local anaesthetic. He stretched and began walking. Outside the briefing room, he turned towards the toilet, but then pushed on the door to the beige cube. Lights flickered and steadied and he reached for his phone. Shona picked up.

'You can have another dose of ibuprofen now,' he began. 'And if you can manage it, have one of those energy drinks.'

'Missed the study unit on bedside manner then,' she teased. After a gripe about general things and what a cow Clegg was for wasting their day, Shona said: 'Went to the toilet. Got the burner out of my bag.'

Jamie waited.

'Had a message from Katya, early hours. I'll forward it.'

Seconds late Jamie got the message.

Boss shout for show. Not really care. No punters waiting. Showed photo of Jakub head. Say no loss. No gays booked in. Jakub okay. Nina keep looking in.

'Good,' Jamie sat back on the edge of the desk. 'She's a good girl. Deserves better.'

After a bit more general chat, Jamie said: 'So, how are you feeling? Think it might be a twenty-four, forty-eight hour thing?'

'Stopped shivering, and opening my eyes isn't a bother now.'

'If you do as you're told you might be through the worst. So, keep warm. And hydrate.'

'I could—' Shona began.

'No. Bed and drink. Faster in the long run. I... those girls need you back, not zombied out for days with your brain AWOL. Go on, Get back under the duvet. I'll call again later.' And he made his way back to another session of arse-end anaesthesia.

Just after two, he clicked save then pulled up Clegg's email address and attached the crucial pro forma. The bullet-point list was straight-forward. He'd already begun a pencil-draft overview.

Finished, Jamie leaned back. The day was a write-off in terms of getting on the street, or having a useful block of uninterrupted time to analyse bank info. He took out his earphones and sat, poring over Katya's sound file. On his third listening, Clegg's name and a thumbs-up emoji appeared on his phone.

'Great,' Jamie closed the message. 'Bout as close as the cow gets to thanks.' He stood, making his way towards the beige cube and the chance of a private phone call.

'Held that plastic strip thing against my forehead,' Shona sounded brighter. 'Said I was normal.'

'Thermometer's on its own there, then,' Jamie imagined Shona bobbing her tongue out at the phone. 'Might bring that thermometer into work. See if Clegg's blood heat moves up and down with the air temperature. That'd be par for a lizard.'

'Let it go, Jamie. At least you know she's tied up all day tomorrow. And, look on the bright side, you'll probably have me back as well.'

'The Lord giveth, the Lord taketh away.'

When he went back to the briefing room, he saw another

email. It was inevitable, but at least he had something to work to – a date and closure.

Jamie let himself in. 'Got you some food, if you're up to it,' he called through. Shona appeared in her dressing gown. 'Back to bed. Keep an even temperature. Don't want any relapses.'

Shona began to protest, but he waved his hand at her. A few minutes later he brought her tea and a Lemsip.

'Pulled up at Waitrose. If you've got your appetite back.' A few more minutes passed and he reappeared holding a tray. 'Soup and artisan bread. Thought you wouldn't want anything too heavy.'

Shona pulled herself straight against the pillow and began to break the bread into the bowl. Jamie watched her, then cleared away the tray. When he returned, her eye-lids were flickering. The thermometer was on the bedside table. Shona smiled up as he held it against her forehead.

'Yeah, fine,' Jamie smiled back. 'Bound to be a bit drained, but with a good night's sleep…'

Jamie was right. After ten more duvet-wrapped hours Shona opened her eyes, then put a tentative foot out of bed and stepped over Jamie as he snoozed on her floor. There was still residual fatigue, but no shivering and the dizziness and aching was gone.

She showered and headed for the kitchen; tea and toast. Two cups, four slices and marmalade. She filled the kettle again and was about to make more tea as Jamie appeared.

'Bread's in the toaster.'

Jamie pushed the switch. 'You look brighter.'

And Shona listed the ways she felt better, then took her tea to the bathroom, finally emerging with her face on for the day. 'Right. I'm ready for the office. Lock up on your way out.'

The briefing room door swung wide and Moonlight strode in.

'Someone's putting on a show,' Jamie whispered to Shona. He noticed the angle of shoulders and jaw. 'We'll wait a bit. This'll be good.'

All over the room Peepos stood, faced the front and stilled. But disdain rippled off them, invisible, but real as gravity. Moonlight flicked on the pre-loaded PowerPoint and began to describe a routine undocumented worker snatch with exaggerated precision. As he finished, his hands were on his hips.

'So... There you have it. Chance to flex our muscles again. The intel says around a dozen targets and the location is in the open, so nowhere to run. Unfortunately, I can't be with you today...'

Jamie took in the looks that flickered between the Peepos.

'I have been selected to attend an initial meeting for a multi-agency approach to border enforcement. But, gentlemen, you all know how this works,' Moonlight continued, his eyes firmly above his men's heads. 'And I have every confidence that you will be ably led.' He nodded towards the Buzzard. 'So, get yourselves out there and do what you're good at. These money grabbing, tax-evading migrants. Pick them up gentlemen. Lock them up. Sweet as, gentlemen... sweet as.'

Jamie and Shona, should have enjoyed it; the token fist pumps and faux enthusiasm, the corrosion of respect. Instead, everything passed them by as the two words sank in.

Shona trailed Jamie across the car park, phone to her ear. Jamie started the engine and revved, then faded to tick-over.

'Sorry. This rushing,' Jamie looked at her. 'Are you...?'

Shona smiled, taken aback. She nodded and he released the clutch.

They parked in a narrow road between a tree-crammed park and the university's school of law. Jephcott's Audi was waiting and they got in.

'*Sweet as.* That's what he said,' Shona's voice and eyes made sure Jephcott absorbed the significance of the phrase. 'Sweet as. He said it twice.'

'So now we know,' Jamie's voice was low.

Jephcott nodded almost imperceptibly.

'We do know,' Jamie looked at him.

Jephcott nodded again, then: 'But no one's going to court on it. Not without physical evidence. Important thing is,' and his voice slowed. 'Is not to get frustrated. Knowing, but not proving,' he straightened in his seat. 'This is great though. Might not be court ready yet, but it stops us looking in the wrong direction. A real positive.'

As Jephcott drove away, they turned into the university building and tucked themselves in the corner of a café.

'Double-edge sword,' Jamie stirred the frothy coffee. 'There's the knowing and then there's the not being able to make the right thing happen.'

Driving back, Jamie was almost chatty. 'Step forward. Knowing it's that bastard. Logical, once we knew it was The Buzzard… if we could get beyond the electronic. An image. Handwriting… why have we taken so long? Dunky knew. Tell by the way he snubbed him.'

As the hours went by, Shona felt his words sliding towards anger and frustration. 'Let's leave it for the morning,' she said. 'New day. Get us positive again.'

But it was like a scab that he couldn't help picking. 'Should've—' he began.

'Christ,' Shona shut him down. 'How many more times, the same thing…'

In bed he was silenced, eventually, by the darkness. But in the early hours, he was still awake. Every time Shona's sleep was broken, she could hear his grinding teeth and feel him clawing at the sheet. Around half-past two, she felt him hitting the side of the bed; only soft, but incessant, in rhythm, as if he were beating out the syllables of circling thoughts. Then his head had turned.

'You need your rest.,' he said. 'Only just better. I'll go home. Give you a chance of sleep.' And he dressed by the light of his phone and slipped into his car.

65

Shona was early for work, but Jamie was already at their desk.

'Hiya. Won't ask how you slept,' Shona leaned over his shoulder. He had the calendar page of his notebook open. 'Counting down to payday. Bit desperate.'

Jamie lifted his eyes and Shona understood she couldn't be further from the truth.

'If we could just get something to tie him in. Maybe Katya...?'

She realised it wasn't a morning for banter. 'Seeing her later. There's a shop. Polish clothing. Back by lunchtime.'

'Okay,' Jamie sat back from his notebook. 'But I'm like a fart in a colander. *Sweet As*... can't focus on paper trails. Clegg's sent over some crap about lorry thefts on the motorway. If I head off to Woodall Services – have a look at their CCTV – might keep Clegg at bay. Give us a clear run when we know a bit more.'

'Girl of many talents,' Shona pulled her chair nearer to Jamie in the canteen. 'I told her about *Sweet As*.'

'And you were in a shop?'

'Yes. It's okay. Small shop. Racks of clothes. You can see all around. Stand close, looking. Whisper. Hold up a skirt or something.' Shona took a sip of tea. 'Said she does the bookings sometimes.'

'Bookings?' Jamie looked confused.

'On the desk,' Shona continued. 'Booking the punters in on the calendar page.'

'So?' Jamie exhaled. 'She sees a few pages of sad shaggers. What use—'

'No, you prat. The computer. You've seen it on the desk. Not a bloody diary. Did all the business admin for her husband before he buggered off, remember? All the office stuff… Word, Excel, Outlook.'

'So?' Jamie cut in.

'Says when it's quiet, the old woman leaves her to it. Puts her feet up, or catches up with the cleaning. Anyway, there's a computer repair shop a couple of streets away, so I bought a couple of memory sticks and we reprised our *drop-in-a-carrier-bag* routine in the corner shop.'

'See you in the morning,' Shona said as Jamie opened the door of his car.

The day had drained her and he'd said he needed a final push on his training, with his dreaded fitness test approaching. There was Sierra Leone too, and a catch-up with Claudette.

Shona had put a selection of frozen meals in his freezer a few days before. 'M&S,' she'd told him. 'Now you're an athlete.'

Setting the oven, he got into his kit and made his way into the night. After a few looseners, he lengthened his stride. Fifteen minutes in, when his lungs fully opened, he began his now familiar interval-training routine, slowing and sprinting, piling up and dissipating lactic acid between streetlight distance markers. As he ran, he felt a sense of release – something to aim at. An endgame.

At home he showered, pulled on his dressing gown and then ate a cottage pie for two straight from the foil tray. Around nine, he sat before his laptop and Claudette appeared.

'Just thought… not always easy to get to say everything when Emmy's around. And I know you and Mandy have been…'

Claudette began to chuckle. Jamie squirmed through the next few minutes. His discomfort accelerating in parallel to Claudette's amusement.

'Mandy emails pictures sometimes,' Claudette looked at her phone theatrically. 'Pretty. This Glasgow woman. Maybe needs a bit more food and hair, but…' Claudette's eyes fixed on him across the ether. 'I have told you. A man is not meant to be alone. They don't cope. One life, and none of us are promised tomorrow. One life, Cara knew that. Anyone who lives in Africa knows that.'

Jamie's eyes dropped and Claudette spoke again. 'Head up, Jamie. No shame in living like a human being.'

Words went back and forth, making Jamie seem more comfortable and Claudette more wise.

'Does Emmy?' Jamie asked, after a while.

'Yes. Called her The Pretty Lady… will we meet The Pretty Lady?'

'She is pretty,' Jamie's voice was low. 'But Cara was beautiful. No one will ever…' his voice trailed away.

'I know,' Claudette leaned towards the webcam. 'I saw you together. I know what my daughter was to you… what you were to each other. But for yourself now. Tomorrow and the next day… they can't all be empty, just because they aren't yesterday. Anyway,' Claudette smiled into the screen. 'Mandy, Jacko and the children, all good, she tells me. And she's met this Shona? Says she likes her. Mentioned phone numbers and emails. Maybe I should ask for copies?'

And the conversation moved on to Baggage and her clubs; fees, musical instruments and clothing. The ritual of offers and refusals followed, then the bartering that ensured Claudette wasn't impoverished by her parental expenses and Jamie didn't feel he wasn't pulling his weight.

'Again soon. Next time earlier, for Emmy,' Jamie smiled at the screen. 'And there'll still be time for you to straighten me out.'

Claudette chuckled again. 'Today, Jamie. You need to enjoy it. Think like an African... even if the weather around you is cold. Do the right thing and don't feel guilty about it.' Claudette blew a kiss, clicked her mouse and the screen darkened.

Do the right thing and don't feel guilty about it. The words confirmed his decision and granted him absolution.

'Hiya,' Shona smiled as he reached the desk. 'On track for the fitness test?' Her voice dropped. 'After your luxury ready meal?'

'Yeah,' Jamie mumbled as he hung his coat on the chair back.

'A day or two, maybe Katya will come up trumps with the memory sticks.'

'Only be Bakula though,' Jamie's head raised a little. 'Moonlight's never been seen near the unit. Realistically, the shit we've got on him? Nothing concrete. Take it to Clegg? She'd laugh in our faces, then give us a bollocking. And she'd love to nail the bastard.'

Shona took a breath. 'It's always this way. Till it isn't. The evidence? It'll come. Give it time.'

'Time?' Jamie finally made a brief eye-contact. 'How many days is it to the end of the month?'

While Shona was fetching a couple of coffees, another Clegg email about car thefts arrived, but he was in court at nine-thirty; a couple of local dealers from months back, open and shut.

Returning to the station, he met Shona for an early lunch. In the afternoon he said he'd pick up the Clegg crap.

'Chance to nose about,' he tried to sound positive, despite knowing the chances of finding something were up there with buying a winning lottery ticket, but it left Shona free to focus on bank accounts and body-cams.

Jamie read the email again. More disappearing cars. The container theory seemed his best lead and, while he was quizzing local haulage firms, he could check any rumours about red vans with Polish plates.He got back around five, no wiser than when he'd left and, as he went to sit opposite Shona, Clegg opened her office door and crooked a finger.

'Enjoy,' Shona looked across as he blew out his cheeks and stood.

'Back early?' Clegg indicated he should sit.

'It's dark,' Jamie reached for a chair. 'There's some paperwork…'

'There always is,' Clegg looked at him. 'But people talk to coppers in the dark. Especially if they think no one can see them. Anyway, now you're here, what did you find out?'

The words *Sweet As* kept circling in Jamie's mind while he took Clegg through the litany of car-related trivia.

'At least the slow-cooker's done its job,' Shona said as she stepped into her hallway and inhaled. 'And dumplings.' She ladled out a thick gravy, loaded with shin of beef, carrots and mushrooms.

After eating, Jamie was fiddling in his pocket and took out his phone. 'Missed call, 15:04. Four hours ago. Must've been when I was driving.' He shrugged as he showed Shona.

'Is there—'

'No. Nothing on voicemail.'

'That's the branch landline, but you've got her mobile,' Shona looked at the screen, then moved towards the oven. 'Phone her back.'

Jamie nodded but, after the dialling tone timed out for a second time, all he could do was leave a message. After he was done, he put his phone on the table.

'So Katya?' he said. 'Working the desk? A couple of memory sticks. Usually cheap enough. How big—'

'Bought the 128 gig ones. Hope it's enough.'

Jamie began chuckling. 'Well, unless they've downloaded the contents of Netflix.'

'So should be easy, with the two?'

Jamie was shaking his head. 'Do you know what the average office laptop holds?'

Shona waited for the mansplaining.

'Like I say, unless there's loads of video, 128 gig. Probably won't reach half full.'

'Well, suppose we'll find a use for the spare,' and Shona stood, reached for a couple of bowls, then walked to the fridge. 'Bring you a tea in a bit. That M&S meal I got you. Three for two, so it seemed a shame.' And she took out a large tiramisu.

'If my nan could see me eating foreign puddings full of vowels…' Jamie shuffled towards the sofa. Shona was a few seconds behind him, carrying two dishes.

'Spoke to Claudette, last night.' Jamie said, as Shona sat and leaned into him. 'Just general chit-chat. She's seen your picture… and Baggage. Our Mandy's work.'

Shona waited, head hovering just above Jamie's chest.

'Pretty Lady.' Jamie looked at her. 'That's what Baggage calls you. Apparently.'

Shona snuggled deeper into his shoulder. The room was warm and she closed her eyes. Then her phone beeped in the kitchen. Then again. And again.

Jamie plumped a cushion as she got up and put his head on the arm of the sofa.

'Jamie… Jamie,' it was only seconds and he was up and moving. Shona was holding the phone, shaking, tears already streaming. 'The number. Not one I…'

Jamie took the phone and looked. A video ran; four, five seconds. Whoever filmed it was stood back a little, but the figure, the blood – the scene was terrible. Jamie clicked – the same few seconds. And again. Pushing the phone back in Shona's hand, he held her shoulders.

'Coat. Quick. I'll drive.'

66

Leaving the car on double yellow lines, they both had their police IDs out as they ran into the A&E reception.

'Katya. Don't know her surname,' Jamie leaned across the desk 'Throat wound.'

'There's no throat wound come in. Not…' the receptionist was scrolling furiously down her computer monitor.

'Dark hair. She's Polish.' Shona was reaching for her phone.

'Polish. Yes.' The woman was reading from the screen now. 'In three. But—'

Jamie and Shona raced beyond the doors into the treatment area, scanning the cubicles for numbers. Then they spotted 3.

Katya was sitting up, her eye-lids flickering, both hands bandaged and a necklace of dried blood cracking across her neck and shoulders.

'Moving her through now,' the doctor squinted at their identification. 'Sooner we sort those hands out the better. Be a while in surgery and then there'll be the anaesthetic. Best if you call ahead.' And he began tapping notes into a tablet.

Shock. Adrenalin. Going straight home wasn't an option. Making their way into the station, the lights felt even more fluorescently sterile than usual. When they reached the briefing room, the overnight Peepos were huddled over distant filing cabinets, illuminated by a dull desk lamp. Using his phone torch, Jamie flicked the main switches.

At their desk, they drank tea. Paced. Swapped theories back and forth.

'Some of those punters. Bound to have a past,' Jamie speculated. 'She was by the reception. If we could get names. Check our records.'

As the early morning cleaners arrived, Jamie said: 'If we go back. Get showered and changed. Might be able to check on Katya again in a few hours.'

It was nearly ten when they arrived at the police station again.

'Moonlight's car,' Shona peered across the car park. 'Looks like a dinner suit hanging in the back. Full black tie rig out.'

'Maybe they've changed the canteen dress code.'

They'd messaged Clegg as they'd left the hospital, so she was expecting them in late.

'Disgruntled client?' Clegg stood in her open office doorway.

'All the drugs,' Shona explained. 'Saw her, but she was woozy. Shock, sedatives. Doctors said try again later.'

'All this?' Clegg was looking at the video on the phone. 'Defence wounds?'

Shona nodded.

'And we know who sent this?'

'No. Not a number I recognise,' Shona shook her head.

Clegg leaned on a filing cabinet and waited.

'Gave her a burner a while back,' Shona explained. 'Said she kept it under the floorboards in her room. But not this number.'

'Hopefully she's in a state to talk this afternoon,' Clegg sat down. 'Keep checking with the hospital. Make sure you keep me posted. When you know, I know.'

'Come bearing gifts,' Jamie said as Dave Collins opened the door. He held a cardboard carrier with three large coffees, and Shona had a bag of sandwiches and pastries. 'Can't face having those bald-headed bastards staring at us across the desk.'

As they all sat around the central table, Shona tilted her phone towards Dave and played the video.

'Christ,' Dave leaned close. 'No wonder you thought she'd had her throat cut.'

'Hospital said give it three hours,' Shona slumped in her chair. 'She's still out of it.'

'Right mess,' Jamie reached for one of the sandwiches. 'Palms cut to bits and severed flexor tendons.'

'Best case scenario? Eight weeks of her fingers immobilised with a splint,' Shona added. 'Then another month or two of physio to get the strength and movement back. So the doctor tells us.'

'So she's fending off the attacker with her hands, as he's slashing at her with a knife,' Dave absorbed the scene. 'She holds her own throat and that was why there was blood on it… but you didn't know that till you saw her in the cubicle.' Dave tapped pause. 'And there were no injuries near her neck. So why were her hands flapping around there?'

All three lifted their coffees. As the silence stretched, Jamie reached for his phone and started to scroll 'Jesus wept.' He held up the screen. 'The bloody bank.'

'Thought you'd have been knocking my door off its hinges yesterday afternoon,' the bank manager sat at her desk. 'Had visions of a TV interview. *Look North* at least, if not the national news.'

'We've had—' Jamie began.

'Someone that's been helping us. Nasty assault. Been at the hospital,' Shona cut in.

Jamie's hand went to the phone in his pocket.

'Evidence,' Shona caught his hand. 'The pictures aren't what you might… young woman. Lots of blood.'

Janine Bowker was quiet for a moment. 'Maybe these pictures might just balance out the karma of your day then. Now, Solar Properties,' she turned her laptop. 'Every few weeks the card gets used and most of our ATMs have a camera. Like I said, the boffins can rig an alert. Which means we've got an image tied to a time and place.'

Shona and Jamie were out of their seats, staring at the laptop.

'Might be a bit hazy for evidence. And the ATM cameras are a bit fish-eyed, But…' and Janine closed one tab and opened another. 'The cashpoint was in our main branch, and that's got CCTV everywhere. So, when we match up the time with the CCTV…'

And there he was. Walking in. Standing in the queue. Looking around in a room with bright marble walls and metres of plate glass on two sides.

Moonlight. Clear as day.

The bank manager flicked the mouse and Jamie's phone beeped.

'Actually,' she went on. 'Worked out for the best. Only had the ATM footage when I phoned yesterday. Coming today, I've been able to tie it together with the CCTV. So, it's all there, nice and clear. And attached to the email I just sent you.'

Shona and Jamie looked at each other, mouths wanting to speak. Then Shona was around the desk, hugging Janine Bowker.

'Thank you so much. You don't know what it means…'

Jamie stood back, shuffling from foot to foot. When Shona stepped away he held out a hand to shake. The bank manager smiled.

'Best you can do, big fella?' but she didn't move to hug him.

Words went back and forth. Just chatter. Social bonding. Then: 'Company's House has the directors listed,' and Janine took a print-out from a folder.

'No,' Shona read down the list. 'Not any name I recognise.'

'Yeah, well, you know what I said about I.D. checks. Anyway, I had everything copied, just in case.'

Shona looked at her watch. 'I can't tell you how grateful… the domino you've pushed over today. Without you, going way beyond… you don't know how much good you've done.' She reached across and took Janine Bowker's hand again. 'But the girl in the hospital. We need to get over. The sedatives… if we're lucky, by now she might be able to…'

'We'll be back,' Jamie folded the photocopy into his pocket. 'It's right what she said. Thanks. You've made a difference. More than you know.'

The ward was windowless and a dozen beds stretched under fluorescent light tubes. The last bed on the left had curtains drawn around. As they got closer, Shona was aware of a hunched silhouette.

Jakub didn't look up as they edged through the curtains. His eyes were on the rosary beads in his hands. There was a bruise and swelling where his jaw met his neck.

'Hi,' Shona smiled and said a few words in Polish.

Jakub straightened a little and Katya's eyes opened, then closed again. Shona stretched towards her hands, but saw the bandages and she reached up, trailing her fingers over Katya's cheek.

'Mind if…' Shona indicated the bed. Jakub nodded and she sat down. Jamie remained at the gap in the curtain.

'Zdrowas Mario, laskis pelna,' Jakub bowed his head again and moved his hand one bead along the chain.

'Hail Mary, full of grace,' Jamie's voice was almost inaudible.

Shona stayed quiet. Then, as one Amen followed the other, she said: 'Never learned that one. My grandad had a Rangers season ticket.'

Jamie grinned a little and Jakub sat up. Shona took out her phone.

'Bakula,' Jakub looked at Katya. 'Bakula,' and he turned back and pointed at the bruising on his own face. 'Video. I send.'

Piecing together from Jakub's broken English and Shona's cracked Polish, they learned how Bakula had come in and seen Katya snatch the memory stick out of the computer. How he'd sent Jakub sprawling as he'd tried to get in the way. How there'd been a craft knife on the desk that was used for sharpening pencils. How Asenka, one of the girls, who was walking from between the containers had dodged back and lifted her phone.

'This?' Shona held out her phone screen, video running.

Jakub nodded and tapped his head, and again an exchange of fractured English and Polish.

'He knew about the burner, under the floor,' Shona's eyes indicated to Jakub. 'Memorised the number and sent the video from Asenka's phone. Then…'

Jamie nodded. There was only one number in the burner's contacts.

'I'm so sorry about…' Shona touched a wrist above Katya's bandaged hand. 'Should never have… and all for nothing. Now he's…'

Katya's eyes opened again and her head tilted towards the bedside locker and her clothes. 'In jeans.' Her eyes flickered. 'All files on one stick, easy.' And she breathed for a few seconds. 'Gave bastard blank one.'

Shona stood, leaned across the bed and kissed Katya. Then her hand went to Jakub's shoulder and his head bowed again. As Shona took the memory stick from Katya's jeans she felt a small metal rectangle. She held it up; gold, dangling from a broken chain.

'Black Madonna.' The icon's gilded haloes glinted, spinning in Shona's fingers. 'From your babcia… grandma.'

'Felt break.' Katya's bandaged fingers moved towards her throat, but stopped short, her hands splayed and stiff with dressings. 'Not lose it. How else I keep pure?' And her eyes fluttered and closed for a few seconds, then she smiled again and slipped into sleep.

At the nurse's station, Shona spoke to the sister on the desk. 'He's her little brother.' She told her. 'You can let relatives stay. Be safer. Assailant's still at large, and gives us time to organise Social Services.'

As Shona was emphasising her points to the sister, Jamie had managed a round trip to the staff canteen.

'Keep the lad fed and watered,' he arrived back at the nurses' station, stacking sandwiches, a banana and a large bottled water. 'And something for your staff.' He took two slabs of chocolate from his jacket pocket and slid them towards the sister.

Driving away from the hospital, Jamie was staring out the passenger side window. 'Drop me back at the station so I can collect my car. Then I'll pick up some odds and ends and come to yours. Don't make any calls yet. We need to talk this through.'

Back home, Jamie reached into his bookcase and pulled out a large sheet of paper, then spread it across his table. A series of flow diagrams. Different scenarios. Suspect A first? Suspect B first? Arrest local? Arrest at port? Escape to Europe? Jamie stared at the strategies and endgames. He didn't need to look at them though. He'd long since committed them to memory.

'So it begins,' he had a pencil clamped in his fist but, lost in thought, he ground it into the paper. The point detached, dark graphite dust formed a small fan and he kept grinding, oblivious to anything outside his head. Twisting, pressing, relentless—

Snap.

His hand slammed into the paper as the pencil gave way, cracking and splitting, splintering across the page and into the edge of his hand. Jamie didn't flinch, didn't blink. Blood and graphite stained the flow diagram lines and letters. Eventually, he looked down.

'Enough now, game face.' And he walked to the sink, washed out the cut and took a plaster from the cupboard.

Less than half-an-hour later, Shona saw Jamie's car turn across the row of shops below her flat. She was at the door, holding a couple of carrier bags, as he bounced up the steps.

'You look ready to go,' she turned the key in her lock.

'Born ready.'

And, reaching the car, Shona saw his best jacket and tie, dangling on a hanger, above the back door.

'Clegg will have gone home,' Jamie said as he turned onto the ring road. 'Give us chance to decide how to play it. Task one: Getting her royal highness on board. Task two: Decide who gets lifted first? For me? No brainer...'

Jamie was right. Clegg was long gone. The briefing room was empty, except for a couple of the older night-shift Peepos.

'So, picking up Moonlight?' Shona eased her chair along the desk.

'Best if you make the call to Clegg,' he leaned towards her.

67

'Sorry to disturb you at home ma'am.' Shona began. 'But, this afternoon, things just...'

Clegg listened and questioned.

'Yes ma'am, once the card registered in the ATM, it was like dominoes toppling. Documented proof. Video ID.'

'So,' Clegg began her summary. 'Provided you lift him without any cock-ups, we're solid. Any slime-ball politician who tries bigging the Peepos up, the Chief Constable can tell him *Fuck off and Told you so*. Okay. The warrant. I'm on it.'

'Be a headline grabber,' Shona continued. 'As we speak, ma'am, we've got cast iron charges relating to fraud and vice, but I'd be amazed if GBH and a menu of sexual abuse doesn't follow,' Shona could almost hear Clegg nodding at the other end of the phone.

'And you say going for a synchronised pick-up is—'

'Well, the way we see it... maybe if Jamie goes through it.'

She handed the phone across to Jamie and leant in to listen as he tapped speaker.

'Ma'am,' Jamie began. 'We know Bakula's in the frame, but given our current relations with European banks and police services, official co-operation could take a while to arrive. Irrespective, coordinating synchronised arrests, never easy. Only got to be a fraction out and one gets to warn the other. So, on balance, go for Moonlight. He makes the biggest headline. *Peepo boss in vice girl murder probe*. More traction than *Another violent, foreign pimp arrested*. And, on the practical side, Bakula's escape routes are limited. Ferry ports have timetables, CCTV and pinch points. Got to go through customs. Worst case scenario, he makes it onto the boat and even then, he's fair game until he clears UK waters. I've sorted a list. Overnight ferries in driving distance. Relevant ports and police contacts. Details on Bakula and his known vehicles. The calls can be started soon as—'

'But' Clegg seemed to be verbalising her own thought processes. 'To arrest Moonlight, you need to be sure of his location. And I'm guessing he's not still at the station?'

'Sadly, no ma'am. But if we leave it until around midnight, I'm pretty sure I know where to find him. And gives us a chance to line up all the calls to the ports and stuff, before we make our move.' Jamie went on, eventually ending with: 'And Dave Collins is on a late shift tonight. Gives us time to fill in the details and let him coordinate the uniform support.'

'And he'll—' Clegg put in.

'And he'll be happy to accept the overtime and unsocial hours money.'

A few more details and Jamie spoke his closing words. 'But Moonlight, when he goes down. Serious dent for any Peepo hopes of upping their profile. I'm sure at HQ...'

'Okay,' Clegg absorbed the point. 'Keep me informed. 'Be worth a sleepless night to look that smarmy bastard in the eye as he's heading for the cells.'

The warrant arrived whilst Shona and Jamie were with Dave Collins.

'If you make sure there's two or three back-up cars,' Jamie turned away from the printer, folding the warrant. 'When all the details are done and dusted.' He sat and they leaned over three coffees.

'So, same routine as before,' Shona took a sip. 'Try not to flash the warrant until we have to. Minimise the chance of someone tipping him the wink.'

'Put you in charge of double checking,' Jamie grinned over his mug. 'Make sure I don't leave it in this jacket when I swap into my casino kit. But what about you? Not dressed to—'

Shona leaned down and opened a carrier bag. There was a sparkle of sequins. 'I'll change in the toilet, and I've got my long coat until the grand reveal.'

'Just going in now Ma'am,' Shona was on the phone as they pulled onto the casino car park. 'Yes, got coordinated uniform response sorted. All goes to plan, the blues-and-twos should be arriving just as we exit with the bastard cuffed.' Shona listened again. 'Yes Ma'am, thanks. We've got the warrant.'

'Miss Fur-Coat-and-No knickers is here. That's her car,' Jamie pointed. 'So we're on.'

Shona chewed a knuckle as she stared out of the car window, waiting for cover but, as the dragging minutes stretched her nerves, only a succession of couples and the occasional four arrived in their cars. Then, just after midnight, about a dozen party animals spilled out of three taxis.

'Bingo,' Shona heard the drink-loosened voices. Striding from the car, she and Jamie slipped alongside the suited, booted and sparkle-dressed gaggle. 'Flirt,' she said. 'Head down, face around my neck.'

The orange light from the four, large imitation flames at the entrance rippled off the sequins on Shona's dress and they huddled in mid-group, keeping bodies between them and the door staff. Jamie did as instructed; head down, somewhere between Shona's shoulder and cleavage. And they were in.

Shona went to the ladies, checked the paperwork was to hand in her bag if anyone should make a challenge, then took out her phone and messaged Dave to stand by. Jamie waited in the corridor, leaning on the wall, backheeling the skirting board.

When she returned, Jamie took Shona's arm and they moved towards the gaming rooms.. The men were split, half in lounge suits and the rest in black tie. The male to female ratio was about three-to-one, but the women stood out, sparkling in their shiniest evening-wear.

'Like flies on horse shit,' Jamie sucked in a breath.

Shona scanned the room. 'There,' she pointed. 'Next to Fox's daughter. She's in the red backless number.'

'Okay,' Jamie's shoulders relaxed. 'Just give it a minute.' He nodded towards a group at the roulette table. 'Might be a way to load the scales a bit more.' And he was walking, Shona hanging on as he pushed through the crowd.

As expected, Fox stood in a circle of acolytes. Jamie stopped just short of the group and waited for Fox to register. At first Fox ignored him and moved away a little. Jamie shifted, again stopping short of the group. Fox looked once more. A slight nod showed he understood he was being given a chance to minimise disruption.

'If you'll excuse me a moment,' he stepped beyond his entourage.

'If we can—' Jamie opened his jacket to show his police ID.

Fox registered and looked to Shona. She lifted her eyebrows and tilted her head. Fox began to move to a clear floor space just beyond the gaming area.

'If you've got some half-baked, penny-pinching…' Fox's teeth were clamped and his eyes seethed.

Jamie stared back, unblinking.

'Whatever it is, you won't get it to court,' defiance crept into Fox's anger. 'Certainly not with my name on. Why would I cheat, when I own the wheel?'

'Because you can. Genetically above the law. Genetically too clever to be caught. It's in your blood. The entitlement.' Jamie held up a hand as Fox went to answer. 'But, yeah, in this case, it isn't you. And I'm here to do you a favour. Chance to maintain a bit of insulation. Your daughter. Might want to drag her away from her boyfriend for a minute. Be a good idea if the two of them weren't in camera phone distance for a while. Or ever again.'

Fox signalled one of the bar staff and a minute later his daughter was squeezing her way between the bodies, leaving Moonlight with a pile of chips and a dice in his hand.

'Arabella,' Fox began.

'Solar Properties,' Jamie cut in. The girl reddened. 'Bit of an anomaly between the money arriving in Vulpes accounts and what the tenants are paying.'

The girl looked to her father, then at the ground. ' I only took him to the office. Told Georgie to help him out.'

'Georgie?' Fox looked at her.

'Georgie, she's the manager. If she's been—'

'She hasn't,' Shona cut in. 'All standing orders to Vulpes match the paperwork and a normal rent.'

'But then there's the bags of cash,' Jamie looked steadily at Fox. 'For every pound going into Vulpes accounts, her boyfriend, well his minion really, was collecting twice as much from the girls in cash.'

'Girls?' Fox stiffened.

'Mostly,' Shona turned to look at the daughter.

'Working girls. Sex workers. Smuggled in'

Fox flinched as Jamie carried on.

'Hence the extra payments. He had them over a barrel.'

'And a few of them against the side of a van,' Shona's focus was locked, straight at Miss Fur-Coat-and-No-Knickers. 'Mr *Sweet As* they call him. Apparently it's his catch-phrase, at moments of high excitement. Sweet As.'

The girl's eyes dropped.

'But you made nothing?' Fox pointed a finger at his daughter. 'Your name?'

'No. Nothing. Signed nothing. Put my name on nothing. Just the intro to Georgie... sorry,' she was fighting to stop her voice cracking now.

Jamie and Shona didn't speak, making sure that nothing intruded on the hostility that streamed towards Arabella Fox from her father.

Eventually Jamie broke the silence. 'If we can make the arrest with the minimum fuss, maybe you'd like to step out. Like I said, there's always someone with camera phone.'

'Might be wise to...' Shona held out an arm in the direction of the ladies restroom and the girl began to walk.

'So,' Shona said as they walked. 'If we asked for access to documents – hard drives at the Vulpes office?'

'To nail that bastard?' Arabella Fox's eyes rippled behind a film of moisture, but no tears fell. 'While he was with me, dipping his wick in those rent-a-shag girls...'

'Not just girls,' Shona held the restroom door open for her. 'Might be an idea to get a blood test.'

Arabella Fox's mouth went to speak, but Shona pushed the door wider. 'Go on, scurry away. Stay out of the way till I'll call you.' Making her way back to Jamie, she whispered to herself: '*Zemsta.*'

'If some of your door staff could position themselves so he can see there's nowhere to go,' Jamie was saying. 'Probably facilitate maximum discretion.'

Shona took the arrest warrant out of her bag and Fox glanced at it, then beckoned to a manager.

Jamie and Shona sidled their way across to the dice table and stood behind Moonlight as he made a couple of losing bets.

'Not your lucky night,' Jamie's voice made Moonlight turn, disconcerted for a moment.

'Probably means I'm lucky in love,' his default arrogance dropped back into place. 'Especially as I was given the chips for free. Very intimate friend of the management.'

Jamie grinned. 'Never got the hang of these games. Dice, roulette, blackjack, all that malarkey. More a dominoes man…'

Shona opened her bag and took out her phone. The message she sent was pre-typed.

'Dominoes,' Jamie went on. 'When you balance them all on end and they just stand there, until you find that elusive missing piece, put it in place and give it a shove.'

'Is there…' Moonlight began. 'I mean, much as I'd love to debate empirical philosophy with you, I've got other people's money to enjoy.'

'Well maybe not anymore,' Shona had folded the warrant so the heading and police crest were just visible.

Moonlight looked around. Eight doormen faced inwards at a radius of about five metres.

'You want me to read you your rights and cuff you here?' Jamie tilted his head. 'Or maybe we could go somewhere more discreet and avoid adding resisting arrest to the charge sheet.'

'What…' Moonlight lowered his voice.

'Dominoes, other people's money. Using an ATM to take it out. We identified the account a while back, when your pal turned up with a carrier bag full of cash. But you'd anticipated that hadn't you? Giving the account a business name, then listing fictitious directors at Companies House. But then there was the ATM. Didn't you think about most of them having cameras on? And bonus, you picked one inside a bank, with all the CCTV. And suddenly it's all fall down time,' Jamie nodded towards the doormen and they maintained their unobtrusive ring until, reluctantly, Moonlight followed Jamie and Shona into a side office.

'You do not have to say anything…' Shona recited the arrest mantra as Jamie pulled Moonlight's arms behind his back.

'When this comes out,' Jamie said. 'Your brother. What will he say? And your dad? Probably need an upgrade on his birthday Merc to get over the disappointment.'

Moonlight thrashed and twisted, but Jamie shoved a knee into the back of his leg, gripped his neck and pushed his head towards the desk.

'Careful, now,' he twisted the handcuff lock into place. 'You nearly resisted arrest then.'

Jamie spread a hand across Moonlight's back and shoved him against a wall, holding him there for a few seconds. With the other hand, he took his phone from his pocket and looked down.

'They're outside now,' Jamie looked up at Moonlight, there was a smear of red across the collar of his white shirt where the blood had seeped from under the plaster on his hand.

They took him through a fire door and the car park was a chaos of revolving blue lights.

'Three cars, Dave. Bloody hell mate, you've left half of Sheffield undefended.' Jamie shoved Moonlight towards the first car.

68

They got back to the station around two in the morning. Clegg was waiting in her office with lime cordial and a bottle of single malt on the desk.

'Seeing him taken down to the cells. Couldn't miss that,' she poured out two whiskies. 'Bit old school TV cop drama, but this needs celebrating.' And she tipped a drop of lime into a tall glass and filled it from a jug of iced water. 'Got the old man to drop me off, but you can do the return trip after Shona and me have drunk a couple of toasts. Thought I'd start with Truth and Justice. You can still join in. Have a drink of squash. Go on. Let yourself go.' A few minutes later her desk phone rang. 'Johnno and Greenie picked his oppo up.' Clegg listened and relayed the message. 'Sitting with his toothbrush and wash bag waiting for them, apparently.'

'Buzzard failed to fly,' Jamie smirked and Shona smiled back.

Clegg looked puzzled.

'The Buzzard,' Jamie said. 'It's what the girls called him.' And he stood, hunching his neck with his arms stretched wide, elbows up and fingers spread. Clegg gave a laugh as the penny dropped.

'What about Bakula?'

'Nothing yet. But we've notified passport control. They'll be checking the passenger lists for the next few days.'

An hour or so later, Clegg eased herself out of Jamie's car and searched her pockets for door keys.

'Good work, you two. Duty solicitor said Moonlight's too tired to be questioned. Good, suits us. We get a rest and he won't sleep anyway. Right, I'm going to wake the old man up. And you two, have a good sleep. I don't want to see you for at least nine hours.'

Jamie said goodnight and drove on to Shona's flat.

'Still awake?' he phoned Dave Collins after parking. 'So we're waiting on airports and the ferries then.' Jamie listened and nodded. 'Okay Dave, thanks. Get some sleep.' He turned to Shona. 'When the patrol cars reached the unit, Bakula was gone. Girls said he'd been in earlier and cleared out the safe.'

'Maybe if we'd synchronised the raid on the unit with the cars arriving for the arrest at the casino…'

Jamie shrugged. 'Might've lost Moonlight then. Timing not spot on, and all it would've taken was a phone call for him to leg it out of there. Don't panic. More than one way to skin a twat.'

'Look at them.' Jamie tilted his head towards the Peepos. Groups splintered, reformed, but the buzz of voices was constant. 'Headless wankers.'

'Do you think they—'

'Yeah. Look at them. They know.' And he continued to enjoy the chaos. 'Anyway, got a report that Bakula was booked on a KLM flight out from Leeds Bradford to Warsaw, at about six o'clock this morning. We had people on hand, but he was a no-show. And a Lufthansa flight from Manchester to Wroclaw at seven. Again, no-show.'

'So, panicked and lying low?' Shona looked back towards Jamie.

'Nah, he'll have had a plan. Those flights? Diversions. His bosses in Poland will have mapped out contingencies, like we role-play major incidents. My money's on send us to the airports, then race to a ferry. False passport, false number plates and cram his Merc's body panels with cash.'

Shona sat and they both started searching ferry schedules.

'Channel ports?' Jamie squinted at his screen. 'Drive time's too long. He'll have to go East coast, or maybe Liverpool and onto Dublin.'

Both carried on scrolling.

'That'll be it,' Jamie turned his laptop round. 'Harwich to the Hook of Holland. Left at nine this morning.'

'Long crossing,' Shona read the arrival time.

'He's gone.'

Shona looked surprised at Jamie's matter-of-fact tone. 'But we could—'

'Nah,' Jamie shut his screen. 'Smart-arsed bastard. Be out of British waters by now and it's a Stena Line ferry, so Swedish. Been a piece of piss if we still had the European arrest warrants.'

'Bollocks,' Shona stood, then kicked her chair.

Jamie stayed seated for a few seconds, then stood. 'Might as well get a cuppa before the interview starts.'

Shona stared at his back. Her fingers tensed into fists and her teeth were grinding. As Jamie crossed the briefing space, Peepo faces turned, but their bodies parted.

'Thank you. Gentlemen,' Jamie eased between them. 'Seems we're a little late getting started this morning.'

Shona followed, not speaking, making no eye-contact, walking in Jamie's track, her anger feeding from the smoothness of his movements.

'Might even try a late breakfast,' Jamie spoke over his shoulder as they turned into the corridor.

A few Peepos had made the same decision. Hobbes was at the back of a group that had just reached the stairs. Jamie lengthened his stride.

Once in the canteen, there were three or four civilian admin workers in the queue between Jamie and the Peepos. Shona was reading a sandwich label when Jamie picked up his tray and squeezed forwards.

'Can I just...' he smiled at the admin group. 'Bit of a rush on this morning,' and he reached over to the woman on the till and handed her a twenty pound note. 'Put the change in the charity box.'

Hobbes turned to see Jamie was smiling.

'Think you're better? One of the masters?' Jamie's voice was cold and measured. 'Think if you do whatever those entitled shits who run this country tell you, you're part of *their* gang? Part of their gang? You're fuck all but a guard dog. Do what you're told for a biscuit.'

Hobbes lip curled.

'That's it, boy... fetch.'

And Jamie snatched the Kit-Kat off Hobbes tray and skimmed it across the floor. As Hobbes lurched forwards, restraining hands grabbed his shoulders.

'Leave it Hobbesy. He's not worth it,' Jamie said, putting on an exaggerated Essex accent. He looked at the pair of Peepos clinging onto Hobbes. Then he laughed and took the doughnut from his own tray and dropped it onto Hobbes's. 'There you go. Wouldn't want to get into a dogfight.'

'At least you've saved a few calories,' Shona whispered as they turned away and headed for a table, somehow relieved to see a glimpse of a spark in the unnatural calm of Jamie's morning.

After eating, Jamie wiped the grease and tomato sauce from his fingers.

'So that's your view of the British class system?' Shona asked. 'Rich smart-arses, balancing on top of a pile of wannabes. Dickheads who've been tricked into thinking they're part of the ruling gang, because they get pats on the head and the occasional biscuit.'

Jamie shrugged.

'But—' Shona began.

'Look,' Jamie cut in. 'I take the piss. If I wanted to preach, I'd be standing in a pulpit, not sitting in a canteen shovelling beans into my gob.'

Shona stared out of the plate glass window at the rise and fall of the Sheffield skyline. Jamie drained the last of his tea and stood. As they moved towards the door, Hobbes' eyes lifted and glowered. Jamie grinned back and mouthed woof.

Moonlight's solicitor arrived. He was given the beige cube room to consult with his client. At least Jamie and Shona had some natural daylight from the window behind Clegg's desk.

'I've scanned the paperwork and the images from the bank,' Clegg was making notes as she spoke. 'Should be open and shut, now the CCTV puts his face on the account numbers. And the stuff we got from The Buzzard, tied up a few loose ends. The Buzzard…' Clegg looked up. 'Christ you've got me saying it now.'

'Been in there an hour. Must be running out of things to say, by now,' Clegg flicked the edge of a pile of documents.

'Not legal aid then,' Shona stated the obvious.

Clegg carried on organising the chain of questions that would be used to keep the interview focused. 'It'll be me doing the first interview,' she picked up a folder. 'And I've asked to borrow Tommo, to be in there with me.'

'Tree-climbing Tommo?' Tension shot into Jamie's voice for the first time that morning.

'Specialist interview trained Tommo,' Clegg looked up from her papers.

'Why?' Shona asked.

'Clue's in the word specialist,' Clegg shuffled more paper. 'And I can't afford emotion getting in the way. You two are too involved.'

'But we're the ones with the relevant information up here,' Jamie tapped his head with a finger.

'And that's why you'll be watching on CCTV, and me and Tommo will be wearing earpieces. That way you can feed us lines, but if you start ranting like a prat, I can just give the wire a pull.' Clegg's phone buzzed. 'Tommo's on his way up.

After about twenty minutes of getting up to speed with Tommo, Clegg's phone buzzed again. 'Solicitor's gone for a cuppa, says he's ready when we are.'

Jamie and Shona stood.

'Specialist interviewer. Master tree-climber. Bloody hell, Tommo,' Jamie turned in the doorway. 'You must've been on more courses than Tiger Woods.'

In the surveillance room, they both fell quiet as they checked the video and audio feeds. Preliminaries began. They adjusted their monitors and microphones. Jamie watched every word, Shona's eyes flicked from screen to notebook. It was all standard. Evidence outlined. A stream of *no comments*. Early days. It was only at the end, when the solicitor mentioned bail, that Jamie became animated.

'Flight risk. Witness intimidation. Prisoner's own protection… could be viewed as possible informant by his organised crime associates.'

Clegg shuffled papers and, looking down, mumbled 'Numerous factors to balance…'

'Leaving him on the streets, he might get careless,' Shona leaned into her microphone. 'Get us closer to a murder charge.'

'Target for media scrutiny,' Jamie jumped in. 'Got enough to put him away now. Imagine the negative publicity if he fled, or got bumped off. Flight risk. Witness intimidation…' Jamie went through his original prompt again.

'Bail will be opposed on grounds of flight risk, witness intimidation and for the prisoner's own protection,' Clegg fell in line with Jamie's words.

There was some further low-level back and forth and then Tommo said: 'Interview ceased at 12:43,' and he switched off the recorder.

'Interview ceased at 12:43...' Jamie opened the door into Clegg's office. 'Christ, did you have to have specialist training for that?'

Tommo looked up from his chair and grinned.

'Before we decide where next, I want you and Shona to watch the interview through again.' Clegg didn't invite them to sit. 'Soak it up. Get ourselves on top of the details. We'll charge him with something financial, so there's no clock ticking down, then let him stew till the morning. See how he is after another night of lying in a cell, too much on his mind to sleep.'

Chairs were pulled close on the same side of the desk. The interview footage was playing on a laptop.

'Watch his reactions,' Jamie leaned forwards. 'And think about other ways we can push the questioning.'

Shona stared at the screen. 'Fraud. Finance, white-collar crap. The bastard needs to pay for more than that,' her fingers were scratching at her knuckles. 'If he was on bail... face in the papers. Bank account suspended. He wouldn't cope. He'd slip up. Give us an opening on a murder charge.'

'See that twitch?' Jamie tapped the screen. 'Look, when Clegg asks him about body-cams and the London Gateway.'

Shona stood. Her movement was quick and she was rocking from foot to foot, as if she didn't know what came next. 'I'm going for a wee,' she said suddenly.

The ladies toilet was empty. She leaned on a sink, looking at herself in the mirror. Late nights. Tension. Temper. Cheap fluorescent lighting. She turned a tap and splashed cold water onto her cheeks, avoiding the make-up around her eyes. She looked into the mirror again. 'Christ, I look like my granny's bus pass.'

As she returned, the laptop was on the desk, but no Jamie. Sitting down, she looked where the video had been paused, then pulled the timeline bar forwards and backward. Just more Moonlight *no comments*. The movement of Clegg's door drew her eye and she saw Jamie turn towards their desk.

'You've been…?' Shona said before he'd sat down.

'Just asking if specialist interviewer Tommo had come up with anything.'

'And has he?'

'No. Think he's more suited to trees.'

Shona stared across the desk at the top of Jamie's head. Occasionally, he looked up from the papers, or computer screen and smiled.

Fuck off, Shona's words were silent, behind clenched teeth.

Jamie cued up the interview recording software, making occasional small-talk and suggesting the odd question. Shona gave minimal answers, not able to trust her voice since seeing Jamie sneaking back from seeing Clegg.

Around four o'clock, Clegg was pulling on her coat. Shona had been watching for signs of movement.

'Getting a coffee. I'll bring you one.' She was on her feet.

Jamie looked surprised and grunted. Rushing into the corridor, Shona jogged to catch Clegg at the lift. When the doors closed they were alone.

'Left my purse in the glove compartment. Should've brought my coat.' Shona shivered, theatrically. 'Did Tommo come up with anything?'

Clegg looked blank.

'When Jamie was in your office earlier.'

Clegg still looked blank.

'Because I think the key to nailing Moonlight properly would be giving him bail, then watching him when the pressure kicks in. The being on his own. The no money, no mates.'

'Bird in the hand,' Clegg looked up at the floor numbers. 'It's still high profile, so we get the headlines. Does a runner or gets bumped off? Not the media coverage we need. And Fox. He knows he owes us one, knows what a leak to the press would mean. Might be a prat, but he knows people. People who could do us good. On balance – bird in the hand.'

'*Bird in the hand*. Bitch.' Shona kicked the lift door as she went back up on her own. A minute later, she sat opposite Jamie. 'Forgot the coffee.'

'Wasn't that all you went for?'

Shona opened a copy of petty crime follow-ups on her laptop and pressed print. 'Making a start. Ready for the morning.' She waved the print-out. 'Might be a case of too many cooks. Maybe better if it's just you on the earpiece with Clegg and Tommo next time.'

Shona was striding ahead as they crossed the car park.

'We need milk.' Jamie spoke to her back.

'It's not enough,' Shona stopped and turned, her jaw angled up. 'Needs to be murder. Charged with people smuggling and rape, minimum. If he was out, under all that pressure. A pariah. On his own. No money… under surveillance. Even if he does a runner, he'll have a shit life.'

'Off the streets,' Jamie's voice was irritatingly calm. 'Bird in the hand.'

'Bird in the hand. Bollocks,' Shona slammed a flat palm against a patrol car's door. 'Sparrow in the hand, when it should be a fucking ostrich.' She stepped closer, hissing. 'And the girls? Jakub? What message does that send? We've traced the money, so fuck off?' And she was moving again.

'Known Peepo in prison. No picnic.' He touched her hand. 'We'll talk about it back at yours.'

'Think I've got a migraine kicking in. There's nothing in the fridge,' Shona strode towards her car and pressed her key.

'I could—' Jamie tried to keep up.

'Hardly any milk. Won't be enough for both of us to have breakfast in the morning.'

And she was in her car, pulling the door shut.

69

Shona sat on the sofa, still in her coat, the light from the hall spilling into the room. Her head was full with so many thoughts, it felt almost worse than a migraine. Her phone buzzed.

Mandy

A tear fell on the screen, blurring the letters and refracting a distorted spectrum. She let it go to answerphone.

'Hiya Shona love. Thought I'd give you a ring. Kids are in bed and Jacko's gone to work. Sorry I missed you. I'll be up and about till at least midnight, if you pick this up. Otherwise I'll try again tomorrow.'

Shona put the phone on the table. Not ready.

An hour later she stood, walked to the hall and took off her coat. In the kitchen, she switched on the kettle and, a couple of minutes later, she was back on the sofa in the dark with a tea and a small whisky. She sipped one, then the other. Then she tilted her head back and inhaled to the bottom of her lungs. She did it again, and again. A little space cleared, but she kept a tissue in her hand.

Another twenty minutes and her phone beeped. She passed her hand over it. It was a calendar reminder – *dental hygienist 12:30pm*. She pushed the phone away, but kept staring. The time flashed 23:26. Lifting the phone, she went to missed calls.

'Oh, glad you got back. Some days I could go mad. Between Jacko and the kids, I feel like I haven't had an adult conversation for about a week.'

'Mandy, I just…'

'What's up love? What's my dozy brother done now?'

Shona mopped her eyes. 'Can't give you names. But if it gets on the news.' Her voice choked.

'It's alright, sweetheart. Let it go. I know what he's like. If there were Olympic medals for insensitivity and being a prat he'd be a double gold medallist.'

The juddering in Shona's voice eased the more she got into the story. Mandy dropped in the occasional *I know, I know* at intervals and there was a smattering of *well you don't have to tell mes* and *always been the sames*.

'Look,' Mandy began when Shona had finished her outpouring. 'Like I say, I know what he's like, but he is my brother. So, if I say anything… you know. It won't have been the way I mean it. Just… you know. But look, I also know what you've done for him. You're the best thing in his life this side of the Sahara Desert.'

Shona could almost feel Mandy holding her hand.

'There's nothing simple about our Jamie. There's always been layers, even when he was a kid.'

Shona listened as Mandy put more flesh on the bones. The conflict. The abandonment: shit flat, after shit flat on shit estates. A grandmother's fierce determination that the grandchildren shouldn't go the way of the mother.

'And then there was Julie,' Mandy said. 'Yulia Radul. Talk about twist of fate. Her and her big brothers, Miro and Vlado. Miroslav and Vladimir.'

And Shona listened as Mandy explained just how Jamie got out of those shit estates. Hearing it all. Seeing the child that was the father of the man as Mandy painted him. Shona felt the knot in her chest loosen. Words, time, understanding, Mandy's patient humanity.

'Thanks. Gave him a hard time tonight. He's on a day off, so at least I can have some headspace tomorrow.' Tension eased in Shona's shoulders now and her voice steadied. 'I can't tell you, Mandy…'

'It's okay love. He's my brother, so I'll always have to take his part. But like I said, you're the best thing in his life since Emmy was born. Best thing to happen to him for years. And I'll tell the stubborn prat when I see him.'

Jamie had been on the road for about an hour when he pulled up by the Big Baps Butty Van on a lay-by just coming into Hyde. He took out his phone and sent two messages – both *on schedule*, *as arranged*, or words to that effect.

First meeting was in the city centre, late lunch, or at least a chance to dive into a snack bar afterwards. The second was on more familiar ground; there wouldn't be food. That'd have to wait until he got to Mandy's. He hadn't had breakfast, so he ordered two big baps; one sausage, one bacon and egg.

About the same time, Shona dived into a café with three mind-numbing visits behind her: an old lady, victim of a bag snatch, a theft from a motor vehicle and a stolen purse by a man with a fake British Gas ID. She'd made notes, gave out the same pointless platitudes and didn't mention the force's eight per cent arrest rate.

Sitting in front of a frothy latte, she took out her phone and began to message.

One primary suspect in custody. Other believed to have fled the country. Be in contact soon. Time to start making good on some promises.

The latte was lukewarm. She looked out the window. It began to rain. Then, a message from Dave.

Sighting of Merc. Same model, different plates. Yesterday, 9am sailing. Stena line, Harwich to Hook of Holland. Looks like Bakula on terminal CCTV. Face matched to Slovakian passport in the name of Ferenc Hossa.

'Bollocks,' Shona sucked her lips. 'Stena line. Harwich. You bastard, Jamie.'

She looked at the rain. At least her car was only the other side of the footpath. She sipped the latte. It felt claggy in her mouth. Then her phone beeped again. Clegg.

Ferry as per. Hope Jamie's as accurate with everything else.

'Oh fuck off, you cow,' she seethed under her breath. An old lady who had just opened the door tutted. Shona stared until the woman moved on. 'Might as well be a ventriloquist's dummy with Jamie's hand up her back.' She pushed the remains of the latte away and prepared to brave the three metres of rain between the café door and her car. Once settled behind the steering wheel, she took a list from her pocket. The allotments with the shed break-ins were only a couple of streets away.

The rain had already passed through Manchester. Jamie headed for the city centre, but turned off the A57 just short. It wasn't far to walk in and he could park for free in the street. Where he was going, the parking would cost more than the fuel from Sheffield and back. He got out of his car and a young lad asked if he could look after it. Jamie gave him a pound.

'Might not be our premium service,' the boy turned the coin in his fingers.

Jamie reached into his pocket. The boy saw his police ID and walked off.

Warehouse walls and factory units rose above the low houses. Jamie was in the back end of Ancoats and its shroud of familiarity wrapped itself around him. A few streets on and there were intrusions of edgy urban between the car body repair shops and textile wholesalers. If he'd been heading through the canal-side border, he'd have already been submerged by metropolitan chic. The further west he walked, the more the city centre money eroded remnants of buildings where people got their hands dirty at work. Reaching the junction of Oldham Road and Tib Street, he crossed into the Northern Quarter, still reassured by the pockmarks of austerity that blistered through cheap paint and the respectable face of graffiti. But the further he walked, the deeper he found himself in the belly of a Manchester that he barely knew.

Passing the Arndale Centre, he crossed into Corporation Street and looked up at the National Football Museum.

'What was it with this city and football?' He turned the other way. He was early, so walked on into Shambles Square; all faux Tudor exteriors and cafes delineated by rows of bedraggled planters. January had put a dent in the boulevard culture, but a couple of hardy souls were sat on an outside table next to the door. Jamie tucked his scarf inside his ski-coat, pulled up his collar and sat at the furthest point from the entrance, surrounded by an expanse of empty tables. A waiter in a waistcoat and shirt-sleeves peered through a window. Jamie saw him mouth *fuck*.

When his tea came it was in a pot. As the waiter retreated, Jamie took out his phone. After brief opening pleasantries, he said: 'Yeah, in about half an hour. It's only a couple of minutes walk.' Jephcott began speaking, but he cut in. 'You're going to hear some legalistic shit about how we need more evidence. Shona, most likely. The financial stuff is watertight, but she's pushing for more.'

Jephcott waited.

'We can get there,' Jamie continued. 'See Moonlight gets what he deserves. And I think I can do the same for his mate.'

'The Buzzard, Hayden?' Jephcott started to ask.

'No, not him. Due process should sort him. Bakula.'

'What exactly are you saying?' Jephcott tried for clarification again.

'I'm saying run with me. Trust me to get the right result.'

'And the right—'

'Back channels. Got it all mapped out. This is important to me, Mr Jephcott,' Jamie heard Jephcott's intake of breath as he called him *Mr*. 'I need you to bump into Clegg. Make conversation. Bring it round to the case. Reinforce the bird-in-the-hand line. Go on about Moonlight as a flight risk. Mention Manchester.'

'Manchester?' Jephcott repeated.

'HMP Manchester. Strangeways. Mention the security. Mention how full the local nick and Doncaster are. Mention he might be safer away from where he's known. Go on about headlines and shit. Say how, if it goes tits up in Manchester, she's still the hero. Sooner he's away, the sooner she's insulated from any future cock-up. Push that line.' And after some low level information passing, Jamie ended with: 'So, you'll be able to do that for me?'

He looked at the waiter when he saw the bill for a pot of tea. He still left a decent tip. It wasn't the lad's fault. Ten minutes. It was only across the road.

The price of parking didn't concern Maria Morcanu, Jamie thought, watching her exit the lift that accessed the store from its basement, surrounded by enough dark coated men to fill two cars. Waiting a few seconds, he let a gap open up, then followed them upwards, maintaining his distance as her entourage stepped onto the escalator. As they closed in on the restaurant, Jamie diverted into an adjacent clothing area, finding a spot that gave a clear line of sight. Hovering behind a display unit, he saw the maître d' lead Marika and her back-up to a block of four tables set in a right-angle of floor to ceiling windows. The maître d' touched the back of her chair and bowed a little. Marika sat alone, her support group spaced on three remaining tables.

'Let her feel like she's waiting for me,' Jamie kept the restaurant entrance in sight, but mooched about for five minutes before making his move.

The maître d' walked him to the table and Maria Morcanu eased from her seat a little and extended her hand. Jamie played along. Looking in, he'd seen the set-up: Marika in the window corner and her men completing a square on three surrounding tables. As he sat, the entourage watched from the corners of eyes, while seemingly engaged in a trio of business lunches.

Jamie leaned forwards. 'Boxing me into a corner?' the faux business diners didn't look up.

'More ensuring a little privacy. Given some of our likely subject matter, I thought it wise to keep a *cordon sanitaire* between us and any potential ladies-who-lunch.'

'Cordon sanitaire,' Jamie gave a slight nod of appreciation. 'Time was, I thought that was a French chef who washed his hands after he'd had a dump.'

'Surprised you chose somewhere so public,' Marika moved things on. 'Especially as you're on home turf.'

'Harvey Nics,' Jamie's laugh was harsh. 'Yeah, the women off my old estate are always in here… when it's raining on Longsight Market.'

'Something to eat?' Marika lifted a menu.

'Will I be tax deductible?' Jamie began reading. 'Bit pricier than the Big Baps Butty Van. I breakfasted there earlier. You must try it.'

One of the cordon sanitaire suppressed a laugh. Marika looked and the man's eyes went back to his plate.

'Cousins,' Marika saw Jamie scan the men and anticipated his thought. 'There won't be any leakage.'

As Jamie looked at the menu, Marika said: 'If we order and get down to business? Are you straight back to Sheffield after?'

'No. Got that other meeting next, then onto my sisters. Stay over. See the kids.'

'So family man as well,' Marika's tone held no irony.

'Just my sister's lot. Well, in England,' Jamie slipped into conversational, then caught himself and stiffened. Marika motioned to a waiter.

'So, your phone call... the way you explained it,' Marika smiled professionally. 'Works for me. Gives my family a chance to get out from under without triggering any Polish reprisals. Moonlight and Bakula? What goes around comes around. And Miss McCulloch?'

'Shona wants to play things by the book. Wants bail for Moonlight. Says he'll slip up, give us more evidence for vice and violence charges. Bakula's already out of the country. Send his case file to the Polish police. Wife's family are organised crime. Gives them a lead into their activities.'

'Anything like Romania and half the police will be on the payroll,' Marika didn't hide her disdain. 'But your solution. At least they pay the price. Doesn't she see that?'

Jamie didn't speak. Marika watched his face. Then his mouth opened. But a waiter arrived and they both sat back while their food was arranged.

'So you couldn't persuade her?' Marika continued as the waiter receded.

'More convincing if she's anti,' Jamie pushed a fork into a pile of green beans. 'It's my inspector's call, but if she felt... if it all looked too rehearsed.'

'But doesn't that risk—'

'I know how the inspector's mind works, which buttons to press.'

They both paused and ate a couple more forkfuls.

'Your phone call?' Marika moved things on. 'You've told me the end game. Don't need to know the hows, whens and whos. And I don't want to know,' she pierced a glazed carrot with her fork. 'Then I can't be blamed if there's a leak.' Marika stared beyond the window, the table was bathed in the orange light of a January sunset, reflecting from a building clad in smoked glass. 'Be good if the family can make it look like a police operation.' She seemed to be thinking aloud. 'Saves sparking retaliations. Face-saving vendettas.'

Jamie finally looked up. 'Vendettas? Seen a few of those. Last tribe standing rules the world. Anyway,' he sat back. 'First reason for our meet. Check you're okay with my proposed solutions for our two friends? And the answer seems to be Yes and Yes.'

Marika nodded.

'And when that side's tied up,' Jamie sat back and looked directly at Marika Morcanu. 'Time to start making good some of your promises re the girls.'

Marika had a small folder next to her chair. She passed Jamie a sheaf of papers. 'I've spoken to Vulpes and I'm taking over the girls' rental payments for the next three months. There's another house, besides the one Katya's in, and a couple of girls in a flat.'

Jamie began reading the papers.

'And there's the skills audits. I've already called Miss McCulloch. Said she'd take them round and help anyone who needs it with the paperwork.'

'With Katya...'

'Shona told me. Said I'll cover all her expenses till her hands heal and then three months beyond. Apparently, she has computer skills; accounting, general business experience.'

'Managed her husband's business before he fucked off with her money and passport.'

'Shona said. Honestly, from what she's told me, Katya will be an asset, and I pay well for assets. Keeping smart people happy is good for business. Nothing hits profits worse than having a revolving door of wasters who are in and out before they know what they're doing.'

'Yeah, I know someone else who thinks that,' Jamie smiled to himself.

'I don't know why I care, but if you understood… our family, no one has ever touched that business but our father. Been a liability for years. Risks high, profits low. But how he started it? Almost by accident. Couple of girls came into his shop regularly. Punter's cars. Stood in alleyways. All weathers. All sorts of nutters. Dad had a storage room. He heated it. Put in furniture. Their pimps only came knocking once. Dad and a couple of uncles…' Marika waited for the smart-arse remark, but it didn't come. 'I know it's a shit way to live, but he didn't recruit. His girls? Already in the business. At least dad's operation kept the rain off their heads and the bastards at bay.'

'And then came Bakula,' Jamie spoke at last.

'Yes, and then came Bakula,' Marika's eyes narrowed. 'One Bakula, when Poppa was old and ill. But without him, two, three decades of Bakula's.'

'So you'll…' Jamie's voice caught a little.

'Yes, I'll… I like your colleague, Shona. But her way? These two bastards? Especially, the Pole – your solution is final. I have a family. Priority one, no comeback, no few months down the line a mafia thug parked outside my kids' school, or an auntie's shop catching fire.'

A waiter arrived with a pot of coffee and a selection of pastries. Jamie didn't bother with his speech about *Remember I've got files on you…* She already knew that.

70

Outside, shop windows spilled harsh neon into the street and the wind had picked up. Walking on a little, Jamie turned left and, funnelled between the valleys of buildings, a gust hit him. Retracing his steps, the tide of fashionable frontages ebbed and, eventually, the last Ancoats warehouse gave way to low-rise streets. Jamie found his car. It had been looked after, or rather permitted to sit unhindered. He got in and glanced at the houses. Most were semis, reasonably new-build and uniformly unadorned; brick, small windows, pointless canopies floating above the doors. Drives were van-length and there was some green space. He felt its nature, but somehow couldn't pin it down – then he saw the lock-up garages, roofs-trimmed with razor wire and all doubt left him. Driving further east his sense of home increased as the houses aged a few decades and became terraced together with late twentieth century efficiency. It'd been a while.

On he drove, street to street, turns made without having to think and then he was there, edging onto a potholed pub car park: *The World's End*. Streetlamps and an array of orange floodlights, some wall-mounted, some on posts, cast overlapping shadows. The flat roof of its large, single-storey bar was edged with an elaborate line of revolving spikes. Jamie picked out a spot that was under a floodlight – close to one of the large rectangular windows – and parked.

He pushed open a set of double doors that were covered with fluorescent, felt-penned posters; Tuesday bingo, Thursday meat auction, another listed TV sports channels. Across the bar, a man was talking to two others. As Jamie approached, the pair moved away.

'Jamie,' the man extended a hand.

Jamie shook it. 'Not getting any weaker,' he grinned and rubbed his fingers.

'Been a while.' The man caught the barman's eye. 'Are you still?'

'Yeah, and driving.'

The man ordered Jamie's lime and soda and another pint for himself.

'I'd ask about business,' Jamie lifted his glass. 'In a different world.'

The corner of the man's lip curled into a slight grin. 'Yeah… mutually exclusive. Probably best way to describe our career choices.' And he lifted his beer. 'Your mam? Not seen her around here for a few years.' He stared across the bar.

'Over in Gorton, stinking of piss.'

'It was your nan dying that did it.'

'Thanks for that, Miro, but we both know she was shit long before the old lady died. Since she left school probably.'

'Yeah, well, round here can do that to you.'

Both men leaned on the bar, motionless for a moment.

'Anyway, guessing you aren't delivering a late Christmas present.' Miro lifted his pint.

'No. Need a bit of favour on a matter of restorative justice. One for Vlado.'

'Been in Strangeways a while now.'

'Yeah. I know. Young copper with a Taser who hadn't grasped the bigger picture,' Jamie took a sip of his drink.

'The bastard was on our patch, trying to get the young kids to do his deliveries. Vlado saw him and took appropriate action. With a tyre iron. Didn't kill him. Just made a statement.'

'Collar bone and knees. Drug pushing twat from the Hulme gang, one of the old desk sergeants told me,' Jamie toyed with a beer mat. 'Said the bastards are grooming kids all over. Sucking them in. Said it was a public service, if it'd been him, he wouldn't have arrested Vlado, he'd have nominated him for a Pride of Britain award.'

Both men smiled and took a drink.

'Look, Miro. I've got a favour to ask. Been on a case. Got this bloke, possible conviction for people smuggling and sexual assault, rape, but honestly, good lawyer... All we're left with is finance stuff. That's rock solid, but the sentence...'

Miroslav Radul waited.

'There's more. He's a nasty bastard. Money. Full of himself. Him and his oppo, force girls onto the game. Smuggles them in. Virtually kidnapped. Industrial unit. In boxes like battery chickens. He rips them off. Triple rent, in cash. Two girls murdered that we know about. Pal of mine,' Jamie paused. 'Silly bugger. Civilian, no threat to anyone. Throat slashed. Professional. This bastard probably helped bankroll the contract. We know it's him, but the evidence isn't there, not for the real stuff. Witnesses? His word against theirs. So all he gets charged with is white-collar shit.'

'Drugs?'

'Hand on heart, Miro. Not a dealer. Not the usual way. And the murdered girls? Dead too long to show on a post-mortem. But there was some. I've seen it with one lad. Doped out of his mind and my main informant says most of the girls use. Deadens the pain. Suits the management. Keeps them compliant. Keeps them in debt. They put a profit margin on, but no, he's not a street dealer. But those girls – good few. Gives them a couple of freebies, then starts charging. Look I don't need to tell you... not after Julie.'

'Sounds like a bastard. And we both know what Vlado's opinion would be. But I can't see what he could do.

'Sorry, yes. I'm pushing to make sure he's remanded. No bail.'

Miro waited again.

'If it goes to plan, I'll convince my boss to push for Manchester. Get him banged up over here.'

Jamie and Miro picked up their drinks, moved to a table and went back over old times and present circumstances. Family, shared acquaintances, normal stuff.

'Anything else I need to know?' Jamie straightened and zipped up his coat.

'Don't buy a white car,' Miro had his elbows on the table. 'Can't nick 'em off people's drives and into the containers fast enough. They love 'em in India and Malaysia.' He turned and winked. 'That's just a bit of advice for you and yours, not for professional consumption.'

Jamie smiled softly. 'You're alright. CPS wouldn't prosecute. Not in the public interest. Any twat who buys a white car deserves all they get.' And he held out his hand.

Jacko was at work and the kids were asleep when Jamie and Mandy finally sat down, one table lamp pooling around them and the television off.

'Been a bit of prat haven't you,' Mandy put down her cup of tea and looked at him.

'You'll have to narrow it down a bit, sis. At least give me the first letters as a clue.'

'Shona, you pillock. She's upset.'

'And?'

'And you lose her and you'll be lucky to get a Facebook ad for *Single Women in Your Area*. She's good for you Jamie. You need to—'

'Look, it's work. She thinks one thing, I think another.'

'And you can't—'

'I'm right. She's wrong. It's not personal. It's not about getting one over.'

'She said you were on a day off today.'

'I am. That's why I'm seeing you.'

'And the rest of the day?'

'Well, there was the Big Baps Butty Van in a lay-by, then I had lunch at Harvey Nic's.'

'Harvey Nic's? Where are you tomorrow? Buckingham Palace Garden party?'

'Nah, not after the Big Baps Butty Van, be too much of a disappointment.'

'Okay, I get it. Business. You have to do what you believe is right. But there's ways. Try and look after that girl. Dickheads like you don't usually get a second chance. Actually, dickheads like you don't usually get a first.' She leaned across and gave him hug. 'You mean a lot to her, Jamie. Don't push her away.'

Be in about half-ten

Shona was already at the station when Jamie's message flashed on her phone. She hadn't expected that. Clegg had been in at eight and Shona had taken the chance to push her *let him out and let him slip up* theory.

'Morning,' Jamie said as he arrived, sitting down. Shona was taken aback by the normality in his voice.

'Thought we could visit Katya in hospital. See how she's doing.' He looked across the desk. 'Might be an idea if one of us gives Marika Morcanu a prod. Make sure she's as good as her word.'

'Tried her yesterday,' Shona said. 'Just kept going to voicemail.'

'Yeah, well maybe she hasn't got as much on today. If we could pin her down to something in the next week? Might be better if you were the one? I seem to rub her up the wrong way.'

Shona shook her head. Clegg was still in her office and Jamie stood. Shona followed.

'I've already heard from Shona,' Clegg was drawing a line across a graph. 'And I know what you think.'

'Just, I've been having a look. At the practicalities,' Jamie sat. 'Remand here means police station cells. But only short term. So, locally we've got Doncaster. Next is Wakefield. Both of them overcrowded. Both Yorkshire. Things go wrong? Shit on our own doorstep.'

'And if he's bailed?' Shona looked to Clegg.

'But Manchester,' Jamie carried on. 'Strangeways. High security. Easy as Wakefield to get to, just not in our region. We hand him over. Arresting heroes. Anything tits up? Manchester gets the shit headlines.'

Clegg's fingertips were touching and flexing.

'And if you're the one pushing that line at Divisional meeting?' Jamie left the thought hanging.

After leaving Clegg's office, Jamie and Shona went up to see Dave. He had the CCTV from Harwich docks.

'So that's him gone, then,' Shona slumped in her chair. 'Down to the Polish police now. Or maybe the Germans, if he's stopped off in the Bavarian house. Suppose we can send off duplicates to Munich and Katowice.'

'Better if you had a named contact,' Dave pushed a packet of chocolate digestives across the desk.

Jamie took one and kept his eyes on his tea.

Outside Katya's house, as they looked through their windscreen, two girls got out of a taxi, each carrying multiple carrier bags.

'Doesn't look like their income stream has dried up,' Jamie watched them go in. 'Have you tried Morcanu again?'

Shona tapped speaker phone as the number connected.

'Miss McCulloch,' Marika's voice echoed around the car.

Shona recounted the taxi and carrier bag scene.

'Yes, I sent one of my cousins,' Marika said. 'Told him to take them to the supermarket. Gave them two hundred pounds cash.'

'Wondered if a face to face might be beneficial at this point,' Shona's tone was business-like.

'Meet, yes. I'm in London tomorrow, but...'

'So the day after?' Shona didn't invite discussion.

'Day after, would be fine,' Marika agreed.

A few brief arrangements followed.

'Promising,' Shona said after the call ended.

Jamie started the engine. The traffic on the roads to the Northern General was quiet and so was the atmosphere in the car; a sense of lull after a battle decided.

Shona and Jamie showed their police ID at the ward desk and were led through. Katya was propped on a pillow with one hand strapped into a curved plastic splint and the other heavily bandaged.

'Katya, how are you, luvvie?' Shona leaned forwards and kissed her.

'Doctor say cancel piano lessons for couple of weeks?'

Jamie smiled. 'The injuries?'

'This hand, just cuts. Few stitches.' Then she held up the other. 'One tendon cut through. Another part way.'

'How long?' he stood back as Shona sat on the bed.'

'Few weeks, some movement and all dressings off. Two, three months, close normal, I hope.'

'Have you had many visitors?' Shona's head was tilted.

'Girls come. Bring Jakub. They look after him.'

'They seem to be okay for now, the girls in the house.' Shona's eyes were reassuring.

'Yes. They phone me. Taxi says call if they need lifts. No charge and he bring money. Said it from old man's family.'

General chit-chat came and went, then Katya asked: 'What about Bakula?'

'We've got all his bank records. Film of him attacking you. And all that stuff you downloaded. He'll be bang to rights if he ever sets foot in the UK.' Shona nodded meaningfully.

'Bang to rights?' Katya looked puzzled.

'And we'll send everything to the Polish police,' Shona jumped in.

'Maybe not just the police,' Jamie's voice was low. Shona turned.

'More than one way,' Jamie looked into her eyes.

As they drove away, Shona leaned back in her seat. 'More than one way?'

Jamie kept driving.

When he got home, he reached for his edgeland chronicle, then laid out his collection of precise pens and ink. The drawing brought him quiet.

As he worked his phone buzzed: Shona.

More than one way… for us to find a way through this. See you tomorrow XXX.

Jamie smiled and texted back a thumbs-up and *XXX*, then returned to his illustration, dabbing blotting paper. Black ink had pooled in a hedgehog's eye, in dark contrast to the crescent of light that gave it life.

'One spikey bastard looking at another,' he imagined Shona behind him, leaning her chin on his shoulder.

Around ten, Shona had a call.

'I called him a dickhead,' Mandy began. 'And he agreed he was. Said it was business, nothing else, but there are ways. He knows that. Knows that you're good for him. He said he knew. Had quite a chat, bit of a late night…'

'Mandy phoned me last night,' Shona said over a canteen breakfast that felt more relaxed, now the end of month deadline was redundant.

Jamie looked across the table.

'Penny didn't drop till I'd rung off. You were in Manchester on your day off?'

'Yeah, like a mooch about sometimes. Old stomping grounds.'

'Harvey Nic's? That's what you told Mandy.'

Jamie raised an eyebrow as he smiled.

'Aye that's what I thought.'

'Harvey Nic's and the arse-end of the world. All there in Manchester, if you know where to look. Mind you, there's bits I don't recognise. Bloody canals in Ancoats. Can't move for waterfront swank. Time was, the only thing you'd get down there was a bike frame and the occasional dead dog floating by.'

'Masterful grasp of the romantic cityscape,' Shona shook her head. 'Maybe we could hire a gondola.'

The following morning, Clegg called Shona into her office.

'Says she needs me to play secretary,' she told Jamie as she came back to their desk. 'Some course at HQ on planning patrol frequency in relation to crime data. Not strictly detective stuff, but she's got the big divisional meeting this afternoon. Told me to go and take notes. But there's time for a cheeky cuppa and teacake, before I set off, if you fancy?' And she took her coat off the back of her chair.

71

When Jamie had finished his teacake, he hurried back and, as he hoped, saw Clegg in her familiar pose, talking into her phone and pacing. With Shona already out of the way on her secretarial duties, he straightened his jacket and went over to the office door.

'Following on from the Moonlight location problem,' he was talking as soon as Clegg beckoned for him to come in. 'Thing is, there might be stuff that we can control from our end, case-wise and publicity wise.' Jamie placed an evidence bag on the table. 'Moonlight's.' And he straightened the polythene over the phone that lay inside.

Clegg looked. It was labelled properly and still sealed.

'Could be all sorts of shit on this. God knows where it might—'

'If we could get it unlocked,' Clegg cut in. 'Presume it must be.'

'Yeah, and has some encryption. But a few weeks back, he cut his finger. And thing is, I'm a nosey bastard.'

And Clegg watched as the screen lit up inside the bag.

'Like I say ma'am. We've got the arrest. We can be the bringers of new evidence. But if we could get Moonlight stored away from his support network, engineer it so he's less local, where there's less potential interaction between his mates and the media, puts us in control of what's released and when. Any potential cock-ups and leaks? Like I said, someone else's patch.'

Clegg leaned back in her chair and rocked a little. 'Division this afternoon. What you just said, and the other stuff before. List it, so I can sound like we've nailed all the angles when I raise it in the meeting.'

Jamie began scribbling.

'You can wave him bye-bye,' Clegg was reading as he wrote. 'He's being moved to Sheepcote Lane custody suite this afternoon.'

Finishing with Clegg, Jamie made his way down to the reception desk. 'Our pal, Moonlight.'

'That snarky bastard?' the desk sergeant was staring at his monitor.

'Clegg says he's being moved up to—'

'Sheepcote Lane nick, yeah,' the sergeant's focus remained on the screen. 'Two o'clock, the transport's due.'

It was about quarter to twelve as Jephcott parked on a drive off Shirecliffe Road. It led nowhere, except to a rough open ground called Parkwood Springs. Jamie pulled up round a corner, walked and tapped on the Audi's window.

'Got this end sorted,' Jamie said as he sat in the passenger seat. 'But Poland. Is there someone we know? Preferably Katowice area.'

'Guessed that's what you'd want,' Jephcott was holding a paper. 'Big city, so we've got a few people. Just need to finish a couple checks. Have something definitive pretty soon. Does Shona…?'

'Not specifics. She's guessing bits, but nothing significant.'

'Well the less she knows, the more she's protected.'

'Thanks. I'll use that line next time she's bollocking me for keeping her in the dark.'

A few more minutes chat and Jephcott concluded. 'Guessed that was your general direction with Bakula. Is it just a matter of—'

'Getting the info in front of the right eyes.'

'Well, I engineered an excuse to see Clegg and gave her the spiel.'

'Yeah, she said,' Jamie faced Jephcott. 'Good work.' And he reached for the door handle. 'Need to get back for two.'

Jamie was standing by the custody sergeant's desk as the prisoner transfer papers were being laid out for signing. A pair of fire-doors swung open and Moonlight was there, handcuffed and chained to two policemen.

'Just wanted to wish you *bon voyage*,' Jamie stood, feet apart. 'Expect you're thinking about the gap between what you've actually done and what we've got evidence to prove.'

Moonlight narrowed his eyes.

'I know, this is all inconvenient. But knowing what it could have been?' Jamie shrugged. 'Brings a bit of comfort. Leaves the old superiority intact.'

Moonlight was smiling now.

Then Jamie lifted up an evidence bag with a phone inside. 'Locked, encrypted. Bit more comfort. Bit more of a smirk, knowing there's so much, so close, but forensics can't access it. My suggestion was cut off your index finger and swipe it across the print reader, but Clegg... you know.' Jamie shrugged. 'So that leaves the back-up pin number. And what would be the chances? No birthdays, or dates when this shithouse of a government got elected for you. Not like some ordinary sap. No you'd go random and that means *what*? Ten to the power of however many digits. So, say four digits? Ten thousand to one. And, obviously, you're the kind of man that would go the extra mile, so I'm guessing five and the big one-hundred K to one against.'

Moonlight's grin was intact, but in his eyes was a sense of *where-is-this-going?*

'No,' Jamie stepped closer. 'You're above all that. Your sense of superiority.' He paused. 'And that's your weakness. You and your sort. It makes you careless, because you can't imagine anyone able to catch you out.' Jamie pushed his face close and spoke through his teeth. 'Remember when you stapled your finger? Didn't give joining the dots a thought did you? Dragging your hand across the pin number,' Jamie pressed the unlock button through the polythene evidence bag.

Moonlight froze as the screen reacted to Jamie's hand. '7, 1, 8, 3, 9 – M.' Jamie was grinning now, 'Fucking M for Moonlight. Fucking M,' and shaking his head. 'Jesus, could you have chosen an easier pattern to follow?'

Moonlight lurched at Jamie knocking him backwards into a bench, before restraining hands pulled him back, folding his waist and neck.

Jamie straightened and looked down. 'Be sharing that with forensics,' and he traced an M in the air. 'But Bluetooth and wireless? Already made a start myself.'

Moonlight was still thrashing and screaming obscenities at Jamie as the doors closed on the lift, taking him down to the waiting van.

'Heard you had a frank exchange of views with Moonlight this afternoon,' Shona stretched her arms behind her head and looked across the desk at Jamie. 'First thing they told me as I signed in after that course.'

Jamie sprawled forwards on his elbows. 'Yeah. He was pissed off when I unlocked his phone.'

'How d'ya?'

And Jamie recounted the stapler incident, and described some of what he'd found.

'Like I said,' Shona sat forward. 'Give it time, evidence will come out. He's careless, there'll be more.'

'Careless,' Jamie made eye-contact. 'That's what I said.

Arrogance, superiority. Makes you careless.' Jamie was looking down now, but sensed Shona was holding her gaze. 'Has its compensations, the working class experience.' He didn't look up. 'That feeling that you're in the wrong place, in the wrong clothes, holding the wrong fork. Standing with your flat Manc vowels, and your flies open. That feeling of never quite being good enough. It makes you careful; aware of your own weaknesses.' He looked up for a second and Shona was smiling. 'Anyway,' he went on. 'Told Clegg about the phone. Told her the new evidence could change everything. So, later… are we…'

'Sorry, previous engagement, as they say. Following up on what you said.'

Jamie waited, trying to work out which particular said she meant.

'Marika Morcanu. Catch-up on how she's sorting the girls out.'

'Good. I've been thinking about that as well. Don't want her getting complacent just because we haven't had a face-to-face for a while. Don't want her thinking I've forgotten what's expected.'

Shona left her car at the police station and walked onto the main road. A taxi arrived, as arranged, and she recognised the streets on the drive to Endcliffe Park and beyond, but was surprised when the driver parked and pointed her towards a small restaurant frontage, that was tucked in next to a large, neon signed shop where a flood of brash furniture sat behind an expanse of plate glass.

Beyond the narrow restaurant entrance, Shona climbed a staircase that opened onto a stylish dining area that spanned the footprint of the garish ground-floor shop. A waiter led her to a corner booth. There was a screen. Marika Morcanu held up the wine list.

'Driving,' Shona sat.

'But the taxi?'

'Car's at the station and I'll need it for work in the morning,' and she looked around. 'Nice. Not what you expect from downstairs.'

'Yes. I said they should call it Hidden Gem,' Marika Morcanu gave her "business lunch" smile. 'Actually, the food is excellent. My cousin's boy, chef and owner. BA in culinary arts from UCB and then worked at a couple of Michelin starred restaurants. Honestly? Belies the location.' She handed Shona a menu. 'We did the market research – university staff and students in the area. Enough of them that would want something a bit more high end. If you're not vegetarian can I suggest…' and Marika picked up her menu, turned it round and pointed.

'Yeah, guided by you,' Shona squinted to read.

'Hopefully, the negotiations won't ruin our appetite.' Marika had the same folder she'd shown Jamie in Manchester and passed it to Shona. 'Enjoy the food better if we're all happy and things are on track,' and she beckoned to a waiter, ordered, and, giving Shona time to read, spoke again. 'Initial assessments show the standard of English is variable, but there's no one who won't be functional in some capacity. Qualifications and skills? We'll give them our own assessments, get them to work alongside people who know what they're looking for.'

'Katya has at least the basics of business and accounting IT skills.'

'And a bit more besides,' Marika was rotating an empty glass in her hand as the waiter arrived with starters and returned with wine and a jug of water. 'Saw her in hospital. Smart girl. Funny. Bit of training, her interpersonals and thinking on her feet will work in her favour.'

'And the lad. Jakub. She says he was a real computer whizz in Poland, before…'

'Yes, she told me,' Marika made eye contact. 'His parents. Tragic.'

'There'll be issues. Mental health. Some drug use, but Katya—'

'Yes, I worked that out,' Marika cut short the potential

drawbacks. 'But with a bit of patience, if he can get back on track? Worth the gamble for us.'

'And if it proves a little difficult?'

'Look,' Marika lifted a bite-sized morsel. 'Your colleague. I know what he'll do if I mess you around. If I don't play fair with the girls. So whether you think I want to do the right thing, or that I'm just scared of the Polish mafia turning up on my doorstep, the end result is the same. I'm going to stick by our agreement. That'll mean explaining what happens if we have drop outs. And I'm under no illusion that you would be seeking the girls' view on matters. As for Jakub? Yes he's a gamble. But, if he isn't coping, how about I organise an independent psychological report? Or you can appoint your own.'

Shona maintained a stoic expression.

'Honestly, Miss McCulloch. I want a line drawn under this. You've looked into our businesses. You know we're not dodgy.'

'Fox said something similar,' Shona's voice was quiet. 'Didn't stop his daughter sticking her fingers in other people's pies.'

'But there's the difference. Our family? Still close enough to the shit-heap to smell it. Being a spoiled brat was never an option.' And she looked around and a waiter appeared, cleared the starters and returned with the main course. Food impeccably plated, he bowed and, as he retreated, Marika continued.

'History. My father was big on history. Family history. History books. Suppose it was like a drip-feed for us. Cause, effect, choices, chance, risk. Early days he took risks. Ducked and dived. Stood his ground, but leaving it behind was always in his mind. Get some security. Build up your seed corn and get to the place where profit outweighs risk. And we've been there for years. The girls? I know it was stupid. We told him, but he's our father. And yes, we had our new lives in London, and no excuse. Out of sight, out of mind. That was down to us. No excuse. But in my father's mind? If not him, then some other brutal bastard.' Marika held her gaze on

Shona. 'But for us, my brother and I, it never stopped. Being told we were lucky, being shown photographs of where our father grew up. Family history? My father always made sure we understood that our future stands on his past.'

'Remember being on a school trip,' Shona spoke at last. 'This food, by the way, excellent. Like I say, school trip, Glasgow kids in Edinburgh, not a good mix. Teacher made us look at the castle. Explained how you never know what's underneath. Old volcanoes, their fires sunk deep,' now Shona looked into Marika's eyes. 'Everything's stable now. Solid. But where fissures haven't long closed,' she pushed her thumbs into a bread roll and split it lengthways. 'Where the pressures are near the surface… people have to claw out a living and deal with the occasional outburst.'

Marika Morcanu blinked, then took a sip of wine. Shona registered her face and it was the first time she sensed her to be lost for words, so she waited for the moment to stretch before smiling and breaking silence.

'Like with your father,' Shona reached for the water. 'Born in troubled times, but worked for the day the ground beneath his family's feet cooled and solidified. That's the narrative isn't it? And we hope you're not selling a fairy tale.'

Marika looked to the waiter and his clearing of plates and return with coffee eased the unease from the silence.

'Level playing field,' Marika eventually spoke again as she dropped two clusters of brown sugar in her cup and stirred. 'I take your point. Easier to make allowances when it's family. Someone you love. Harder when you don't know the whole story. When the other person is—'

'An irritating Manc bastard. Yeah,' Shona laughed and Marika felt the tension ease. 'But what's that crap they used to say in school assemblies? Walk a mile in another man's shoes… That's what you're asking us to do with your father. But it's not an exclusive right. So yes, Jamie's seen stuff, done stuff. Good stuff most of it.

Stuff beyond my ken. But from what I do know, I'm willing to bet he's helped more people than you and me put together, even with your charity dinners. A day in his shoes and we might both see the world differently. If we were the ones with no one but a grandmother clinging on for dear life while we grew up on estates with shit-heaps bigger than anything on your poppa's farm. Gang turf,' Shona sipped coffee through a layer of cream. 'And now he's in the police, when so many of his mates went the other way.'

'The power of a good grandmother,' Marika mirrored Shona as she broke a small, chef-baked biscuit.

'Power of random chance and school swimming lessons,' Shona looked at Marika. 'Mandy, his sister, she told me the other night. How he got himself, and her, a free pass. Local gang, growing power, the Raduls. Where they lived, you were with them or against them. And no one was against them. The grandfather had come over in the sixties. Yugoslav,' Shona held eye contact. 'Hard man. Hard sons when the time came. The grandchildren were Jamie's age. The Radul's asked you? Mandy said it wasn't a request. Refusals couldn't be tolerated… loss of face. But Jamie…'

A waiter appeared at the screen to enquire if more coffee was needed.

'But Jamie?' Marika waited until the waiter moved away.

'The canal. Julie, Yulia Radul, fell in. She was seven. Jamie was nine. He jumped in. Made himself ill. Cuts and the dirty water. Septic. But anyway, free pass. No one questioned why he was never subject to requests from the Raduls like the rest of the able-bodied youths on the estate. He was left alone. Everyone knew he was the boy who saved Julie Radul.'

'Happy ending then?' Marika cut a sliver of stilton.

'Not really,' Shona fiddled with a fork. 'When she was fifteen, Yulia Radul went off the rails. Hard being that age and not knowing if you've got friends, or just people who are scared of your brothers. Drugs. Ran away. Returned. Same again but longer. Bad cycle… and her brothers? Controlling a sister isn't like controlling a gang. She was eighteen when she committed suicide – the drugs and what she had to do to pay for them,' Shona paused and let Marika think about the irony.

'Anyway, Jamie,' she spoke again. 'Gang free. Granny hanging onto him and Mandy like grim death. Came out of school not doing too badly. Few years on, qualified nurse, then joins the territorials, medic, and…' she reached for her water to dispel the claggy film of coffee that had coated her mouth. 'A few years later he's fighting Ebola in a biohazard suit. So…'

'More than meets the eye.'

'Aye, that's what I said.'

A waiter brought Shona's coat and she stood.

Marika poured herself another coffee. 'The records you've seen tonight. I'll keep them up to date, email weekly so you can track progress.'

'But not just documents and data,' Shona straightened her collar.' No substitute for face to face.'

The taxi dropped Shona behind the police station and she walked down the ramp to the car park. There was a note under her windscreen wiper.

Back home, Shona was propped on a pillow.
Got your note. Should've let yourself in
And she pressed send. An instant reply appeared on the screen.
Not sure how you've been feeling last few days X
Shona typed straight back.
I'm in bed, wearing your t-shirt… See you tomorrow
S XXX

72

Clegg pointed to chairs as they entered the office. 'Went well.' She was walking a tight figure-of-eight across the carpet on her side of the room. 'Division liked it. The cordon around our role – around the good headlines and pushing the potential for cock-up into another division.'

'So, decision made? Done and dusted?' Jamie relaxed into his chair.

'Barring a prat in the court,' Clegg leant on a chair back. 'Likely scenario? Remanded in custody as per police recommendations. Fly in the ointment would be an appeal.'

'And that's?' Jamie put in.

'He'll have a good lawyer.'

'So, maybe bail?' Shona looked at Clegg.

'Unlikely, but if it happens then we go to surveillance. As things stand?' Clegg placed her hands flat on the desk. 'Very much plan B.'

Jamie went to speak as they walked away from Clegg's office, but Shona held up a hand. 'Don't,' she said. 'Don't throw me a bone, when you know it's bollocks. It'll be remand. No judge is going to risk the consequences of putting a high profile prisoner on the streets against police advice.'

The day was a mixture of Shona splitting herself between paperwork and searching for new links between the Bakula, Buzzard and Moonlight bank details. Jamie was dragging and dropping an eclectic selection of text, images, video and audio files onto a memory stick. It was almost four in the afternoon when the WhatsApp arrived from Clegg.

Just received notification. Moonlight bail hearing set for day after tomorrow.

Jamie pulled up behind Shona's flat. Preparing the meal together, he was aware that he was speaking in sentences and Shona in monosyllables. Neither raised the subject while they ate. Shona went over the position re: Marika Morcanu and the plans for the girls. Jamie didn't mention that he'd seen them the day before her. She talked about the restaurant and its food and recounted the conversation, leaving out the potted history of Jamie's family. There was washing-up and make-up sex, a pattern re-established, hostilities on hold.

The next day dragged. More of the same. Couple of drive-outs to thefts from the forecourt of local car dealers. At lunchtime, Shona met Dunky's mother. The following morning started tense. Three hours of faffing around. Staring at screens and papers, minds elsewhere. Then, just before twelve, Clegg walked over.

'Remanded to Manchester. Result,' she pumped a fist.

The evening followed the previous one, though emotions were diluted by the power of fait accompli. Shona spoke more sentences, Jamie less – and the sex wasn't make-up. Around midnight Shona was asleep and Jamie eased himself to the bathroom. He had his phone.

'Yeah, pretty much as I said. Cell number. Wing and stuff? I'll dig tomorrow, then message... Vlado?... He's on board?'

The conversation went back and forth.

'Good, good. Appreciate it, Miro.'

'Yes. Both on the side of the angels this time.'

And on in a series of memories and scenarios, but all moving to one conclusion.

'Well, today. Spate of car thefts…' Miro began.

'No, no, I know it wasn't. Random selection of colours. Not a white one among them.'

'Thanks again. I'll get you details. Best if it happens sooner rather than later. Might get moved. Kick up a fuss and stuffed in solitary. You know better than me.'

'Sooner the better. Tell Vlado, thanks.'

When he got back into bed, Shona's eyes were still closed. He set his phone alarm to vibrate and put it under his pillow, but knew he wouldn't need it.

He woke at four and tapped cancel twenty minutes before it was due. He collected his clothes from the bathroom and tip-toed out. Shona stirred, but didn't wake. He showered and dressed. He'd get breakfast back at the station, after he'd borne witness.

Jamie watched from a pool of darkness, cast by a grey brick wall, that projected beyond the exit of Sheepcote Lane nick. There was a prison transfer van waiting in the car park. It was a little before six. Early start to avoid the worst of the rush hour. He didn't speak and Moonlight didn't notice him. It was enough, seeing the door slam and the van pull onto the dual carriageway. He turned for his car. The canteen would be racking up their breakfast selection by the time he got back to his own station.

'Might go for a celebratory full English,' he said to himself as he turned right onto Sheffield Parkway. 'Wait till they've settled him.'

He'd already got the phone numbers he needed to make the right connections at HMP Manchester.

The morning came and went. Shona had read the note he'd left, letting her know he'd gone in early to crack on.

'Crack on with what?' she arrived around eight. 'Can't have cracked on that much if you've had time for breakfast.' And she picked a tissue off the desk and wiped ketchup and egg yolk off his mouth.

Around noon, Jamie said he was going to stretch his legs and disappeared towards the lift. Standing on a patch of green not far from the front of the station, he took out his phone.

At shift end, as he drove to Shona's, his phone rang. He answered on Bluetooth.

'So, Manchester?' Jephcott's voice echoed from the speaker.

'Yeah,' Jamie was devoid of emotion. 'Be tucked up in his own little room by now. Apparently, the en-suite piss buckets have been replaced since the refurb.'

'What will—' Jephcott began.

'Just standard,' Jamie cut in. 'But your bit of research?'

'Two names,' Jephcott sensed to move on. 'Katowice police. First one for preference. Fluent English. Real star.'

The conversation petered out and Jamie heard the message beep, but was still driving. Parking next to Shona's car, behind her flat, he checked his phone. Two names and contact details.

An evening of studied avoidance passed. Shona put the television on, but ignored it in favour of YouTube and Instagram on her phone. In his hand, smaller than Shona's phone, Jamie held a small, decades old book. Another of *The Observer* series, *British Wild Animals*.

'1962 edition,' he'd said at one point. Shona had nodded. Later, the spoons lay back to back.

'Need to speak to Clegg about getting a link-up with the Polish police,' Jamie was talking to Shona's back as she buttered some breakfast toast. 'Be good if we have an evidence file ready for when we open a dialogue.'

'Role for me, with my computer wizardry and legendary Polish speaking. Best if you pick up the general theft and crap. Give me a clear run.'

The atmosphere of the evening seemed to have eased overnight.

'Get this eaten and make a move,' she pushed a plate of toast across the table. 'I'll be in when I've had my shower.'

Jamie checked Katowice time on his phone before he started the car. An hour ahead. 'If I'm up, he should be.' He dialled the number. Three or four rings and a voice answered. Female. 'Bakula,' Jamie began. 'I was told you were the contact.'

'Yes, I was told to expect your call.'

'You're English is—'

'A relief? I was a liaison officer with the Met. Few years back, before the vote. Pilot project. Tracking Polish villains coming to London. Getting local Poles to tell us what they knew. Worked well. But then...'

Jamie could almost hear the shrug.

'Wasn't expecting—'

'A woman,' the voice completed for him. 'Growing force in the world.'

'Yes, I'm painfully aware of that. No, it's fine. Just the name Lucja. Was thinking Luca, like Italian, Luke.'

'LooSha,' she corrected his pronunciation.

'Okay, *Lucja*. Just want to check we have the same understanding of—'

'I've read the notes.'

'So you—'

'We know this man. Like you, we know what he's done, but evidence...'

'There'll be an official approach. Today or tomorrow.'

'I'll keep an ear open. Probably me on the official side as well, with my background.'

Jamie waited as Lucja outlined her time in the UK. Two years joint operations.

'Liaised with the community leaders, legit Polish businessmen, priests, cutting off the oxygen to the gangs. The people like Bakula's father-in-law.'

'But the files I've sent you. Much fuller,' Jamie began outlining likely scenarios when Lucja's nostalgia had run its course. 'Official stuff?' he continued. 'There'll be a gesture. UK and Germany, mainly financial offences. But ultimately—'

'Polish courts will say foreign. Not our problem.'

'So it's left to us to apply justice,' Jamie was saying what they both knew.

Moonlight and the Buzzard's replacements seemed to have been tasked with providing safe hands. The Peepos were kept busy and all meetings were low key. Voices and movements were damped down and almost apologetic.

Jamie pushed a memory stick into his laptop. He managed to get a couple of folders started, but pressed save and put the stick in his pocket as Shona crossed the room.

'Corporate bland,' Jamie nodded towards the new Peepo leaders. 'Calm, polite. But they never take their eyes off the troops.'

'Moonlight's done a lot of damage politically.'

'Yeah. Be a few of our lords and masters trying to put a bit of distance. Quicker and quieter that Moonlight disappears.'

'Clegg's not in until ten. Had a message.'

'I'd suggest a visit to the canteen,' Jamie checked for a thaw.

'Full English? With your compulsory fitness test so close?'

'Spaghetti hoops on toast. What elite athletes call carb loading.'

When Clegg called them into her office, Shona was surprised that Jamie suggested she take the lead on the Polish liaison.

'Speaks some Polish, ma'am and she's better at organising documentation than me.'

'Making the call in an hour,' Clegg nodded towards Shona. 'Get yourself back here fifteen minutes before. And you,' her gaze turned on Jamie. 'Make yourself useful.' And she handed him a list.

Back at the desk, Shona switched on her computer. Jamie folded the paper Clegg had given him into a pocket and picked up his laptop.

'Be back this afternoon. Fill me in then.'

Shona cracked on, making sure she was across any queries the Poles might make. At ten past eleven, Clegg reached for her phone and pressed speaker.

'Dzien dobry,' Shona opened with.

The man's voice at the other end was halting. 'Good afternoon… today, just introductions. Have asked colleague to lead. Gave folder, so up to speed when make call.'

Shona made polite Polish noises, but everyone recognised the process of delegating and distancing.

Jamie spent the next couple of hours tracking down a random rainbow of missing cars, mainly budget, ten-a-penny models. Most of the lots were a rectangle of tarmac and a portakabin and he built up a list of local scallies who specialised in cash pub transactions and dodgy websites. He'd pass it on. Uniform could ask questions on the likely estates and get a civilian admin to trawl the internet.

Sitting in the car, he took out his laptop and memory stick. He left the engine running, to ensure the heater kept blowing warm air.

'Glad you could get across,' Shona spoke as she and Marika entered the ward. 'Thought it'd be good if you were here.'

Katya was sat in the armchair by her bed. 'Scuse if not shake hands,' she said as Shona bent to kiss her cheek.

Marika smiled and sat in the visitor chair.

'Thought you'd want this back,' Shona sat on the bed and rummaged in her bag. 'Been photographed and swabbed.' She stretched a gold chain between her fingers and leant forward to fit the clasp around Katya's neck. 'Got it fixed in town.'

'Black Madonna,' Katya smiled. 'Keep me safe.'

Marika was sat back as Shona and Katya chatted fashion and other irrelevancies. After a minute or so Katya looked to Marika.

'Ms Morcanu. I hope these…' she held up her hands.

'No, not a problem. I think your abilities with computers – tracking accounts, analysing costs and profits – will be worth the wait,' Marika smiled. 'And your ability to think on your feet.'

'But your business. Much more than I…' Katya looked.

'Big business, small business. Lot of things the same,' Marika's smile was relaxed. 'Just bigger numbers.'

'And Jakub?' Katya smiled back. And then she reinforced Jakub's narrative with the already known litany of parental tragedy, failure of foster care and abuse, before moving to the things she'd seen him do with a computer; the speed and complexity of his spreadsheet building, the way he explained the algebra, the coding and app design. His place on the school fast-track before his world fell apart. 'But he is …' Katya's eyes made her point.

'Fragile,' Shona nodded.

'But he can be with me,' Katya fixed her eyes on Marika. 'If patient. Forgive cracks. In time.'

'Sounds like he'll be worth the wait,' Marika moved closer.

Shona leaned on her car as Jamie crossed from the lift. Light spilled across the police station basement but, beyond the ramp to the road, it was dark.

'Saw it in her face. Katya likes her,' she said as Jamie got nearer.

'I think she could be the real deal.'

'Good. Hope you're right,' Jamie fumbled through pockets. 'Might see you later. Maybe not. That fitness test. Been lazy last few days. Need to push on. See how I am after a session.'

'Okay. Wouldn't want you short of your peak. Give me a call later.'

Jamie sorted his kit onto his bed. The usual mix of random colours and fabrics. Looking at his watch, he remembered it was an hour earlier in Poland, then reached for his phone.

'Lucja. Can you talk?'

'Yes. Just finished my meal for one.'

'About our way forwards.'

'Be speaking again tomorrow. My boss received the request from UK police, an Inspector Clegg. And I'm to liaise with a Sergeant McCulloch.'

'Yeah, Shona,' Jamie cut across. She's good. She's on board with nailing the bastards. Really wants the right result. But…'

'But?' Lucja prompted.

'Playing it by the book, even though she knows where that'll end up,' Jamie disappeared into thought for a moment, until Lucja coughed. 'So what we do is separate,' Jamie was back. 'Official approach? Your bosses will say banking irregularities. Someone else's country. My bosses will fake being affronted. Everybody shrugs and moves on.'

'I like British films,' Lucja took a seemingly non-parallel line of her own. 'That old one with the Spandau Ballet guy, *The Krays*. Have you seen it?'

'And the new one, where Tom Hardy plays both twins.'

'Yeah, well. Like Katowice today, except the cars are modern and there'd be no Ronnie. Polish gangsters are less tolerant of gay rights. Anyway,' Lucja came back to the matter in hand. 'You know the family background?'

'Way I was told, Bakula's a loose cannon. An embarrassment that married the boss's daughter. Sent to England to get him out the way.'

'Pretty much.'

'And if they found a way to keep face?' Jamie's voice slowed. 'And give the daughter a get-out clause, there wouldn't be too many tears. If I can supply that, you could…'

'Not me personally. No. It would need to be someone who was, what did they say in the Met? Taking a bung. Someone who's in the family's pocket.'

'And you could find someone?'

'Spoiled for choice. Is that the right phrase? Anyway, tomorrow – the official phone call. This Shona? You say she thinks Bakula is a bastard? So, maybe if she hates where the official approach is going, she might come round.'

'Maybe. But my way, less chance of cock-up. And I've got other balls to keep in the air.'

'Cock-up. Balls in the air. Haven't heard that one for long time. Like old times, speaking to you.'

73

Jamie pulled the flat door behind him. The cold air hit his legs as he set off towards the park. Tonight he didn't want interval training. This close to the test it was just about keeping loose, opening up the tubes. It was about getting out of the car fumes and into the zone. The park had gate posts, but no gates, so closing time was aspirational. Moving beyond the borders where the street lamps bled, he clicked on his head-torch. A band of white LED light picked out the tarmac path ahead. Moving deeper in, the air freshened as the sky opened up above him. Across a couple of hundred metres of grass, he could see two other torches, bouncing white, like sparse fireflies appearing and disappearing between the islands of shrubbery. Kindred spirits, Jamie thought. Brothers of the night.

'God, you're getting poetic in your old age,' it was Cara, laughing. 'Fireflies and foolishness. Man, have you seen yourself in those nylon shorts and baggy socks?'

'Last lap before the test, then I can get back on the doughnuts.'

'Not with that pretty, young woman you've got in tow. Need to think about how you appear to her now. And not just in the way you look.'

Jamie veered towards a bench, sat and turned off his head-torch.

'Not an African sky, Jamie. Different world. Narrower. Colder.'

Searching for words he could hear the pulse in his head.

'Maybe she's closer to your way of thinking than you realise? Never know till you trust her.'

'Too much at stake in Manchester,' he felt the sweat run into his eyes and waited for the sting. 'Too finely balanced.' He looked around. The jogging lights seemed to have disappeared.

'Maybe,' Cara's voice was close and quiet. 'But Poland? Do you really think she wouldn't come on board, rather than let some Polish version of Clegg shrug their shoulders and say it's some other country's problem?'

Jamie sat, taking it in. Shona's hatred for what was done, for those that did it. Her fierce defence of the girls' best interests. 'Okay, point taken. I'll give it some thought. The Polish end anyway.'

Then he saw the bobbing dots of light easing around a curve towards him. He stood and flicked a switch. A narrow LED beam washed across the path, promising safe passage. Behind him, the fireflies were closing in, and, a hundred yards on, the shadows of shrubs closed around a pair of tall, brick gate posts. Jamie adjusted his head torch, checking there was nothing to cause injury, lengthened his stride, and he was beyond the gate posts, under the streetlights and slowing to a jog. Just inside the park perimeter the fireflies passed him. His brothers of the night were taking another lap.

It was gone ten when Jamie got out of the shower. Sitting with a tea, he opened the latest edgeland chronicle. There was a pencil outline. He shook his needlepoint pen to clear the dried ink. Between Shona and the murders, he'd let things go. It felt good, the total concentration and, as he looked at the drawing, the knowledge of a job well done. After about twenty minutes he leaned back and reached for his phone.

Been on a run. Thinking of you. Messaged rather than rang in case you were asleep. See you at work J X

Shona had been asleep, but she'd got into the office first. When Jamie arrived it was general chat and a couple of hours of writing up car thefts and ringing neighbouring towns to see if it seemed like an organised gang.

'Just finishing off this Bakula stuff,' Shona stared into a computer monitor. 'Phone call booked later with some Katowice detective. She'll be all shit by the book. Make a gesture. Fuck all else.'

Jamie's eyes narrowed.

'Anyway, need the little girls' room,' and she stood.

Jamie lifted his phone. 'South Yorkshire Police. I'm writing up the paperwork on a remand prisoner, Moonlight. One of our's. Arrived with you recently. Just checking all is okay and if you could give us his admin details. Need to come over for some follow-up questioning at some point. Hope we can find him, what with …' Jamie listened. 'Yes, ten wings of cell blocks. Knew it was huge.'

And he went back to his car thefts.

Shona re-appeared and slumped into the chair. 'Nearly done. All neatly zipped in its folder and ready to be emailed.'

Clegg called them in to talk about the liaison, about fifteen minutes before the call was due. Jamie skimmed through some notes and looked up. 'This liaison officer? What do we know about him?'

'Her,' Clegg squinted at her papers. 'Luk-ja Kalinska. Detective sergeant equivalent. Done extensive liaison with the Met. Lived in London nearly three years.'

'Sounds like you can stand down your legendary Polish,' Jamie grinned at Shona.

Clegg passed across the paper.

'*Loo-Sha*,' Shona said. 'The name…'

And the phone rang.

Jamie and Shona walked out of the reception and the wind hit them.

'Should've just braved the canteen coffee,' Shona pulled her scarf over her mouth.

'Nah,' Jamie jammed on his woolly hat. 'Need privacy and something drinkable.

The lunchtime rush had waned, so they had a corner to themselves. The coffee arrived in a hybrid cup come soup bowl. The heart in Jamie's froth had distorted so it looked like an arse.

'That Kalinska woman, Lucja. Anyone check her DNA. Could've been Clegg's long-lost twin. *Official procedure* this, *outcomes assessed against resource costs* that.' Shona lifted her eyes to Jamie, but he kept staring at his coffee, so she had to fill the void.

'So she knows what he's done. They'll have reams on his activities there as well, but hey, it's okay to ignore because you can say Bavarian Bank, UK operation. Murdered girls, Lithuanian and unknown. Not Polish. Not our problem.'

Jamie lifted the arse to his lips.

As they headed back to the police station, Jamie checked his watch. 'Kit needs washing and I'm out of laundry gel. Go on. I'll catch you up,' and he turned in the direction of a convenience store.

Shona disappeared beyond a wall and Jamie took out his phone.

'Miro, Wing—' he began.

'Yeah, we know. That photo you sent. Vlado had some boys keep an eye out for new arrivals. Like you said. No point hanging around, while we've got him in the open. And, psychologically they say the shock of the first few days. Hits the first-timers hardest.'

Jamie did need laundry gel and he dropped a couple of bottles in his car boot before making his way back up to the briefing room and Shona.

After their shift, when Shona opened her flat door, the warmth of the central heating and the smell of unctuous winter-warmer food wrapped itself around Jamie like a single entity. Walking into the kitchen, the slow cooker gave an occasional gasp of released steam from under its lid. Jamie walked across to Shona, kissed her and began laying the table.

Later, in bed, as Shona was dozing on Jamie's shoulder, his words seemed random. 'But that Polish woman. If there were back channels? If Bakula's father-in-law got sight of the bank accounts. Let him see what finished up in Bavaria instead of Katowice. Might—'

'Close the gap between evidence and justice,' Shona completed his thought, without opening her eyes. 'Aye, well if you do, make sure you build in a get-out clause, so Bakula cops his, but the daughter looks like the wronged woman. Let the boss pretend his little girl was a victim too.' Shona lifted her head and brushed his lips with hers. 'Night, now.'

The only light was Jamie's phone, flitting from work emails, to personal messages and a couple of new photos from Mandy. There was a sense of a line drawn and he could've slept, but Shona kept him awake – her words and how she felt on his chest. He wanted to hold onto that a while longer. His burner phone was on the bedside table and, ten minutes after he sensed Shona's weight sink into sleep, he reached out. There were only a handful of contacts. He scrolled down and tapped VR.

The message was simple:

Do it for Julie.

A few seconds later there was a reply. No words, just a thumbs up.

He went back to his smartphone and flitted from page to page on the BBC News site, but there was a sense of job done. It wasn't long before the phone slid from his hand into the duvet's folds and he slipped into sleep.

74

With his fitness test imminent, Clegg had said Jamie could do a short shift, so it was around eleven when he finally crossed the briefing room.

'Silhouette like Usain Bolt,' Shona was grinning as he arrived at their desk.

'Time was, I'd get abused crossing the Peepos' space, not when I get up my own end.'

'So, what've you done?'

'Stretching and light jogging. Just been keeping loose, this close. Avoid injury and it should be a piece of piss.'

After about twenty minutes of chit-chat and paper shuffling, Jamie said: 'You know what you said about Bakula?'

'What? The gap between evidence and justice.'

'If they had a file implying he was shagging the girls. Maybe Katya, or she could get one of the others. Set it up like a police interview and then send the sound file.'

'Yeah,' Shona was flat and factual. 'You could shove in something from Jakub for good measure. We've got him recorded saying about Moonlight coming in his arse. Just crop the audio so the name's missing. Let them join the dots.'

'And—'

'And,' Shona cut across him. 'The bastard's murdered at least two girls. Probably arranged Dunky's. Fuck him. We both know the alternative. Everything the Polish police get via the official channels gets filed under *Forget it, it's foreign*.'

For a moment after speaking, Shona stared into a distant nowhere.

'Tomorrow ma'am,' Jamie leaned through the door of Clegg's office. 'Fitness test. Not sure how long it takes, and then there'll be the inevitable interview with Sky Sports.'

'Best rest up tonight then,' Clegg turned from the filing cabinet. 'Keep away from activities that could sap your strength.'

Jamie phoned Shona when he got home.

'Going straight there in the morning. Drive's worse than the test.'

'Rod for your own back,' she said. 'Telling Clegg you'd hit level twelve in the marines, then betting her you could still manage nine.'

'Didn't tell her the marine test uses twenty metres and the police is only fifteen. Anyway, pasta just hit boiling. Maximising the blood chemistry ready for tomorrow.'

A couple of closing endearments and he was in the kitchen, spooning his way into a bowl of fusilli with cheese and a tin of tomato soup for a sauce.

Jamie washed up, tidied and showered. Clean kit was bagged and ready and he had the postcode in Google Maps. Relaxation and a good night's sleep. He reached for his edgeland chronicle and laid out pens. Black ink and needlepoint detail worked its own mindfulness and, around ten, he went to bed and sent his final message.

See you tomorrow pm wearing gold medal. J X

Almost immediately there was a beep.

My hero. Will arrange bunting and open-top bus XXX
Jamie set an alarm and plugged in the phone charger. Then he reached out to the lava lamp and his world was green.

Breakfast was light with honey and a glucose tablet. In the car, he sat and tapped Google Maps on his phone.

'Shit traffic,' he cursed over the Radio 4 news. It would be a long drag up to Rotherham, this time of the morning. Then, after Rotherham, he cursed the rest of the way to Swinton and beyond. Eventually he pulled onto a soulless industrial estate; silver clad office complexes with grey and blue doors and windows. NHS, Police, and IKEA buildings all sharing the same anonymity.

There were seven for the test. When Jamie had phoned to confirm his attendance he'd explained about his bet with Clegg and how the loser had to pay fifty pounds into the Police Benevolent Fund. A bit of pointless banter and Jamie and the others shuffled into something like a school gym. The instructors went through the regulations with all the enthusiasm of a metronome. They explained about the pass mark and Jamie's bet with his inspector. A tall, lean man in his forties came and stood next to him. 'Mind if I give it a go as well?' His t-shirt said *Rotherham Harriers Vets*.

Fifteen metres beep, level by level. Jamie was still smiling as the instructor called: 'Five. Finish,' and all but Jamie and the Harrier stopped, content with their morning's work.

At level eight, Jamie was scowling and reddening. 'C'mon kid,' the Harrier stayed on his shoulder. Nine, Jamie's mouth was open. 'Last push,' the Harrier was grinning through clenched teeth. Ten and Jamie hit the floor, still gasping when the Harrier finally came up short. 'Good effort, kid,' he bent over, alongside a horizontal Jamie. 'Suck it in. Nothing like air hitting the bottom of your lungs to make you feel alive. That and getting one over on your inspector.'

Back in the station Jamie breezed across the briefing space towards Shona, smiling.

'Test? Piece of the proverbial, pushed the envelope an extra level.' He reached their desk. 'Glory days. Just going to knock on Clegg's door and tell her to get her purse out.'

Then he registered Shona's face and followed her eyes. Through her open door, he could see Clegg, phone in hand, agitated and striding in circles. His eyes scanned the room and he saw it: what he'd missed on his triumphant passage, the edginess in the air and the two replacement Peepo officers huddled together.

'Moonlight,' Shona said. 'Found dead in his cell. Looks like he killed himself.'

Jamie sank into his seat.

'I know,' Shona carried on. 'First thought is *Oh Shit, doesn't look good*, but then.' And she gave a little fist pump. 'You think, Yes, Justice... only downside is thinking it was the bastard's own choice.'

Jamie looked at Shona. 'Yeah,' he said, 'The bastard's choice...' and then his thoughts and words petered out.

'Haven't heard many details,' Shona carried on. 'Wasn't on suicide watch, apparently.'

'Been a long drive,' Jamie looked across to the still striding Clegg 'Just need a wee.'

Shona went to speak, but he was heading for the corridor. The toilets were empty. Jamie chose a cubicle and, pressing mute on his burner, he opened a missed message. It had no sound, just a photograph and two words.

For Julie.

The image showed a face, blackened and bloodshot, tongue out, a sheet around a neck and a chair on its side, feet dangling above it.

When Jamie returned from the toilet there were even more Peepos standing around. As he crossed to Shona, he could see Clegg leaning against a filing cabinet. Turning, she saw him, pointed to Shona and beckoned. As Shona stood, another group of Peepos came through the door.

'Shona's told you then?' Clegg was still on her feet. 'Found him hanging about the time they were testing your fitness.'

'And it was—' Shona began.

'Looks it,' Clegg glared above the frosted glass line. More Peepos had arrived. 'Appears he stood on a chair and kicked it from under himself. Initial conclusion? No clear evidence of others involved, no sign of violence. Been a slight scuffle in the meal queue day before. Usual new boy stuff. A couple of the old lags shoving him to the end of the line. Just grabbed hold and pushed him to the back. Something and nothing.'

'No sign of force in the cell? Unexplained bruising? Being tied, or anything?' Jamie shuffled from foot to foot.

'Early days, but nothing at first glance.'

'Can't say I give a fuck,' Shona's face matched her words.

Clegg looked for a second, then said. 'Manchester. They weren't happy, but… maybe every cloud…'

The briefing space was filled with Peepos now and the new commanders were standing. Clegg, Shona and Jamie moved towards the door so they could hear.

'Gentlemen,' the new commander's voice was unhurried. 'I know you have heard the news and I can guess your emotions. The way former commander Moonlight abused your… well, I'll leave it to someone who appreciates your work. Someone who knows that the only thing any of you can be accused of is loyalty. She'll be on the news later, but she wanted to speak directly to you first.'

The other officer was at a computer, the wall screen blinked and a cerise jacket walked towards a camera and began to speak. 'My friends, we have worked to establish a new force that puts the ordinary people of this country first. And you have fulfilled that purpose honestly. So the shame is not with you, it is with a commander who abused your diligence for personal gain.' The cerise jacket droned out a few more party line platitudes, then looked into the camera. 'I never forget that we all serve in different ways, but with equal value. Support the cause, as you have always done, and you are the equal of anyone in our nation.'

The new commander began to clap and the room followed seamlessly.

'Pat the animals on the head,' Jamie looked across the room. 'Tell the minions "We're all equal." Just another day on Animal Farm.'

Clegg pursed her lips.

Lifting a hand to silence the clumps of Peepos that were littering the briefing space, the replacement officers dismissed them to the duties of the day, then returned to their laptops and whatever was next on their list.

Clegg closed her office door and Jamie and Shona returned to their desk. Once sat, he tapped Shona.

'She's moving something her way.'

Clegg was on the phone again, but her face seemed lighter, with the occasional outbreak of banter.

'Anyway,' Jamie looked over at the Peepo officers, still huddled together. 'See they got the troops split up and working with minimum fuss.'

'Devil finds work,' Shona whispered.

'Yeah, got them on board. Now keep them busy. At least that'll mean the canteen's quiet.'

Jamie slid a certificate across the canteen table.

'Bloody hell,' Shona said 'Level ten. Bet you had a celebratory doughnut.'

He shook his head. 'Fucking muesli bar. What have I become?' Over two teas and a shared Kit-Kat, Jamie recounted the run and the Harrier. Then his voice dropped. 'So, Moonlight?'

'Well, I won't be wearing black,' and she stared into her cup. 'Okay, courts, checks and balances. But when you know… it's the right result. Hanging with his tongue out, dripping with his own piss and shit.'

'And Bakula? If there were a way?' he knew the question was redundant.

'Like I said. Need to give the daughter a get-out clause, so the family can save face, paint her as a wronged woman.'

Jamie let the thought settle for a few seconds, then said: 'Lucja Kalinska.'

'That Clegg clone.'

'Yeah,' Jamie was looking at his own hands. 'Plays it well. Jephcott said she was a star. Anyway, got a couple of things to do. Starting with this.' Jamie picked up his coat and waved his beep test certificate at Shona. 'I'll see you in an hour or two.'

She watched him go into the office and hold up the paper.

'Fuck off.'

Shona could lip-read Clegg's reaction as she wafted Jamie away, but then she was grinning and reaching for her handbag.

Jamie winked as he left the office.

75

It was too early for visiting time, but by now the staff knew he was police.

'Halfway there,' he pulled his chair close to Katya before rummaging for his phone. 'Moonlight. Thought you should be first. And Jakub. If you think it would help him.' Jamie held up the burner and its dim image of the dangling Moonlight.

'Help, yes. Think he like poster on wall.'

'*Zemsta*,' Jamie almost smiled.

'Zemsta? Yes. But Jakub need be certain. See with own eyes.'

'Means he'll have to see this. Can't send it. Needs deleting and the phone dumping soon.'

'Tell Nina. He like her. Slovak, but speak some Polish. How you…'

'Best you don't know.'

Katya nodded.

Beyond the hospital, Jamie turned into a narrow cul-de-sac; long walls, Victorian buildings. It was dark, no signs of life. He took out his phone.

'Miro. Hi. Can you talk?… Vlado, yes. Got the images… Did it go… Yeah, as you say. Not like the boys aren't used to getting people into car boots. And after a few months locked up with nothing to do but weight-lifting and wanking…'

Jamie listened, occasionally uttering monosyllables. Then, when Miro paused: 'Can't tell you how much… tell Vlado. Tell him there's another bastard, fucked off back to Poland, but I'm dealing with him. Tell him the girls… can't give you details, names, but we think we're giving them a chance. Let him know. A way out. Not just retribution.'

Jamie bought flowers on the way to Shona's.

'Hoping they're for me, not Moonlight.' She was wearing an apron. There were two large steaks lying on a plate. She lifted one on a fork, so he could appreciate the slab of dead flesh. 'Thought a Level Ten body could cope with a chunky chip supper, but I'll get a shower first.'

Jamie nodded. 'Yeah, fine. I had one lunchtime.'

When she came back, she was wearing a white towelling robe. She smiled and turned on the grill. 'How was Clegg when you told her she was donating fifty quid to charity?'

'Surprisingly, cheerful. Still, been a good day for her.'

'Yeah,' she was rubbing his hair dry. 'Busy doing what she does best. Manipulating the politics, enhancing her image. Won't have time for us.' She opened the oven door and put in trays of tomatoes and mushrooms. 'That stuff for Lucja. The back channel stuff?'

'All done. Except the Jakub audio. But that's just editing. I'll—'

'Thought so,' Shona slid two steaks under the grill. 'I've done it.' And she wiped her hands and took an SD card from her purse. 'Meant I only had time for frozen chips though.'

They were both at their desks just before eight the next morning. 'Halcyon days,' Jamie was staring round the office. The Peepos came and went on their appointed tasks.

Shona looked up.

'Calm between winter storms,' he carried on. 'Make the most of it. I called Cozza when I first got in.'

Shona waited.

'Thought he might use his professional status to get a look at the body.'

It was around eleven when Clegg beckoned them over. 'Getting a few more details. Everyone's on board with the press strategy. Official line: regrettable suicide. Unofficial? Encourage the media to push the *got what he deserved* angle. And, as planned, any come-back – Manchester. *He was safe when he left us.* But there won't be. In no one's interest to dig.'

'Have you…?' Jamie waited for the details.

'Suicide. Nothing to suggest otherwise. Hadn't been there long enough to make enemies. The meal queue stuff? Like I said. Nothing. Just letting the new boy know his place. Time of death? Average morning, bit before there was an altercation at the other end of the wing. Handbags, everyday stuff. Guards jumped on it. And nowhere near him. It was activity time. Blokes watching telly, some playing pool, table-tennis, in the gym, usual stuff.'

'CCTV?'

'Well, not in the cells. Only if there's been threats. Nothing on psych reports to say suicide watch.'

'But the galleries and landings?' Shona didn't look at Jamie as she asked. 'All operating? Nothing jammed?'

'Funny you should say jammed,' Clegg smirked. 'Actually, it was peanut butter. Some prat had gone along smearing peanut butter on the lenses. Regular annoyance, apparently. The guards had just started cleaning them up when things kicked off. Bloody peanut butter.' Clegg's grin widened. 'But that's not for public consumption.'

Jamie joined in the laughing, even though he'd heard it before.

'Messaged our pathological friend,' Jamie was holding his phone as he and Shona stepped into the corridor. 'Hopefully, he'll be in his office later. Don't want another pork pie and mustard evening.'

Then his phone buzzed. He answered and mouthed *Cozza*.

'He'll be there till six,' Jamie turned to Shona as he rang off. 'And this Lucja,' he continued. 'Sooner we move things on with her, the sooner its job done and we're into monitoring Morcanu. Making sure she doesn't backslide.' He pushed the beige cube's door open and held it for Shona. 'Saw Katya last night,' he said, taking the burner from his coat pocket. 'Need to see Jakub. Be useful if you were there. Katya said ask for Nina. But going to the house. Might not open the door for a man.' And he began typing into WhatsApp.

Can you speak?

His phone beeped and he tapped recent contacts.

'Lucja. Glad you were available,' he listened for a moment then: 'Moving things on quickly this end. The emailed files…'

Shona gave him a nudge and he pressed speaker.

'Yes. Had a look,' Lucja said. 'Foreign financial, that's all they'll say. UK, German banks. Not Polish business.'

'Nice to know that bureaucrats and office politicians are flourishing everywhere,' Shona leaned into the phone.

'Same all over,' Lucja sounded world-weary. 'Every country. Sewers run everywhere and it's always the turds that float to the top.'

'So Bakula? The real stuff. You can…' Jamie pulled things back on track.

'Like I said, plenty to choose from.'

'And you can be sure—' Jamie's question was cut short.

'Rock and a hard place. Once they have the file. If they don't deliver it, but someone else does. Explaining to the father why they hadn't passed it on? Not a conversation I'd want to have.'

'Delivery?' Jamie cut in. 'Post, obviously so there's no trace. If we send a stick or—'

'SD card,' Lucja said. 'Less bulky in the envelope. Pay extra for express, usually arrive in two days. Pay cheap? God knows.'

A few more details went back and forth and then Lucja sent a WhatsApp – pick-up address and the express postal link. Jamie replied with a thumbs-up and stood. Shona did the same, but he made no move towards the corridor.

'This visit to Jakub,' he began tapping a finger on his burner phone. 'Katya says this will help. Help him towards closure.' He flicked the photos app and hit the light switch.

Shona peered into the darkness and the burner came to life. It took a few seconds for her eyes to process the jumble of shapes and colours.

'When Jakub's seen this, it'll need deleting and the phone dumping.'

'How? Who?' Shona's voice was calm.

'Don't ask. Not again,' he switched the light back on. 'Different universe. Got its own laws on crime and punishment. Clear and easy to understand.'

Shona felt the finality in his voice.

Just before five they were driving. The last light was gone before they pulled up on Katya's street. Jamie handed her the burner, but stayed in the car as Shona approached the door. She knocked and a triangle of light spilled from a lifted curtain. Jamie saw Shona lean towards the letter box.

The door opened and Shona went in.

About ten minutes later Shona messaged. The door opened again and she beckoned to Jamie. In the light, he could see the glaze of tears on Shona's eyes. Nina and Jakub were wet-cheeked and red-eyed. Jakub stepped forwards and hugged him. When he stepped back, Nina did the same and kissed his cheek.

'Thank you,' her lips were by his ear. 'From all in house. You do good thing.'

Jamie backed away smiling, not knowing what to say. Then he whispered to Shona: 'Cozza.' And as she turned, he tapped his watch.

The end of day traffic was heavy, as usual, but they were outside Cozza's lab at about quarter to six. Jamie took out his phone.

'Helluva a day,' Shona leaned her head on his shoulder as they waited for the door to open.

They heard the push bar rattle on the other side.

'Greetings, earthlings,' Cozza appeared.

'So, what did you see?' Jamie asked as they walked along the corridor.

'Not much,' Cozza held the door to his office open. 'Saw a waxwing at the weekend. Nearly as beautiful as your lovely companion.'

'But you managed to get in?'

'They'd moved him to the Manchester Royal Infirmary. Good facilities there. Better for the family.' Cozza went to the kettle. 'The brother did the ID.'

'The millionaire?'

'Don't know. Girl on the desk just said he was nice. Asked about making a donation to the hospital. Anyway, showed her my home office pass and said I was here at the request of the arresting force. Said she hadn't worked for the hospital long. Christ, I bet she got a bollocking after they kicked me out.' Cozza placed three teas on the table and sat down. 'Like I say, they kicked me out. Just had time for quick external once over, before they fucked me off with a lengthy lecture on the vast number of forms my superiors needed to fill in, if they really wanted a look at their case.'

'Not like Manchester folk to be unfriendly,' Jamie smiled over his cup.

'Weren't Manchester staff. I know the Royal Infirmary lot. Forensic pathology. Small world. Anyway got a look. Nothing too unusual, but—'

'Bruising. Like he'd been held?' Jamie flicked at a post-it. 'Upper arms, wrists, ankles.'

'Some on the arms. But I'd expect more if he'd been held tight enough to stick his head through a noose and kick a chair from under him.'

'Tied?' Shona put in.

'Again, expect clear marks? Even if they used ripped sheets. Be a real struggle to hold someone still enough to tie knots.'

'What about Velcro straps?' Jamie asked. 'Big ones, like for weight training? Top and bottom of the limbs? Wide. Don't need tying.'

'Yeah. Less likely to dig in,' Cozza held his gaze on Jamie.

'And he'd been in scuffle the previous day,' Jamie went on. 'Grabbed and pushed to the end of the meal queue. There'd be marks.'

'Yeah, but the—'

'But if you wanted to find suicide?'

Cozza shrugged. 'Valid interpretation. Right photos and a friendly coroner? Nothing anyone would challenge.'

The moment of silent understanding was broken when Jamie took a sip of tea. 'Anyway, where was this waxwing?'

76

'Be back in a bit. Need to lose the burner and that photo.' He watched Shona reach the door of her flat and waited until the lights came on before driving.

Pulling into the builder merchant's drive, where Rutland Street crossed the river, he deleted everything from the phone's memory. Then he cracked it open and removed the SIM card. Locking the car, he walked to the centre of the bridge, looked around, leaned over the wall and dropped the card into the water, followed by the phone. There was a satisfying plop. The streetlights reflected fragmented orange as the wind flicked across the river. Jamie watched.. A vee-shaped trail of ripples was moving out from a clump of reeds. It was a rat. Jamie kept watching until it disappeared into the shadow of the bank.

'Always a rat, baby.' Cara was suddenly there. 'Out of sight, but always there. Spreading their nastiness. All over the world. But maybe one or two less tonight. You did good honey. You and Shona.'

Jamie used his key to let himself into Shona's. He guessed she'd be asleep. He was right. He'd had a new burner in the glove compartment. Sitting at the kitchen table, he pushed in a new

SIM card. There was plenty of milk in the fridge, so he warmed a mugful in the microwave and began dipping digestive biscuits.

He closed his eyes. Miro, Vlado: the attention to detail, even down to engineering a scuffle to explain the upper arm bruising. Had the feel of a well-rehearsed routine. He dipped another biscuit and tried not to think of the possibilities.

Shona had left her bedside lamp on, but her eyes were closed. Long, audible breaths wobbled her lips. Jaime reached across for the off switch. She didn't stir, just carried on breathing as Jamie lay in the dark, watching the slit of light that arced across the ceiling every time headlights passed on the main road.

'Outside chance that SD card will reach Lucja today,' Shona was surprisingly breezy at breakfast.

'More likely tomorrow, or the day after.'

'That's why I said *outside* chance.'

The day was predictable. Jamie kept going to his car to check his burner and kept coming back disappointed. Clegg was in and out of meetings and seemed to be elevated to the status of strategy guru, if the number of phone calls was any indication.

'Brisk, smug.' Jamie watched her moving above the frosted line. 'If I was asked to describe her in a couple of words.'

Shona shook her head and carried on.

Clegg walked towards them. 'Stretch my legs. Got the Assistant Chief Constable calling at ten. By all accounts he's loving the *We made the arrest, he died in Manchester* aspect. And I've seen a draft from the pathologist. Should be open and shut in the coroner's court. Suicide. Nobody wants publicity.' She tilted her head towards the Peepo commander's desk. 'Not that lot. No love lost with the brother, either. Owns all those shops, Jyoshna.. Apparently, half the station's seen him talking about it on YouTube. So, he'll want it done, dusted and under the carpet. Not the brand image you want if you're selling family groceries.

Anyway, Assistant Chief.' And she breezed back to her office.

'Unexpected consequences. Flavour of the month.' Shona's eyes followed Clegg. 'Be telling them everything. Bound to be giving you full credit. Especially Manchester.'

Jamie stood. He had his car keys again.

It was around four when he came back. 'Jephcott messaged,' he said. 'Wants a meet. Nothing from Lucja.'

Clegg was standing again, visible above the frosted glass line, brushing her hair. A couple of minutes later, she was on her way out. 'Official post-mortem's out. Assistant Chief wants my input on the press release.'

Jephcott was parked close to the red brick wall. Jamie checked his burner again as he and Shona got out of their car.

'She's contacted me,' Jephcott said as they shuffled into his Audi. 'Says she'll look properly overnight, but initial assessment... expect the expected.'

'So tomorrow?' Jamie cut in

'Maybe a tad over-optimistic but, bit of patience and trust, I'm confident she'll get things where they need to go.'

'And all without my legendary Polish language skills,' Shona spoke into a pause.

'When this is over,' Jephcott moved on. 'The organisation thinks you need a break.'

'But—' Jamie began.

'Can't operate like this forever. In the end it catches up. Causes mistakes. Things you do.' Jephcott moved his attention between their faces. 'We need you sharp. There'll be something else soon enough. Might be a chance for some family time. If we can arrange Africa?'

'Great,' Shona huffed. 'And I get Glasgow.'

'Thought the Gambia might be a joint trip.'

'Joint?' Shona's eyes widened.

'Come on,' Jephcott was smiling now. 'Everyone knows. Clegg was laughing about it the other day.'

'How'd she—' Shona began to redden.

'Gossip. Body language,' Jephcott was still smirking. 'She said "Once it's common knowledge? Fun's over." Said it's more entertaining watching you two trying to be clandestine. Not like either of you would pass a RADA audition.'

Shona looked away.

'Anyway,' Jephcott went on. 'There's a place we use sometimes. We'll work out an exit strategy. But this, today? Lucja will get the details done and dusted and let you know. You push on with Morcanu.'

Shona was on her side, eyes away from the light, trying to sleep. Jamie was propped up, his pillow turned vertical, reading the RSPB magazine.

'Jephcott. Do you think he's right about Morcanu? Too smart to risk reneging? Too much to lose?'

'Yes, I do actually,' Shona didn't open her eyes. 'She earns so much legitimately. This must just be eating her time. And she's got kids. Way too much at stake.'

Clegg had been in her office for about twenty minutes, when she knocked on the glass, beckoning Shona and Jamie.

'Couldn't have gone better,' she put three cups on the table. 'Coffee? Bought this on the way home from the meeting with the Assistant Chief yesterday.' A new espresso maker was simmering on top of the filing cabinet. 'Seconded me to the Joint Force Steering Committee. In the room with the top brass. Doing the liaison with the other Yorkshire forces. Bit more driving around, but…' she poured coffee into the cups. 'But this job. Moonlight. Couldn't have gone better. That's the view from the top. Good arrest, good publicity. Perfect ending, avoiding a court case.

And politically? That's what the bosses really love. Those Peepo bastards? Toxic brand, for a while at least. Sound of our lords and masters rowing backwards? Deafening.'

'Still got stuff to follow up,' Shona took a sip of espresso. 'Forecourt thefts and the spate of post-January credit card bill shoplifting at Meadowhall.'

'No, give it a day or so,' Clegg topped up the coffees. 'You two deserve a breather. Maybe you could have a nice lunch. You could even arrive in the same car.'

'Piss-taking cow,' but Jamie was suppressing a smile.

Shona wasn't suppressing. 'So, lunch?'

'Honestly? Not today. Not till we've heard from Lucja. It'd be a waste of money, way my stomach's feeling.'

'Maybe see Katya? Then you could take me for a nature ramble.'

'Ramble…' Jamie snorted.

'Marika here again,' Katya was in the chair by her bed. 'This one feel better,' she held up her left hand. 'Cut not so deep. Miss tendons.'

Shona leaned forwards and hugged her.

'And girls. Three come. Bring Jakub. He getting better, Nina say. Little steps. But knowing Moonlight gone… better.'

'Marika,' Shona perched on the bed again 'Has she contacted the girls yet?'

'Says will go to house soon. Talk. See how girls feel.'

'She said about a skills audit,' Shona put her hand inside her coat.

'Yes. She show me. It good. But I tell her, speak girls first. Get to know them.'

'Take them some fashion magazines,' Shona smiled.

'Soon, she visit. Girls will message. I balance phone on knee.' And she held up her left hand and her fingers moved a little in the bandages. 'Can just about turn page. Creases sometimes.' A tiny oval of flesh peeped from the bandage on her index finger.

'Jamie...' Shona handed him her car keys. 'In the boot, two or three in there,' she turned back to Katya. 'Only *Reserved!* Catalogues, sorry. But tomorrow? I've got some more upmarket magazines at home. *Vogue Polska*, *Elle*, I'll have a search.'

Shona chatted, filling Katya in on as much as she could, talking about where things could go with Marika.

'Three,' after a few minutes Jamie appeared at the end of the bed, holding the magazines. 'Good job we weren't in my car, you'd have got the Observer Book of Birds.' He resumed his position of redundancy and the two women carried on chatting, flicking through pages of glossy photos.

'C'mon. You just need warm and dry. A woolly hat and if you've got waterproof trousers...' Jamie was standing in Shona's hall. 'You're not going on a photo shoot for Polska Vogue.'

At Jamie's flat, she waited in the car. He was less than five minutes: full kit.

'Wish I had shares in Gore-Tex,' Shona turned as he dropped his rucksack on the back seat.

Pulling up outside Abdullah's shop, Jamie nipped in and came out with two packets of sandwiches and a couple of bottled waters. Shona moved towards the car, but Jamie pointed at the gap between the houses.

'Thought we were seeing nature,' Shona looked towards the patch of scrubland and the tunnel of bare hawthorns beyond. 'Somewhere scenic.'

Jamie locked the car and they moved beyond a pair of gable-ends. 'Meant to warn you about that,' he grinned as Shona jolted backwards. 'Quiet, Kaiser. We're staying this side...' Jamie tapped a wooden gate. 'Nearly filled my boxers first time he did that to me.'

'This is…' Shona stared at the brown tangle of briars and uncut grasses.

'Teeming with life. Even this time of year. There'll be voles and mice using the brambles like barbed wire to keep safe from birds and foxes.'

'Birds?'

'Owls at night. Buzzards daytime, kestrels most common, maybe sparrowhawks. You need to look,' Jamie carried on. 'It's changing all the time, the light. These tiny green seedlings. Come back in a fortnight and they'll be ankle height and as wide as your fist. End of May, above your waist.'

Shona was drawn in by his voice. Trying to see things with his eyes.

'People go on about blossoms and leaves, but there's always something,' he held her hand as she stepped down a small dyke into the tunnel of hawthorns. 'Look at the shape. The architecture of the bare branches. Gothic, like a church.' Stepping out, he pointed at spoil-heaps of orange soil. 'Rabbits; they like a rise and sandy soil. Helps keep their warren dry.'

Jamie took out a camera and his sketchbook and for the next hour recorded the intricacies of the landscape and the animals, all the time talking, a flow of information that was neither forced nor showy, but just there.

'Wind's dropping,' Jamie looked up. The last fragments of blue sky were shrinking. 'Come on,' he smiled. 'Enough for an introduction.'

'No, enjoyed it, but maybe a cuppa and a cake?' Shona said. 'Hopefully, that bloody Rottweiler hasn't got over the wall.'

She dropped her wellies in the car boot and pulled on trainers. 'So, you and Cozza do this sort of thing together?'

'Yeah, when we can. He's the real bird expert. I'm just a dabbler, bit of a generalist.'

'I'll just nip in and change,' Jamie pulled up outside his flat, but Shona followed him in. He took a pair of jeans off the back of the door. Shona saw his chronicle on the desk and opened it.

Just as before, she was absorbed by the precision; the drawings and the writing. She flicked to the page he was working on and saw pencil marks, some framing out, light sketched forms, some lining and margining of handwritten text.

'Never guess there was all this going on under your work.' Shona traced a finger across the page. 'You even write in light pencil, before using the pen.'

'Need to know I've got everything where it needs to be, before going to ink: spacing, spelling. Too late once you've committed and it's permanent.'

Jamie's burner phone began buzzing. He froze for a moment then, recognising the number, picked it up from the table and tapped speaker.

'Jamie, thought you'd appreciate a progress report.'

'Thanks Lucja. Yes. I've got Shona with me.'

'Okay, good. Progress report, job done. Well, will be soon. The SD card is probably with the father now.'

'So you—'

'Yes,' Lucja continued. 'At least three in the gang's pocket, just at this station. Taking their bungs. Copied the card and left it and a set of print-outs on Bent Copper One's desk with a note. Watched him open the envelope. Watched his face. The note told him the card contained information that must be passed on. Told him the same card was on its way to one of the other corrupt bastards.'

Jamie looked up at Shona and her suppressed smile.

'Quite entertaining,' Lucja's voice echoed from the phone again. 'Watching him scroll through the card. Few minutes, he was in his car. Just a matter of time, now. Two, three days, maybe to get organised, then however long the boss deems Bakula needs to spend in purgatory before the inevitable.'

'Zemsta,' Jamie said.

'Zemsta... yes,' Lucja was surprised for a second. 'But also, education. A lesson for anyone else who might fall into temptation.'

'So now you'll...?'

'Avoid the kabanos at the local market. Stick to the vacuum-packed supermarket brands for a couple of months.'

'Bloody kabanos,' Shona opened the passenger door. 'Right, well... we'll need to pick up a curry on the way to mine. Didn't get anything out of the freezer. Wasn't expecting an afternoon of wildlife and nature.'

It was a stare-out-of-the-side-window sort of drive. Shona watched the normality of people walking on pavements. The city sat under a flat, grey sky; one of those weatherless winter days, shadowless and muted. Any sun, or rain, or breath of wind seemed far off in the dull calm.

'You choose,' Jamie said as they pulled up outside the curry house. Shona went in and he waited in the car.

After their meal, they watched television. Jamie slouched on the sofa as a procession of antique shops, amateur cooks and people who wanted to move house went past. The news came on, but they went to bed.

It was dark when they drove into work.

'Suppose we're back on that list? Stolen cars and shoplifters,' Shona said. 'Her ladyship will be busy with higher things, if we see her at all.'

Jamie nodded and turned down the car park ramp.

They walked in together. Nobody even noticed. They took two teas to their desk and divided up the jobs.

'You've made a start on the cars,' Shona said. 'I might as well head for Meadowhall.'

The next day was similar and so was the next, except Clegg

phoned Shona and told her to go to a meeting for her and take notes.

'Called in to see Katya on the way home.' Shona shook some pasta into boiling water. 'Took her some more magazines. She said the girls told her Marika had visited and asked if people were interested in talking about a change of life-style.'

'Maybe give her a call, Morcanu. Maybe make it like a thanks. But it won't hurt that she knows we know.'

'Soft skills.' Shona shook some frozen prawns into a colander.

She was washing up and Jamie was drying when his phone rang.

'I've got some brochures,' the call began.

Jamie was confused for a second.

'For that holiday complex.'

Jamie went to the window. He could see Jephcott's car in the shadows of the car park behind Shona's flat.

'Just taking some crap out to the bins,' he called through. He couldn't make out Shona's reply, but he guessed it meant she'd stack things on the draining board.

Jamie was at the top of the concrete steps when the courtesy light came on. He looked back a couple of times as he went down to the large Audi. He opened the car door and saw them. Brochures on the front seat.

77

'Gambia,' Jamie spread the brochures across the table and called through to Shona from the kitchen. 'Self-contained complex with a private beach, Jephcott says. They have an arrangement, apparently. Two weeks and they'll organise travel for Claudette and Baggage.'

Shona sat down. As she stared at the glossy pages, she gave Jamie a hug, then pulled off her washing-up gloves and passed them to him. 'Go on, you finish off, while I go through this lot.'

'Says they've got a way of getting us there, so no one knows,' Jamie re-emerged after he'd finished at the sink. 'Especially, with my background.'

Shona looked and waited for him to go on.

'Issues both ends really. Africa for a holiday? Passport numbers, various destinations? Can't afford anyone pulling on the loose ends in my backstory. There'll be watch lists. Don't want either of our names setting the lights flashing at border control.'

'Both ends?' Shona asked.

'Sierra Leone. There's people I pissed off. People with connections. Not a wasps' nest I want to kick again. Not for me, or Claudette and Baggage.'

'So when?' Shona went back to flicking pages.

'Says whenever we can get leave.'

'Hours we've done? Both got loads owing. And,' Shona was drinking in the photos of sea, sand, pools and rooms. 'Needs taking before the end of March. That's the regs. He say if we can let anyone know?'

'Yeah, says we can tell Claudette and Baggage, but not *where*... Got people to arrange their pick-ups and flights.'

'So...' Shona gave him a nudge and he took out his phone.

A few seconds later, Claudette was sounding surprised.

'She says Baggage is asleep,' Jamie told Shona. 'But they'll be waiting by the iPad in the morning."

Shona was up early, showered, made-up and was endlessly tweaking her hair. Jamie opened facetime.

'We've been waiting,' Claudette's smile appeared. 'Where are you?' she was looking beyond him. 'Looks comfier than your flat.'

'Claudette...' Jamie reddened and handed the iPad to the side.

'Hi, Claudette. I'm Shona. Not sure what Jamie has been telling you.'

'Glasgow girl. We meet at last.'

'So, he's told you.'

'Well, let's say good job he doesn't play cards,' Claudette began to chuckle. 'Emmy...' and the girl's face filled the bottom half of the screen.

'Hi, I'm Shona.'

'Daddy's girlfriend?' the gap in her teeth appeared.

'I'm going to pass this over to your daddy,' Shona blushed slightly. 'There's something he wants to show you.'

Jamie and Shona had gone through the magazine, scribbling out and sticking bits of post-it over any text that could give away the location and, holding the iPad over the photographs, going from page to page, they explained about the holiday.

'Not got a definite date yet,' Jamie explained. 'But we have friends. They'll sort everything. You just need to pack.'

'Just need to pack. Such foolishness,' Claudette was chuckling again. 'We need to shop… and then pack.'

'Quite right,' Shona's smile was more relaxed now. 'Need to be beach-ready.'

They scanned over the pages one more time. Shona said her *lovely-to-meet-yous* and she sat back as Jamie and Baggage blew kisses back and forth and he said his good-byes to Claudette.

'Speak again, really soon,' Jamie was waving. 'Keep you posted on the holiday.'

Baggage was behind Claudette, jumping around the room, singing about going to the beach.

'She's a beauty, Jamie. I can't imagine…' Shona kissed his cheek. 'That Claudette…' And she chuckled.

The holiday request went through. Dates finalised. Jephcott had arrangements delegated and under control and Jamie watched the accumulation of online clothing deliveries. It only took two days before he heard Shona mid-conversation with Claudette, and by the end of the week girlie face-time exchanges of new bikinis, sun-hats and sarong modelling between Shona and Baggage became the norm. On the odd occasion he got to the iPad first, Baggage dismissed him to fetch Shona.

Two weeks after Lucja mentioned kabanos, Jephcott messaged. Jamie's phone had been on silent. When he saw the name he slid the phone out of his pocket and under the desk.

Find somewhere quiet and phone back.

'Toilet.' Jamie stood. 'Maybe a while.'

'Thank you for sharing,' Shona didn't look up.

Jamie walked down, sat in his car and took out his phone.

'Lucja called,' Jephcott began. 'Only a rumour, but Bakula's wife has been seen shopping and in restaurants. She's always got her sister and a couple of aunties in attendance, but no sighting of the man himself. And the guy who had the SD card and the other policemen that Lucja says are on the payroll? Chinese whispers, but the chatter is, Bakula won't be seen anytime soon.'

'So it's…'

'As close to a confirmation as we'll probably get. Will you tell Shona?'

'Have to, I suppose. Then Katya, so she can let the others know.'

Back at Shona's flat, Jamie waited for the right moment, but somehow it never arrived.

'Anyway, had a call off Clegg,' Shona began. 'Wants me to stand in at Harrogate tomorrow. She's double-booked. Perils of her new guru status.'

The next morning, Jamie walked down with Shona to her car. As he hugged her, he looked at his watch.

'Plenty of time. Be able to sneak in a cheeky Danish pastry before kick-off.' Then, as he disengaged and opened the car door. 'Forgot to mention. Had a call off Jephcott yesterday. Information from Katowice is Bakula's wife's been seen a good few times around town, but no sightings of him. Do you want this bag in the back or the boot?'

Shona just looked. Only at the traffic lights did it begin to sink in.

Around seven o'clock that evening Jamie put his key in the lock and stepped into the hall.

'Another bikini. So that's three.'

After he hung up his coat, he followed the sound of Shona's voice 'Three bikinis, Claudette? What are you—'

He leaned on a kitchen chair and ducked into view of the iPad's camera.

'Me, not nanny. Silly.'

The face on the iPad was alive with mock indignation. He looked at Shona. She was smiley, chatty. He breathed a little deeper.

After about twenty minutes of alternating between Baggage and Claudette, the video call ended and Shona fixed her attention on him. Smiley, chatty made an abrupt exit.

'You can face down Ebola, but me? You think, *tell her as she's driving off, then she can be angry in her own time*.'

Jamie went to answer.

'Don't. It's bollocks. You only use apologies for damage limitation. Eat your tea. Say nothing. Probably see you later. I'm going to the gym. Might see what's on at the multiplex after.'

Jamie looked around for his meal. It was plated up in the fridge. He lifted it into the microwave and took out a tray. As he ate, some expert on the television was valuing an old jug.

'Looks like a glazed turd,' he hit the off button.

When he'd washed up, he went to the door and pulled on his coat. He thought about going home for his edgeland kit, but he needed movement, not stillness and the night. He strode beyond the University, beyond the Royal Hallamshire hospital.

Cara arrived as he reached Endcliffe Park.

'So, Africa? And you're taking your girlfriend to meet our daughter. And my mother.'

'Both seem to like her,' Jamie's shoulders formed a resentful hump.

Cara started to laugh. 'I know. Be good for Emmy to have someone to talk girl's stuff with. And Claudette, what did she say about her? "Pretty, but could do with a good dinner."'

He kept walking, keeping the woods on his left. Cara stayed with him for a while, as he headed off down Rustlings Road, teasing. Then it started to rain.

The light was on when he got back. Shona was sat on the sofa, arms folded, legs crossed, up on the coffee table.

'You were right. Took the coward's way out. Shouldn't have—'

Shona turned and saw him dripping, his hair stuck to his head.

'Went for a walk. It started to rain.' He blew a droplet off the tip of his nose.

'I can see that,' Shona's head moved in disbelief.

'I was just passing Whitely Woods when it started,' he slid his coat off his shoulders.

'It was forecast.'

'I wanted a walk.'

'She was on her feet now, opening a cupboard. 'Here.' And she threw him a towel.

They were both owed nearly three weeks holiday.

'So, the fortnight in Gambia,' Shona was checking the calendar in her notebook. 'Have Friday and Saturday to pack and drive to the docks. Then the extra couple of days for laundry when we get back.'

Jephcott had explained the travel arrangements.

'Got you a hired campervan and you're on the Hull to Rotterdam ferry. That's the nearest. Then on to our guy in Blokland. I'll get you the postcode. He'll have your false passports. Stop overnight, and he'll drive you to Schiphol for your flight to Gambia. Two weeks in the resort and when you get back everyone thinks you've been camping.'

'Because every sane person goes camping in Northern Europe in March,' Jamie shook his head.

'More believable than trying to tell people you'd gone to Holland for the tulip festival,' Jephcott laughed. 'I'll email the fictional itinerary to memorise.'

'But what about—' Shona began.

'Sun cream,' Jephcott anticipated. 'That's the one thing. We've got you a load of total block.'

On the Wednesday before they left, Katya arrived at Shona's in a taxi.

'Brought him to open doors,' she smiled at Jakub. 'Marika said text when ready and she send taxi back. Her cousin. I talk to him in office on Monday.'

'How're your hands?' Jamie was stirring a sauce.

Katya wiggled her left hand, but held up the right to show the finger splints still rigid. 'Scans looking good, doctor say.'

'She hit me with elbows,' Jakub smiled and his eyes were lively as he demonstrated.

Over the meal they discussed the job and accommodation situations.

'She give us all contracts. Four months paid, so extra month. Seen everyone now. Knows all qualifications and she send women from office to test our English, maths and stuff. Some of girls have had days training – stock control, talking to customers.'

'Sounds like you're ahead,' Shona put in.

'Jakub had tutor come in. Marika say help get ready for college. Special computer stuff, not just office and accounts like me – coding, programming. Egg-head, nerd stuff.' And she lifted an elbow.

Clegg was in on Thursday, their last day. 'Love's young dream,' she poured them all an espresso coffee. 'Who'd have thought it, that day he was stood in my office sprinkled with doughnut sugar. Anyway, right result.' Clegg leaned back in her chair. She was wearing trainers. 'Not you two together. God knows how that's right. Moonlight. We know what he did, right. Not just the money, the girls, the smuggling. And if he wasn't hands-on with the murders, he was complicit. So no tears. Pity about the other bastard getting away on that ferry. Still, never made the papers and he wasn't on our crime figures. Anyway, you two, have a good break. And come back ready to work without being lippy.

As they drove home, Shona said: 'Drop me at Dunky's mum's. I'll call when I'm ready to be picked up.'

'Shall I—'

'No,' Shona put her hand on his arm. 'Easier with just me. We'll talk.'

Jamie collected the camper van on Friday afternoon and parked it as close to Shona's steps as he could.

'Good fun, driving that,' he was smiling as he dropped the keys on the kitchen table. 'Make a fortune with them, festival season. The bloke was telling me, Glastonbury week, be cheaper to buy one, use it and sell it again when you got back.'

There was a final video call.

'Next time face to face, not facetime,' Shona blew a kiss to Baggage.

'Alright for you,' Jamie called to Claudette. 'Taxi, flight, taxi and in your swimsuit. We've got two long drives and an overnight ferry. Then on a plane for seven hours. You pair? Less than an hour and a half.'

The camper van was packed and they were in Hull with two hours to spare. The drive to Blokland was uneventful. Johan, their contact, was waiting with the passports. Jamie followed him to his lock-up and the camper van disappeared. Johan drove him back and gave them a meal. Then they loaded their bags into his car and headed for Schiphol airport.

The plane lurched, like planes do as they turn into position for take-off. Everyone was strapped in and three stewardesses spaced themselves along the cabin. Wearing coordinated life-jackets, they gestured towards emergency exits, then went through their routines in sync with an audio track. Jamie wasn't listening. No one was.

Shona leaned across and whispered: 'So then, first time you've seen her in the flesh for what? Four years?'

Jamie's eyes lifted towards the nearest stewardess, indicating that Shona should wait until the girl had finished her demonstration.

Shona's voice lowered. 'Just saying. It'll be good to meet Baggage in the flesh. Hope she takes to me, at least a bit.' And she smiled.

Jamie continued looking down as he spoke. 'If you can call her Emmy... that would... Baggage is like my name for her... Claudette, everyone else calls her Emmy.' His eyes remained fixed, as if he were interested in the leaflet that was open in his lap.

The plane's engines were shrieking now and the stewardesses hurried towards their little fold-down perches. Jamie slid the unread safety leaflet into the magazine net on the back of the seat in front. A diagram of an oxygen mask was visible through its elasticated diamonds. Jamie pushed back into his own seat, waiting for the first steep climb from the runway. He wanted it over. His tensions usually eased as the plane levelled out. After that, he knew he had to accept that he was where he was.

Acknowledgements

I spent many years knowing no one else who wrote fiction, so it was a road to Damascus moment when I drove to Birmingham to attend the National Writers Conference. Since then, *Writing West Midlands* has been a constant source of knowledge and support, as I was, subsequently, accepted for their flagship writers' development programme – *Room 204*. This has led to many opportunities, most notably a critique from *The Literacy Consultancy*, who asked award winning author and screenwriter (and musician) Ray Robinson to read my work. My particular thanks to Ray for his unstinting wisdom, advice and encouragement.

Less formally, and with more beer, my thanks go to the *Page-Turner Writers*, who read my work and offered sound advice – and to Liam Brown (find his speculative fiction on Amazon and in all good bookshops) who taught and brought us together. I am also indebted to Paula Pawlus for knowledge way beyond Google Translate. And, finally, I am grateful to Crescent Swan for believing I could tell a tale and to Joe Chadwick, for his patient and skilful editing.

About the Author

Tim was born in Wolverhampton, and grew up on the sixth floor of a block of flats. He spent his career as a teacher, and later a headteacher in the Black Country. After retiring, he worked part-time at Wolves Academy tutoring young footballers. He lives with his wife, who was a nurse on a specialist cardiology unit for many years, and has two daughters: one is a garden designer and the other a landscape architect.

Tim has written a variety of educational textbooks, including one on Ancient Greece and two English textbooks. His short story, *Through My Own Fault*, was broadcast on BBC Radio 4. *Days of Long Shadows* is his first published crime novel. His next projects include a story set during 1940 in Blitz-torn London and a Young Adult novel.

A note from the Publisher

Thank you for reading this book, we hope you enjoyed it! If so, we'd really appreciate you leaving a review on Amazon and Goodreads, to help others find and enjoy this story. Also, if you'd like to keep informed about our latest releases, please sign up to our mailing list at: www.crescentswan.com/news

Whilst our books are edited with great care and attention, being an independent micro-publishing house, there is a chance that the occasional typo or error goes missed. If you happen to spot any in this book, please do let us know at publishing@crescentswan.com